BLADES OF THE OLD EMPIRE

Kara is a mercenary – a Diamond warrior, the best of the best, and a member of the notorious Majat Guild. When her tenure as protector to Prince Kythar comes to an end, custom dictates he accompany her back to her Guild to negotiate her continued protection.

But when they arrive they discover that the Prince's sworn enemy, the Kaddim, have already paid the Guild to engage her services – to capture and hand over Kythar, himself.

A warrior brought up to respect both duty and honour, what happens when her sworn duty proves dishonourable?

ANNA KASHINA

Blades of the Old Empire

THE MAJAT CODE
BOOK 1

**ANGRY
ROBOT**

ANGRY ROBOT
A member of the Osprey Group

Lace Market House, Angry Robot/Osprey Publishing,
54-56 High Pavement, PO Box 3985,
Nottingham New York,
NG1 1HW NY 10185-3985,
UK USA

www.angryrobotbooks.com
Diamonds are forever

An Angry Robot paperback original 2014

ISBN: 978 0 85766 412 9
Ebook ISBN: 978 0 85766 413 6

Printed in the United States of America

9 8 7 6 5 4 3 2 1

To VKB

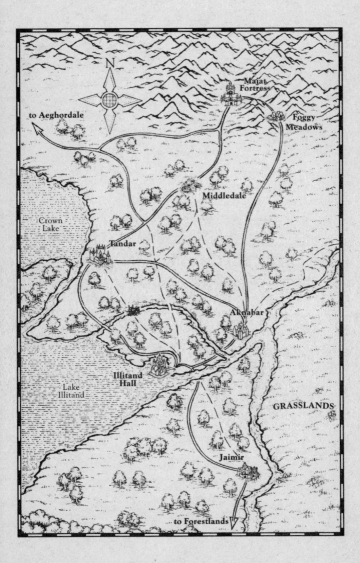

1
KADDIM

Prince Kythar Dorn waited for his friends at the entrance to the small courtyard. It was a perfect, secluded spot. A cool breeze wafted through the columned gallery at the far end, carrying the fresh smells of lake water and bread baking in the palace kitchens. Up above, a lonely watchtower crowned the jagged line of the battlements looming against the clear morning sky. A hawk shrieked overhead, out on its early morning hunt.

Feet rustled on dry stone and a shadow fell across the pavement by his side. Kyth turned and met Ellah's sharp hazel-green eyes. He nodded to the girl, his gaze sliding past her to where his foster brother Alder had just emerged from the garden passage behind. He looked sleepy as he hurried toward them, straightening out his shirt.

Kyth's smile faded as he realized that the passage behind Alder was empty. "Kara couldn't make it?"

Ellah shook her head. "She said to start without her. She'll try to join us later if she can."

Kyth nodded, swallowing his disappointment. Without Kara, a Diamond-ranked Majat warrior and the girl of his dreams, it wouldn't be the same. Her fighting skill would have allowed Kyth to test the true level of his newly mastered ability to focus the wind onto the tip of his sword. Not that he could ever hope to match her.

He glanced at his foster brother, who was rolling up his sleeves to expose the impressive muscle of his forearms. Alder reached for the axe strapped across his back, then caught Kyth's gaze and grinned. "We don't need Kara – let's first see if you can handle me, brother."

"Just don't lose your axe." Kyth drew his sword and moved into position.

Ellah's eyes darted across the yard and to the top of the wall. "Are you sure this is a good idea?"

Kyth inhaled a full breath of the Lakeland wind, feeling it course through his body with new energy. He grinned. "You *did* want to see how my gift worked, didn't you?"

"Yes, but suppose someone sees us."

"No one's going to see us."

"What about the guards on that watchtower?"

Kyth narrowed his eyes, glancing at the massive stone structure overhead. "Empty. This one overlooks the lake, so it's rarely manned. Besides, even if anyone saw us they'd just assume we are out for weapons practice."

"With a sword against an axe?"

"Come now, it'll be all right. Trust me."

Ellah pursed her lips, subsiding into silence.

Kyth edged further into the yard–

–and froze.

A sense of foreboding, just at the edge of consciousness, held him in place. He hesitated, feeling the small hairs on his neck stand on end.

Ellah frowned. "What is it, Kyth?"

"I'm not sure." He strained his senses to penetrate the corners of the courtyard, all the way into the deep shadows under the columns, but couldn't detect anything out of place.

"Well," Ellah said. "Why don't you get on with it, then?" She shielded her eyes against the sunlight and swept past, heading for the shade by the far wall.

A warning cry caught in Kyth's throat as he finally realized what was wrong.

There were no sounds.

He could no longer feel the wind. Morning air wavered over the smoothly hewn stones of the ancient pavement with the rising heat of early sunbeams. Ellah's short brown hair and the folds of her dress hung limply as she strode across the yard.

"Ellah, stop!"

She paused and glanced at Kyth with a questioning look. Alder lowered his axe, his eyebrows shooting up in surprise.

Kyth's skin crawled. An invisible blanket of power descended onto the small courtyard. It rolled over his head, smothering sounds, absorbing all movement into its blunt softness.

Someone nearby was using a strange sort of power. A gift, strong enough to penetrate the entire area.

A lot stronger than Kyth's.

Great Shal Addim.

"Ellah, get back. *Now!*" Kyth locked his eyes with Alder's, both raising their weapons.

"Greetings, Highness." The voice that echoed behind them crept through the yard like a snake poising to strike.

Kyth spun around.

Shadows by the wall shifted and became a hooded shape, wrapped in a black priest-like robe.

Kyth gasped and backed off. He could have sworn there was no one there when they first arrived. Too late, he noticed the deep protrusion of the wall by the arched courtyard gateway. He had never realized the niche was so deep. *How the hell did he get in here?*

The hooded man chuckled. He clicked his fingers, answered by movement beside the columns at the far end. At least a dozen men stepped out of the shadows and fanned out, blocking the way to escape. They were dressed for action, folds of their black robes tucked into their belts, loose pants girded at the ankles by the tall cuffs of their leather boots.

Kyth recognized their weapons, spiked balls hanging on long, thin chains. Orbens – powerful, but extremely hard to master, banned for centuries after the fall of the Old Empire. A sword was all but useless against them, at least for someone with Kyth's limited skill. *Pits of hell*. He edged further away, keeping as many men as he could in his line of sight. They idled, holding their weapons but not attacking.

The hooded man stepped forward. Sunlight fell onto his face illuminating gaunt features, his eyes of such pale brown that they looked yellow. Animal-like.

"So, we finally meet, Prince Kythar."

"Who are you?" Kyth demanded.

The man's smile wormed over his thin lips. "You may call me Kaddim Tolos."

Kaddim. The strange title echoed in Kyth's mind with a half-memory. A blend of opposites in the old tongue, *Kadan* – Destroyer, and *Addim* – Creator. Where had he heard this before? His skin crept. "What do you want?"

"You." The man raised his hands, palms downward.

A silent thunder rolled through the courtyard. Waves of smothering force pounced onto Kyth's head. Alder and Ellah gasped and doubled over, sinking down to the stone pavement.

Kyth rushed to his friends but the attackers closed their ring, forcing him to a halt.

"Ah," Tolos said. "I can see your gift has grown strong enough to resist our power, Highness."

Kyth clenched his sword. *How does he know about my gift?*

The attackers drew closer, spinning their weapons with a short leeway. Spiked metal balls blended into gleaming circles. Kyth felt the wind on his face as he edged around their line searching for a possible gap.

"They will not harm you," Tolos said. "Unless I order them to. All in all, we would like to capture you alive, but if we have to injure you in the process…"

Kyth swept his eyes around the group. Too many to face by himself, but he would be damned if he gave in without a fight. He concentrated. As the attackers neared, he feinted at the closest one and countered the anticipated block by shifting the other way. He aimed low. His sword ripped through the cloth with a satisfying crack, but didn't graze the flesh as the attacker twisted out of the blade's way with snakelike speed. *Damn.* He crouched, trying to keep as many attackers as possible in sight.

Too late, he noticed more shapes sliding in from behind. *Where the hell are they coming from?* He yelped as hands gripped his elbows with a numbing force. Their clammy fingers once again made him think of snakes. Constrictors, judging by the way his arms were rapidly losing feeling. His sword clanked on the stone pavement, an oddly loud sound in the smothering stillness of the windless air.

Kaddim Tolos chuckled. "There, Highness, see? No need to trouble yourself with pointless fighting." He nodded to his men. "Let's go." He headed for the outer castle wall, but a new sound at the courtyard entrance forced him to a halt.

A lithe, muscular figure burst into the yard. A woman, moving so fast her shape blurred as she darted toward Kyth's abductors.

Kara. Despite the danger, warmth rushed through Kyth's body at the mere sight of her. Slim and neat in her closely tailored black outfit, she wielded two narrow swords as if they were a natural continuation of her hands. Her short blond hair gleamed against her dark skin, the ranking diamond in her Majat armband shining in the sun.

The air exploded with steel, Kara's blades hacking through the hooded men's line. The grip on Kyth's elbows eased. He dropped to the pavement, searching for his sword.

Kaddim Tolos raised his hands again.

Waves of smothering force pounced onto the courtyard. Kara stumbled, hovering like a tightrope walker losing balance. Then, to Kyth's horror, she swayed and collapsed onto the stone pavement, swords sliding out of her hands.

He gasped.

No one in the world should have the power to disable a Diamond Majat.

Great Shal Addim.

The attackers regrouped, fanning out among the bodies of their fallen comrades.

"Finish her off." Tolos held his hands steady to maintain the flow of force.

No! Kyth's mind raced. He would be damned if he stood by uselessly, watching Kara die. He would fight for her to his last breath.

If only Kaddim Tolos didn't smother the wind. Without it, Kyth couldn't use his gift. There was no power he could focus.

Except...

Could he use Kaddim Tolos's force?

He opened up his senses, absorbing the smothering waves rolling through the courtyard. The dark power felt strange, bitter as it entered his body. He steadied himself, letting it flow freely into his calm center, out to the limbs.

New strength coursed through his veins. He focused, concentrating its flow on the tip of his sword.

It wasn't the same as the wind, but it would have to do. Grasping his sword, he took a running leap through the hooded men's line. They met him with spinning orbens, but he was faster this time. He sidestepped the figures rushing at him without really seeing them, his entire senses focused on Tolos standing motionlessly by the wall. He had to get to this man, take him out before he did any more damage – before his men killed Kara, who was sprawled helplessly on the courtyard stones.

A spiked metal ball whizzed by Kyth's ear. He half-saw the surprise on his enemy's face as he danced around the weapon. Ducking and jumping, diving and rolling over the ground, he broke through the attackers' line and launched himself on Tolos, using the momentum to thrust an upward blow straight at the man's chest.

Tolos moved with unexpected speed. Kyth's sword harmlessly brushed the black robe and the man's fingers caught his wrists in an iron grip. The sword slid out of his hand, but the pressure stayed, until he could no longer feel his hands.

He slowly raised his head and looked at the sharp features framed by the hood. The man's yellow eyes were hypnotic. Kyth felt like a fly trapped in a web.

The attackers surrounded them.

"No more distractions, I think," Kaddim Tolos said with a smirk.

"Think again," a deep female voice echoed through the yard.

Kara. Kyth's heart pounded. Was the delay provided by his attack enough to give her the advantage she needed?

"Blast," Tolos said through clenched teeth. "Didn't I tell you men to finish her off?" He raised his hands again. A new wave of force hit the courtyard.

Kyth's eyes locked on Kara's.

This time she remained upright, caught in the onflow of force, her violet eyes shining like amethysts against her dark skin. Her face became hollow, ashen gray with the strain. A streak of blood oozed down from her nostril. The attackers closed in on her like vultures.

Kyth groaned, uselessly struggling in the hands of his captors. He couldn't bear to see her die. If it wasn't for his stupid, careless wish to sneak out to a remote place to practice his forbidden gift–

Resist them, Kara, he prayed. *Please, don't let them win.*

He held her gaze.

Fight them, Kara, he thought, sending the feeling toward her with such force that he was sure she would sense it even without words. *Fight, for I cannot bear to lose you.*

Her eyes widened. She hovered for a moment, then slowly steadied herself, straightening against the oppressive flow. Her muscles rippled, a barely perceptible wave that ran down her body, restoring her graceful, confident posture.

The attackers sensed the change. They raised their weapons with renewed urgency, but none of them could possibly be fast enough to match her. She slashed into their line, her shape a blur as she swept through like a human whirlwind. Men fell to her blades left and right, their blood painting the stones dark crimson. Others backed off, their faces showing fear as they kept their distance.

In mere moments the impressive attack force was reduced to a disorderly group, huddled together in a fight for their lives.

"Retreat!" Kaddim Tolos commanded. His yellow eyes sought out Kyth's and fixed him with a chilling stare. "We'll meet again, Highness."

He turned and darted toward the castle wall. A small grappler hook shot out of his sleeve. He flung it up to catch on the edge of the wall high above his head and flew up the rope so fast that he looked like a grotesque black bird with his wing-like robe flapping in his wake.

His men followed. In a blink of an eye they were gone, leaving their fallen comrades, black heaps on the bloodstained pavement of the courtyard.

The smothering blanket of power lifted as the attackers disappeared. Sounds of the outside world filled the courtyard: the chirping of sparrows in the palace gardens, the high shriek of a rivergull out on the lake, the distant hacking of an axe chopping wood by the kitchens. A fresh morning breeze gently touched Kyth's cheek.

A group of Kingsguards poured into the courtyard.

"Your Highness!" The guard captain looked badly shaken.

"I'm fine," Kyth snapped. "Help Ellah and Alder!"

But his friends were already getting to their feet, looking dazed. Kyth rushed to their side.

"I'm all right," Alder said. "I think." He rubbed his face, smearing the drying nose blood all over his cheek. Kyth reached past him to help Ellah, struggling upright. She looked pale, her hands shaky as she smoothed her dress with a nervous gesture. "Th-thank Shal Addim Kara arrived when she did."

"What kind of a power did this man have?" Alder wondered.

Kyth shrugged. No power he had heard of, for sure. No power any man should ever have.

"Their leader called himself Kaddim," he said. "It sounds familiar, but I can't remember why."

"The Keepers would know," Ellah said.

Kyth nodded, watching Kara coming up to them.

"There was a boat waiting for them on the other side of the wall," she said. "They took off before I could catch them."

Kyth shivered with relief at seeing her alive. If his attackers had been faster carrying out their leader's orders; if she hadn't recovered when she did–

"Thanks," he said quietly.

She merely nodded. Her full lips quivered as she glanced at the bodies scattered over the yard. With a quick movement she flicked her blades into their double-ended, staff-like sheath strapped across her back. Then she slowly raised her hand to wipe the blood off her face. Kyth had never seen her so shaken before.

Gasps from the far end of the courtyard caught their attention. Kingsguards crowded over one of the bodies.

"This one's still alive, Highness," the guard captain said as Kyth approached. "And he has... this..." He pointed.

The fallen attacker was slowly coming to, pale eyes dazedly watching the people leaning over him. A gash on his left temple oozed over his closely shaved scalp. But these details swept by as Kyth's eyes fixed on the man's left shoulder, bared by his ripped shirt.

A black brand mark, a triangle with elongated corners, marred the man's skin. The shape resembled an arrowhead pointing to the ground. It also looked vaguely like a head, with a pointed beard and long, protruding horns.

The sign of Ghaz Kadan.

Kyth's eyes widened. Did his attackers worship the *Cursed Destroyer*?

He suddenly remembered what he knew about the Kaddim. An ancient brotherhood, rumored to play a key part in the fall of the Old Empire. As far as he remembered, the Kaddim cult had been outlawed centuries ago, all its followers hunted down by the Church.

Maybe he remembered wrongly?

We'll meet again, Highness. Kyth shivered. Who were these men? What did they want with him?

2
BAD NEWS

"What the hell were you doing in that courtyard?" King Evan demanded.

Kyth hesitated, glancing at the two Keepers standing beside the throne. The pristine white of their cloaks made a stark contrast with the black outfits of the King's bodyguards, a Pentade of five gem-ranked Majat forming a semicircle around the King.

"You're busy, father," he said. "I didn't mean to hold you up."

He wasn't about to discuss his gift in front of strangers, even if Mother Keeper and her right-hand man, Magister Egey Bashi, already knew of its existence. His eyes flicked to the table by the King's side, holding three pieces of parchment and a throwing star set with a huge diamond in its center. The token symbolizing the Diamond Majat's contract. *But why?*

The King pinched the bridge of his nose. He looked as if he hadn't had enough sleep. The weary look he exchanged with the Keepers told Kyth that this meeting had been going on too long and couldn't possibly have been a pleasant one.

"Just tell me more about these men, son," the King said.

"Their leader called himself Kaddim. He…" Kyth paused

as he noticed his father's widening eyes and the frown
Mother Keeper exchanged with her subordinate.

"Kaddim?" the King echoed. "Impossible."

"Anything's possible, Your Majesty," Mother Keeper said.

"But here? Now? After nearly five hundred years?"

The older woman nodded. "Unlikely, I agree. Yet, Prince
Kythar's description of this man's power–"

"What about it?"

The older woman frowned, her full lips twitching at the
corners to set her mouth into a straight line. The stern look
in her eyes reminded Kyth that this frail-looking woman
commanded a power that rivaled that of the Church and
extended a huge influence over the kingdom. "Kaddim
brothers possessed what used to be called 'power to defeat'.
It seems possible, Your Majesty, that the power Prince
Kythar described could be of a similar nature."

"For some reason," Kyth said, "this power failed to affect
me. This man – Tolos – seemed to expect it."

"He did, did he?" Magister Egey Bashi's deep voice
reverberated through the chamber with a startling force.
The man's piercing dark eyes bore into Kyth, the disfiguring
scar across his bear-like face making him look frightening.
"Did he also expect Your Highness to give up without a
fight? Or did he think playing with orbens – and possibly
injuring or killing you – was a good way to make you more
agreeable?"

They didn't care about injuring me. Kyth swallowed. "I'm
lucky Kara was able to resist them." *And that she showed up
when she did.* Against reason, the thought filled him with
warmth. Kara clearly made the effort to come early, despite
her numerous duties. Did it mean that she actually cared?
*Don't be a fool, it's not like she is available. Her life belongs to her
guild.* He swallowed again, catching his father's intent gaze.

"What about the prisoner you took?" the King asked. "Did he have any unnatural powers too?"

Kyth shook his head. "As far as I could tell, only the weapon."

"Orben?"

"Yes."

"As I recall," the King said, "these weapons were outlawed around the same time as the Kaddim."

"Which makes these men fit the description even better, Your Majesty," Mother Keeper said.

"Almost too well."

The older woman raised her eyebrows.

"They surely made a point of letting us know their leader's name and title," the King went on. "Is it possible that somebody is eager to mislead us into believing the Kaddim are still around?"

"To what end, Your Majesty?"

The King shrugged. "Only one way to find out."

The prisoner. Kyth shivered. Kara took charge of overseeing the care and confinement of the prisoner until arrangements could be made for a formal interrogation. Kyth, Alder, and Ellah were supposed to attend, in case their presence brought up any additional memories. Kyth wasn't looking forward to it.

Mother Keeper bowed. "With your permission, Your Majesty, the Magister and I would like to be present at the interrogation."

"I would be obliged, Mother Keeper," the King said. "No one knows as much as you and the Magister about the Kaddim. Aghat Mai will accompany you. I'm placing him in charge. His methods can be very effective, or so I've heard."

He signaled to the Diamond-ranked leader of his Majat Pentade. The man bowed and stood to attention. Kyth looked at him in wonder.

It was hard to imagine anyone who looked less appropriate than Mai for his high post of the leader of the Pentade. A slender youth with soft blond curls and a face of an almost sexless beauty, he seemed far too young to be in charge and much more fit to hold a lyre than a sword. Yet, a ruthless glint in his tranquil blue eyes – and the deadly rumors that spawned around him like dust around a tornado – warned Kyth not to underestimate this dangerous man.

"I'll walk with you, Aghat," he said. "Alder and Ellah are waiting by the dungeon."

"In a moment." The King gestured for Kyth to stay, waiting for the door to close behind the Keepers and Mai. "Now. Is there anything else you can tell me about the attack, son?"

Kyth glanced at the four Ruby Majat standing still beside the throne.

"I've been to this courtyard several times before," he said. "The attackers must have been watching me for days – they knew exactly when and where to catch me unprotected."

The King shook his head. "I don't like this at all. After we're done with the questioning, I will ask Aghat Mai to oversee the security of the grounds. It appears the Kingsguards aren't really up to the task. And you – you should be more careful, Kyth. It is fortunate Kara arrived when she did."

Kyth nodded. "She was able to overcome their power. Quite possibly, this resistance, along with her Majat skill, makes her the only warrior able to protect us. Isn't that reason enough to keep her at court?" His gaze faltered as he saw his father's pursed lips.

"She can't stay," the King said.

Kyth's heart fell. He knew his father disapproved of his affection for a hired guard, but Kara's unique value was more important, wasn't it?

"Is it the gold?" he asked. "I know her services cost a fortune, but–"

"Not quite." The King gestured toward the parchment on the table next to the Majat token. "This letter from the Majat Guild came today. Her assignment here is over, and they want her to return as soon as possible. While I believe that eventually this could be resolved by money, for now we have no choice but to send her back."

Kyth stared at the letter, fighting the sinking feeling in his stomach. The Majat obeyed no one except the Code of their Guild. This arrangement made them invaluable as mercenaries, loyal to their contract until it was fulfilled. But it also meant that even the King had no power to keep Kara at court if she had been recalled. Not until a new contract could be negotiated.

"I know how you feel, son," the King said softly. "But you must understand. You are the heir to the throne. The sooner you forget her and seek a proper match among the ladies of the royal blood, the better. As for your protection, we still have Aghat Raishan. When Aghat Kara leaves, I'll send a letter along, requesting to extend his services as your personal guard."

Kyth shook his head. He knew he should listen to his father. Raishan was a decent man, and a superb fighter whose skill and rank matched Kara's. But to forget her, and turn his attention to other young ladies? That didn't seem possible.

The King's chest heaved with a sigh. "Right now, this isn't the only one of our worries." He handed Kyth a parchment marked with a black glossy imprint of the Holy Star. "This letter came from the Holy City today."

Kyth's eyebrows rose in disbelief as he ran his eyes over the parchment. "A new reverend? But Father Boydos was elected less than six months ago."

The King nodded. "I don't like this any more than you do. Father Boydos's sudden illness sounds highly suspicious. And all this business about holding an emergency election by the conclave, without my knowledge and with less than half its members present..."

Kyth looked at the letter again. "I guess we'll learn the details soon enough. It says here that the new man, Father Cyrros, will arrive shortly, possibly even this afternoon."

"Yes." The King frowned. "He's in a damn hurry to see us, that's for sure."

"He had to start his trip to the capital on the day of his election, as soon as he sent off this letter..." Kyth's voice trailed into silence. Such a rush could only mean one thing. The new Reverend had pressing business at court, and Kyth could just guess what it was.

My gift.

By the ancient law of Ghaz Shalan, a man with magic could never succeed the throne, an old rule that put not only Kyth's but his father's position into question. Old Reverend Boydos had been willing to look the other way, possibly even to speak in favor of reconsidering the law. But now that a new man had taken his place and was on his speedy way to the capital.

Will this ever end? Kyth bit his lip, glancing out of the window to where the blue haze of the lake interceded with the jagged roofline of the city. From the throne room he couldn't see the stretch of the main road leading up to the castle, but he had a clear view of the Holy Gate and the wide street that led from there to the Fountain Plaza. People lined it as far as the eye could see, a colorful crowd carrying flowering apple branches and banners with the signs of the Holy Star.

"News travels fast."

The King frowned. "Especially bad news. In any case, we'll know as soon as His Reverence is sighted from the main gate. Which leaves me a bit of time to show you the last of the three letters I received today." He handed Kyth the rolled-up parchment tied with the green and gold sash of the Royal House Illitand.

Kyth ran his eyes over the neat lines of writing. Duke Daemur Illitand was regretfully informing the King that due to an illness he won't be able to attend the meeting of the High Council due in six weeks. He also mentioned that Princess Aljbeda of Shayil Yara, currently enjoying his hospitality at the Illitand Hall, found the air of the south lakes so agreeable that she may not be able to make the trip either.

Kyth lowered the parchment in disbelief. "But this... this..."

The King nodded. "Yes. This borders on mutiny and is bound to cause a major uproar. The other noble families would never take me seriously unless I can get the Duke's and the Princess's support. If I cannot change their minds, we might end up in a civil war."

More trouble because of my gift. Kyth sighed. When his father won the contest for the crown, he thought all their troubles were behind them. But it seemed that Kyth's cursed magic, an ungodly gift that should have marked him for elimination at birth, would haunt them forever.

"What are we going to do, father?" he said quietly.

"Change the law. It's the only way."

"But–"

The King ran a hand through his long black hair with a scarce touch of gray and leaned back into his chair. "I know. Without the full vote at the High Council, this couldn't be done. Which means, I'll just have to travel to Illitand Hall and personally convince the Duke – and the Princess – to see things my way."

"Travel?"

"Why the hell not?"

"Too dangerous."

The King grinned. "Beats the boredom of sitting in the royal chambers all day reading letters."

Kyth held his father's gaze. The merry sparkles in the King's blue eyes showed him as he was before – not an aging man buried in the kingdom's affairs, but a dashing nobleman and a renowned swordsman, the only man at court who played by his own rules. Against reason, this confidence caught Kyth. No matter what the new Reverend had to say about his gift, no matter what the nobles thought, they were going to have it their way. And, he was going to keep Kara by his side even if he had to go to the Majat Guild himself to talk to their Guildmaster.

He lowered his eyes to the three parchments. If he became king, would he learn to deal with bad news like his father, with a smile on his face?

"I think," the King said, "you'd better go. The Keepers are waiting."

Kyth looked at his torn, dirty shirt. There was nothing he wanted more than a nice, warm bath. But before he did, he had to go to the dungeon and do his duty.

3

THE PRISONER

The open doorway to the interrogation cell oozed with smells of rot, mold, and dirty wash water. Ellah, hovering close to the entrance, looked green in the face as she cast nervous glances inside.

"Where's Alder?" Kyth asked as he approached.

"He went in already." She glanced at the dark doorway. "Are you sure it's necessary for us all to be there?"

"Why don't you wait outside," Kyth said. "I'll call you if you're needed."

She nodded gratefully.

The light of two torches fixed into the sconces at the far wall painted the white Keepers' robes with a blood-red sheen. The Majat's black outfits blended with the shadows. Kyth had to strain his eyes to see Kara and Mai standing beside the prisoner, their slim shapes partially shielding him from view. The third Diamond, Raishan, hovered nearby, his face set into a calm mask.

The presence of three Diamonds, a deadly force capable of withstanding a small army, made the cell safer than any fortress, yet Kyth shivered as he made his way toward the chained prisoner crouching at the far wall.

At close range the man didn't seem menacing. He looked like a regular mercenary, no match for the Diamonds that stood guard over him. A bandage covered his head, a torn shirt exposing the muscles of his arms and chest. The cursed mark was hidden from view, yet Kyth couldn't keep his eyes from sliding to the cloth covering the man's left shoulder.

"Where's Ellah?" Alder asked. "I thought she was right behind me."

"She's outside," Kyth said. "I think she's not feeling all that well. We should start without her. We'll call her if she's needed."

"In this case we're ready, Your Highness," Mother Keeper said.

Kyth looked past her to the Majat. "You may begin, Aghat Mai."

The Diamond nodded, then flicked a slender staff out of its sheath at the back and gave the prisoner a slow, appraising glance. His long fingers ran along the dark, polished wood in a caressing gesture, answered by a sharp click of a hidden spring. A blade sprang out of each end of the staff, lengthening the weapon by a foot on each side.

Kyth gaped. He had never seen this weapon at work before, always assumed it was a regular staff. He looked at Mai with new wonder.

The prisoner's breath quickened. "Keep the pretty boy away from me!"

Mai surveyed him calmly, like a child studying an insect in a jar. "Why did you attack the Prince?"

The prisoner paled and shook his head, pressing against the wall.

Mai tilted his staff, a blade point touching the prisoner's skin. The man squirmed. His lips acquired a bluish tint, ragged breath coming in gasps. He gulped, as if trying to speak but failing. It seemed that no matter how hard he tried he wasn't able to produce any words.

Keeping his hand steady, Mai glanced at the other two Diamonds. Kara shrugged, her face impenetrable. Raishan remained still.

"Perhaps–" Kyth began.

Mother Keeper's hand touched his wrist. "Forgive the interruption, Your Highness, but I have a suspicion what the problem is. If you'd permit the Magister to interfere–"

The prisoner's eyes darted to her with hope. Mai balanced the staff in his hand, looking at Kyth with silent question. Kyth nodded. The Diamond stepped aside, sliding a calm glance over Magister Egey Bashi.

The Keeper rolled up his sleeves, exposing his hairy muscular arms. His scarred, bear-like face looked outlandish in the flickering torchlight. He reached forward and tugged at the prisoner's torn collar, exposing the black downturned triangle branded into his shoulder.

"Tell me," he said in a quiet voice. "Who marked you with this sign, and why?"

The result was the opposite of what Kyth expected. Instead of calming down as the threat of the weapon was removed, the prisoner's face twitched in agony. He bared his teeth, throwing his weight against the chains. "*Damn* you, Keeper!" he rasped.

"Tell me," Egey Bashi pressed. "Or we'll let Aghat Mai do his worst."

The prisoner growled. His lips foamed. Egey Bashi straightened and nodded to Mother Keeper.

The woman spoke, looking the prisoner straight in the eyes: "*Kados g'zakkur ahlghalim.*"

The words of the strange tongue cut like ice as they echoed through the stone cell. Torchlight wavered. The room darkened, as if a shadow ran over the ceiling.

The prisoner's body shook from head to toe. His lead lolled, hitting the wall. Arms twisted against the chains as he fell, his eyes bulging, face turning purple. With choking screams, he clawed at his throat as if trying to tear it open, thrashing over the floor as far as the chains would allow.

The fit ended as suddenly as it began as the man collapsed, twitched one last time, and went still.

A silence fell onto the chamber. Then Mother Keeper slowly reached down and felt his pulse. "He's dead." She let out a short breath and wiped her hands on the edge of her robe.

"Dead?" Kyth's voice came out as a whisper. "But–" he faltered.

Mai leaned over the prisoner. His long fingers punched the pressure points at the base of the neck, but failed to produce an effect. Finally he straightened out and exchanged a look with his fellows in rank.

"I doubt this was what His Majesty had in mind when he asked us to conduct the interrogation," he said.

Mother Keeper shook her head. "It was useless to question him, Aghat. He wouldn't have told us anything."

Kyth found his voice again. "Wh-What did you say to him?"

"A few words in the old tongue. This used to be the Kaddim Brotherhood's motto, crudely translated as '*he who destroys in faith is rewarded*'."

"Why would these words kill him?"

"It's an old way of conditioning, Your Highness."

"*Conditioning?*"

"Yes."

"What the hell does it mean?"

The older woman's gaze slid over him with a semblance of pity. Kyth clenched his fists until his nails bit into his palms, forcing himself to relax. Whatever happened, he had no business to raise his voice at this woman, who was a lot older than him. The prisoner was dead, nothing to be done about it.

"It's the most effective way to ensure one's secrets are safe, Your Highness," Mother Keeper said. "The Magister and I suspected it after seeing the way he reacted to Aghat Mai. The mere threat of an effective interrogation made him sick. When pressed, he died rather than reveal any information. I'm afraid the fact that this man reacted to the Kaddim motto confirms that this was indeed the true identity of your attackers."

Kyth slowly let out a breath he hadn't realized he was holding. "Don't you think we should have tried to extract the information in milder ways first?"

The older woman shook her head. She looked weary. "It wouldn't have worked, Your Highness. He wouldn't have been able to give us any information at all. All he brought was danger."

"Danger?"

Her gaze darkened. "The Kaddim were known for their ways to communicate with each other through the same link that protected their secrets from the outsiders. Keeping this man alive would have been like keeping a spy in your midst."

Kyth looked down at the prisoner's body, dead fingers clenched around his throat as if tearing at an invisible garrote. He thought he knew a lot about the Keepers. But in all his knowledge there was no room for an explanation of how this frail woman with a kind, motherly smile could kill a man with a few words. Or, how she could be so calm about it.

"If it's of any consolation, Your Highness," she said, "I didn't kill him. His own brotherhood did. The same would have happened if Aghat Mai proceeded with his interrogation."

Perhaps. But now we'd never know, would we? "How can you be so sure? Perhaps his death was a coincidence? Perhaps he had a poisoned pill under his tongue." Kyth had read about spies and assassins ordered to take poison and die if caught. He supposed this was also a conditioning of sorts, just one with a more rational explanation.

Once again there was a touch of pity in Mother Keeper's gaze. "The signs were clear, Your Highness. We couldn't possibly mistake them. You see, such conditioning was first invented by the Keepers."

"You –" Kyth felt at a loss for words. The image he had of the Keepers, peaceful scholars traveling the lands as healers and teachers, fighting to save the lives of gifted children, had just been shattered. He had always thought that their order had earned its high standing because of their selfless quest to improve people's lives through studies of the Book of Knowledge. Perhaps it was naïve of him, given their proficiency in politics, but he had never thought of them as anything but kind, generous, and somewhat idealistic. This short scene in the dungeon changed this view forever. To think that each of them was conditioned to die in agony if interrogated about their Order.

He looked at the two figures in white robes. They were supposed to be on the same side. And yet now, for the first time, he wondered what it truly meant to be their allies.

4
REVEREND FATHER

Kyth barely had time to wash and change before the news of the reverend's arrival was brought in by a group of Kingsguards, armed to the teeth and determined to accompany him to the throne room whether he liked it or not. Their fervor made Kyth wonder if his father had made it a priority to discuss the castle's security issues with their captain. He felt pity for these men as he marched inside their ring, tight enough to shield him against a minor avalanche.

When he entered the throne room, the greeting party was in assembly. The King sat on the throne, surrounded by the Majat. Next to him lingered the royal house priest Brother Bartholomeos, his bald head covered with a hood, his chain of office resting over his black robe in glimmering golden links. The other side of the throne was taken by the Keepers, their white cloaks a pale spot in the gray afternoon light.

There was a newcomer in the Keepers' group. A young woman with an oval face and dark almond-shaped eyes stood between Mother Keeper and Magister Egey Bashi. As Kyth approached, he noticed a loose strand of her dark hair coil up her neck like a miniature snake and wind its way into the tight bun at the back of her head. He blinked. The woman noticed his gaze and gave him a conspiratorial smile before sinking into a deep curtsy.

"Allow me to introduce Odara Sul, Your Highness," Magister Egey Bashi said. "Initiate of the Inner Circle and a member of the Keeper's Council. She arrived from our Order this afternoon."

"A pleasure, my lady." Kyth kept his eyes on the woman's hair. A few loose wisps wavered in the light draft, but their movement didn't seem to be anything but natural. I must have imagined it, he thought. Then he caught Ellah's and Alder's prompting gazes from the side of the crowd. He edged closer.

"That woman's hair," Ellah whispered. "I saw it *move*!"

"I saw it too," Alder boomed, in his version of a whisper. Kyth opened his mouth to hush him, but the sound of fanfares prompted him to hurry to his place at the side of the throne.

The doors at the end of the hall opened, letting in the newcomers.

The hooded man walking through the central aisle toward the throne had a slight build, shorter and slimmer than many in his retinue. The richly embroidered ceremonial cloak draped down to the ground, its ends sweeping the floor. Clearly, the new owner had no time to shorten the garment properly before the trip. Twelve priests moved in his wake with a stalking grace not usually seen in the peaceful servants of Shal Addim. For a moment their silent approach made them look like an attack force. The Majat closed their circle around the King, forcing the procession to halt.

"Father Cyrros, I presume," King Evan said.

The man bowed, pulling his hood back to reveal the thin features of his hollow face. "At your service, Your Majesty."

A chill went through the chamber as he spoke. Kyth's skin crept as the reverend's glance paused on him briefly, singling him out of the crowd.

"We were sorry to hear about Reverend Boydos's illness," Evan said.

Cyrros's pale lips twitched. "*Brother* Boydos," he made a slight emphasis on the title, "is regretfully highly unlikely to recover. The conclave was forced to make a speedy decision in replacing him. I took the liberty of bringing a letter detailing his condition to Your Majesty." At his sign, one of the priests brought forward a folded parchment, handing it to Brother Bartholomeos. There was a pause as the King received the letter and read it through.

"This is highly unusual," he said. "It's my understanding that each meeting of the conclave is arranged in advance and the King must be properly notified before the event."

"I have a notification letter right here, Your Majesty, as well as the attestation to the conclave's decision." More documents passed hands. "I must apologize, but we had to act so quickly there was no time to send a separate messenger. I assure you, Majesty, I was properly elected, and these venerable brothers," the priest nodded at the silent figures behind him, "could testify to my words." He paused and once again Kyth had a sense of a strange power reverberating through the chamber.

"I appreciate your bringing the news in person, Holy Father," the King said. "Your willingness to make the trip on such short notice is commendable."

The reverend held a pause. His eyes flicked to the Prince and hovered over the Majat surrounding the throne. Kyth imagined they stayed on Kara longer than the others, but he couldn't tell for sure.

"Actually," Cyrros said, "I came to discuss another matter with Your Majesty. One that perhaps merits a more private setting?"

Here it comes. Kyth bit his lip, trying to quiet the pounding in his chest.

King Evan glanced around the assembly, a dangerous glint in his eyes. "State your business, Reverend Father. I have no secrets from my loyal subjects."

The priest hesitated, then bowed. "As you wish, Your Majesty. First, allow me to congratulate you and Prince Kythar on the joyous event of his eighteenth birthday. Age-coming, for a royal heir."

"Thank you, Your Reverence." The king smiled, but a tense cord in his neck told Kyth how alert his father was.

"A pity the celebration had to be cut short by King Daegar's demise and the preparations for your coronation, Your Majesty."

Evan raised an eyebrow. "Forgive me, Your Reverence, but while it is a joy to hear your birthday wishes to my son, such a matter can hardly merit your request for privacy – or a trip to the capital, for that matter."

The priest's face became still. "The matter I wish to discuss concerns Prince Kythar's gift."

Kyth held his breath, but his father did not look in the least disturbed.

"What about it, reverend?"

"According to the standing law of Ghaz Shalan Testing, prince Kythar should not… be alive."

A smile creased King Evan's lips. "Isn't it too late to discuss that, Reverend Father? By Shal Addim's will, the Prince is alive and well. Or, is there a suggestion somewhere in your words?" His voice rang with a hidden threat as he looked over the reverend's head to his hooded suite.

The priest bowed again. "I believe, Your Majesty, I may indeed have a solution to this problem. If you agree to relinquish the Prince – temporarily – into my care, I will be honored to escort His Highness back to the Holy City and perform an exorcism to rid him of the curse."

"An exorcism?"

"Yes, Your Majesty."

The King shifted in his chair, leaning closer to his visitor. "And does such exorcism actually work?"

"With our Lord's blessings, there is a chance that—"

"A *chance*."

"Yes, Your Majesty."

"And what if it doesn't work?"

The priest swallowed. "Surely Your Majesty is prepared to do anything possible to ensure that this court is not harboring an outlaw?"

The silence was so complete that Kyth's skin prickled. He never imagined such a large chamber could be so utterly still.

The King leaned back in his chair, throwing a meaningful glance at his Majat escort. "Did you bring enough men to enforce this... this solution?"

The priest lifted his chin. Again it seemed to Kyth that his eyes paused on Kara before returning to the King. "Please, Your Majesty. We are peaceful servants of our Lord Shal Addim. We don't *enforce* anything. I merely hoped that—"

"You hoped wrong."

The reverend held his gaze. "The dilemma must be resolved, Your Majesty. My sources tell me that people of Tallan Dar are having trouble accepting the rule of a king whose heir possesses a cursed gift. I see no other solution but to attempt to clear Prince Kythar of his unfortunate problem."

The King's smile froze. "It's funny that you mention other solutions, your Holiness. I fancy I have just the one that would settle this once and for all."

The priest fixed him with a heavy stare.

"Since this particular law is giving us such trouble," the King went on, seemingly oblivious to the reverend's expression, "I think our only option is to change the law. Incidentally, this would save the lives of many gifted children that right now are being purged by the Church. I am certain the people of Tallan Dar would find such a solution more agreeable than yours, Reverend."

Not to mention easing the control that the Church has had over our lands for the past hundred years. Kyth saw the thought reflected in the reverend's face.

"This course of action, Your Majesty, is not only treacherous, but extremely difficult to accomplish." The priest's eyes flicked to the Keepers. "I hope you are not overestimating the value of Mother Keepers's support, which she has undoubtedly offered to you in taking this shaky path."

Evan raised his eyebrows. "Shaky, Holy Father?"

Cyrros drew himself up. "The Church will never support this, Your Majesty. No matter what you do, this change of law isn't going to happen. So, if you've been planning any steps in that direction, I suggest you proceed no further."

Evan leaned forward in his seat. "I believe your support is not technically necessary, Your Reverence. The High Council has authority to overrule the Church with a unanimous vote."

"*Unanimous* vote, Your Majesty."

"Exactly."

"The council meets in six weeks, doesn't it?"

"Yes, it does."

The reverend's thin lips twitched. "Are you certain you can bring all the members to assembly in that time, Your Majesty?"

The King exchanged a quick glance with the Keepers. "I understand that my predecessors relied on the Church in all their decisions, but since we are having this conversation I should inform you that matters will be different from now on."

The reverend bowed. "I'm glad we have this chance to begin by stating our positions openly, Your Majesty. However, I will take the liberty to offer you a small piece of advice. I fully understand your wish to be, shall we say, independent, but this course of action isn't necessarily wise."

"Given that you are new to your position, Your Reverence, I shall give you some advice too. I don't *like* unsolicited advice."

"I assure you, Your Majesty, I'm only trying to help."

"Why don't we leave this until the council meeting, Your Reverence," the King suggested. "In the meantime, I expect you must be tired after your long and hasty journey. Our house priest, Brother Bartholomeos, has prepared accommodations for you and your men."

The reverend bowed again, his neck muscles bulging as he briefly clenched his teeth. "You are most gracious, Your Majesty, but I fear I must decline. I will be taking my residence in the Crown Temple. I humbly request to take my leave now."

At the King's nod, he bowed and signaled his men. In the deadly stillness, they turned and left the hall.

5
PLANS

"*Exorcism*," King Evan said, looking into space. "Just what we need, a bloody fanatic on our hands."

Kyth kept to the shadows of the small chamber, watching his father's contorted face. He had never seen the King so angry before.

"Give me one reason," Evan went on, "why I shouldn't arrest this man and throw him in the dungeons for threatening my son and heir."

Mother Keeper leafed through the pile in her lap. "The paperwork appears legitimate, Your Majesty," she said in her calm, soothing voice. "We are facing the Reverend Father of the Church himself. I don't believe arresting him would go well with the people."

Evan's chest heaved as he settled back into his chair. "Next you'll be telling me I should entertain his suggestion."

Mother Keeper exchanged a quiet look with Magister Egey Bashi and Odara Sul, seated by her side. Then she looked across the table at Brother Bartholomeos.

"Barring that, Your Majesty," she said, "it seems we do need to ensure the full assembly at the High Council, so that the law could indeed be changed. If we manage it, the matter of Prince Kythar's ability won't arise again."

The King frowned. "Damn well I'm going to ensure the full assembly. I'm leaving for Illitand Hall tomorrow. If needed, I'll *drag* the Duke and the Princess here to sit at the council. Whatever they think of me, they won't stand for the Church dictating to the King."

Mother Keeper bowed her head. "I pray Your Majesty succeeds in this embassy. And, with your permission, I would like to accompany you. I hope this evidence of the Keepers' support might further sway the Duke's decision in your favor."

Not to mention keeping tempers at bay. Kyth remembered the scene in the dungeon. How did this frail, elderly woman manage to maintain such a soothing demeanour while commanding such a horrifying power?

"Thank you, Mother Keeper," the King said. "I'm certain your presence would speak volumes for our cause."

She bowed again. "Thank you, Your Majesty. However, I feel it is my duty to remind you that the Illitand's and Shayil Yara's seats are by far not the hardest to fill for the full assembly of the council."

The King stared at her for a moment without blinking.

"The Cha'ori, Your Majesty."

The King leaned back in his chair. "You can't possibly mean that. Those savages–"

A smile touched the older woman's lips. "Hardly, Your Majesty. The Grassland Wanderers are in command of the most ancient magic in existence. And, they're at odds with the Church. Their alliance – if we can achieve it – may prove valuable in more ways than one."

Evan spread his hands. "But, for Shal Addim's sake, our feud with the Cha'ori goes back to the Holy Wars. Their seat in the council chamber is a historic relic, no more."

"Nonetheless, their chair still has a place at the table."

"Couldn't we just *remove* it by a special decree?"

Mother Keeper shook her head. "Council seats can only be removed by a unanimous vote of the full assembly, Majesty. The reverend included."

"But how in the world would we ensure their support? They won't let our messengers within an arrow's flight of their camps!"

"Actually..." Kyth began.

All heads turned to him.

"I'm sure if I go they would at least listen."

"But–"

"I've met the Cha'ori before," Kyth went on. "Back when Ellah, Alder, Kara and I traveled from the Forestlands to the Crown City so that I could take my place by your side, father. We rode with their hort for a while. A Cha'ori wisewoman even gave me a medallion to wear. I'd say if you send me, father, we do have a chance. Besides, what do we have to lose?"

"Your Highness has a point there," Brother Bartholomeos said.

The King shook his head. "Too dangerous, son. This morning you were attacked in this very castle. What do you think would happen if you go all the way to the Grasslands?"

"Even in this very castle," Kyth said, "the only one who could defend me was Kara. Without her, I would be just as vulnerable here as anywhere else."

"But Kara is due to return to the Majat Guild."

Kyth shrugged. "So, I'll make a detour. I'll go with her to the Majat Guild and hire her back. There's enough time."

"Barely. Besides, she may already be bound to a new assignment. You know the Majat rules."

"I'll bring Raishan with us. If there is indeed an assignment waiting, I'll suggest him as a replacement. He shares Kara's rank and should be as good in every respect."

"How can you be sure that Kara can resist these attackers again? Or that Raishan is not immune to them as well?"

"If I may speak, Your Majesty," Magister Egey Bashi interrrupted, "I think Prince Kythar is right. We already know Kara can resist them, and Raishan is an unknown quantity. It's worth a try."

"Hiring a Diamond by name costs triple," Brother Bartholomeos said.

"If Kara can indeed resist the Kaddim, it's worth the money."

The King hesitated. "You really believe it will work, Magister?"

"With your permission," the Keeper said, "I will accompany Prince Kythar. I've dealt with the Majat before. Perhaps I could be of assistance in the negotiations."

Kyth nodded. "I would be grateful, Magister. I believe Alder and Ellah should also come. The Cha'ori know them. Their presence might be of help once we get to the Grasslands."

"Actually, Highness," Mother Keeper said. "I was hoping your friend Ellah could come with me."

"Ellah?" Kyth stared. "Why?"

Mother Keeper gave him a long look. "I have been watching her for a while. She has an interesting ability – I want to learn more about it."

"Ability? Do you mean magic?" Kyth shook his head in disbelief. Ellah was one of the most normal people he knew. Surely Mother Keeper was mistaken.

"If you don't mind, Highness," Mother Keeper said, "I'll have her come to my chambers later tonight. If I can convince her, I'd be glad of her company. If not, no harm done."

"You don't need my permission, Mother Keeper," Kyth said. "Ellah is a free person." *With enough mind for two.* He was curious how this meeting would go. Would Ellah actually choose to travel with Mother Keeper rather than coming with him and Alder?

One way or the other, he'd know soon enough.

Brother Bartholomeos rose. "We have no time to lose. I'll start the arrangements for the official royal trains to accompany Your Majesty and the Prince. Fifty riders of the Kingsguard and—"

"No need," Evan said. "I'd rather we keep our trips a secret. His New Reverence seems to have too long a nose."

"But—"

"Don't argue with your king, Holy Brother. The prince will need no other protection but the two Diamonds. As for myself, I will travel in disguise with a small retinue, under the Pentade's guard. Let the reverend think I am still here."

"How exactly do you intend to avoid being recognized, Your Majesty?"

Evan shrugged. "You'd be surprised how little people notice. If Mother Keeper is indeed set on going with me, I could travel, for instance, as a stableman."

"A *stableman*?"

"I'm not that good with horses, but with a certain amount of humility, I believe I can pass."

Mother Keeper smiled. "That is possible, perhaps. I could assume the identity of Lady Eyandala Ellidorm, a lesser noble house of the Illitand Clan. I do share kinship and likeness with that house. And you, Odara, can be my handmaiden."

Odara Sul bowed her head, but Kyth saw her frown before she lowered her eyes.

"We must all leave as soon as possible," Magister Egey Bashi said, "if we are to make it back for the High Council. With Your Majesty's permission, on my way back from the Majat Guild I would also like to make a detour to the Holy City and find out more about the circumstances of Father Cyrros's election."

The King nodded. "Every bit of information would help, Magister," he said. "But this may be a challenging task for a scholar like you. Perhaps more of a military force–"

"The Magister has been on such missions before," Mother Keeper put in. "He's very resourceful and, importantly, he can blend in. I assure you, Your Majesty, that there isn't a better man we could send."

The King spread his hands. "I'll trust your decision on this, Mother Keeper. Besides, there seems to be very few we could trust with such a mission. So be it. And with that, shall we conclude our gathering?"

As they made their way along the passageway Evan fell in pace with Kyth, leading him away from the others. The Pentade followed, five noiseless figures blending in with the shadows.

"You must be careful, Kyth," the King said quietly. "Don't let your feelings for Kara get in the way. A thing like this could give your enemies an easy advantage over you."

Kyth felt color creeping into his cheeks. He didn't feel like discussing this, especially when the Majat were so close by and could probably hear every word. In the depth of his heart he also knew that his father was right. He couldn't allow his feelings for Kara to stand in the way of his mission.

Yet, how could he possibly let them go?

6
A CUP OF TEA

Ellah paused in front of the heavy double doors leading to the Keepers' quarters. She frowned and looked over her outfit before raising her hand to the massive wooden handle. It was her favorite dress, green with a brown bodice. Probably too simple for this audience, but wearing it made her feel more like herself. If the Keepers had anything to say about her looks, let them say it to her face.

Raising her chin high, she opened the door and stepped inside.

Two women sat in deep armchairs beside a fire. A third chair across from them was empty. A tray with a steaming teapot and three cups occupied a small table in between. As Ellah walked across the floor, one of the women turned and beckoned toward the empty chair. Ellah approached, trying to look confident, and lowered onto the corner of the soft seat.

Only now did she realize that the woman who beckoned her was Mother Keeper. Without her white robe she looked just like an ordinary woman with a kind face and thick graying hair.

Seated on her left was Odara Sul, wearing a loose soft dress of washed-out blue. Her hair coiled rope-like around her head. As Ellah looked at it, she imagined a tiny strand worm its way into the coil and smoothe itself against the shiny dark mass. She shivered.

"Make yourself comfortable, child," Mother Keeper said. "Have some tea."

She poured the tea and handed a cup to Ellah. A breath of fragrant steam met her face, coating her skin with a warm mist. Ellah took a careful sip. The tea had a heady flavor that made her feel lightheaded.

"I can see you have questions." Mother Keeper's quiet, tranquil eyes rested on Ellah.

There was no challenge in this gaze, but Ellah still felt she was being tested. She sat up straight and turned to Odara Sul. "Why does your hair move?" Her voice came out louder than intended, echoing clearly in the large room.

Odara Sul smiled. "I was experimenting with a new elixir. It's a revitalizer that can bring dead tissues back to life. It was meant to heal wounds. Very serious wounds. But I didn't realize at the time that the substance has more effects than we anticipated."

Ellah held her gaze. Some of these words were not familiar to her. *Tissue. Revitalizer.* It was perhaps part of the test, but Ellah knew better than to play by their rules.

"Can you control the way it moves?" she asked.

Odara Sul shrugged. "Not quite. But it's getting better. For the most part now I can make it go still when I really want to. But it's hard."

Ellah looked at the hair with fascination. "Is that what Keepers do? Invent new elixirs?"

"Among other things." Odara Sul glanced at the Mother Keeper as she spoke. Ellah did her best to keep her face straight and took another sip from her cup. A rich, herbal taste rolled through her mouth. The wind echoed on the outside of the thick window panes, dancing with the leaves in the garden and rippling the mirrored waters of the Crown Lake beneath the castle walls.

With a start, Ellah came back to her senses and noticed the two women looking at her intently. She carefully put her cup back on the table.

"What did you put in my tea?" she demanded.

Mother Keeper smiled and set down her own cup. "This tea comes all the way from the Eastern Empire. You can never get such a flavor from the teas grown in Tahr Abad or Bengaw. I myself enjoy it immensely. Yet, I can assure you, child, that there is nothing in this tea that would affect your mind."

Ellah regarded her with caution. Surely, what she felt right now couldn't be a coincidence. "You didn't answer my question. About what Keepers do."

Mother Keeper nodded. "What we do cannot be explained in one simple conversation. But I can try. Our name, Keepers, used to be longer. We used to be called 'Keepers of the Book of Knowledge'. That's what we are, but very few people remember it now. Back in our stronghold, the White Citadel, we study the Book of Knowledge and attempt to unravel its many mysteries for the benefit of mankind. We also try to preserve unique abilities that humans possess, and to make certain that these abilities are properly developed. And this, child, is why you are here. We sensed an ability within you that is quite unique."

Ellah sat up straight. "Ability? You mean magic?"

Mother Keeper smiled.

"I have no such ability!" What was this woman accusing her of? Ellah glanced at the door, prepared to jump up and run out of the room, but something in Mother Keeper's gaze held her in place.

"There's no need to be afraid, child," Mother Keeper said.

"I'm not afraid!" *Blessed Shal Addim, what did I get myself into?* Yet, she remained in her chair. She had a unique ability, Mother Keeper said. She, an ordinary girl, too skinny and sharp-featured to be attractive, was being called *unique* by this woman, who commanded one of the biggest powers in Tallan Dar.

"Then," Mother Keeper said. "Let's find out if I'm right."

Ellah bit her tongue. All this may not be true, after all. She was surprised that instead of relief she felt a small pang of disappointment.

"I know," Mother Keeper said, "that you sense a power within yourself and you are trying to suppress it, because you believe it's a curse. We think," Mother Keeper exchanged a quick glance with Odara Sul, "that you are gifted with the ability to sense the truth. This is a rare talent that needs to be developed. That's why you are here."

"*Truthseeing*?" Ellah stared.

"That's what common people call it, yes."

"But…" Words were failing Ellah. To hide her embarrassment, she picked up the cup from the table and took a lengthy sip.

Mother Keeper smiled. "You wanted to object, didn't you? But then, you sensed I was telling the truth. So, you didn't say anything. This is a simple example, but we believe you are capable of much more. If you are willing to find out, of course."

"Find out, how?" The words came out in a half-whisper. She felt frightened. She did *not* have a gift! She was normal, like everyone else.

"Allow us to teach you how to control it," Mother Keeper said. "If you do, you will always be able to tell true from false. You will speak to people and know if they believe what they're telling you. Don't you think such power is worth something?"

Ellah continued to stare, unsure what to say. Off hand, it sounded ridiculous. *No one* could have such power. Yet, if she could know true from false, *really* know without guessing…

"The Keepers," Mother Keeper went on, "pick up gifted children and save them from the Testing at birth, before the priests could identify and eliminate them. We take them into our White Citadel and teach them how to control their gift. We make them powerful, so that they can do good for others. And we rarely offer such privileges to adults, who have been brought up with different values and could do more harm than good if they learned to control their gifts. Yet, we offer this to you. Would you refuse?"

Ellah hesitated. "What would I need to do?"

Mother Keeper leaned forward and met her eyes. "Travel with us. Odara and I are going to accompany King Evan to Illitand Hall. You can go with us and on the way we'll teach you to control your skill. At the end of the trip, if you succeed, you can go free and use your gift as you will."

"And if I don't?"

"Then," Mother Keeper said, her eyes filling Ellah's vision like two pools of liquid light, "you will go back to what you were. A girl who denies her gift and tries to pretend it's not there. An extraordinary person who tries to fit in with the ordinary people. Whether you accept my offer or not, if you choose to bury your talent, this choice is up to you."

Ellah held the woman's gaze. "Whether or not I have this talent, I have a feeling you're not telling me everything."

Mother Keeper smiled and leaned back into her chair, breaking eye contact. She picked up her cup and finished the cooling tea, then put the empty cup back on the table.

"This is the first step in your learning," she said. "I dare you to find out what I am not telling you. We leave tomorrow. If you can tell me by then, you're ready to go with us. If not—"

"I don't need that long," Ellah said. "I can tell you right now. You *need* for me to come. You're going to meet someone with whom my truthsense would prove useful to you. Maybe the Duke of Illitand himself? That's why you want me to go with you, isn't it?"

For the first time she saw hesitation in the older woman's eyes. Then it dissolved into a broad, overwhelming smile.

"Consider this the start of your training, child," Mother Keeper said. "I look forward to our trip."

7
NIMOS

The road through the city's north gate ran up toward the hills, barely visible in the distant haze. The plains spread around it as far as the eye could see, in a gradual ascent to the distant Ridges' outskirts, a jagged line of peaks rising out of the blue haze at the horizon. Kyth turned in the saddle for a last look at the stone lace of the Crown City of Tandar, bathed in the beams of the rising sun. Behind it, the golden glow of the lake swallowed the horizon, making it seem as if the city, with its roofs, domes, and spires, was hanging at the edge of the world. Kyth held still for a moment, taking in the view. Then he urged his horse around the bend of the road, to level up with Kara riding in the middle of their small formation.

Kara was silent, her eyes fixed on the road ahead. As Kyth's gaze fell on her hand, he saw a fresh wound grazing her dark skin, half-hidden by the long sleeve of her shirt. Mesmerized, he leaned forward in the saddle and pulled the cloth away. "What happened?"

She shrugged. "Practice fight."

He looked at her in disbelief. There were very few people in the world capable of reaching through Kara's defense in a fight, and they were all her equals in rank. Diamonds. Did they do such things often? Wasn't it unnecessarily risky for Diamonds to be practicing with real weapons?

She grinned. "Mai has a wicked left hook."

"*Mai?*" A chill ran down Kyth's spine. He thought of Mai's staff with retractable blades. A treacherous, vicious weapon. To think that this ruthless man used it to fight Kara and wounded her.

"Do you often practice with real weapons?" he asked.

Kara's eyes glittered with mischief. "We don't. Our trainers could have our hides for this. It was just too… tempting."

"Tempting?" Kyth made the effort to adjust the mental picture again. It didn't quite work.

"Mai and I are well matched," she went on, seemingly oblivious to his emotions. "*Really* well. It's almost as if… as if he's my *shadow*." The last word trailed off into silence, the pause so long that it seemed she wasn't going to say anything else. But after a while she continued in a steady voice. "I guess I just wanted to find out."

"Your *shadow*?"

She turned to look at him, her gaze becoming distant. "Sorry, Kyth. It's something only a Majat can know."

Shadow. He didn't like the sound of it. "Did you also wound him?"

She shook her head. "No. Couldn't get through at all. Anyway, we only fought until first blood, and it happened to be mine."

Kyth's gaze slid to the scratch on her hand again. It was deeper than he had first thought, running along the edge of her wrist down to her fingers.

"Do you think it was a good idea?"

She grinned, mischief back in her eyes. "Definitely not. I was surprised he accepted my challenge."

Kyth's eyes widened. The image of Kara challenging Mai to a deadly fight was difficult to accept. Or was it the fact that she'd found it *tempting*? He was about to speak, but saw Raishan slowing down ahead. The Majat's downturned hand balled into a fist. Kara kicked her horse to level up, leaving Kyth behind.

The road ran around the bend into a small grove of mountain hazel, similar to those scattered here and there among the hills. As they neared the trees, Kyth imagined he saw movement in the low shade of the bushy growth by the roadside.

Kara and Raishan pulled their reins, bringing the party to a halt. They remained still for a moment, like two tightly strung bows ready to fire.

"Twelve," Kara said eventually. "Maybe thirteen."

"Right." Raishan urged his mount on at a walk. Everyone followed.

As the shadows of the first hazels fell on them, Kyth noticed several black-robed figures moving through the thicket parallel to them. Raishan rode to the outside of the formation, closest to the trees. Kara stayed in front.

Kyth kept his eyes on the bushes, trying to catch sight of the moving shapes. When he finally looked at the road ahead, he was so startled he almost fell off his horse.

Five hooded men stood across the road side by side, blocking the way. Kyth's heart raced. For a moment it seemed like a repeat of the scene back in the castle courtyard. His eyes darted to Alder, whose face mirrored his alarm. The brothers moved their horses closer together, pulling up behind the Majat.

Kara's face remained calm. She directed her horse at the roadblock, but the hooded men stood their ground, forcing her to stop. Then, the one in the center stepped forward and took off his hood.

He had a slight build, sharp bird-like features, and short brown hair that stood atop his head in an unruly mop. His eyes were so black that Kyth couldn't see the irises, just uniform ebony disks set deep inside the eye sockets. He shivered as the stranger met his gaze.

"Your Highness. What a pleasure." The black-eyed man slid forward and took Kyth's horse by the reins.

Raishan drew his sword. Alder freed the axe from its strap and weighed it in his hand. Egey Bashi crowded on them from behind.

Kyth stopped them with a raised hand. "Let go of my horse," he said.

The man smiled, glancing around the group. "Or what?"

"Or I'll take your arm off," Raishan said.

The man's hand dropped away, but his face did not show proper fear as he turned to face the Majat. "So, the boy's under protection, eh? Is he paying you, Aghat?"

Raishan kept his silence, adjusting the grip on his sword in a short, meaningful gesture.

"What do you want?" Kyth asked, still keeping his hand up.

The man turned back to him, his black eyes drawing light into their dizzying depths.

"All I want," he said, "is to become your friend. Close friend, Your Highness. Perhaps, close enough so that we could travel together?"

Kyth slowly lowered his hand. "Who are you?"

The man chuckled. "I'm Nimos. And I'm really so glad to meet you, *Kyth*."

Kyth narrowed his eyes. "You've met me. Now what?"

Nimos's dark eyes searched the party and stopped on Alder.

"What about you, handsome lad? Don't *you* want to be my friend? Convince your foster brother that we aren't so bad after all?"

Alder raised his axe. Its thick, polished handle sunk into his large palm. His menacing look spoke without words.

Nimos winked, an expression of mischief on his face. "No? Such a pity. For a moment there, you seemed like a smart one."

Kyth shifted in the saddle. "Why don't you leave us alone before someone gets hurt?"

The man chuckled, turning to his hooded companions as if inviting them to laugh with him. "So sweet of you to worry about your friends, Highness. But don't worry. If you go with us, we won't harm anyone."

"Actually," Kyth said. "It wasn't my friends I was worried about." He glanced at Kara, who moved her horse between Kyth and Nimos, forcing the man to shuffle back.

Nimos turned to Raishan. "How about it, Aghat? We'll pay you handsomely to take the Prince off your hands." At his signal one of his men held out a small but clearly heavy bag. It jingled as he took it and weighted it in his hands.

"You can also keep the gold the Prince is taking to the Majat Guild," Nimos went on. "Three times the price of a Diamond, if I am not mistaken." He glanced at Kyth's saddlebags.

Kyth's skin prickled. *How does he know?*

"All I'm asking is that you and your charming companion" – Nimos winked at Kara – "continue on your way and leave the Prince to us."

Raishan raised his sword, exchanging a quick glance with Kara.

"Clear the road," Kara said. She urged her horse another step forward, forcing Nimos to edge away.

"I can double my offer, Aghat."

"*Now.*"

"Or what?"

"Or," Kara said distinctly, "I'll take your head off."

Nimos cast a slow, deliberate gaze over her.

"Don't you want to draw your weapon to threaten me first?" He flicked his eyes to Raishan. "*He* did."

"I don't threaten," Kara said. "Neither does he."

"Ooh, what a pity. I heard Diamonds' weapons are unique. I *so* much wanted to see yours!"

"You'll see enough of it, if you don't clear the road."

Nimos gave her another appraising glance. "Is that a promise, Aghat?"

"It's a fact."

He hesitated, then signaled his men. Black hooded shadows slid out of sight, so quickly that they appeared to glide over the ground. In a moment the road was clear, the black figures nowhere in sight. Only the retreating sound of rustling in the roadside bushes indicated their recent presence.

"We'll meet again," Nimos told Kara. "I am sure of it."

"I'm not."

The black-eyed man sighed. "You sadden me, lady. I'd never forgive myself if I failed to meet you again. Something tells me we'll know each other really well. Perhaps even travel together?"

"I don't think so."

Nimos swept a glance around their group and it seemed to Kyth as if a cold wind passed through.

"It's been a pleasure," Nimos said. "Until next time."

He turned and disappeared into the hazel thicket. Leaves rustled in his wake. Then everything became quiet.

Kyth slowly woke from his trance as he watched Kara and Raishan relax in their saddles.

"What do you make of this, Aghat Raishan?" Kara asked.

Raishan shrugged. "No idea. I thought they were going to attack."

"It seems to me they knew what they were up against."
Egey Bashi glanced at the two Diamonds.

"They looked very similar to those men who attacked us in the castle courtyard, Kyth," Alder said.

"Yes," Kyth agreed. "And this Nimos reminded me of Kaddim Tolos, too."

"In what way?" Egey Bashi asked.

"Something about his power."

"*Power?*"

Kyth hesitated. "There was something about him… As if he was about to use magic, but changed his mind. Or maybe, he knew it wouldn't work?" He glanced at Kara.

Egey Bashi shook his head, but kept his silence.

They started up the road again at a fast trot, keeping a tight formation. Thinking back to the strange encounter, Kyth shivered as he thought of the way the man, Nimos, looked at Kara. As if he knew everything about her. As if he was sure he was able to defeat her. He seemed so *confident*.

8
THE ROAD

Ellah hated side saddles but her elaborate travel dress, befitting a maid to the Lady Eyandala Ellidorm, made it unthinkable to ride the normal way. She envied the King, a natural on horseback, as if he was born in the saddle.

King Evan had been right about his disguise. Dusty road clothes and a plain brown cloak indeed made him look like a common servant. A hood hid the long black hair of a Westland royal and threw a deep shadow that concealed the paleness of his skin. Only his piercing blue eyes still stood out, but it took a very close look to notice.

The Majat looked even more impressive. All five of them rode horses with an ease that made any other form of travel seem like a chore. As for Mai, he looked absolutely breathtaking riding his black stallion. No man had the right to be that handsome, the way his soft blond curls rested against his muscular neck, the way his dashing black outfit accented his white skin, making it seem smooth like silk. His relaxed pose in the saddle, with one hand on the reins and the cloak thrown back over one shoulder, was so graceful it was painful. Every glance in his direction made Ellah feel clumsier, sitting on the horse sideways, holding on for dear life to keep up with the slow trot of the others.

They rode in a tight formation, with Mai and King Evan in the lead, followed by Mother Keeper, Ellah, and Odara Sul, and the four Ruby Majat bringing up the rear. Despite their relaxed poses, Ellah could sense their alertness, eyes darting in response to every move around the King and his suite.

In addition to the usual guard station, the city gate was manned by four Holy Knights who sat on their mounts peering into the faces of the passers-by. They gazed with disinterest at the King, who rode through with lowered eyes, and followed Mai and Mother Keeper, the two people in the group whose confident postures suggested they were in charge. Ellah's heart raced as she made her way past the armored figures, but no one made a move to stop them.

After the gate the road became wider, enabling their party to ride close together.

"It seems, Your Majesty," Mai said after the city gate disappeared from view behind a road bend, "that if you really want to go unnoticed we should keep off the main road."

"I thought we were past the danger, Aghat. They didn't recognize me, did they?"

"Still." Mai appeared calm, but Ellah heard an edge in his voice. "I didn't like the Holy Knights at that gate. They looked far too alert. Something's not right."

The King raised his face into the breeze, inhaling the fresh smells of ivy buds and apple orchards. "Aren't you worrying too much, Aghat?"

Mai kept his eyes on the road. "It's my job to worry, Your Majesty."

"Aghat Mai has a point, Your Majesty," Mother Keeper put in. "If we travel back roads, we run less risk of being recognized."

Evan shrugged, then nodded. "I suppose you're right."

"If I remember the maps," Mai said, "there should be

a trail coming up soon. It bears east, and will take us to Illitand Hall faster than the main road."

A distant smile creased Evan's lips. "It's a rather small one, if I remember correctly. The Duke of Illitand and I used to take it on our hunting trips, years ago. But," he turned to Mother Keeper, "taking this trail would mean no inns to stay at. We'd have to camp."

"The Keepers are used to camping, Your Majesty," Mother Keeper assured him. "We'll be just fine."

Ellah bit her tongue. She was used to camping too, but not in her ridiculous outfit, designed for court outings rather than traveling in the wilderness. She thought of her own comfortable clothes stowed in her pack, and vowed to change on their very first stop.

"If I remember correctly, Your Majesty, " Mother Keeper said. "There's a river out east, running through a deep canyon before it reaches the lake. Would we be able to cross it if we take that path?"

"There's a bridge," Evan told her. "I'm told the locals keep it in good order."

"Very well. How far ahead is this trail?"

"Not far enough," Mai said.

"What do you mean, Aghat?"

Mai pointed.

A patrol of a dozen Holy Knights had just appeared from around a road bend ahead. Their mounts were lizardbeasts, the glint of their scaly hides accenting the glow of the knights' polished armor. The black-and-red banner flying over the group bore the sign of the Holy Star.

"I swear," Evan said quietly, "the roads of our kingdom are creeping with holy vermin. There's no place for peaceful travelers to ride by anymore."

Mai's lowered hand flicked a complex sign. The Rubies

responded, straightening up in their saddles and riding to the outside of the formation to surround the group in a protective ring.

As the knights approached, the one in front lifted the visor of his helmet. His pale eyes gleamed in the setting of his reddish suntan.

"Identify yourselves."

Ellah's skin prickled. Something was wrong, she just couldn't quite catch what it was.

Mother Keeper straightened in the saddle. "I'm Lady Eyandala Ellidorm," she said haughtily.

"And these?"

"*These* are my suite. How dare you stop us!"

"We're under orders," the knight said. "To look for travelers in disguise."

He is lying, Ellah realized with a chill. *He's not what he says he is*. She glanced around desperately, trying to think of a way to relay this to Mother Keeper, but the older woman wasn't looking at her. Ellah looked toward Odara Sul, but couldn't catch her gaze either. She couldn't risk turning around further.

She took a deep breath. "Whose orders are you following?" she asked the knight.

All heads turned her way. Mother Keeper's look of surprise turned to suspicion as she held Ellah's gaze. Ellah gave her a barely perceptible nod, but the exchange didn't escape the knight.

"For a noble lady's servant," he said, "you are much too ignorant."

Ellah turned to Mai. "They're lying to us! They're not who they say they are!"

Mai nodded. "Get behind me. Now!" He threw off his cloak, his horse prancing into the way of the advancing knights. His lowered hand flicked three fingers, then one. Three of the Rubies moved forward to form a line behind him, shielding the rest of the group. The fourth one stayed at the back, beside the King.

The knight at the front pulled his lizardbeast to a stop and measured Mai with a mocking glance.

"Stay out of the way, boy," he said. "We wouldn't want to spoil your pretty face, now would we?"

Mai smiled. "Tell your men to back down before anyone gets hurt."

The knight's laughter echoed hollowly inside the iron helmet. He lowered the visor and signaled to his men.

Five knights at the front rushed at Mai, aiming their short spears. The Majat leaned out of the way. His horse steered aside and leapt past, into the depth of the attackers' line. In a moment he was surrounded by knights lashing at him from all sides. He slid through their midst like black lightning, leaning one way or the other, seemingly within reach but always avoiding contact. His horse danced between the lizardbeasts, sidestepping the attackers, circling around them as Mai threw his weight left and right to dodge the blows. Without drawing his weapon, he rode through the gauntlet and came out on the other side unscratched.

"What's he *doing*?" Odara Sul gasped by Ellah's side. "He's not going to *fight*?"

Mai stopped his horse a little way up the road and turned, facing his attackers. Some of them were reining in their lizardbeasts to chase him, others turned around to face the line of the three Rubies standing their ground. They looked furious.

"Now we're *really* in trouble," Odara Sul whispered. "They–"

She paused as the leading knight swayed in the saddle. He hovered, grasping the air with his hands, and crashed onto the road. The one on his left followed, armor clanking like a blacksmith's scrap pile. A beast further off flipped onto its back, weighted down by its owner desperately clinging to its long neck for support.

"Blessed Shal Addim!" Odara Sul gasped. "He cut the straps of all their saddles!"

All around them the knights were collapsing. The road became a chaos of kicking and rearing lizards, crawling men, and heaps of metal armor tangled in leather harnesses. Some lay still, others made awkward attempts to get up, struggling against the heavy armor. A lizardbeast ran past, its harness flapping loose. Another beast made an attempt to escape and was pulled down again, landing legs-up in a heap of groveling shapes.

Mai maneuvered his horse around the fallen enemies back toward their group. A dagger glinted in his hand. With a quick movement he tucked it into his boot. Then he swung down from the saddle to pick up his cloak from the roadside.

"I suggest we get out of here quickly," he said. "I wouldn't want to be around when they recover."

They took off at a gallop and soon left the group of knights far behind. Glancing over her shoulder, Ellah could see metal gleaming in the sun as the fallen men struggled to get up and regain control of their lizardbeasts. They were clear for the time-being.

After a while Mai followed Evan's pointing finger off the road onto a side trail, so small that they had to slow to a trot and ride single file. Two Rubies fell behind. The rest of them continued, eventually slowing down to a walk.

They rode until sunset and camped by a large ivy grove next to a brook. Ellah was so tired that she could barely sit straight. She slid off the horse, steadying herself against its steaming side and thinking of how much this was going to hurt tomorrow.

Mother Keeper, Odara Sul, and the King didn't look much better. Only the Majat were as fresh as ever. Before Ellah could even unstrap her saddle bags, one of the Rubies collected wood for the fire and the other went to the brook with a small kettle. Mai disappeared into the bushes on one end of the glade and soon reappeared on the other side. He nodded to the Rubies, then settled by the fire, using his boot dagger to cut the supports for the kettle from the prepared wood pile.

Ellah wanted to participate in cooking, but soon found that she was no match for Odara Sul. The Keeper's deft hands seemed to be everywhere at once as she peeled, chopped and stirred, adding pinches of substances from small boxes and pouches packed into her travel bag. Even the Majat looked at her in awe as she moved around the fire, in control of the ingredients that appeared in her hands as if by magic before making their way into the pot. The result was a meat stew so juicy and rich with flavor that it seemed like the best meal Ellah ever had. She scraped her bowl clean with a piece of bread and sat back sipping tea and enjoying the warmth spreading over her tired limbs.

Somewhere during the meal the two missing Rubies appeared from the direction of the road and took their places beside the fire. Odara Sul handed each of them a steaming bowl, but before starting their meal they exchanged glances with Mai. Only after receiving his nod of approval did they direct attention to the food, which they wolfed down in no time.

Ellah took it upon herself to clean up. She collected the bowls and spoons into the empty pot and made her way down to the brook. Pulling out a patch of tall grass she rolled it up into the likeness of a washing sponge, using sand and mud on the bank to scrape off the grease.

Halfway through her washing, she turned her head searching for a fresh patch of grass, and jumped.

Mai was standing behind her, only a few paces away. She had no idea when or how he got there. She scrambled up to her feet, shaking the unruly strands of hair out of her eyes and trying to keep her greasy hands out of sight.

"How long have you been standing here?" she demanded.

He didn't respond. In the gathering dusk his eyes were in shadow and his hair glimmered like gold against his pale skin.

"How did you know they weren't the Holy Knights?" he asked.

Ellah was taken aback. She didn't expect this. Should she tell him about her gift – if indeed she had one? She wasn't sure what to say at all. It was so hard to think with him looking at her like this. She was beginning to feel hot and was grateful for the dusk that hid the color of her face.

"I just – it seemed to me that they were lying," she said.

"It didn't just 'seem', did it?" he insisted. "You wouldn't have risked everything if you weren't sure."

Ellah lifted her chin. She didn't like it when people thought they could read her.

"How do you know I wouldn't have?" she challenged.

He stepped closer, looking into her face. From this distance she was no longer sure she could hide her blush. She wanted to back away, but there was nowhere to go. Behind her, there was only water.

His eyes were still in shadow, but she could feel the intensity of his gaze.

"Call it a hunch," he said.

He was so close now that she could smell his skin – a faint fresh scent of spring water with a touch of pine. The blush rolled down her neck. Her heart pounded, making it hard to think.

"All right," she admitted. "I knew."

"How?"

She forced herself not to blink. Her helplessness against his closeness made her angry. She gathered all her remaining wits and took a deep breath.

"Call it a hunch," she said.

He held her gaze for a moment longer. Then he turned and slid off into the darkness in the direction of the camp.

When Ellah finally made her way back with a pile of clean dishes in her arms, Odara Sul was waiting.

"You took a while."

Ellah didn't respond. Her gaze drifted toward the fire, where Evan and the Majat were sitting, deep in conversation. Mai had his back to her, his eyes fixed on the shadows.

"Mother Keeper is waiting," Odara said.

"For what?"

"To begin your training. Come."

Intrigued, Ellah followed Odara to the side of the camp. Mother Keeper was sitting on the corner of a blanket, her back straight, legs crossed with the knees flat on the ground, in a pose that Ellah was sure she could never manage.

"Come, sit," Mother Keeper beckoned.

Ellah approached and lowered onto the opposite corner of the blanket. "I can't sit like you."

Mother Keeper smiled. "Just make yourself comfortable."

Ellah relaxed, trying to find a comfortable position on the blanket. After a day's ride it wasn't an easy task. She glanced toward the center of the camp. She knew she shouldn't be visible to the people sitting in the bright circle of the fire, but she could swear Mai, from the far side of it, was looking her way.

"It's essential for our lesson that you are able to concentrate," Mother Keeper said, following the direction of Ellah's gaze. "Do you think you can?"

Ellah tore her eyes away from the distant group and looked at the woman. She was blushing again, but she hoped it wasn't too noticeable in the darkness.

"Yes," she said.

"Good," Mother Keeper said. "Now, tell me what happened on the road today."

"I'm not sure. I just– suddenly I *knew* this man was lying."

"You did fine," Mother Keeper assured her. "I was the one who was slow to react. It is fortunate for all of us that King Evan has such formidable guards."

Ellah couldn't help stealing another look at Mai, but he was now sitting sideways, engaged in a conversation with Evan. She relaxed.

"I did feel this way before," she said, "but usually no one believed me. And then it always seemed to me later that I was wrong. But this time…" She paused.

Mother Keeper nodded. "This time we believed you, and you were right. I can teach you how to control it, so that you could always tell. Now, listen." She moved closer and put her hands over Ellah's. Her touch was warm. "Close your eyes. Make yourself very comfortable. Lie down, if you want. And listen to my voice. Try to distinguish if I am telling the truth."

"But how?"

"There is a method to it. You should think past my words. You should try to separate my voice into tones and undertones, so that you could tell whether I am thinking in harmony with what I say."

"Past the words? I don't understand."

"When you listen to people and recognize that they are lying," Mother Keeper said, "it's not the words that you recognize, it's the feeling behind the words. Every time you hear a lie, there's something you can detect in the speaker's feelings that other people can't. The purpose of our lessons is to try to identify this something, to separate it from the rest, so that you can sense it every time. Try."

Ellah leaned back and lay down on the blanket, facing upward to the clear night sky. It felt good after the hard day. She closed her eyes, listening to Mother Keeper's voice.

"When a king of Tallan Dar dies without an heir, succession must be decided by the majority vote at the High Council, with House Dorn holding the principal claim against the other royal houses," Mother Keeper said.

"True." Ellah hesitated. "But I don't think I need my gift to tell. This is how King Evan won the crown."

"Try another one. If the Royal House Dorn has no eligible heirs, the next in line to rule is the head of the Royal House Illitand."

"It's the truth." Ellah's eyes widened. "Really? But that would make the Duke of Illitand eligible to contest –" she clasped her hand over her mouth. The information put a new spin on their current trip. If King Evan was the last in his line, wouldn't he be in danger right now, riding in disguise straight into Illitand's stronghold? *Relax*, she told herself. Kyth, Evan's rightful heir, was alive and well, under the Majat's protection. There shouldn't be any problems, should there?

Mother Keeper only smiled, as if oblivious to the unspoken question. "Now, let's try a different one. Odara Sul learned to cook from her grandmother, who was also a Keeper of high standing."

Ellah hesitated. "A lie."

"Which part?"

"I am not sure. Both?"

Mother Keeper shook her head. "The first part is almost true. Odara Sul's grandmother *was* a great cook, but she never was a Keeper. She died when Odara was very young, so Odara never had a chance to learn much cooking. We continued her training as a cook in the White Citadel."

"There is something wrong about the way you said it just now."

"Which part?"

"The last one. You almost believe it, but not quite. Which makes it not exactly a lie, but…"

Mother Keeper gave her a long look. "You're better than I thought. The part you are sensing is about cooking. We didn't exactly train Odara to *cook*. But it's not important now. Your purpose is to try to understand how you can tell."

Ellah closed her eyes again and relaxed back against the blanket, listening to Mother Keeper's next statement.

"Ghaz Shalan Testing was first instigated in the Old Empire, when the court alchemists came upon a substance that can boil when it comes into contact with the blood of the gifted. The gift was later proclaimed to be a curse, and the liquid was adopted by the Church as the way to test all the newborns in the Empire."

"It seems like the truth," Ellah said, "but it shouldn't be. The Holy Book says that Ghaz Shalan Elixir was discovered with Lord Shal Addim's guidance by Father Bertoldos, nine hundred years ago, to help eliminate ungodly creations of the Cursed Destroyer."

"Yes, the Holy Book does say this, doesn't it?"

Ellah sensed a smile behind the older woman's calm tone. She sat up. She knew that many in their kingdom opposed Ghaz Shalan Testing, and that quite a few people – including Kyth and Ellah herself – would have been dead if the priests had their way all the time, but to say that the holiest elixir in existence came from anywhere else but Shal Addim's grace was blasphemy. At least it had been, in the world where Ellah had grown up.

"And you think *you* know better, don't you?" she asked.

Mother Keeper smiled. "*You* tell *me*."

Ellah hesitated. *This is just a lesson,* she reminded herself. Besides, what Mother Keeper said didn't have to be the truth – she just had to *believe* she was telling it.

She closed her eyes and lay back again.

There was a brief pause before Mother Keeper went on. "A large part of the Bengaw province is covered in swamps that originate from the Dark Mire in the Forestlands."

"True."

"Aghat Mai is looking at you," Odara Sul suddenly said.

Ellah sat up so quickly she felt dizzy, and spun around toward the fire. Mai was still turned sideways, deep in conversation. He wasn't looking her way at all.

Ellah glared. "You lied, didn't you?"

"Yes, and you believed me!" Odara doubled over with laugher.

"But –"

Mother Keeper's glance silenced them.

"It's the most important part of your lesson today," she said to Ellah. "You can't sense the truth where your emotions are involved. And this is your most vulnerable spot. We must learn to overcome it."

"But how?" Ellah felt helpless. Despite Mother Keeper's words she found it so difficult to draw her eyes away from Mai's perfect profile. Why did he have to be so handsome? Why did he have to catch her alone this evening and sneak up so close to her? Why did his smell, the faint scent of pine and spring water, make her feel so weak inside?

"Try to think," Mother Keeper said. "What makes you

feel something is a lie?"

Ellah closed her eyes one more time.

"Colors," she finally said. "When you speak, I see colors. Blue or green when it's true. And red or pink when I think it's a lie."

"What about the times when you cannot tell?"

"They kind of shimmer. And when I think harder they can turn any color I want."

"Now he's *really* looking at you," Odara Sul said.

Ellah made a move to rise, but Mother Keeper's hand held her in place.

"Try to tell if this one is true. Then you can look."

Ellah relaxed back into the blanket. She tried to think, but when she imagined that he could see her sprawled like this, with her hair in disarray, with the collar of her shirt folded away showing too much of her neck, she couldn't possibly think straight. She tried to tell herself that no one could possibly see such details looking from the brightly lit fire into the darkness, but it was hard.

"Probably a lie," she finally said.

The hand let go. She rose up to a sitting position and looked.

Mai's head was turned her way. It was far, and the blaze of the fire was right in front of him, but she could swear that he looked all the way to where she sat and met her eyes. Then he smiled and turned away.

Ellah blushed so deeply even her neck went crimson. Mother Keeper watched her intently.

"He's quite dashing," she said quietly. "But you must be careful around him, child. Remember, he's a hired killer, cold-blooded and ruthless. If he gives you any attention, it's either for his amusement or to serve some hidden purpose."

Ellah looked away. She knew Mother Keeper believed her words to be the truth. But what if she was wrong about this one? What if Mai really was different?

9
NIGHT-TIME ENCOUNTER

"These hazels are too young," Egey Bashi said. "It would be hard to find any firewood."

They had been riding well into dusk and camped at the edge of a hazel grove beside a small brook, tethering their mounts to the low hanging hazel branches with enough leeway to reach the water and the rich grass pasture on the other side. A semicircle of stones piled waist-high on the far side of the glade created a primitive shelter to protect travelers from the bitter flatland winds. A pit filled with old coals lay in the center of the protected area. A small pile of firewood was propped under a protruding stone ledge, an aid to stranded travelers trying to start a fire.

"This should be enough for a bit," Raishan said. "But we'll need more later on. It's going to be a cold night."

"I'll go gather some wood," Kyth volunteered.

"I'll go with you," Kara said, exchanging a short glance with Raishan.

Kyth laid down his pack next to Alder, busy unpacking their food supplies, and wrapped himself tighter in his cloak before following Kara into the deep hazel growth.

It promised to be a cold night. As they picked their way along the uneven ground, Kyth could see his breath coming out in thin streaks of vapor. The hazel branches spread above them, their deep shade making it difficult to see ahead. Kyth strained his eyes to focus on Kara's cloaked figure creeping away into the gloom.

"There really isn't much dry wood in here," she said after a while.

"Maybe we should just cut some fresh branches?" Kyth suggested.

She shook her head, her hair a pale gleam in the forest dimness. "Fresh wood would never burn. Let's go further. Maybe we'll find a dead tree or something."

Further ahead the trees were scarce , letting in enough moonlight to illuminate the eerie landscape with a suffused, silvery glow. Kyth caught up with Kara, watching the soft line of her profile, barely visible in the forest shade.

"When Nimos looked at you," he said at length. "I... I..." He took a deep breath. "I was afraid," he confessed.

"Afraid?"

"I don't want anything to happen to you because of me."

She let out a short laugh. "Me? What could possibly happen to *me*?"

Kyth hesitated. On one hand, it seemed ridiculous to fear for her; she was one of the best fighters in existence. Only her fellows in rank could match her skill. She was also immune to the disabling power wielded by their mysterious Kaddim attackers. And yet, since their encounter with Nimos, Kyth couldn't escape the nagging feeling that something was about to go terribly wrong.

"My presence puts you in danger," he said. "I can feel it."

She laughed again. "What's gotten into you? I'm here to protect *you*, remember?"

He shook his head. He didn't know how explain it to her. In the face of her certainty he was beginning to doubt himself. Perhaps deep down it wasn't concern for her that made him feel so insecure, but fear of the possibility that after they reach the Majat Guild he might fail the negotiations and lose her.

"Do you think your Guildmaster will let you go on with me?" he asked.

She shrugged. "He will, if you pay the price. He cannot refuse. Unless–"

"Unless what?"

"Unless he's already committed me to another assignment. But even then, someone would have to hire me by name to take precedence over you, and no one has hired a Diamond by name for hundreds of years."

"Really?"

"It costs triple, and it really makes no sense. Everyone knows all Diamonds are truly equal in skill, so why pay triple for the same thing?"

Kyth nodded. Her words were reassuring. "I'm glad we'll be together," he said quietly.

She stopped and turned to face him, her eyes two dark spots in the forest dimness.

"Kyth–"

"I'm sorry, I shouldn't have said it." Kyth lowered his head. He was a prince, a man whose wishes mattered very little when it came to choosing a bride. His feelings for Kara, if pursued, could lead to a scandal, maybe even a war, but they could never lead to a proper marriage. He cared too much to put her through that. It seemed much better never to mention his feelings to her. Yet, when she stood in front of him, so close that he could detect her faint natural scent of wild flowers, it was too hard to control himself.

"I… I know we're not a proper match," he said.

"It's not that." She reached forward to touch his hand. Her warmth made him shiver as he closed his fingers over hers.

"It's not you," she said. "It's me. I'm not allowed to *have* any feelings, for anyone. It would go against my training and everything I am. I do care for you, but–"

Her breath burned his cheek. Her eyes filled his vision, beckoning. Her faint scent was driving him mad. He wasn't sure what he was doing anymore.

As Kyth drew closer, she turned and met his lips. The kiss echoed through his body like silent thunder. His head swam, his mind retreating to give room to raw senses. He immersed in her closeness, her warmth, her smell. He didn't know how long it lasted. Her skin was smooth under his lips, the silk of her hair caressing his cheek. Her kiss drowned him and brought him back to life and drowned him again.

After an eternity he emerged, weak and senseless, his entire being driven by the sole desire to hold her close, so close that he couldn't tell the two of them apart anymore. He felt her body go tense in his arms as she made a move to draw away. He *couldn't* let her go, but through their incredible closeness he sensed that she wanted him to stop. It was the hardest thing he'd ever had to do; to lower his arms and step away, weak and trembling, helpless as if he had just been reborn and didn't know how to make his first steps into the world.

"Kara," he whispered.

She drew away, shivering. "I shouldn't have done it. Sorry."

He didn't move, waiting for her to continue. He felt dizzy. It took all he had to be so close and not to touch her, to force his arms to stay lowered by his sides.

"We can't let this happen again, Kyth," she said quietly.

"Why?" He kept his voice to a whisper, so that she

couldn't hear the plea. The thought that one day they would part forever was unbearable. There *had* to be a way to make this work.

"Like you, I'm not free to choose my fate," she said quietly. "My life belongs to my Guild. Whatever our feelings for each other, I can never be more than a bodyguard to you."

In the darkness he couldn't see her eyes, but he could sense the tension in the set of her neck, in her guarded voice that hid the emotions inside.

"Isn't there another way?" he asked.

She shook her head. "We must let it go, however hard it is. I *can't* be with you, Kyth. I may look like a normal girl to you, but I'm not. You can't even begin to imagine how *different* I am."

He longed to hold her again, to comfort her. He could sense that behind her composure she was aching inside, just like he was. But he stood still. He didn't want to cause her more pain.

She faced him a moment longer, then set off into the dark.

When they finally emerged from the shade of the trees with piles of dry wood in their hands, Kyth sensed something was wrong even before Kara froze in front of him, her still shape melting into the shadows. A moment later a long, thin lash whizzed through the air, aimed at her face. It looked like an unfolding whip, except that in the moonlight it gave off a faint metal gleam.

Kara dropped the pile of wood, keeping one thick branch, which she put up in the way of the advancing menace. There was a crack and the stick broke in two, a clean cut that didn't seem possible for a whip-like weapon.

The lash came back, but this time she had her sword in hand. The blade met the whip with a screech. She flicked her wrist, sending her sword forward in a snake-like movement, answered by a thud and a curse. The whip came free. She caught it at the base and pulled it free of the sword.

"A *shektal*," she observed calmly. "Is there a reason for attacking me, Magister?"

The bushes rustled and a cloaked shape emerged from behind the boulder.

"Sorry, Aghat," Magister Egey Bashi said. "I thought you were someone else."

"No problem." Kara's full lips twitched as she handed him back the weapon.

Raishan and Alder rose out of the bushes on the other side and made their way toward them. Alder looked shaken. He held his axe, its crescent blade gleaming in the moonlight. A long oozing scratch crossed Raishan's cheek.

"What's going on here?" Kara demanded.

"What took you so long?" Raishan's voice had a hidden edge.

A snigger from the far end of the glade made them spin around. A hooded figure came into view.

Nimos. Kyth's skin crept.

The flickers of the dying fire painted his black cloak with blood-red shades. His hood was pushed back, revealing the sharp, drawn features of the hollow face and the deep eye sockets that remained in shadow. Behind him, hooded figures emerged. Each had a weapon in hand, a spiked metal ball on a long chain.

Kyth suppressed a gasp. *Orbens! Just like the men who attacked us back at the castle.*

"An excellent question," Nimos said, his voice echoing clearly in the night air. "Why should it take so long for two capable people to gather a simple bundle of firewood?" He stepped into the moonlit center of the glade.

"A piece of advice, Aghat Raishan. Never send a boy and a girl together into a dark forest. They'd do more than just collect firewood."

Kara and Raishan closed around Kyth, swords in hand, watching Nimos cross the glade. He stopped in front of Kara, the lusty gleam in his eyes making Kyth's guts wrench in revolt.

"It brings joy to my heart, Aghat Kara," Nimos said, "to finally see your weapon out in the open. You only bring it out to fight, don't you? Are you going to fight me? It would be… oh, so sensual. It makes me excited just to think about it."

"What do you want?" Kyth demanded.

Nimos's lips stretched into a smile that didn't touch the rest of his face.

"All I want is to be your friend, Highness. We're not that different, after all. There's at least one passion we both share." He glanced at Kara, licking his lips suggestively.

"Get out of here!" Kyth could barely hold his anger.

Nimos laughed. "You'd force me to go? Without even a proper goodbye?"

"Unless you want to fight us," Raishan said.

Nimos turned and gave him an appraising glance. "Tempting, but regrettably I didn't bring enough men to fight two Diamonds."

Raishan shrugged. "Tough luck."

"I was hoping, however," Nimos went on, "that you and Aghat Kara might have reconsidered my offer."

"Sorry you had to go through all this trouble for nothing."

"Come now, Aghat Raishan, you're a reasonable man. I'm offering you a fortune for this boy. Should I double it?"

"Should I count to three?" Kara asked. "I don't normally say this, but my sword hand is getting restless."

Nimos licked his lips again with slow deliberation. "Oh,

you're such a tease, naughty girl. I know that you have two swords. Hence, two sword hands. You wouldn't be a Diamond if you couldn't use both hands equally well, and ooh, the mere thought of it excites me. I love a woman with a grip. I can show you so many things you could do with your, as you call it, sword hands, rather than hold weapons. Something your boy here can't possibly dream of. You have but to say the word."

"*One.*"

"Oh, please, don't change the subject. We were just getting started, weren't we? By the way, you look so pretty when you're angry!"

"*Two.*"

"You break my heart, beautiful Kara. But if this is your final word—" Nimos waved a hand, a gesture answered by a rustle from across the glade as his men retreated back into the shadows. With a last glance at Kara he darted toward the bushes. In moments, the glade stood empty, the sound of rapidly retreating footsteps disappearing into the distance.

Kara stood still for a moment, then flicked her swords into the sheath at her back. "Let me take a look at your wound, Aghat," she said to Raishan.

The Diamond shook his head. "No need. It's just a scratch."

"What happened?"

He shrugged. "I'm not quite sure. It was as if I lost focus for a moment. I've never felt that way before."

"They used their power on him," Egey Bashi said darkly. "It was short, and very deliberate. I had a feeling it was some kind of test."

Power. They wanted to know if other Diamond Majat besides Kara are immune to them. Kyth's heart raced. He had no doubt now that Nimos and Kaddim Tolos were connected.

Worse, they were after him. And it was clear now that no one except Kara could protect him.

The fact that Nimos didn't bother to hide his connection with Tolos – displaying orbens and openly wielding his power – was even more frightening. As if he was really sure he would succeed in whatever it was the Kaddim had planned. *What do they want with me?*

"We should eat," Kara said. "And get some sleep. Tomorrow's a long day."

Raishan nodded. "We should keep watch," he said. "I believe we may be in for a very eventful trip."

10
CROSSING THE GORGE

Ellah straightened in the saddle and looked around. For the past two hours the path had been climbing steadily upward, until it finally ascended above the line of bushes onto a plateau. After riding through the undergrowth, with low branches slapping across her face or holding on to her with sticky fingers, it was nice to feel the wind and enjoy the view that opened up around them. A wavy line of bushes to the left marked the path of a stream, carving its uneven way from the distant hills barely visible on the horizon, down to the Lakelands. On their right, the blue haze descended to the flatness that concealed the wide waters of Lake Illitand.

The path was so narrow they had to ride in single file. In front of her was the tail end of Odara Sul's sand-colored mare. Whenever she glanced behind, Ellah could see Lothar, a Ruby Majat, riding a chestnut gelding at a measured distance of exactly five strides. It was a comfortable arrangement that left her with very little to do except dodge the branches and enjoy the view.

She realized the interruption when Odara Sul's horse came to a stop, halting everyone in her wake. At first Ellah didn't make much of it, using the extra time to stretch her back and take a full breath of air. Then she started to hear the sounds of argument carrying down the line of riders with the gusts of wind.

"…find a way around," Mother Keeper's voice floated in.

"…knew there was a bridge but didn't know it was just a…" Evan's voice replied.

"…for the locals. They probably don't want anyone else to…"

Odara Sul rode off the path onto the grass and made her way to the head of the procession. Ellah followed, bypassing another Ruby, Brannon, to level up with Mother Keeper.

The sight that opened up in front of her was so unexpected that she pulled on the reins too hard, causing the horse to toss its head and make an abrupt stop. The path ahead ended in an abyss. From where she was, Ellah could see steep cliffs cascading down the gorge to the stream, so far below that the sound of running water was no more than an echo on the rising wind.

A narrow bridge made of two logs placed side by side and tied together with waxed coils of rope ran across the chasm. It was barely wide enough for one person to walk across. There was no rail on its side.

Ellah froze. She had always been afraid of heights. Back in the Forestlands where she grew up with Kyth and Alder, she could never climb a tree, no matter how much fun other children made of her. Despite her longing to share their games, she had always stayed clear of the observation platform the brothers built up on the tall oak at the edge of their grove when they were twelve. She was even afraid to stand up on a stool at home to get the dishes from the top shelf. And now, staying on horseback within three lengths from the chasm, made her stomach turn.

Everyone was dismounting and Ellah followed, anxious to feel the firm ground beneath her feet. She stood aside, listening to the conversation.

"Isn't there another way?" Mother Keeper insisted.

King Evan shrugged. "Not that I know of. Finding a way around might take days. For all I know, our best chance would be to retrace our steps all the way to the main road."

There was a pause as everyone surveyed the scenery. It didn't look any better now that Ellah's pounding heart had slowed enough for her to be able to think straight. There was absolutely no way they could go forward from here. They would have to return to the main road and take their chances with the Holy Knights.

It didn't seem so bad a choice, considering.

"The bridge looks sturdy enough," Mai said. "I'm sure it can hold the horses, if we lead them across one by one." He exchanged glances with the Rubies, each of them giving a barely perceptible nod.

Ellah's heart missed a beat. Was he *out of his mind*?

"*Horses*?" Odara Sul exclaimed, echoing her thoughts. "You can't possibly mean it, Aghat! Horses would never be able to walk on logs. You know how they tend to prance sideways? They'd step off to their deaths! And even if they don't pull any of us down with them, how far do you think we can get in this wilderness without mounts?"

Mai shrugged. "You should give horses more credit, my lady. They can walk in a straight line just like everyone else."

"But –"

"Aghat Mai is very good with animals, my lady," Lothar put in. "If he says it can be done–"

"However good with animals he is, I don't think –"

A short glance from Mai made Odara stop.

"I'll lead my horse over first," Mai said. "If you have any doubts after that, we can discuss it further."

Odara Sul didn't seem convinced, but she had obviously run out of arguments. Mother Keeper came to her aid.

"Horses are like people, Aghat," she said. "They're all different. *Your* horse may be able to do it, but if any of the others are not as well trained, or, by chance, are afraid of heights—"

A smile glimmered in the corners of Mai's mouth. "Leave this to me," he said.

"But—"

"Aghat Mai never says things unless he means them," another Ruby, Brannon, joined in. "You should trust him, my lady."

Ellah's stomach knotted, her legs soft like rubber. She was afraid to even glance in the direction of the chasm, so wide, with just a thin streak of wood running across. She could vividly imagine horses stepping sideways in the middle of the crossing and sliding off to their deaths. What she could *not* imagine was herself, out on that bridge, with the emptiness all around her and nothing to hold on to.

She clasped her arms across her stomach to prevent nausea from rising up to her throat. Luckily, no one was looking her way, busy with the preparation.

The Majat took off their cloaks and wrapped them loosely over the horses' heads, so that the animals were effectively blindfolded without suffering any discomfort. Mai, standing the closest to the chasm, gave his reins to Brannon and walked across the bridge and back again. Ellah could barely bring herself to look at him, a slim figure over the emptiness beneath, but Mai was walking as easily as if he was on flat ground. He stopped here and there, rocking the bridge with his feet to feel how sturdy it was. Apparently, the result satisfied him. He came back to the waiting group and took the reins. Then, he stepped onto the bridge, leading his horse.

Everyone held their breaths. Ellah forgot her own fears, caught in the moment. Mai walked slowly this time, stepping sideways with one hand on the horse's forehead and the other holding the reins with a very short leeway. His horse followed every one of his footsteps precisely, to place its hooves in rhythm with his feet onto the surface of the narrow bridge. Once, Mai stopped and brought his face very close to the horse, whispering in its ear and patting the side of its long neck. Then he continued, over the end of the bridge and onto the safety of the turf on the other side.

"I'll be damned," Odara Sul whispered.

Ellah was aware of the collective breath let out as the area on their side of the bridge resumed its activity. From the other side of the chasm, Mai gestured to Brannon and the Ruby Majat stepped onto the bridge, leading his horse. He walked even slower than Mai. Everyone watched as he made his way across, following the pattern established by his leader, with the reins very tight and one hand on the horse's muzzle. Once his horse attempted to stop. Mai gave a short command from the other side. Brannon nodded and grasped the reins firmer, tugging on with a steady hand. The horse followed without further interruptions as Brannon led it off the bridge.

The Ruby took the reins of both horses and led them out of the way. Mai walked back along the bridge.

Two more horses crossed. Ellah stood as far away as she could without causing suspicion, watching the wind cascading along the valley blow the horses' tails and the cloaks wrapped around their heads. Lothar, on the closer side of the chasm, was handing the horses to Mai, who led them over one by one; calm and easy.

The routine broke when Odara Sul's sand-colored mare was led toward the bridge to be blindfolded. At the sight of the chasm, the horse reared, breaking free of its hold. Lothar tried to catch the reins and was knocked backwards as a hoof caught him on the shoulder. The horse bared its teeth and rolled its eyes in panic.

Mai appeared as if out of nowhere, stepping up from the side to avoid the flailing hooves. He placed a hand on the mare's back, catching the long end of the trailing reins, and held steady as the horse reared again, thrashing its head against the hold. When the horse came down, Mai used his free hand for support and swung into the saddle. The horse bucked, trying to throw him off, but he managed to hold on. It took no more than a few moments for him to calm the horse enough that it would obey the reins. He turned the panicked animal away from the bridge, directing it on to ride a few paces back along the path, down to a standstill. At his silent signal, Odara Sul handed him the cloak and he fastened it around the horse's head, all the while keeping the animal away from seeing the chasm. Then he dismounted and took the reins.

It was like magic. The horse followed him like a trusting child. It never wavered as it stepped onto the bridge and made it across, into the safety of Brannon's receiving hands.

Ellah let out a breath.

"Damn it!" Odara Sul said. "He's an animal whisperer!"

Ellah didn't know what she meant, but she didn't try to find out. As her turn to cross the bridge neared, weakness spread over her body, rising in a nauseating fog that made everything around her seem unreal. She was vaguely aware of her own horse being taken away, of Odara Sul disappearing from her side, and of Mother Keeper beckoning her before making her own way across. And then she was alone, standing in front of the bridge with everyone else on the other side.

She couldn't do it.

But there was no way she could show any of them that she was afraid.

She took a step forward.

Don't look down.

The bridge under her feet was steady, and not as uneven as she thought. Still, she could vividly imagine her foot failing to find a hold on the roughly hewn logs covered by the slippery coils of rope, making her stumble and fall down into the gorge below.

So deep.

Don't look down.

She took another step, trying to look calm and focus her eyes on the group of people on the other side. They weren't paying attention to her, busy with their horses and saddlebags. But Mai standing by the side of the bridge was watching, and there was no way in hell she was going to show him that she was afraid.

Don't look down.

She tried to focus on the trees on the other side, so far away as she made her way along the narrow bridge. She stepped forward, trying to find a foothold.

And then the wind caught her.

A sideways gust caught the folds of her shirt and tugged, swaying her off balance. Her foot, searching for a hold, found a twig and slipped. She threw her arms out, trying to find something, anything to hold on to. As she swayed, trying to regain balance, her eyes moved against her will, down to her feet and below.

Blessed Shal Addim.

From this height the river looked no thicker than a rope coiling on the ground. She could barely hear the sounds of the rushing water, much more distant than the sound of the wind that was trying to knock her off the bridge and send her down, tumbling over, into the chasm. Her searching hands grasped for support, but all they could find was air.

Blessed Shal Addim.

She was losing balance.

She was going to die.

And then, suddenly, her hand came upon a solid object. She felt someone catch her arms and steady her.

She forced herself to look up and met a pair of steely blue eyes..

Mai.

"Close your eyes," he ordered.

His voice was quiet, but its commanding tone was impossible to disobey. She closed her eyes, feeling the world sway around her in the gusts of wind. She held on to him, her hands going numb from the strength of her own grasp, and yet she couldn't possibly feel safe.

Blessed Shal Addim, we are both going to fall.

We're going to die!

He is going to die saving me.

I can't let that happen.

"Let go of me!" she pleaded. "You can't save me! I'm going to fall!"

He put an arm around her, drawing her closer. His hold was steady, like iron. She swayed against him, but he stood still, supporting both of their weights against the impossible shift of balance.

"Don't move," he told her.

The wind tugged at her. The bridge rocked with it, a barely perceptible movement that made the thick, solid wood seem like a hammock. She swayed.

"I can't!" she wailed.

He held her so close that she could feel his breath on her cheek, his soft golden curls brushing her skin. His body against her was light as the wind, yet hard as the rock. It seemed like nothing could possibly throw him off balance.

She grabbed on to him, trying to keep still. But she couldn't. She was going to fall, and she couldn't possibly let him be pulled down with her.

"Let me go," she sobbed. "Please, I can't let you die saving me!"

"Don't try to fight me. Just relax. I've got you." This time there was no command in his voice. It was soothing, no louder than a whisper. It crept to her gut, making her feel warm inside. She suddenly became aware of his arms around her, of his perfectly sculpted muscle, iron-hard under the silky cloth of his shirt. She was helpless against his closeness. She couldn't resist it anymore. She relaxed into his arms, giving in to the incredible sensation of strength and balance that he emanated, to his warmth and closeness that made her forget where she was, forget everything else except his body next to hers.

His skin had the faint smell of spring water and pine. Inhaling it, she suddenly felt stronger. She took a deep breath, steadying herself on her own feet.

"Now," he said. "Let's walk."

They were so close now that their bodies felt like one. As he moved, she felt that his sense of balance had become part of her, so that she had no trouble stepping along with him.

"Keep your eyes closed," he whispered, "and follow my feet. You're safe. I'm here. I've got you."

He is leading me like a horse, a part of her mind thought. But she didn't care. All she cared about was the steadiness of his body against hers, his soothing voice that kept talking to her, engulfing her in the incredible feeling of warmth and safety he emanated. It seemed that nothing could possibly happen to her as long as he was near, so strong that even if she swayed and lost her footing he would never let her fall.

She didn't remember how she made it to the place where, instead of wood and waxed rope, there was real soil under her feet. Mai's hands disappeared. Ellah's knees gave way and she sank to the ground, sobbing.

After a while she felt arms around her, soothing, calming, but different. A voice sounded close by her ear.

"It's all right," Mother Keeper said. "It's over. You're safe."

Slowly, Ellah raised her head and forced herself to look. She knew they were probably all watching her now, thinking how stupid and useless she was. She couldn't bear the shame of having everyone see her like this, her face swollen with tears. Not after she had been such a *coward* and needed rescue where everyone else was fine.

To her surprise, Mother Keeper was alone.

"Where's everyone gone?" Ellah asked, her voice hoarse with tears.

"There's a clearing up ahead," Mother Keeper said. "They're setting up camp."

"But–" Ellah turned to look into the older woman's eyes.

Mother Keeper smiled. "I think," she said gently, "we've all had enough excitement for one day."

Ellah lowered her head. "Aghat Mai risked his life for me. I did nothing to deserve it. He must think I am so–"

"Human?"

Ellah stared.

"It's normal to be afraid of heights," Mother Keeper said. "I myself was very afraid of heights once, a long time ago. At home, I couldn't even stand on a stool to get dishes from the top shelf."

"*You*?" Ellah looked at her in disbelief.

Mother Keeper's smile widened. "Yes."

"But–"

"We all have our weaknesses." The older woman shook her head. "It would be foolish of Aghat Mai to think badly of you just because of what happened. I think you'll agree with me that whatever else he is, he definitely isn't foolish."

"But he…" Ellah paused. How could she possibly say this? That he held her so close that their bodies felt like one, and that this breathtaking closeness made her forget everything, even the danger she was in. That he led her like a horse, blindfolded and trusting, ready to follow him anywhere, even to the ends of the world. She met the older woman's eyes, feeling helpless with the new sensation, for which she had no name.

"He did what he could to save you," Mother Keeper said. "And he succeeded. This is all that matters, and all that you should remember from this incident. Don't think that if you're weak somewhere you can't be strong in other things. And, above all, don't let your weaknesses weigh down your strengths."

She got up from the ground and shook the grass off her clothes.

"Now, come," she said. "I can smell Odara's cooking. Dinner must be ready soon."

She walked off along the path into the gathering dusk. Ellah hastily got to her feet and followed.

11
PURPLE

Ellah found Mai at the edge of the camp. He was sitting on the ground behind a large elderberry bush, polishing his weapon. She stopped a few paces away, waiting for him to acknowledge her presence, but he was deeply absorbed in his task and showed no awareness of her.

Finally, she cleared her throat.

"I wanted to thank you," she said.

There was another long pause, in which she started to doubt if he knew she was there. His eyes were half-closed as he ran his polishing stone in turn along each blade at the ends of his staff, listening to the resulting sound.

Ellah was beginning to wonder whether she should just leave, when he finally raised his head and looked up at her.

"No need." He set aside his polishing stone and took out a piece of soft cloth, running it along the length of his weapon. The new procedure was soundless, but seemed to absorb his attention no less than the previous task. Ellah felt very tempted to retreat back to the fireside, where everyone else gathered to discuss the events of the day, but stopped herself. She *had* to go through with it.

She took a deep breath.

"You could have died," she said. "I could've pulled you off balance. If we both fell, there would have been nothing you could've done. And, I know you didn't have to do it. I know your duty is to protect King Evan, not me."

She paused. Now it *really* felt like a good time to retreat. If she turned and ran, she wouldn't even have to see his face when he looked up. She wouldn't have to know if he thought of her the same way as she imagined herself this afternoon, a foolish coward with no more sense than a horse.

She clenched her teeth and stood her ground.

Mai slowly put aside his polishing cloth and raised his head to look her straight in the eyes. To her surprise, he was smiling.

"You couldn't have pulled me off balance," he said.

She stood back, unsure of what to say.

"Like I said," he went on. "There's no need for you to thank me. It was no trouble at all."

She looked into his eyes. It suddenly felt so easy talking to him, as if he was one of the youngsters she grew up with.

"Whatever you say," she said. "But even if it was no trouble for you, you *did* save my life. So, I wanted to thank you. Really. And," she glanced at his weapon lying beside him on the grass, "I'm sorry for interrupting."

She turned to go, but his gaze held her.

"Want to sit down?" he asked, gesturing to a place next to him.

Her heart quivered. She approached on stiff legs and sat, conscious to keep a clear distance from him. She was careful to look ahead and not at him, but she could feel his eyes on her. It was almost too much to take.

"So," he said after a lengthy pause, in which Ellah's cheeks made it through several shades of pink to a steady red color. "Tell me about yourself."

"What do you want to know?" Ellah heard herself say.

He didn't respond. After a moment she dared a glance and caught his eyes. His gaze was steady, so direct that it made her feel exposed as if she was naked. Yet, she couldn't look away. His quiet interest held her tighter than any bond.

"You're Prince Kythar's friend," Mai said. It wasn't a question, but since he didn't continue, she felt like an answer was needed.

"We grew up together," she said.

He nodded, glancing at the distant campfire through the thick elderberry growth, and back to her face. "So, how come you're not traveling with him?"

She hesitated. She really wasn't sure what to tell Mai. Even if she was starting to believe she had the gift, it didn't seem right to share it with a near stranger. On the other hand, this man *did* save her life. She owed him a huge debt. At the very least, he deserved to know more about her.

"Mother Keeper asked me to go with her," she said.

"Why?"

"Because," Ellah took a breath, "she thinks I have a… a talent and she wants to help me learn to use it."

His eyes lit up with keen interest. "You mean, magic?"

"Sort of." Why was it so hard not to blush?

"What kind?"

"I can sense whether someone says the truth. At least, Mother Keeper thinks I can."

"Can you?"

She hesitated. "Most of the time. But not always."

He gave her a long look. "That's how you knew those men back on the main road weren't the Holy Knights?"

She nodded.

"So, you're going to become a Keeper?"

His smile challenged. It made her want to impress him. But she couldn't lie to him now, could she?

"No," she said. "I'm just along for a few lessons."

His expression didn't change. She wasn't sure what he thought, but the look in his eyes had her trapped.

"So, you can really sense the truth?" he asked.

She swallowed. "Yes."

"Let's try," he suggested. "You ask me something and see if I tell you the truth."

"Ask you what?"

The smile faded from his lips and for a moment he looked almost serious.

"Anything. Anything at all."

"And you'll answer?"

"Yes."

She thought about it. "How old are you?"

The smile was back, teasing, challenging. It made him look even younger than he already seemed.

"Twenty-four," he said.

She looked at his face, at his smooth skin, at the soft blond curls and the slim body that made him seem so much like a young boy. She could have sworn he was not much older than her, nineteen at most.

"Really?"

"You tell me." He laughed.

She hesitated. It was certainly possible. Despite his boyish looks, he had to be quite a bit older than Ellah to get a Diamond ranking among the Majat and serve as the head of the King's personal guard for the past four years. And yet–

See the colors, she reminded herself. Red or pink if he was lying. Blue or green if he was telling the truth.

She closed her eyes, trying to focus his words into the color palette.

The color filling her mind was purple. She strained her inner vision, but there were no other colors.

"I – I don't know," she finally said.

He laughed. "What about your power? Can't you use it?"

She met his eyes. "I just... I can't tell."

"Let's try one more time," he suggested.

His direct look was difficult to bear. She suddenly felt like she did back on the bridge, with his arms around her, and his muscle hard against her skin. The draw was irresistible like the draw of the wind pulling her over into the abyss.

She looked up at him helplessly. His face was serious, but in the depth of his eyes she saw laughter.

Mother Keeper's words floated up in her mind. *He's a hired killer, cold-blooded and ruthless. If he gives you any attention, it's either for his amusement or to serve some hidden purpose.*

Looking at Mai, at his handsome face, at his graceful form and soft blond curls, she couldn't believe it. But now she had a chance to find out.

"Why are you doing this?" she asked.

He kept her gaze. "Doing what?"

She took a deep breath. "Acting like... like you *care*."

He didn't respond at once. He continued to look at her. Except, there was no more laughter in his eyes.

"Maybe because I do?" he said quietly.

She felt dizzy. Now she almost wished for him to laugh, to show her that it was a joke. Yet another, deeper part of her wished that it was true and that she could once again fall into his arms and feel the closeness that made them, for a moment back on the bridge, feel like one. But he didn't move. He just sat there, his gaze comforting and disquieting at the same time.

"Don't," she whispered. "Don't do this. You can't possibly mean it."

"Can't you tell?"

She looked deeper into his eyes, feeling that she was losing hold. The purple color filled her mind, overpowering all the rest.

"No," she whispered.

"Use your power."

She only shook her head.

His gaze wavered and became normal again, laughter dancing in its depths.

"One last question," he said. "Make it easy this time."

She took a breath, forcing herself to calm down.

"How many people have you killed?" she asked.

Once again, there was a flicker of seriousness before she saw laughter back in his eyes.

"About two hundred," he said.

Colors. See the colors. Ellah focused, trying to see past his words like Mother Keeper taught her. She closed her eyes and relaxed, trying to distance herself from his eyes that rested so boldly on her blushing face. Yet, the only color she could see was purple.

She opened her eyes.

"I don't know," she said. "Somehow, with you, I can't tell."

There was a gleam in the depth of his eyes. For a brief moment she thought she saw triumph, but she dismissed the thought. What could he possibly gain from her confession?

She felt exhausted. Even if Mai *did* care, she had enough sense to know that there was an abyss as deep as the one they crossed today between caring for someone and being close. She had no business playing these games with a Diamond Majat. She wasn't a romantic like Kyth. She should know better.

Yet, never in her life had she felt the way she was feeling now. Everything inside her was turning over with this new, frightening and blissful feeling.

12
MIDDLEDALE

"This man, Nimos, is really strange," Alder said. "His behavior doesn't make any sense. I mean, he *knows* he doesn't have enough force to attack us. Why bother to show himself twice in a row and alert us to his bad intentions?"

For a while no one responded to the question, busy as they were with the meal – wild duck wrapped in clay and baked over the coals. Kyth had been skeptical about the recipe, watching with distaste as Kara and Raishan spread mud over the feathers, not bothering even to pluck the bird beforehand. But when the duck was fished out of the coals and the baked clay removed, the feathers came off with it to reveal the skin roasted to a perfect golden brown. The meat, carved into pieces and sprinkled by a fragrant spice from Raishan's pack, was surprisingly tender. It was their best meal in days.

"He must be desperate if he's willing to offer us so much gold just for leaving Prince Kythar without protection," Raishan said.

Egey Bashi lowered his bowl, his eyes thoughtful. "It seemed to me Nimos had something else in mind. Did you see the way he looked at Kara?"

"Yes." Kyth's voice came out more forcefully than he intended. He bit his lip, hiding his embarrassment by staring into the fire. One question continued to bother him all this time. Did his gift help Kara to become immune to the Kaddim? When he looked at her and thought of his feelings toward her, did he transfer some of his resistance to her?

He was still thinking of it when he went to sleep, sinking into a disturbing dream where hooded figures with orbens crowded in on him from all sides.

When he woke up, dawn had already lit up the horizon in the east. Alder was still sleeping, but Kara's and Egey Bashi's cots were empty. Raishan was busy by the fire. A faint streak of smoke carried the reassuring smell of burning wood and the promise of a hot breakfast. Splashing and voices came from the creek down at the bottom of a shallow ravine beside the camp. Kyth jumped to his feet and made his way down the muddy slope.

This close to the Ridges, the stream was fast and much too cold for comfort. The chill emanated by the water enfolded him as he approached. Kara rose up to greet him, shaking back her wet hair. The halo of droplets around her head caught the rising sunlight and burst out in tiny rainbows. Then it was gone as she smoothed down her hair, squeezing out the water. She looked so beautiful, her dark skin lit up by the glow of the rising sun, wet hair resting against her neck in a smooth golden wave.

"Too cold," she remarked. "Makes your hands stiff."

"Damned right," Egey Bashi said from beside a deeper pool further downstream. He had his robe off, his hairy muscular torso naked down to the waist. Steam rose off his skin as he dipped his arms into the water, splashing it over his back.

Kara stepped aside, letting Kyth on to the flat patch of the bank where the protruding stones formed a path, reaching the deeper part of the stream. Kyth met her gaze as he walked by and caught her brief smile. He smiled back, but she had already turned away, heading up the muddy bank back to the camp.

The water was indeed icy cold and as Kyth splashed it onto his face and hair his hands went numb. He hastily finished washing. As he stood up and turned away from the brook, he saw Magister Egey Bashi standing there, watching.

"Are you all right, Highness?" he asked.

Kyth hesitated. Since the start of the trip he never found time alone with the Keeper. And now, finally, he had a chance for some answers to questions that had been troubling him for a while.

"Can I ask you something, Magister?" he said.

Egey Bashi nodded.

Kyth swallowed. "Why do you think the Kaddim are after me?"

Egey Bashi's face darkened. "I can only guess, Highness. I can't know for certain."

"But you do have an idea, don't you, Magister? I could see it in your eyes when I first told you and my father about the Kaddim's attack."

The Keeper shook his head. "Guessing serves no purpose, does it?"

Kyth met his eyes. "Please, Magister. You think I'm facing something terrible. It is important for me to know what it is."

"Very well, Highness." The Keeper spoke with reluctance, averting his eyes. "My guessing amounts to little until we know for sure – and I hope we never will – but here's what I know. The Kaddim's magic is very old and powerful. Their ability to subdue their opponents is only a small part of it.

Their leader – rumored to be the reincarnation of Ghaz Kadan himself – has the power to absorb magic through a long and torturous process that destroys the original bearer of the gift."

Kyth shivered. "You think they're after my gift?"

The Keeper nodded. "Your gift, Highness, has to do with controlling the elemental powers. No one knows how it really works, but combined with the Kaddim magic of mind control, it would give them command of virtually everything in this world. These gifts complete each other, multiplying the Kaddim power to make them undefeatable. There would be no stopping them if they succeed."

Kyth shivered. "But even with the gift, someone immune to their power can kill them, right?" He thought of Kara and the way Nimos looked at her. Did her immunity make her enough of a threat to the Kaddim?

Egey Bashi frowned. "Something not commonly known about the Kaddim is their ability to reincarnate. Even though their bodies can be killed, they are technically undead."

"But we saw a man die in the castle's dungeons after Kaddim Tolos's attack."

The Magister shook his head. "That man wasn't a Kaddim Brother. He was a servant, no more. The true Kaddim Brothers are very few, but they are rumored to have survived in different bodies for centuries, ever since the fall of the old Shandorian Empire, whose last emperor was a Kaddim Reincarnate. If the Brotherhood is on the rise, he is also around somewhere, you can be sure of it."

Kyth nodded, his mouth dry. He hoped he wasn't going to create a dark page in his kingdom's history by surrendering his gift – and his life – to the Kaddim. Would Kara's protection be enough to spare him such a fate?

They returned to camp and, after a quick breakfast, set out on their way.

During the day the road slowly ascended to the higher grounds, making the horses shift from a trot to a slow walk. The jagged line of the distant Ridges became more substantial, looming in the northwest. In the clear air Kyth imagined he saw snow peaks on the horizon, ghostly shapes above the line of the distant clouds.

The trees became scarcer, hazel groves giving way to sickly, crooked mountain oaks rising here and there out of the yellowing grass. Protruding boulders painted the surrounding fields with brown and gray spots. The sun was hot but the wind was getting cooler, forcing them to wrap tighter in their cloaks.

Watching the road ahead, Kyth slowly became aware of a distant patch of greenery, getting more and more visible as they drew closer. It looked like a green grove of oaks, healthier and fuller than their sickly counterparts scattered around the hills. Kyth imagined he could make out houses among the growth, their domed roofs as gray as the boulders around them. Smoke coiled out of the low chimneys, mixing with the afternoon haze.

Kyth rose in his stirrups to see further ahead.

"Is that a village?" Alder asked by his side.

"Middledale," Raishan said. "There're hot springs around this place. Very popular with travelers going up to the Ridges. For a moderate price you can get a room with your own bath."

This seemed too good to be true.

"Are we going to stop there for the night?" Alder asked hopefully.

Raishan and Kara exchanged glances.

"We were planning to be further ahead by now,"

Raishan said. "But horses are not as good on the uphill as lizardbeasts. I guess we could use the break."

In another half hour they neared the outer buildings of the strange settlement. Kyth looked around in wonder.

Low, domed houses rose out of the ground in front of them like giant rain mushrooms. Some buildings consisted of several mushrooms planted side by side, connected by passages and spreading around for a hundred yards each way. Their outside walls were half-hidden by the thick, fleshy crowns of the mountain oaks, whose low thick trunks heavy with lichen sprouted multiple branches in every direction. Each dome had a smoking chimney, but up close Kyth could see that the smoke rising out of them looked more like steam, settling in water droplets over the surrounding greenery.

"Where's the moisture coming from?" Alder wondered.

"Each house has a hot spring inside," Raishan told him. They need no other heating source here. In fact, it can get downright hot at times."

They rode to a larger building toward the middle of the settlement, whose battered sign with a foaming mug on it identified it as an inn. The words underneath it were covered in lichen, making it impossible to read.

Warm fog enfolded the large vaulted space of the inn's common room. Scant daylight found its way through the narrow windows, leaving the dome overhead in shadows. Tables surrounded with sturdy wooden chairs filled the space as far as the eye could see. Some of the tables were set with lanterns, flickering with small tongues of flame.

As Kyth's eyes adjusted to the gloom he realized that the center of the room was occupied by a stone basin, where water bubbled and poured over the edges, running along a narrow paved trench into an opening of the wall at the far end. He also realized that the smell of boiled eggs with a faint touch of rot that dominated the room came from the basin itself and not from any of the dishes on the customers' plates.

There were very few customers. A large group of men wearing patched travel cloaks sat all the way on the other side, partly hidden from view by the vapors rising from the basin. Several lone figures occupied small tables with lit lanterns along the wall. The rest of the room was empty.

"Let's find a table," Raishan said. "Once we're settled, Master Olren will be sure to show up."

They sat around a table and threw down their gear. Kyth's clothes and hair were slowly getting damp in the humid air, but the warmth emanated by the water in the basin was a welcome change from the bitter wind outside.

The innkeeper emerged from the depth of the room and stopped in front of the table. He was short and slim, with thick brown hair and pale gray eyes, wearing an oversized apron over a baggy brown outfit and carrying a damp towel over his shoulder. As he paused to survey the newcomers, he used the edge of the towel to wipe his forehead.

"Welcome, Master Raishan," Master Olren said. His northern speech, with hard vowels and softer consonants, told of the man's local upbringing. "Such a pleasure to have you back with us."

Raishan nodded in acknowledgment.

"We'll have whatever you're serving today," he said. "And a pitcher of ale."

"And rooms later on?"

"Please." Raishan flicked a coin out of his purse and handed it to the innkeeper.

Kyth knew the ritual. These small coins that looked like no more than simple coppers came from the Majat Fortress and had a lot of buying power throughout the lands. The price was included in the Majat's services, making it unnecessary for Kyth to reach into his own purse. The innkeeper took the coin with a solemn face and put it away with such care as if it was a precious gem.

Today's meal was a thick goat stew with herbs that gave the dish a slightly bitter taste. It seemed unusual at first, but became better with every bite. By the time Kyth finished his bowlful, he was ready for more. The bread that came with it was dark and sour, but made a perfect accompaniment for the stew. The brew was sweet and smelled of honey. It rolled through the body with warmth, making Kyth realize how tired he was after days of intense riding.

When they were almost finished with their meal, they saw movement in the large group of men seated on the other side of the room. One of them got up from the table and walked over.

As he made his way through the fog, his features became more and more familiar. With a sinking heart, Kyth recognized the slight build, short brown hair standing around his head, hollow cheeks, and dark shadows of the eye sockets.

Nimos came up to their table and stopped beside an empty chair.

"Long time, no see!" he exclaimed. "Fancy running into all of you here. Mind if I sit down for a moment?"

"Yes," Kara said distinctly. "I mind."

The man looked her up and down in such a suggestive way that Kyth's stomach turned.

"Oh, come now, it won't even be a minute." Nimos put his hand onto the chair back and made a move to sit down.

Kara reached down to her belt in a sweepingly fast gesture, bringing out a fan of throwing knives. Her look became appraising as she balanced the entire pack in her hand, blades out. Then, with a short flick of her wrist, she sent them flying across the table. Knives whizzed through the air and arrived, hitting their target with dry thuds. Everyone gasped.

Nimos backed away from the chair, his face pale. From where he sat Kyth could see the chair seat covered in protruding knife hilts, sticking out of the wood at even intervals that made the chair look like a balding porcupine. Kyth counted twelve knives, their blades buried deep into the wood.

It took incredible skill and strength to one-handedly throw so many knives at once. It took even more to have them all go in at such even intervals and penetrate the wood so deeply. Kyth knew how hard it was to provoke the usually composed Kara into such a display. He glanced at her sidelong, but she looked calm as she leaned back into her chair.

Nimos looked up. Behind the shock, there was a strange satisfaction in his face.

"Impressive," he said. "I must learn that trick one day."

"I have more knives, right here," Kara said. "It seems, however, that there isn't much room left on the chair. I'd need another target for the next throw. Want to stick around for a moment?"

Nimos cocked his head to one side. "I was hoping you'd reconsidered my offer, Aghat. We did, after all, leave you alone for quite a few days now. As we're all getting close to the Majat Fortress—"

She flicked out the knives. Nimos backed off.

"Only six left," Kara said. "But I think it would be enough if I only target the vital organs. In fact, I could probably make do with two."

Nimos swallowed. "I guess this means we will have to do things the *other* way, then. Well, maybe it's all for the best. After all, this way will allow us to see so much more of each other, Aghat Kara. I shall look forward to it."

He turned and walked away.

"He certainly knows a lot about us," Egey Bashi said slowly.

"What the hell did he mean by the *other* way?" Raishan wondered.

But nobody had any answer to that.

13
ILLITAND HALL

Evan pulled his mount to a stop. The fortress city of Illitand Hall loomed up ahead like a giant beast crawling out of the water. The jagged stone wall spiraled around it like the spine of a stone dragon curled up for sleep. Inside its protective circle the city rose up in cascaded steps toward the distant castle, its elegant shape reigning over the lake.

The entire city was built on a hill protruding out of the lake near the shore. Technically it was an island, but the strip of water that separated it from dry land was so shallow that a tall man could walk across without getting his shirt wet. Evan had heard stories how during droughts the water receded to make the city stand on land, and how in spring the lake swallowed the stone bridge that connected the island to the main road, keeping carts and wagons away for days at a time. Now, in high summer, the waters stood low, and the bridge lay wide open to the travelers on their way to the lake dwelling of the Illitand lords.

Evan urged his mount on toward the bridge, but Mai placed a hand on his reins, bringing the horse to an abrupt stop. He used his other hand to signal to the Rubies, who rode up and formed a line at the front of the group, with the King and the women behind.

"Forgive me, Your Majesty," Mai said. "But we can't approach the city on horseback."

Evan looked from his bodyguard's alert shape to the city wall ahead, its massive stones bathed in the warm afternoon sun. The blue haze of the lake made the city look peaceful, like a serene painting by a countryside artist. Yet, from everything he knew about Mai, the Diamond was not prone to sudden panic attacks.

"Why not, Aghat?" he asked.

"There're archers on that wall," Mai said. "See those slits?"

The King narrowed his eyes.

The outer ring of the city wall was composed of roughly hewn boulders that rose to a height of at least three houses out of the lake waters. A row of narrow openings ran along its jagged top, placed at even intervals as far as the eye could see. Looking carefully, Evan could now see movement inside those openings, arrow points protruding just enough to be visible to a careful observer. But surely this was no more than a precaution?

"They wouldn't attack their king," he said.

Mai's lips twitched. "Begging your pardon, you don't look like a king at the moment, Your Majesty."

"I'm sure they'll recognize me when we get closer."

"They *might*. Once we get closer." Mai met his gaze. In the pause that followed Evan felt a chill run down his spine. The very thought that these men could fire at him from the wall was preposterous. The silent implication that they wouldn't stop after they recognized their king made it an outrage. Duke Daemur Illitand *couldn't* give such an order and risk being beheaded for high treason. And yet–

"What do you propose to do?" he asked at length.

Mai raised his hand and pulled his weapon from the strap at his back.

This was the first time Evan had seen Mai draw his weapon for anything other than the daily polishing ritual. Unwittingly, he gathered his reins tighter to make sure his horse didn't bolt.

"I trust you don't plan to attack the fortress with only five men, Aghat?" he asked.

Mai shrugged. "We can get you close enough to the wall for them to recognize you."

At least two hundred yards of open road separated them from the bridge and the tightly shut gate. The stretch lay open, not a single tree in sight.

"You propose to *walk* all this way against the Lakeland archers, Aghat?"

"Would you rather go back, Your Majesty?"

Evan looked at Mai in disbelief. He should have stopped questioning the Majat's skills by now, but he found it hard to imagine five men, armored in no more than light leather doublets, withstand a direct attack of arrows. It was rumored that a skilled Lakeland archer could pierce a metal breastplate from a hundred yards.

Yet, from everything he knew about Mai, the Diamond was not known for idle boasting. Besides, after all the trouble of getting here, there was no going back.

"Lead on, Aghat," Evan said.

Mai nodded. "We must dismount and leave our horses here, Your Majesty. The Pentade will walk in front to deflect the arrows. Please stay very close behind." He turned to the Rubies to signal orders.

"What about Mother Keeper and everyone else?"

"If we get a proper welcome, they'll join us. If not – we'll have a better chance to retreat. I suggest you move away to a safer distance," Mai said to the women. "Behind the road bend should be far enough." He lifted his leg over the horse's neck and jumped down to the ground. Then he ran his hand along his staff, drawing the blades at its ends. "Make sure you stay as close to me as you can, Your Majesty."

"Like your shadow," Evan assured him.

Mai's back became tense, but Evan had no time to wonder about this show of emotion, because at that moment he heard a rapidly approaching whizzing sound. Mai's hand shot up and caught the arrow right in front of Evan's face. Evan let out a breath, feeling an unpleasant weakness in the area of his knees.

"Let's move," Mai said.

The Majat formed a line, with Mai in the center and two Rubies on each side. As they started to move, arrows came down from the wall to meet them, a dark cloud descending onto their group at high speed. The Majat raised their weapons, their blades a blur in their hands.

Mai held his staff in front of his body, rotating it with two hands to create a wide, impenetrable circle more than big enough to protect Evan behind him. On his sides, Brannon and Lothar moved their swords in figure eight-shapes. The Rubies on the outside completed the semicircle, surrounding Evan with a front of force.

As the formation advanced in slow, steady steps, broken arrows cascaded to the ground around them. Walking behind Mai, Evan could feel the wind on his face, splinters of wood falling like a cracking rain as if the arrows hit an invisible shield.

The Majat's faces were calm; their breath, even. Eyes, fixed on the oncoming flow of arrows, held expressions of detachment, making this violent head-on advance onto a line of the kingdom's best archers seem no more than a training exercise, a curiosity that absorbed their minds but did not occupy the rest of their senses. Only by being so close could Evan see the ripple of muscles under their silky clothes as they moved forward with the ease and grace of attacking panthers.

Leaving a trail of fallen arrows in their wake, they stepped onto the bridge and made their slow way across, raising the weapons higher as the speed and angle of the arrows flying from the walls became steeper and harder to deflect. From this distance Evan could clearly make out the men hiding behind the narrow openings of the wall. There were two archers in each slit. They shot arrows in turn, sending them evenly upon the advancing group.

Evan judged the distance. They were close enough to hear clanking coming from behind the tall protrusions of the wall, and the muffled swearing as each new wave of arrows failed to reach the target. From this distance he would have no trouble being heard.

He raised his hand.

"Gate captain!" he shouted. "Cease your fire! We come in peace!"

The man in a tall plumed helmet signaled, sending down a new wave of arrows. Evan waited until the cracking of the broken shafts quieted down.

"We pose no threat to you! All we want is to talk!"

He stepped sideways, making sure the slanting beams of the setting sun fell on his face. The man hesitated and lowered his arm.

Bows lowered everywhere in sight. Several shapes appeared behind the gate captain, engaged in a frantic conversation Evan couldn't quite hear.

"They'd need a gracious way out of this," he said quietly to Mai.

The Diamond kept his eyes on the wall openings above.

"They wasted far too many arrows for a simple group of travelers approaching the gate. I'd say you were expected, Your Majesty."

Evan shook his head. "Daemur Illitand is many things, but he's surely not suicidal. He wouldn't give an order to shoot his king."

"If you say so, Your Majesty."

"No one in this city would follow such an insane order," Evan insisted, feeling less and less confident as the conversation on top of the wall showed no sign of ending. "I'm sure the only reason they didn't stop sooner was because they felt too threatened by the Pentade's skill." He strained his eyes for a better look at the man in charge. He thought he'd recognized the voice. Besides, he knew of only one man in the Illitand city guard who could take so much time with an important decision. He decided to try.

"Captain Ragan, if I'm not mistaken?"

The activity on the wall ceased. The gate captain slowly stepped into the opening, his figure coming into full view. "M'lord Evan Dorn? Sire?"

Evan gave the gate captain a radiant smile. "Good to see you finally recognize me, captain. Now that's settled, I hope you'll let us in at once. I am sure Lord Daemur wouldn't want you to keep us waiting any longer."

There was a commotion behind the wall as more figures appeared at Ragan's back.

"Your Majat guard will have to stay outside," the captain said.

Evan's smile became wider. "Out of the question, captain. They go where I go. You do remember, captain, that their job is only to protect me. They pose no threat to anyone who isn't trying to harm me."

He made sure these words rang clearly enough through the battlements to reflect even in the dimmest of minds. It never hurt to be careful.

The captain disappeared from the wall, and Evan saw shapes move past the stone openings. After a long while the heavy gate rattled and rolled open. A group of men came forward, led by the slightly disheveled Captain Ragan. His dirty blond hair cascaded down his shoulders from underneath the tall pointed helmet. Small eyes that looked even paler on the background of his sunburnt skin studied Evan and his retinue with suspicion.

Ragan and his men saluted and stood to attention in front of Evan.

"Forgive us for not recognizing you sooner, Your Majesty," the captain said. "Your clothes and your retinue were quite unusual. We thought—"

Evan waved a hand in dismissal. "No harm done, captain. Your defenses are commendable. I'm guessing you don't get many visitors, do you? At least none that make it as far as the gate?"

The captain showed no reaction to the irony. "Not ones so heavily armed, Your Majesty. Before we let you into the city, your Majat guards must surrender their weapons."

Mai changed the grip on his staff in a swift movement that made the entire welcoming party back off. The Rubies held their swords bare, blades lowered as they all looked at Mai for a signal.

"They're my bodyguards, captain," Evan said. "How're they supposed to protect me if they're unarmed?"

"But they're Majat of the top gem ranks," the captain said with uncertainty.

"Exactly."

The captain's eyes darted from the silent figures of the Majat to the open gate and back to Evan, who gradually realised that the entire gate garrison was probably not enough to stop the Majat now that the defenses were lowered.

"Sire." He bowed.

Evan smiled. "Good man. I'll be sure to commend you to Lord Daemur, captain. I'd appreciate it if you see to our mounts and to escort our companions into the city. They are waiting over there behind the road bend."

The houses lining the streets of the Illitand city were several stories high, their flat roofs perched against each other as they rose step-wise along the slope to the upper city. The main street ascended steeply from the gate, but after the first bend it became almost level, enabling them to ride side by side.

Ellah ended up at the back of the procession, between Mother Keeper and Odara Sul. The two women rode in silence, their side glances making Ellah uncomfortable. Yet, when the question came, it nearly caught her unawares.

"So," Mother Keeper said in her most innocent tone of voice. "How is your power working with Aghat Mai?"

Ellah jumped in the saddle. *Can Mother Keeper read thoughts?*

"It isn't working, is it?" Mother Keeper insisted.

"What makes you say that?" Ellah tried her best to sound nonchalant.

Mother Keeper smiled. "Gem-ranked Majat have very controlled minds. Especially Diamonds. Even in a normal situation he would have been a challenge. But with the way he makes you feel emotionally–"

"I'm not emotional!" Ellah blurted out. She immediately bit her tongue, but it was too late.

Mother Keeper gave her a knowing look. "You blush every time he looks your way. You lose your voice every time he speaks to you. You're so overwhelmed by him that you become all but senseless when he's around. If you want to become good at using your gift, you must overcome this."

Ellah kept her eyes on the road. She was afraid to open her mouth, of saying something foolish again. She knew Mother Keeper was right. But there was no way in the world she was going to admit it. She really wanted to be able to use her power with Mai, to learn if he meant what he said to her that evening. But every time he spoke, the color purple filled her vision, overpowering everything in sight. She was helpless against it.

"However dashing he may seem," Mother Keeper went on, "you must learn to see him for what he is. He's a ruthless killer. He never does anything without a purpose. He might find it irresistible to play with you, and I don't blame him. Any man would be flattered to see a girl blush so deeply every time he looks her way. But, do you really think such a man would take a fancy in a girl like you?"

Kara could, Ellah thought. Kara had the same training as Mai and was no less ruthless or capable of killing, but it was obvious she really cared for Kyth even if she never acted on it. In fact, Ellah was pretty sure that their feelings for each other went far beyond simple fancy. Why couldn't it be the same for her and Mai?

At the same time, a more reasonable part of her realized that Mother Keeper had a point. There was no way that Mai, so handsome, so competent, the best of the best, would pay any attention to her, a simple girl who couldn't in all honesty even call herself pretty.

And yet, what if? After all, by Mother Keeper's own admission, he found her *irresistible* to play with. The mere thought brought color to Ellah's cheeks.

Mother Keeper studied her intently.

"I can see it will take more training than I thought," she said. "Unfortunately, we don't have much time. So, listen carefully. We're about to reach Castle Illitand. Whoever meets us there will try to convince King Evan to do things their way. You must make yourself unnoticeable among the King's retinue and keep a very close eye on everyone who talks to us. It will be critical to know if they are telling the truth. Stay in my line of sight and keep at least one of your hands visible to me. If you hear the truth, I want you to hold out one finger. If you hear a lie, two. Can you do that?"

Ellah nodded. She watched Mai, riding in the lead next to Evan. He was so handsome in the saddle, his posture graceful and alert, his eyes darting back and forth in search of possible danger. *Could such a man take a fancy to a girl like me?* Ellah forced herself to look away.

After the last bend the street opened up to a wide plaza, ending in an ornate gate; it was open. Beyond the gate, Castle Illitand shot its tall jagged spires up into the clear Lakeland sky. Its slender towers connected by arches and galleries made the stone structure look airy. It almost seemed as if a strong gust of wind could dislodge the entire castle from its perch on the hilltop and carry it off into the blue.

They entered a large yard, paved with marble so white it hurt the eyes in the bright sunlight. On the steps leading up to the castle stood a slender young woman of about sixteen, clad in a green dress with a golden trim. She had a heart-shaped face, rich auburn hair, and deep green eyes that shone with chilling intelligence on her porcelain-smooth face.

Ellah had seen this girl before during the Duke of Illitand's visits to the King's court. Lady Celana, the Duke's daughter.

The party dismounted. Ellah hurried on after Evan, with her hand in view. She rested it against her thigh, fingers half-closed so that she could easily hold out one or two without drawing attention to the gesture.

Lady Celana stepped toward Evan and dropped to a deep curtsey.

"What an honor, Sire." Her voice was clear, with a sharp ringing timbre that echoed through the stone court. "Welcome to the Castle Illitand."

The deep green of Lady Celana's dress made Ellah's mind fill with this color, but as the royal lady started to speak, waves of pink washed over it, slowly turning into a deep red. Ellah held out two fingers and caught Mother Keeper's barely perceptible nod.

"Please forgive my father, Your Majesty," Lady Celana said. "Urgent business prevents him from being here to greet you. He sends his deepest regrets and will be along as soon as he can."

The color was still red. Ellah kept her fingers steady as Evan nodded to the royal lady's greetings.

"It is a joy to see you, Lady Celana," he said. "Lord Daemur couldn't have pleased me more than by sending you in his stead."

"Your Majesty is too kind." Lady Celana bowed her head. "Please allow me to escort you to your chambers and see to the comforts of you and your suite."

They followed the royal lady up the marble steps. Servants wearing green and yellow Illitand livery joined them as they entered the cool shade of the castle. From where she walked, behind the Pentade, Ellah found it hard to catch the conversation, but she did her best to guess by the fragments that floated her way. It was mostly polite nonsense. And the colors in her mind mostly wavered between pink and red. She let her hand swing as she walked, with two fingers out.

They moved up the stone stairs, through ornate hallways, along narrow and wide galleries. Through the arched windows Ellah could catch the light breeze that brought in smells of fresh water and sunlight. Most of the windows faced the lake, so big that the strip of greenery on the other side was just visible in the distant haze.

As they reached a wide hallway located at least five flights of stairs up from the castle entrance, Lady Celana stopped. At her signal a servant flung open a large door, letting in the breeze and the Lakeland sunshine from the windows in the suite of chambers beyond.

"Thank you, my lady," the King said.

"Mother Keeper." Lady Celana turned to the Keepers. "We have prepared chambers for you and your ladies in the North Wing. My father and I would be honored if you–"

The older woman smiled. "I regret that I must trouble you, Lady Celana, but I would be very obliged if I could stay close to King Evan. It has been my privilege to accompany His Majesty on this trip, and I prefer not to be separated from him now that our mission is so close to completion."

The royal lady returned her smile without a flinch. Ellah marveled that someone so young could have such composure.

"Of course," Lady Celana said. "Forgive me for being so inconsiderate, Mother Keeper." She signaled to her servants and they moved to another door down the hall which, when opened, revealed a similar set of chambers as the one offered to Evan.

"My servants will see to your needs," Lady Celana said, "and will escort you to my father once you are refreshed and rested."

She bowed deeply to King Evan, gave a lesser bow to Mother Keeper and her eyes flitted over Mai before she departed. Most of her retinue left with her, but several servants stayed, moving through the guest chambers to set out basins of water and arrange the pillows on the tall, massive beds.

Ellah walked into the Keepers' suite and looked around. The doorways of the three adjacent rooms opened into a long gallery. Each room contained two curtained beds that looked large enough to accommodate at least five people. Coming closer, Ellah could see a lace of castle galleries and towers cascading down the steep hill toward the distant roofs of the city and the water beyond.

As she lowered her gaze to the inner castle grounds, Ellah saw two figures standing together in a small courtyard below. One of them was dressed very brightly, a bold splash of color in the calm grays of the castle decorations. His scarlet and blue robes accented the color of his deep chocolate skin and brought out the glimmer of his pale bronze hair. Ellah was fairly sure she recognized the man. It was ambassador Tanad Eli Faruh, the trusted advisor to Princess Aljbeda of Shayil Yara.

But it was the other man who drew Ellah's attention, making her heart jump. He was lean and muscular, wrapped in a black hooded robe that revealed just enough of his face to notice his gaunt features. From up here, Ellah couldn't see his eyes, but she had no doubt that the way he wore his hood deliberately left the eyes in shadow. He had the composure of a trained fighter, his movements so light and precise that it reminded her of the ranked Majat.

Ellah could swear she knew who that man was.

Kaddim Tolos, the man who had attacked Kyth back in the royal castle.

14
COURTYARD ENCOUNTER

"Are you sure the man you saw down in the courtyard was the same one who attacked Prince Kythar?" Mother Keeper insisted.

Ellah hesitated. She had been sure when she first saw him, but after all this questioning she wasn't anymore. The way everyone in the room was looking at her didn't help. There was a range, all the way from Evan's quiet curiosity to Odara Sul's open mockery, but worst of all was Mai, whose indifferent gaze, fixed on the wall just past Ellah's shoulder, suggested that her words didn't matter at all.

Ellah took a breath. "No, I'm not sure," she said.

Odara Sul patted her on the shoulder. "There, see? You're probably mistaken. It happens."

Ellah swallowed. No matter how patronized she felt, she *had* to say it.

"It's just that there was something unusual about that man. As if…"

"As if what?" Mother Keeper's voice rang with impatience.

"As if – as if he had lots to hide," Ellah managed. "The two men I saw talking down there, I'm sure they were talking about something forbidden. Something they wouldn't want anyone to know."

"But you were so far away you couldn't possibly hear them!"

Ellah paused. She really didn't have much else to say. It was a hunch, no more.

"You still have a lot to learn," Mother Keeper said. "Next time, talk to me first. There's no need to alarm everyone unless you are sure."

Ellah lowered her head, wishing she could make herself invisible.

"Forgive the interruption, Mother Keeper," King Evan suddenly said, "but I had a chance to observe Ellah during our trip, and it seems to me that she doesn't usually speak up unless there's something that needs to be said . Shouldn't we at least consider that she could be right?"

Ellah's eyes widened at the unexpected support, but Mother Keeper's glance cut her off.

"With all due respect, Your Majesty," the older woman said, "this is Keepers' business. I know how many – or rather, how few – lessons the girl had. I also know her shortcomings." She glanced at Mai. Ellah hoped she was the only one to notice. "She would have to be far more advanced in her training before she could make claims like this. Trust me, Your Majesty."

Evan smiled. "I trust you completely, Mother Keeper, and I would never dream of questioning your judgment or interfering in Keepers' business. Yet, if we find out later that Ellah was right and we dismissed the possibility, we would never forgive ourselves, would we?"

"What do you suggest, Your Majesty?"

Evan turned to Mai. "Do you think you could look into this, Aghat? With your usual tact, of course. Remember that we're guests here."

Mai nodded, a brief smile on his face mirroring Evan's. Then, he looked past the Keepers straight at Ellah. "Will you come with me? You're the only one who knows what he looks like."

Ellah's mouth fell open. Was he *asking* her to come with him because he needed her *help*?

"Yes."

"Thanks." Mai's face was straight, but she caught a merry gleam in his eyes.

"If you feel it necessary to organize this search party, Your Majesty," Mother Keeper put in, "I think it would be prudent to send Odara Sul along. She has a lot more experience than Ellah."

Evan shrugged. "I just placed Aghat Mai in charge. You'd have to ask him. However omnipotent he seems, he can only protect so many people on a dangerous mission."

"I can protect myself, thank you," Odara Sul snapped. She loosened her dagger in its sheath and went over to stand by Ellah's side. From up close, Ellah could see a strand of hair tighten onto the knot on Odara's head, as if trying to choke it to death.

Ellah followed Mai around the bend of the corridor, trying to mimic the way he slid along the wall, smooth and sleek like a shadow. She could hear the rustle of Odara Sul's dress close behind.

As they neared the corner, Mai's hand shot up, making them freeze in their tracks. They waited as the shuffling steps of the patrol went by, echoing in the large stone hallway. Out of the corner of her eye, Ellah saw Odara Sul draw a thin, curved blade from a sheath at her belt. Anxious to be as useful as she could, Ellah reached for her own dagger, but Mai's hand stopped her.

"Do you know how to use it?" he asked quietly.

Ellah opened her mouth to say "yes", but his look made

her bite her tongue. He really needed to know, she realized. And, however much she wanted to impress him, saying yes wouldn't be truthful. Despite some weapon lessons she had taken, she had never felt comfortable handling a blade, even one as short as a dagger. She could use it, say, to clean fish or cut bread, but wielding it against an opponent…

"Not for fighting," she admitted.

He nodded. "Put it away then. And focus. The courtyard you spoke about is through that door."

He pointed to a tightly shut door at the end of the hallway. A chill went down Ellah's spine. She never realized they were so close.

"If someone opens the door from the other side, they'll see us," she whispered.

Mai's hand closed over her wrist, pulling her along the wall into a deep niche behind a column. Odara Sul followed. The three of them huddled into the tiny space. Ellah did her best to distance herself from the warmth of Mai's body, so close that she could feel the hardness of muscle under his shirt. She caught Odara Sul's mocking gaze and turned away, forcing her attention to the small door.

"Now!" Mai whispered, as if giving a command.

The door swung open. A shadow blocked the light and stepped into the hallway, a tall man wrapped in a hooded black robe.

He approached their hiding place and stopped. His nose twitched, as if he was sniffing the air. Then he turned and looked straight into the niche.

"I know you're in there," he said. "And I know you're waiting for me. Why don't you show your faces?"

Mai disengaged from the wall and stepped forward, keeping to the shadows and shielding Ellah and Odara Sul from view. "You first."

The man chuckled. Then in a quick gesture he swept the hood off to reveal a bony face with heavy eyebrows and a strong jaw. His eyes were pale brown, almost yellow.

Ellah's heart raced. "It's him! Kaddim Tolos!"

Mai nodded and stepped all the way out of the niche. Tolos stood still for a moment, studying him with an unreadable expression.

"Ah, a challenge," he said at length. "I enjoy a challenge."

He raised his hand and gestured into the depth of the hallway. A dozen hooded figures emerged from the shadows, fanning around Mai. The Diamond's eyes widened. Following his gaze, Ellah realized why. There was no mistaking the face of the man in the lead, his square jaw and small, beady eyes. He was at the head of the patrol of the false Holy Knights that tried to stop them on the road out of the Crown City.

But how was it possible?

It was clear that the man recognized Mai as well. His face folded into a grin as he and his companions drew their weapons, spiked metal balls hanging off chains.

"Orbens," Odara Sul whispered.

Mai drew his staff from the sheath at his back. Tolos measured him with his eyes.

"How good are you with that stick of yours, Aghat?" he asked.

"Good enough."

"Shall we test that?" At Tolos's signal the hooded figures came into motion all at once. Orbens shot out, the whizzing of spiked metal balls filling the narrow hallway.

Mai flicked the blades out from the ends of his staff. When the front line attackers were in range, he thrust his weapon sideways in a rotating motion, catching an orb on the blade. Moving like lightning, he twisted his grip and thrust to the other side. With a screech, both orbens came free, chains wrapped around the blades on the ends of Mai's staff.

Mai lifted his weapon, the orbens extending its length by two spinning chains. He made a forward sweep with it, sending the frontline attackers down to the floor. The others stood back, hesitating.

Tolos stretched out his hands. Ellah felt as if an invisible wave hit her, rolling on through the hallway. The wave stilled all sounds in its wake, pressing on the ears with disabling strength. Standing behind Tolos, Ellah imagined she could see the air waver in front of his outstretched palms, a cone of force trapping Mai as he faced his attackers.

Mai's weapon hand wavered. An orben lashed through his defense, hitting the end of his staff. Another whizzed past, narrowly missing his head. There was a smirk on the attacker's face as he recomposed for a new blow.

As Mai struggled to regain his footing, orbens came at him from all sides. One brushed the side of his face, metal spikes biting into his cheek. He staggered, trying to recover his balance. Blood gushed down his face.

Ellah gasped, eyes fixed on the mess of Mai's face. Torn flesh hanging in pieces made him almost unrecognizable. As another orben swayed past, he made no move to avoid it. *The next one would kill him!*

Don't just stand there, do something! Shaking off the terror, Ellah took a running leap out of the niche straight at Tolos. She landed on his back, grabbing on with all her might, squeezing and twisting, digging her nails into flesh, trying to do as much damage as she could. The man, unprepared for such an attack, stumbled, grasping on in a vain attempt to shake Ellah off. The pressure of the force subsided. Out of the corner of her eye Ellah saw Mai recover. As a new orben shot toward him at full speed, he leaned out of the way and sent the attacker down with a clear blow of his staff.

Tolos's hands closed on Ellah's wrists with numbing strength. She kicked and screamed, but was unable to hold on. The man pulled her off like a sack and threw her against the wall. Winded, she lay there, watching the fight with blurry eyes.

Mai's remaining opponents were backing up the hallway, more anxious to keep out of the way of his weapon than to continue the fight. They were throwing hopeful glances at their leader, but he seemed in no hurry as he straightened out his robe and hair, keeping his thoughtful gaze on Mai, whose movements, no longer suppressed by the strange power, regained their usual speed and precision.

"You may stop, Aghat," Tolos said. "I trust we've both satisfied our curiosity about each other, haven't we?"

Mai lowered his staff, keeping the blades bare. Tolos looked past him to his men. "Is anyone dead?"

"No, Kaddim," came a reply.

Tolos nodded. "Of course. Diamonds don't kill, unless they're paid to do it. Or," he looked at Mai, "unless they fight for their life. I take it, you didn't feel challenged enough, Aghat?"

Mai responded with a calm stare. The wound on his face looked bad. Streaks of oozing blood caked his cheek, concealing the true extent of the damage.

Tolos chuckled. "Fair enough. At least you've got a small token on your face to remember me by. And now, I hope you'll excuse me, Aghat. I am expected elsewhere." He turned and strode away along the hallway. The robed men limped off in his wake, throwing fearful glances at Mai.

When they were gone, Odara Sul brushed out of the niche and stopped in front of Ellah.

"That was a stupid thing to do," she snapped. "You could've been killed! What were you thinking?" She paused, but instinct told Ellah that it would be best to keep her silence. "Are you all right?" Odara added at length.

Ellah nodded and shakily got to her feet. She looked at Mai, his disfigured face a mask of blood and gore. Tears filled her eyes. He was a *Diamond*, the best fighter that ever walked the earth. What kind of evil power did Tolos possess that could make *this* happen?

Odara rushed to Mai's side and pushed his blood-caked hair out of the way to take a closer look at the wound. Mai tensed and drew back. Odara gave him an exasperated glance.

"For Shal Addim's sake, Aghat! Let me look at that!"

His guarded expression warned her to keep her distance.

Odara sighed. "Come now, Aghat. We both know your wound isn't deadly. But you probably also know enough about orbens to realize how long it will take to heal, and what kind of scar it will leave. Believe me, it'd make your face hard to recognize. It would be a great pity to let that happen. Not if something could be done about it."

His lips twitched. He winced as the smile touched his wounded cheek. After a long pause, he nodded.

Odara Sul stepped up to Mai and drew his hair back again. This time he didn't resist as she took a piece of cloth from her shoulder bag and pressed it to the wound.

"Hold it, Aghat." Odara turned, pushing several dry towels out of her bag into Ellah's hands. "Take these," she commanded, "and soak them in the fountain out in the courtyard. We have some washing to do."

Ellah grabbed the handful of cloth and made her cautious way out into the empty courtyard. She approached the basin and dipped the towels into the cool water. Then she scooped them out and hurried back inside.

Mai was sitting against the wall at the courtyard entrance, with Odara leaning over him. Now that the bleeding had stopped, the wound looked even worse. Mai's left cheek was completely disfigured. Skin hung off it in pieces, the torn flesh underneath slowly acquiring a deadly leaden color. Ellah resisted the urge to look away.

"Keep very still, Aghat," Odara Sul said. "This is going to hurt."

She took the wet towels from Ellah and thoroughly cleaned the wound and the skin around it. Mai's face remained calm, but as Odara's fingers moved along the gash, slow and careful not to destroy any more flesh, Ellah saw his lowered hand ball into a fist until his knuckles went white. He noticed Ellah's gaze and slowly relaxed his hand. Ellah hastily looked away.

When the wound was clean, Odara Sul carefully took a small vial of dark glass from a pouch at her belt.

"You must help me to hold his head," she said to Ellah. "It's going to hurt, but we can't let him move. You must hold him very still."

Ellah glanced hesitantly at Mai and made a move to approach, but his gaze kept her in place.

"I appreciate the thought," he said, "but I can hold my head still all by myself, thank you."

"It's going to hurt like hell," Odara warned. "You'll think your flesh's being burned alive. I've seen grown men scream and go berserk with the pain. Yet, I can't have you move when I am doing this. A slight movement and you'll have a permanent scar. Or worse."

Mai's face twitched into a crooked smile. "If I went berserk, with pain or anything else, the two of you wouldn't be able to do much about holding me still, would you?"

Odara sighed. "Probably not. But if you want me to heal

your wound, the only way I can do it is my way. Please trust me."

He held her gaze for a moment longer, then relaxed and leaned back against the wall. Following Odara's nod, Ellah approached and kneeled by his side. She carefully pushed back his blood-caked hair and put her palms on the sides of his head. The gesture felt too intimate, but Ellah did her best to distance herself from it. She pressed her palms tighter. A shadow ran over his face and she knew that she caused pain, but there was no time to change the grip. Odara drew forward. In one hand she had the open vial. In the other, a small brush glistening with dark, sticky liquid.

"Hold on tight," Odara said to Ellah. "And, for Shal Addim's sake keep his hair away from the liquid!"

Ellah had no time to wonder, because at that moment the brush connected with the open flesh of the wound. In an instant blood drained from Mai's face and he became so pale that he seemed almost transparent. Holding on with all her might, Ellah sensed his body go tense and shiver against her. Yet, he didn't move. His face remained calm. Only his eyes betrayed the pain, the dilated pupils making them look black instead of the usual blue.

If Ellah wasn't so close to him, she would never have guessed how much pain he felt. But now, through their touch, she almost felt his pain as hers. The strength of it made her want to sob.

Odara Sul showed no awareness of any of it. Her hand slowly worked the small brush with the precision of an artist putting finishing touches onto fine detail of a painting. Ellah sensed each touch echo through Mai's body. His lips became gray, yet he didn't move any muscles on his face.

Finally, Odara Sul put the brush away, closed the vial and tucked it back into her belt. Then she moved her long, deft fingers around the wound, closing it. The sticky liquid covering the flesh kept the wound edges together, like glue. She made several passes over it, until all that was left on Mai's cheek was a narrow, winding scar. And then–

Ellah could scarcely believe her eyes. As Odara's fingers moved, smoothing out the wound, the scar *disappeared*. Its edges grew together, healing until there was only a pink line in the place of a recently open wound. And then, the pink subsided into white, and all that was left was the smooth skin of his cheek.

The scar wasn't there anymore. There was no trace of the recent wound on Mai's face. Only his blood-caked hair spoke of the predicament he had been in, just a short while ago.

Odara Sul drew away, surveying the results of her work with satisfaction. Then she took out a wet cloth and wiped Mai's cheek, careful to remove all traces of the strange substance.

"You may let him go," she told Ellah.

Ellah nodded and dropped away her hands. She felt almost as exhausted as Mai looked. She sat and stared at his face, fresh and smooth as if there never was a wound. Tears blurred her eyes, but she had no will to blink them away.

Mai raised his hand, running his fingers along the skin, first lightly, then pressing down searchingly. His eyes met Odara's with wonder.

She smiled. "This is my best one yet. All because you didn't move a single muscle on your face. How did you manage that, Aghat?"

He smiled back, his face slowly acquiring faint traces of color.

"Clearly," he said, "you don't know much about Majat training, do you?"

Odara slowly got to her feet and shook the dust off her skirt. "Let's go back. King Evan and Mother Keeper must be worried about us."

15

THE MAJAT FORTRESS

Kyth pulled his horse to a halt, unable to draw his eyes from the sight that opened in front of them. The valley ahead descended and then rose again, in a gradual climb up to the next ridge. In its center stood the most impressive stronghold Kyth had ever seen.

At this distance it looked like a giant monolith, surrounded by a wide trench of water. Its smoothly hewn walls rose up to at least fifteen men's height, topped with a double line of jagged stone teeth. Signal towers marked each wall bend, positioned to make sure that no piece of land in the vicinity of the fortress could be missed by the watchmen stationed on top. The city itself was barely visible inside the ring of the outer wall, its size traceable only by the transparent wisps of chimney smoke that made the air waver as they rose up to the sky. Inside the city, another, taller wall separated the center of the fortress into a stronghold of its own. Its ornate towers were much more elaborate than those on the outside wall, reaching their slender spires toward the bright afternoon sun.

Sunlight painted the stones of the fortress into a palette of reds and yellows, reflecting off the surrounding water and enfolding the massive structure in a radiant golden glow. The narrow vertical slits creasing the walls and towers looked like dark watchful eyes. As Kyth sat looking at the Majat Fortress from horseback, he couldn't escape the feeling that the fortress watched him in return, alert like a powerful nesting beast.

The road wound down the hill and around the city, across a drawbridge, to a tall double gate in the east wall. The bridge was lowered, but the gate was tightly shut.

"Let's go," Raishan said.

He took out his Majat armband from his saddlebag. The diamond glistened in its dark metal setting as Raishan clasped the band onto his upper left arm. Kara had already donned hers. Now she unfolded a piece of black cloth and pulled it over her head, covering her face all the way down to the neck.

"I'm an Anonymous," she said in response to Kyth's questioning gaze. "Trained in the Inner Fortress. I can't show my face anywhere in the outer grounds."

Kyth nodded. He heard of the Anonymous training before. Some of the Majat were raised separately from the others, so that they wouldn't be recognized in case they ever needed to be pitched against each other on assignments outside the Fortress. The Anonymous Diamonds were special, even more feared than the regular ones. And now, her masked face made her so distant, a deadly warrior whose life belonged to her Guild. She looked ominous, an all-black figure with the only bright spot about her the diamond in her armband. *When will I see her face again?* He turned away.

The road was wide enough for two horsemen to ride side by side. As they started to descend, Kyth took care to end up next to Kara.

"What will happen after we get there?" he asked.

"You will be taken to the guest quarters," she said, "and eventually to the Guildmaster. You'll explain your needs to him and present the payment. Then, he'll send for me and we'll get on our way."

Our way. The thought filled him with warmth. The sooner they got this over with, the sooner they could be on the way again, together. Then he could see her face again.

"And you? What will you do in the meantime?" Kyth asked.

She shrugged. "Both Raishan and I will report to the Guildmaster. Then we'll be given time to check our weapons and refresh our travel gear. Raishan may be able to stay to get some rest, unless he has another assignment waiting."

Kyth glanced at Raishan riding in the lead. It all seemed simple enough, a mere formality. Besides, Egey Bashi was with them and he had dealt with the Majat before. Before long, he and Kara should be on the road again. But he couldn't escape the feeling of danger that hadn't fully left him since they first encountered Nimos.

The main gate to the Majat Fortress was a tall wooden structure covered with sheets of metal for reinforcement. There was no grate or window on the gate's smooth surface, and no other visible way to draw the attention of those inside. As they approached, Kyth was beginning to wonder how they were going to announce their arrival, and whether they would just have to wait outside for someone to notice their presence. But his worry was needless. As soon as Kara's and Raishan's horses set foot onto the bridge leading up to the gate, the heavy doors creaked on their hinges and slowly swung open.

The entrance courtyard was packed with guards. Muscular men, whose graceful movements and plain-metal armbands indicated advanced Majat ranking, stood to attention, forming a corridor for the travelers to ride through. They pressed fists to their chests in a silent salute as they watched Kara and Raishan ride by.

A man ran up to them from the entrance to the guard tower. Unlike the others, his armband was set with a stone, but not a shiny one. This stone was grass-green and non-transparent. It gave off a suffused surface glint that made the metal around it look brighter by comparison.

The man pressed his fist against his chest and bowed his head. "*Shelah*, Aghat."

"*Shelah*, Gahang," Raishan replied. Kara only nodded. They followed the man through the rapidly parting row of guards that continued to eye the two Diamonds with awe.

Kyth, Alder, and Egey Bashi stood waiting, while Kara, Raishan, and the man with the green stone exchanged quiet words. Finally, Raishan turned back to them.

"We're all going to leave our mounts here in the lower stables and walk on to the inner grounds. Gahang Amir will send word to the Guildmaster of your arrival. I'll show you to your quarters."

Raishan's restrained look and Egey Bashi's raised eyebrows told Kyth that they weren't following the proper procedure, but no one offered objections.

"What does Gahang stand for?" he asked Raishan when they were out of hearing range.

"His rank. Jade."

Kyth nodded. He wanted to ask more about the Majat gem ranks and where a Jade stood in their Guild's hierarchy, but the Diamond's frown warned him off.

At first glance, the Majat Fortress seemed just like any other city. Tall houses perched against each other, their walls connected to make best use of the space. Smoke rose out of the chimneys, tainting the cool gusts of mountain wind with a bitter tinge of burning. Smells of freshly baked bread, roast meat, and sweet medicinal herbs filled the air, mixing with odors of stale hay and road dust.

The streets boiled with the normal activity of a busy afternoon. Women hurried by with buckets of water and bags of household goods, men stood in groups talking on the corners, and children ran around like flocks of restless birds. But, despite their ordinary looks, the inhabitants of the Majat Fortress weren't like any other common townsfolk Kyth had ever seen. Every man, woman, and child had a weapon strapped to their belt or sheathed at their back. Everyone seemed to have a clear ranking relationship to each other, so that if two people collided on a corner there was never any question about which one should go first. As a result, the streets seemed much more orderly than in other cities Kyth had been to.

There was another thing. As Kara and Raishan went by, all the activity stopped. People watched them in awe. Most gave a silent salute, with a fist across the chest. Others bowed, or even knelt on the roadside. An old woman with shaky hands flung herself on the ground in front of Raishan and tried to kiss his feet, and a girl of about Kyth's age took her away, throwing wistful glances at Kara's and Raishan's diamond armbands. A little boy pointed at Kara's mask and said something. His mother hastily grabbed him and carried him into the house.

The Diamonds didn't look surprised at this kind of welcome. They nodded to acknowledge the attention, but didn't break their stride. Seeing it, Kyth started to realize what Kara meant when she spoke about her rank that made her so special among the Majat. Here in the fortress she and Raishan were treated like royalty.

The street they were following ended with another gate. It opened as Kara and Raishan approached, timed so that the Diamonds didn't have to slow down. Inside, men with non-gem armbands lined the passage, heads bowed, fists pressed to their chests.

Across the wide courtyard ahead loomed another wall. Raishan stopped and gestured for the rest of them to stop in his wake. He exchanged a brief nod with Kara and she walked on alone. They stood and watched as she entered the low gateway at the end. A door swung open to let her through, as if whoever was on the other side had been waiting for her approach. She never looked back.

Kyth swallowed, fighting a sinking feeling in his chest. He couldn't escape the nagging sensation that something was about to go terribly wrong. Suddenly, seeing Kara's face seemed to be the most important thing in the world. But he would never be able to do it without following her through the tightly shut door. It was up to the Majat Guild now to decide if he was ever going to see her again.

Alder's voice woke him from his trance. "I think we have to follow Raishan."

Kyth turned. Raishan and Egey Bashi were heading in the direction of a low stone building adjacent to the wall. He and Alder hurried to catch up.

"What was behind that other wall?" Kyth asked Raishan as he fell into stride.

"That's the Inner Fortress, where the Anonymous are trained."

Kyth nodded. Everything was going to be fine. No Majat Guildmaster had ever refused to dispatch a named Diamond for an assignment. Not when the King did the bidding. Not if he was willing to pay the price.

He was going to see Kara again soon.

The guest quarters greeted them with a breath of old stone chill. Inside, a long hallway ran off to the left and a narrow stairway led up to the second floor. An open door on the right let in the clanking of plates and the rank smells of dirty wash water and food cooked in large quantities from very cheap ingredients. Kyth twitched his nose as they went by.

They followed Raishan up the stairs to another long hallway that ran on both sides of the landing, lined with closed doors. Raishan pushed open the nearest one and led them inside.

The room had a low ceiling and at least a dozen beds occupying most of the free space. There was a washbasin in the corner and a weapon stand by the far wall. A small window covered by a thick, cloudy pane let through very little of the afternoon light. Everything was spotless, but Kyth couldn't escape the feeling that this room had been empty for a very long time.

Egey Bashi threw his travel pack onto the nearest bed.

"When I was here last," he said, "I was offered better accommodation."

"I have very little experience with our guest quarters," Raishan said, "but I must admit, this is not what I imagined when Gahang Amir relayed the Guildmaster's instructions on where to take you."

"So, he knew we were coming, did he?"

Raishan shrugged. "As you saw for yourself, no one can approach the Majat Fortress in secret. In addition to the guard towers, the road can be clearly seen from the Guildmaster's study. He had an hour between the time he saw us descend into the valley and the time we reached the gate."

The Keeper shook his head. "Master Oden Lan and I have done a lot of business over the years. I expected the sight of my face to bring a better welcome. Or is it the fact that this time I'm escorting the royal heir?"

"I can only hope he didn't recognize Prince Kythar," Raishan said. "Still, it doesn't seem right. But I'm sure Master Oden Lan will see you right away to offer his explanations."

"Let's hope, Aghat."

Raishan had another look around the room.

"I don't know about you all," he said. "But I'm starving. Why don't we go downstairs and grab a bite?"

"Are you sure you want to eat here with us, Aghat?" Egey Bashi asked. "I couldn't help but notice that the gourmet chef in this dining hall seems to be on leave. If you show up, the cooks would have a fit. Apart from the quality of the food, they'd probably have a hard time finding a throne to put you on, or a golden plate to serve your meal on."

"I'm sure they'll come up with something," Raishan said.

Egey Bashi was half right. When they entered the large chamber filled with the clanking of dishes and the smells of cheap stew, there was a feeling of indrawn breath that momentarily froze all activity. A large man in an apron and a tall chef's hat approached them from the depth of the room, maneuvering between the long tables.

"*Shelah*, Aghat," he said weakly, fumbling with his hands to produce a Majat salute and settling for a very deep bow instead.

"*Shelah*." Raishan looked past the man at the scarce inhabitants of the hall.

"Such an unexpected honor, Aghat," the man went on in a trembling voice. "Please, come in. The stew is not our best today, but surely you're not here to eat–"

Raishan met the man's eyes. "My friends and I'd like to have some food, thanks. Unless, of course, it's a problem."

Color drained from the man's face. He grabbed a corner of his apron as if searching for support.

"Of course, Aghat," he bleated. "Of course. Please, take a seat wherever you like."

Raishan dismissed him with a wave of a hand and walked between the tables in his smooth, springy steps. Kyth followed, Alder and Egey Bashi in his wake.

There was only one other group in the dining hall. About a dozen men wearing road cloaks over leather armor sat at the far end of a long table. As Kyth and his friends walked past, the men stopped eating and watched them in a tense silence. They looked like mercenaries. It was strange to see them here in the guest quarters of the Majat Fortress, where people normally came to hire mercenary services rather than to offer theirs.

Raishan settled in the corner with his back to the wall, a position that gave him the best view of the entire room. Kyth took a place by his side, keeping the group of men in sight. Something about them bothered him.

They barely had time to settle when the cook rushed out of the back door with a tray holding four steaming bowls, a jug of brew, and four mugs. He set the table, then took out a warm loaf of bread from the bundle tucked under his arm and placed it on the table between the mugs. Smells of yeast and hops filled the air, mixed with a heady aroma of spiced meat, much more appetizing than anything they sensed when they entered the hall.

"It pays off to come here with you, Aghat," Egey Bashi observed.

Raishan shrugged.

The stew had more potatoes than meat, but showed a clear effort to whip up a decent meal in a very short time. The brew was sour, but flavorful. It was also unexpectedly strong. Kyth took a big gulp and felt his head swim.

"They really do treat you like royalty here," he said to Raishan.

"It's more practical than that," the Majat said. "A Diamond's assignment can support the entire fortress for half a year. These people have food and shelter because we earn the money to keep this all going. So, the respect we get is proportional to the worth that we are to the Guild. You can call it royalty if you like, or plain wealth."

"A diamond," Egey Bashi intoned, "is the costliest of gems."

Raishan nodded. He glanced over to the other table and Kyth suddenly realized that the Majat's thoughts were no longer on the conversation. His eyes followed the other men who had just finished their meal and were rising to leave.

"What is it?" Kyth asked quietly.

Raishan shook his head. "Probably nothing. It's just… there's something familiar about these men. I keep having this feeling I've seen them before."

Egey Bashi turned and watched as the last few of the group disappeared through the open doorway.

"Do you think they could handle orbens, Aghat?" he asked.

Raishan shrugged. "I wouldn't be surprised, Magister. Not surprised at all."

16
GUESSING GAME

Ellah sat on the windowsill in the Keeper's quarters, looking down into the lower castle courtyard. It was empty. From her place she could see the white stone basin over by the far wall. She thought it looked like the water in the basin was pink with blood, but she knew this couldn't be true.

The rest of their party had gathered in the King's quarters to discuss the situation, but she couldn't bring herself to get up and go. She was too exhausted. Her fight with Kaddim Tolos had taken away all her strength. Or was it the way she felt Mai's pain, as if it was her own?

She suddenly became aware of someone standing by her side. Startled, she turned and came face to face with Mai.

He had changed into a clean outfit. His hair was damp, but bore no trace of blood. He looked just like always, elegant and composed, dashing in black. There was no way to tell he had recently fought twelve men and had miraculously recovered from a very serious wound.

"How long have you been standing there?" she asked weakly.

Mai didn't respond. He approached and lowered himself onto the other end of the windowsill across from Ellah.

"I wanted to thank you," he said, "for your help today."

She stared. It was nice to hear him say it, but in truth there was no way in the world *she* could possibly do anything to help *him* in any way.

"I don't think I made a difference," she said earnestly. "You didn't need my help with the wound. All I did was cause you more pain."

He smiled. "You did more than that. But I was actually talking about the fight. Given the odds, what you did was damn brave."

She continued to stare. Did he just call her *brave*? Did he just thank her for helping him in a *fight*?

"And reckless," he went on. "What were you thinking, attacking a man so much more powerful than yourself?"

Ellah looked at him, so amazed that she even forgot to blush. "I wasn't thinking," she admitted. "I just… did it. So…" She took a breath, keeping her eyes steady on his face. "I guess it means there's no need for you to thank me."

He smiled and leaned back against the windowframe. "I guess it means we're even."

She nodded.

He continued sitting there looking at her, but she felt too weak to be flustered by it. It was so much better to try to relax and pretend that nothing in this conversation was out of the ordinary. He was her travel companion, and lately they spent a lot of time with each other. They could just act like friends, couldn't they?

She made an attempt at it.

"This man's power," she said. "What did it feel like?"

Mai appeared to consider it.

"It was strange, nothing I've ever felt before. It seemed that I was still able to move but unable to… to focus, I guess. There was a mist in my head, and every movement I wanted to make came too late."

She kept her eyes on his face. "It was so scary when they hit you," she said, her voice sinking to a half-whisper.

His fingers traced the smooth skin of his cheek in an absentminded gesture. For a brief moment he looked vulnerable, like a child. Ellah had a sudden urge to hold him and stroke his hair, to touch his face and feel for herself that the ugly, deforming scar wasn't there, that all this had been no more than a horrible dream. She couldn't forget the way his face had looked, torn flesh caked with oozing blood. She would never forget the pain that echoed in her own body through their touch. So much pain. And such incredible control. What kind of training could form this ability to remain so still under such excruciating pain?

She shivered. "Does it still hurt?"

He smiled. "Only as a memory. I'll live, thanks."

"Kaddim Tolos's men were the same ones that attacked us back on the road," she said. "Probably the same as back in the King's castle, too – except that I didn't have a chance to take a good look back then."

He nodded. "Back on the road, you recognized they weren't real Holy Knights. I guess now we know for certain you were right."

"But why? Why did they try to attack us then? And why are they here?"

"Something tells me we'll soon find out." A strange gleam lit up in his eyes.

She suddenly became aware of a thought that had been nagging at her for a while. Something that related back to her earlier conversation with Mai. Something Kaddim Tolos had said.

"Remember when we played the guessing game?" she said slowly. "When you were testing if I could sense the truth?"

He nodded.

"You lied to me back then, didn't you?" she said.

He shifted in his seat. His eyes became innocent, but there was mischief behind them.

"About what?" he asked.

"About killing."

He looked at her with sudden interest. "What makes you say that?"

She swallowed. "I watched you fight. You could've killed those men today, but you didn't. None of them. And, back on the road, you could've killed them too, but all you did was cut their saddle straps."

"So?"

She kept his gaze. "Kaddim Tolos was right, wasn't he? You only kill if it's part of your assignment."

He laughed. "So?"

"You haven't *really* killed two hundred people, have you?"

He leaned forward, his face becoming serious in a flash. The change was so fast that she drew back in fright.

"Why do you think that?" he asked.

She forced herself to stand her ground. "You *couldn't* have killed two hundred people. Not with the way you avoid killing, even accidentally."

"How do you know?" he insisted. "Maybe before I became the King's bodyguard I had an assignment to kill two hundred people."

She looked into his eyes searchingly. It was possible, of course. In theory. But she just couldn't believe it. *No one* could kill two hundred people in cold blood and keep looking so young and innocent. No ruthless killer could have such laughter in his eyes. And yet – how much did she really know about the Diamond Majat?

"Tell me," she insisted. "Please. Have you really killed so many?"

He leaned back against the wall. His gaze wavered.

"No," he said.

She let out a sigh. "How many have you killed?"

He smiled. "If I told you, you wouldn't be able to know if I told the truth anyway, would you?"

"No. But you could just tell me the truth, couldn't you?"

"Perhaps."

"Please," she begged. "Just this once."

He shrugged. "If you *must* know, four."

"Really?" she whispered.

"Really." He met her eyes. There was no laughter in them anymore. But it was too late to back down.

She took a deep breath. "What about everything else you told me that time?"

He smiled, but his eyes were in shadow. "Which time?"

"You know which time." She sensed the blush creep to her cheeks and did her best to ignore it. "The time we– the time you tested my gift. Did you lie about everything else?"

His smile became wider, mischief gleaming behind the outward innocence. It was clear that he knew exactly what she meant, but he wasn't going to make it easy for her.

"If I did," he said, "it wouldn't be much of a test, would it?"

"What do you mean?"

"Think about it. If you wanted to know if someone could tell true from false, you should tell this person…" He paused, looking at her expectantly.

Ellah nodded. Of course. What a fool she had been!

"You should tell at least one lie," she said. "And at least one truth."

She looked at him with wonder, almost fright. It *did* make sense. To know if one could tell true from false, you should put both true and false into the game. It would be foolish not to.

And yet, how could he have been so *calculating* when talking about *feelings*?

Mai leaned forward toward her. She didn't draw back. She waited until his face came so close that she could feel the warmth of his breath on her cheek.

"Right," he said quietly. "At least one thing I told you was the truth."

She shivered. She wanted to indulge herself in this wild hope, to believe, if only for a moment, that the truth he had told her back then was about his feelings for her. Since that time, she couldn't think of anything else. She *needed* to know. And now, with his face so close and his voice so quiet, it was *so* easy to think that it was indeed what he meant. But another, sensible part of her mind stirred up, watching her from aside with cool logic. In all likelihood, it said, he'd probably told the truth about his age. Really, no matter how young he looked, he had been the head of the Royal Pentade for the past four years. He should be at least twenty-four. At least.

And yet–

At least one thing was the truth, he said. *At least one*. But no one said anything about *only* one thing.

"One?" she asked quietly.

He smiled and leaned back. "Now, if I told you *that*, it wouldn't be a challenge anymore, would it?"

Ellah sighed. Why did everything in life have to be a challenge?

She shook her head. "I'm not good enough for this. I have no real power."

He laughed again, but there was something behind the laughter that she couldn't read. "Of course you have power. Just not with me, right?"

She looked at him helplessly. "Not with you."

"And that bothers you?"

Yes, she wanted to say. It *did* bother her that she couldn't tell whether he meant what he had said to her back at the camp. But it was clear that she wasn't going to find out. Not this time.

"I don't belong here," she said instead. "I shouldn't have come with Mother Keeper at all. If I was meant to travel, I should've gone with Kyth and Alder."

He reached forward and touched her arm. His hand was warm, slightly roughened at the fingertips. He slid them down her wrist in a brief caress that made her shiver. Dazed, she raised her eyes to him.

"There's no use in thinking what you should've done in the past," he said. "The *future* is ahead of you. Think of that." He dropped away his hand and sprang to his feet. "We should go. It's time. I think you're about to earn a place in the King's retinue."

Before she could ask him what he meant, Mai swept away. Ellah got up and followed.

Everyone was gathered in the King's chambers. As Ellah walked in, Mother Keeper looked her up and down with eyes that seemed to notice everything, including Ellah's flustered state, and the blush that simply wouldn't leave her cheeks. The older woman took her time before glancing over to Mai, who had taken his place by the King's side with the calm ease of a cat reclaiming its rightful spot on the back of the master's armchair.

"You need to change," Mother Keeper told Ellah.

Ellah raised her eyebrows in surprise. After the fight she had been in, her other outfit needed mending. She had changed into her spare dress when they came back from the lower courtyard. She had nothing else to wear.

"Don't you think it would be better if she went the way she is?" Evan asked Mother Keeper. "They're going to know she's a girl anyway."

"And how would you explain her presence in your suite, Your Majesty?" the older woman asked. "I'd say she should change. She's tall enough. With her slim build and short hair she could pass as a boy."

A boy? Ellah looked at her in disbelief.

Evan shrugged. "A boy in what capacity, Mother Keeper? Surely not a bodyguard. Not when the Pentade is present. And I wouldn't be able to tell Daemur that she was my manservant, would I?"

Manservant? Ellah gaped. Why were they talking about her as if she wasn't here?

The Ruby Majat, Brannon, cleared his throat and glanced at Mai for permission to speak. Getting no objection, he said:

"She could be a weapon carrier. She could carry His Majesty's sword. It's not uncommon. We could outfit her, with Your Majesty's permission."

Ellah found her voice. "Where am I going?" she demanded. And, as an afterthought, added: "Your Majesty."

Evan's face softened. "Forgive us. We've been impolite discussing you like this. I'm going to meet with Daemur Illitand. Mother Keeper believes your gift may be useful to me during this meeting. If you could stand in my line of sight and show me whether he is lying or telling the truth, our negotiations could go a lot better. If you would, of course."

She met his eyes. He looked so much like Kyth it made her feel homesick, her resentment melting away like spring ice. Suddenly she didn't mind at all.

"I would be honored to help, Your Majesty," she said. "And if I must wear a man's clothes and carry your sword as part of my disguise, I would be glad to."

Evan gave her a warm smile. "Thank you."

17
THE NEW ASSIGNMENT

Sitting at his desk in the corner tower of the inner grounds, the Majat Master Oden Lan watched the slim, elegant figure clad in black approach the tower at a fast walk. A wave of short golden hair bounced against her dark skin in rhythm with the stride, the distinct coloring that marked her Olivian origin. The narrow hilt of her weapon showed from above the shoulder, the double-sworded staff whose elegant, efficient design made it one of the deadliest of weapons in the history of their Guild. Oden Lan knew of only one Diamond's weapon that could boast the same elegance and uniqueness, but he hadn't seen that weapon in over four years.

As she approached, Oden Lan admired her grace and precision that made her stand out even among her fellows in rank. Each Diamond was special, but Kara was more special than all.

He had overseen her training since she was four, and even at that age her talent had been incredible. At twelve, she had defeated a Jade in a face-on combat with blunt training swords. At fifteen, she had become an artist with her blade, her fame spreading like wildfire through the inner and outer grounds. When she turned eighteen, she had been pitched against a Diamond and after an exhausting melee she got through, leaving a mark on his face with a particularly wicked backhand blow. Soon after, she became the youngest Diamond to get ranked in the history of the Guild.

She was his prize champion, the proudest of what Oden Lan, the Majat Master for over twenty years, considered his creations. But even more important than her skill was her incredible life force. A passion drove her, filling her entire being with the creative power of her gift. Oden Lan never ceased feeling amazed that such a perfect creature was serving under his command.

She made no sound as she walked up the stairs. She merely disappeared into the opening of the tower at the bottom to reappear in the Guildmaster's study a few moments later. Despite the height of the stairway she had to ascend in such a short time, she wasn't in the least bit out of breath.

She stopped in the doorway and met Oden Lan's gaze. "*Shelah*, Aghat."

"*Shelah*."

She approached his desk and placed her token in front of him. The diamond set into the center of the throwing star glittered, and her name rune carved into the ornaments around the gem echoed with a suffused light.

Oden Lan nodded and picked up the token, tracing his long fingers against the name rune. Each of these runes spelled a secret nickname, one given to every Majat at the time of their ranking, so that no two Majat tokens would look alike. Kara's rune meant "black", a word which in the old Ridges' dialect sounded similar to her name.

"You did very well on your first assignment, Aghat," he said. "I am very proud of you."

She bowed her head in acknowledgment, but kept her silence.

Oden Lan would have hesitated to say a thing like this to any other Diamond. But Kara was different. If the Guildmaster had been allowed to have personal bonds, he would have loved her, almost like a daughter.

"Now," the Guildmaster said, "I'm sending you on a new assignment."

She looked at him with question, but still didn't speak.

"Your new assignment will be relatively easy," Oden Lan went on. "You will escort a group of travelers from here to the Bengaw Crest and ensure their safety on the way. There will be no complications and no true challenges you'll have to face. Your new employer paid enough for a promise that no other Majat will be dispatched to conflict with your assignment. I gave him my word."

She kept his gaze. There was a strange gleam in her eyes.

"From *here*?" she asked.

"Yes. Your employer arrived in the fortress a few hours before you and waited for you to come back."

"Waited for *me*?"

The Majat Master shifted in his seat. "He hired you by name. And paid the price for it in full. Three times the cost of a Diamond."

To his surprise he saw alarm in her eyes.

"Who is he?" she asked slowly.

Oden Lan reached for the bell on his desk and rang. A guard noiselessly appeared in the doorway. Oden Lan nodded to him and turned back to Kara.

"Your new employer insisted that I brief you on the details of your mission in his presence. He wanted to make sure there would be no mistakes."

Light steps echoed up the stairs and a man appeared in the doorway. Oden Lan gestured toward him. "Allow me to introduce Master Nimos."

Kara's eyes widened. Her cheeks flushed and went pale, making her dark skin seem ghostly gray. She watched with an entranced expression as Nimos approached and stopped in front of her.

They stood for a moment, eyeing each other in silence.

"Glad to see you again, Aghat," Nimos said.

She continued to stare at him.

"What the hell is going on?" Oden Lan demanded. "Do you two know each other?"

Nimos's thin lips twitched into a crooked smile. "Aghat Kara and I met on the way here. I can see I left an impression." He smirked, his eyes resting on Kara with such lust that even the Guildmaster felt uneasy. "I told you, Aghat Kara, one day we would be traveling together. Aren't you glad the day has come so soon?"

Kara looked past Nimos and met Oden Lan's gaze.

"What will be my assignment?" she asked.

Oden Lan leaned back in his chair. The way Nimos was eyeing Kara, practically eating her up with his eyes, made the Majat Master wonder if this man really understood what the services of a Diamond consisted of, and what wasn't included. He knew Kara was perfectly capable of taking care of herself, but to see this going on in front of his eyes was unsettling.

"Perhaps it would be best if we all sit down and discuss the details?" he suggested.

"Of course." Nimos approached the table and lowered himself into a chair. Kara remained standing. Oden Lan waited for her to come over, but she didn't move.

"Master Nimos," the Majat Master said after a pause, "wants your help to escort two youngsters, Kythar and Alder, to a secret stronghold in the Bengaw Crest. You know who I'm talking about, of course. You accompanied them here."

He glanced at her but she didn't respond.

"There's a possibility," Oden Lan went on, "that they wouldn't go willingly, but that won't be your concern. Master Nimos has his own men to take care of that. To assist with the operation, I have placed the youngsters in the guest barracks next to Master Nimos's men. These men will handle the capture and the upkeep of the prisoner. Your job, Aghat, will be to ensure that they reach their destination safely and without delay. Since I gave my word not to dispatch any Majat on a conflicting mission, the trip should be easy and fast."

Kara stiffened. "One of these young men is the King's only son, crown prince and heir to the throne."

"I know that." Oden Lan's voice became stern. "And I assure you, Master Nimos has paid enough to cover the boy's high station. You do remember, Aghat, that the Majat Guild doesn't participate in politics and doesn't take sides."

"Prince Kythar is under the protection of the Guild," Kara said. "He came here to seek our help. We can't capture him on our own grounds."

The Majat Master smiled. "*We* can't. But we're not obliged to interfere if *Master Nimos's* men capture him."

"But His Highness is here to hire a Diamond."

Oden Lan spread his hands. "Master Nimos was here first. And the agreement we made with him makes it impossible. If the young man tried to hire a Diamond now, it would certainly qualify as a conflicting mission."

She continued to stand still, tense like a coiled spring.

A triumphant smile flickered on Nimos's lips. "We wish to leave tomorrow at dawn, Aghat Kara. Shall we, say, meet you at five in the morning by the East Gate?"

She didn't respond, looking past him to the window outside. Oden Lan wasn't sure she even heard these words.

"She'll be there," the Guildmaster assured. "Here's her token." He handed Nimos the glittering throwing star. "You may go and make your preparations, Master Nimos," he went on. "And please don't hesitate to ask if you need anything."

The slight man got up from his seat and strode to the door, brushing past Kara on the way. She shuddered at the contact, but didn't step aside or otherwise acknowledge his presence. She didn't move even after the door closed behind Nimos. She stood so still that Oden Lan began to wonder if she was all right.

"Something bothering you, Aghat?" he asked.

She looked at him, her face blank like a mask. "Forgive me, Master Oden Lan. But I must ask you to send someone else on this mission. I– I can't go."

He shook his head. "Impossible. He paid to hire you, and not any other Diamond. In fact, he told me in no uncertain terms that if you're unavailable for the mission he will not hire anyone else. As it happens, though, you are available. And, you are currently between assignments. You cannot refuse, Aghat. You know the Code."

Not a single muscle changed on her face, but suddenly she seemed so vulnerable that Oden Lan's heart quivered.

"Is something bothering you, Aghat?" he asked again.

Her lips twitched as if she was about to speak, but kept her silence.

"I trust," Oden Lan went on after a pause, "that you remember your training and the Majat Code. The Majat do not take sides. We work for money. We don't pledge loyalty to anyone except the Guild. And, we don't judge our employers. We do the job, and we do it well. That's why our services are valued so highly."

She continued to stand still, staring ahead.

"Whatever your quarrel is with this man," Oden Lan persuaded, "you must not let it get in the way of your duty. I saw the way he looked at you, but I'm quite certain he understands what kind of services he has paid for and won't give you any trouble of *that* kind. More than that, even if he *did* try to force himself on you, alone or with all twelve of his accomplices, with your skills in combat you can't possibly be afraid of it. Are you, Aghat?"

She shook her head. She still didn't say anything. Oden Lan was beginning to get angry.

"I am certain, Aghat," he said, "that the years of your training make it unnecessary for me to further remind you of your duties. I've said enough. Now, go and rest. You're leaving tomorrow at dawn."

She raised her gaze to him.

"And if I don't?" she asked quietly.

Oden Lan lifted his chin abruptly, as if he had been slapped.

"If you don't," he said distinctly, "you will become an oathbreaker and will be expelled from the Guild. You do remember what that means, Aghat, don't you?"

She kept his gaze. "Yes."

Oden Lan nodded, forcing his voice down to its normal tone. "Good. Since I know that you didn't have time to rest after the completion of your previous assignment, I will pretend, just this once, that this conversation didn't happen. Now, go and get ready. I look forward to another successful report."

She hesitated for just a moment longer. Then she turned and left the room.

18
DIPLOMACY

Ellah felt strange in a man's outfit, walking next to Evan inside the protective ring of the Majat. Evan's long sword was heavy. She had to clutch it with both hands to keep the weapon from hitting her legs as she walked. She hoped this was a permitted way to treat the King's sword. She looked at Evan for reassurance, but the King kept his eyes firmly ahead.

They followed their honorary guards in green and gold Illitand colors through a maze of white marble corridors, awash with sunlight streaming through tall arched windows. Unlike the ominous strongholds in Tandar, the dwelling of the Illitand Dukes was open and airy, full of white marble staircases and big windows framing the sky and the lake outside. The majority of the castle's space came from the vertical dimension, arranged around the top of the mountain like a large, ornate crown. Ellah guessed that this slender architecture was possible only because the castle was so well protected, surrounded by water and the impenetrable city walls on all sides.

As they neared the large double doors at the end of the hallway, Mai broke off from the formation and caught up with the guard captain walking in front. The man threw a nervous glance at the Majat and signaled the guards ahead to open the heavy doors to the audience chamber.

"His Majesty King Evan Dorn!" he announced.

Evan stepped forward, but Mai's hand shot up, halting the procession. Two Rubies in front closed in, shielding Evan with their bodies. The two at the back drew their swords and crouched, ready to attack.

Mai spun forward and around, his outstretched arms unfolding with two long swords that weren't there just a moment ago. The blades whistled as they cut the air, and Mai completed his movement, coming to a standstill. Ellah blinked, trying to understand what had happened.

Mai stood, arms out, holding two swords at the throats of the armored guards on the inside of the open doorway. Behind were more guards, drawn out of hiding by Mai's display. Ellah realized that the swords Mai was holding at their throats belonged to the guards themselves, and that with his quick movement Mai had disarmed them before they had a chance to react.

There was an awkward pause.

"I'm sorry, my lords and lady," Evan said, looking past Mai into the open doorway. "We seem to have spoiled a surprise."

Only now did Ellah notice their welcoming party. The tall, pale man with long auburn hair falling on his shoulders was certainly Duke Daemur Illitand. He would have been quite handsome if it wasn't for the look of cold displeasure in his green eyes as he surveyed his guests. Ellah felt an instant dislike for the man.

On his right was Lady Celana, the young girl who had welcomed them into the castle. On the left – Ambassador Tanad Eli Faruh, a dark-skinned Olivian with pale bronze hair and deep purple eyes. Ellah's heart raced as she recognized him as the man who had been talking to Kaddim Tolos down in the courtyard.

"Your Majesty," the Duke said. "Forgive the confusion. My guards should've stayed in sight, but you see, they're new at their jobs."

Evan smiled. "I feel honored, Lord Daemur, that you chose to assemble such a force to greet me. But I must say, if this happened on the high road, I would've thought we were being ambushed."

The Duke spread his hands. "Come, Sire. You don't think we'd plan an ambush, knowing that you're coming here with your Majat guard? That would have been utterly foolish."

"Indeed." Evan's eyes gleamed with mischief. "Two dozen men seem like an insult to Aghat Mai's skill." Ellah saw his glance wander her way and took care to keep the two fingers in sight on top of the sword hilt she was holding.

"You may stand down, Aghat Mai," Daemur Illitand said. "No one's trying to harm the King."

Mai didn't move. Evan gave him a thoughtful glance.

"I think, Lord Daemur," Mai said, "we may have run into some protocol issues here. Something about armed guards in the presence of the King?"

Illitand's face twitched.

"How foolish of me to forget," he said. "As always, Aghat Mai's knowledge of protocol is commendable."

"What should we do, Aghat Mai?" Evan asked.

"The guards must leave, Your Majesty," Mai said.

Daemur Illitand raised his head. "You heard the Aghat. Move!"

The men edged along the walls out of the room. Daemur watched them go, his face folded into an expression the Duke probably considered to be a smile.

"You came here well protected, Sire," he said.

Evan nodded. "I am impressed. Frankly, I never thought before this trip that the Pentade served more than a ceremonial purpose."

He glanced at Mai, who lowered the swords and stood aside with his back to the wall, so that he had a perfect view of both the room and the hallway outside. The Rubies loosened the ring around Evan, but kept their swords bare.

"I admire Aghat Mai's style," Daemur observed. "His predecessor in the Pentade – Aghat Seldon, I believe – was quite different. He never rushed into action himself. He always sent the Rubies in first. To me, it makes more sense. A commander should stay out of danger to oversee his troops, don't you think?" He turned to Mai, who continued to stand still, staring straight ahead as if the conversation didn't concern him at all.

"You're quite right," Evan agreed. "However, I understand that Aghat Mai hasn't yet found himself in danger while being in my service. It's all been quite uneventful so far, thanks to his care."

"So far," Daemur echoed.

Evan gave him a square look. "What exactly do you mean, my lord?"

Daemur bowed. "I heard of the unfortunate incident at the city gate, Sire. My deepest apologies. It was quite reckless, if I may say, to come here in disguise."

Evan waved his hand in dismissal. "No problem at all. Your archers were most gracious in letting us through, thanks to the quick wit of your gate captain. Captain Ragan, I believe. Most commendable."

The two men stood for a moment, glaring at each other. Ellah's mind was full of a steady red color as she continued to hold two fingers out. If diplomacy meant lying all the time, both King Evan and Duke Daemur seemed to have mastered it to perfection.

"In any case," Evan said, "now that we're done with the formalities, there's nothing to prevent us from having a pleasant conversation, is there, Lord Daemur?"

The Duke of Illitand continued to smile, but his eyes were still. It made an unpleasant contrast.

"I look forward to it, Your Majesty," he said. "Now that you have honored us all by accepting the hospitality of the Castle Illitand."

Evan smiled. "It is a joy to see that Tanad Eli Faruh is also your guest." He turned to the Olivian ambassador. "The Duke was kind enough to inform me in his letter that your ward, Princess Aljbeda, is also here?"

The Olivian bowed. "Lord Daemur has graciously offered his beautiful castle for Her Highness's entertainment."

Ellah's hand holding out two fingers was beginning to feel stiff. Was it possible that during diplomatic talk no one *ever* told the truth?

"Very prudent of you, Lord Daemur," Evan said. "I can see that your castle indeed has a lot to offer someone in need of refuge. I myself would have liked nothing better than to stay longer, but I am afraid I came with a different purpose. It is my intention to convince Your Grace – and Her Highness – to return to Tandar with me."

Daemur shifted from foot to foot and exchanged a glance with Lady Celana. Even though the red color in Ellah's mind hadn't changed, she sensed that the conversation was finally coming to an important part.

"I'm afraid, Your Majesty," Illitand said, "your departure would be quite impossible."

"Whatever do you mean, Lord Daemur?"

The Duke of Illitand exchanged another glance with

his daughter. "The business we need to discuss with Your Majesty might take considerable time."

Evan smiled. "Surely you don't propose holding me here against my will?"

Daemur's gaze wavered. "Regretfully, I must, Sire. Until we resolve our little… issue."

Evan shook his head. "Aren't you being a bit careless, Lord Daemur? The Pentade–"

"The Pentade is capable of keeping you safe within this castle. However, I doubt they could break you out of here with a guarantee that no harm would come to you in the process, Your Majesty. Isn't that right, Aghat Mai?"

He turned to Mai, who responded with a calm stare. There was a feverish gleam in Daemur's eyes. Ellah had a sense that the Duke himself couldn't quite comprehend the boldness of his words. She folded away one finger as the color in her mind suddenly changed from red to deep royal blue.

Evan drew himself up. "Holding me prisoner, Lord Daemur, qualifies as high treason."

"Only if the man I hold is the rightful king." The words rang clearly through the deadly silent hall.

"I see," Evan said.

"Since the Keepers took part in placing House Dorn on the throne," Daemur went on, "it is also fortunate that Mother Keeper is here with you. Her presence will allow us to resolve this once and for all."

"Resolve? What exactly do you have in mind?"

"We're not barbarians," the Duke said. "We'll stick to diplomacy as long as we have a choice."

Evan glanced around the room. "There's one person I don't see here. I believe, he should've been included in the greeting party, for I could distinctly sense a touch of his unique style. I heard some refer to him as Kaddim Tolos."

Daemur stepped back, eyes wide. "Kaddim Tolos?"

Evan smiled. "Yes. The title is quite historical, as you know. Some believe the Kaddim Brotherhood has been extinct for centuries. However, strangely enough, a man addressed by this title has attacked my son back in Tandar. And, even more amazingly, shortly after our arrival here, the same man ambushed Aghat Mai in one of your castle's hallways."

"*Ambushed* Aghat Mai?" Daemur stretched the word in mockery. "Is this possible?" he turned to Mai again, and again received nothing but a blank stare in response.

"This man," Evan went on, "seems quite keen to destroy House Dorn. And, his appearance here is an amazing coincidence with your decision to perform this outrage toward your king."

"Your kinghood," Daemur said slowly, "remains to be determined."

Evan's eyes narrowed. "And what, pray, makes you say that, my lord?"

"Ghaz Shalan Law," the Duke said. "We both know, Sire, your house is tainted with the cursed blood. Your heir–"

"Are you questioning the last thousand years of history, Lord Daemur?"

"You're a royal," Daemur said. "And as such, you should know why the King cannot possibly place himself above the law."

"Funny you should mention that," Evan said. "For I made this trip to your castle to talk exactly about this particular law. However now that you have the audacity to question my entire bloodline–"

"Not yours," Illitand said through clenched teeth. "Your son's. He's cursed, and should have been eliminated at birth. If you truly wish to rule, you should first order his execution!"

Evan's nostrils flared. "This law has kept us in the clutches of the Church for centuries. It's overdue for a change, Daemur, and you know it. Don't tell me you're in support of it now!"

"It's a *law*. Does the word still mean something to you, or is it that after you were crowned–"

"Have you seen our new Reverend?" Evan asked.

"No, but I've heard that he is a man of high principles. Unlike you."

"I see," Evan said slowly. "Did your new ally, a Kaddim Brother, tell you these things?"

Daemur's face reddened, but before he could speak Tanad Eli Faruh hastily stepped forward.

"Perhaps, my lords, this is not a good time to discuss our differences. You have a proposition for His Majesty, don't you, Lord Daemur?"

Daemur slowly let out a breath. "Yes. Indeed, Sire, I believe there is a way out of this situation. A union between our families, to seal the rightful heir for the kingdom."

Evan raised his eyebrows. "What happened to the execution I'm supposed to order? After all you said, you are proposing a marriage between your daughter and my son?"

"Not your son. You."

Evan's eyes widened, noticing Ellah holding out one finger and back to the Duke. "You're serious, aren't you?"

"Really, Sire," Tanad Eli Faruh's reverberating baritone easily carried through the hallway. "Lady Celana is a lady of rare beauty and virtue. You should be pleased by this suggestion."

"I quite agree," Evan said. "Lady Celana's beauty and wit are famed. She deserves a brilliant match. She is also young enough to be my daughter. It's shocking to me that her father would use her as a bargaining chip in his political games."

"But think about it," the Tanad insisted. "You're still in your prime years, Your Majesty. If you had a young wife, you could sire children that share the proper bloodlines of not one, but two royal houses, and will once and for all stop the endless games of succession that have drowned our kingdom in blood for generations. Houses of Dorn and Illitand united – wouldn't that be glorious?"

"Glorious, yes. But in the present circumstances it's utterly inappropriate to offer this match to me. The Duke should be offering it to my son."

Illitand's face twisted in anger. "Your son's an abomination! Don't you *dare* bring him up in connection to my daughter!"

Evan's face froze. Stepping back, he ran his eyes around the room.

"It seems to me," he said into space, "that we've overstayed our welcome. I wish to return back to my chambers immediately, Aghat Mai."

Mai stepped away from the wall and threw down the two captured swords he had been holding. Steel rang loudly through the hall. At his signal the Pentade regrouped into a travel formation. Evan turned and strode away along the corridor, surrounded by the Majat. Ellah hurried to keep up.

"Go ahead!" Illitand shouted to his back. "Walk away! You'll *rot* in my castle, Evan Dorn! You'll never be able to leave these walls! *Never*!"

Evan didn't change his stride, but Ellah saw knots of muscles move under the skin of his neck. His glassy gaze frightened her.

She wondered if the two royals were ever going to make up. If this was what diplomacy was all about, she wanted no more part in it.

19
FLIGHT

"It's getting late," Egey Bashi said. "We should get some sleep."

Kyth surveyed his bed. Its roughly hewn wood was barely covered by a thin straw mattress, dry stems sticking through the holes. The blanket thrown over it resembled a thick grain sack. A small hard pillow was filled with something heavy and dense that felt like sand. All in all, the bed didn't look too inviting, but Kyth was tired enough to try.

Alder had already stretched on top of his blanket. Kyth envied his foster brother's capacity to fall asleep anywhere, without giving too much consideration to simple human comforts. He reached over and covered Alder with a cloak. Alder mumbled sleepily and pulled the cloak over his head.

As Kyth bent down to take off his boots, he heard a creak outside in the hallway. A thin blade slid into the gap between the door and the frame and threw the latch off the hook with a click.

Kyth quietly reached for his sword, exchanging a meaningful glance with Egey Bashi at the other side of the room. But before any of them could move, the blade disappeared and the door swung open.

A cloaked figure stepped into the room.

"Kara!" Kyth breathed out.

He was so glad to see her he was at a loss for words. He wanted to rush forward to greet her, but he noticed the paleness of her face, the feverish gleam in her eyes, and the set of grim resolve in the lines of her full mouth.

"What's wrong?" he asked quietly.

She closed the door behind her and brushed past, flinging a bag off her shoulder onto an empty bed. "We're leaving. Now."

"*We*?" Alder sat up, pulling the cloak off his face.

"You and Kyth are coming with me."

"Where?"

She ignored the question as she undid the strings of the bag and took out a bundle. After further unfolding it revealed two black outfits, similar to those many Majat wore throughout the grounds. She handed one to Kyth and threw the other one to Alder.

"Put it on," she said. "Quick."

"But why? Where're we going?"

"To the Grasslands."

Kyth looked at her in disbelief. "But we haven't even seen your Guildmaster yet. Did you tell him about me? Did he send you to protect me?"

She averted her eyes. "No."

"What's going on, Aghat?" Egey Bashi demanded.

She turned to him. Again, she hesitated before answering. "There's been a change of plans. The Guildmaster's not going to send anyone with you. And believe me, it's best if you don't question me any further."

"Best for whom?" Alder asked.

Her gaze hardened. "Get dressed."

Alder looked at the heap of clothes in his lap. "Aren't you going to step outside while we change?"

"No. But if you're *that* shy, I'll turn around and count to ten. You'd better be done by then." She turned her back and stood still.

Kyth and Alder exchanged a glance.

"Better do what she says," Egey Bashi suggested.

"Four," Kara said.

Kyth and Alder rushed over to the heaps of clothes on their beds.

The Majat outfits consisted of loose shirts and tight pants. They were surprisingly comfortable. Silky cloth fell right into place, the folds fitting exactly – comfortable with no suppression of movement. When Kyth finished dressing and pulled on his boots, he felt fit and ready for action.

"Done?" Kara asked, her back still turned.

"Yes," Kyth said.

"No!" Alder exclaimed almost at the same time.

She turned around. Alder was still struggling with his boots. She came over and picked up his gear, waiting. Alder finished and hastily straightened up.

He looked dashing in the new outfit. Gray eyes and blond hair made a striking contrast with the black cloth, whose loose folds, tucked into the wide belt, made his shoulders seem even wider and the waist even narrower than they already were. He looked graceful and fit, just like the ranked Majat they'd seen today. Even under the circumstances Kyth couldn't help but admire his foster brother. He hoped he looked half as handsome.

He stuffed spare clothes into his pack and flung it onto his shoulder.

"Let's go," Kara said.

Kyth hesitated. "Aren't you going to tell us *anything*?"

"There's no time," she snapped.

"Really, Aghat," Egey Bashi joined in. "This seems like

a major change of plans compared to the time we last saw you. You should tell us *something*." He was also putting things into his pack.

Kara's eyes fixed on his face. "You're not coming."

"Out of the question," Egey Bashi said calmly. "Unless you give me a *really* good reason."

She looked around the room in exasperation. "We're out of time!"

"Why?"

She paused, her gaze wavering.

"Nimos and his men," she said quietly, "are stationed in the room next to you. At dawn, they're going to capture Kyth and Alder and take them away. And the Majat Guild is not going to interfere."

Egey Bashi looked at her in disbelief. "I thought that as long as we're here to hire the Majat services, we're all under the protection of the Guild."

She met his eyes. "Nimos hired *me* to help with the capture and ensure that Kyth and Alder can be safely taken to his secret stronghold. He also paid our Guildmaster to ensure that no Majat will be sent on a conflicting assignment. Which means the Guild won't protect Kyth and Alder against Nimos's men, here or anywhere else."

They all gaped. What she said seemed impossible.

"Hired *you*?"

"By name. He paid three times the price of a Diamond."

"And what do you intend to do?" Egey Bashi asked slowly.

"I'm going to take Kyth and Alder out of here and to the Grasslands, to meet with the Cha'ori."

"Why?"

For a moment she was very still.

"Is there any other choice?" she asked quietly.

Egey Bashi looked at her, and it seemed to Kyth that there was a silent conversation going on between them.

"No," the Keeper said.

She nodded. "At dawn, they'll notice our absence. This is why we have so little time."

"And why don't you want me to come along?" Egey Bashi asked.

"Because," she said, "there's nothing you can do to help."

There was another pause as their gazes held on to each other, a conversation going on within.

"What about your Guild?" Egey Bashi asked quietly. "It can't possibly be good for you to disobey your orders."

Her gaze became stern. "That's none of your concern."

"If we're putting you in danger because of helping us," Kyth protested, "we can't go. I won't. I'd rather face Nimos and his men."

"Danger?" Her lips twitched and folded into a distant smile. "There's only a handful of warriors who can match me, and none of them can beat me in single combat. What possible danger could there be for me?"

Kyth hesitated. Her words made sense, but he had a feeling there was something she wasn't telling him.

"One thing doesn't make sense," Egey Bashi said.

"What?" Kara asked.

"Nimos's behavior. First, he makes very sure that we all know of his bad intentions and that all of us, especially you, can't stand his presence. Then, he pays an exorbitant sum of money to hire *you* for this mission. If I'm not mistaken, any other Diamond would do the job just fine. And any of them would certainly be more agreeable than you."

She shrugged. "It may be so. But whatever his plan, it leaves us with very few options." She took out three pieces of black cloth and handed two of them to Kyth and Alder.

"Put these on, and get your packs. Hurry."

"What's this?" Alder asked. But before he could get the answer, she already unfolded hers and pulled it over her face.

"The Anonymous mask?" Alder asked in disbelief.

She turned to him, eyes gleaming through the slits in the black cloth. "I said, *move*. Or do you want me to knock you out and carry you?"

Given the difference in their size the suggestion seemed ridiculous, but Alder didn't laugh. He pulled on the mask at double speed and flung the pack and the sheathed axe over his shoulder.

"Wait, Aghat!" Egey Bashi called out.

Kara's shoulders stiffened.

"Are you certain there's nothing else that could be done?" the Keeper asked quietly.

She turned around slowly, her look forcing the Keeper to take an inadvertent step back.

"Yes, there is," she said. "I could knock *you* out and stop you from interfering with our departure." She nodded to Kyth and Alder and put her hand on the doorknob, then paused.

"Actually, there *is* one thing you could do, Magister. I'm sure you can't wait to run off to warn Raishan, or to attempt to talk some sense into the Guildmaster. If you want Kyth and Alder to survive, don't do any of this until they notice our absence. We can't have anyone raise the alarm before we're well out of the city."

She turned and waited for his nod of acknowledgment. Then she opened the door and noiselessly slid through. Kyth and Alder followed.

They didn't talk as they sped down the sleeping streets to the East Gate. The occasional guards they came across shied sideways as soon as they saw the masks and the gleam of the diamond in Kara's armband. No one dared to interfere with the Anonymous, especially if one of them was of the Diamond rank.

As they saddled the horses and made their way to the gate, Kara gave a hand sign to the Jade guard captain. The Jade hastily signaled ahead to open the gate. Kara didn't say a word as they rode past the saluting guards and out of the city. In less than ten minutes they were halfway up the hill, chilly night wind finding its way through the holes in the masks and the gaps in the travel cloaks. As they rode on, Kara never looked back.

20
THE CODE

Oden Lan unclenched his fist and looked at the broken glass in his hand. Some of the pieces went deep into the skin. Blood trickled down his wrist and onto the polished table.

He took out a handkerchief and carefully wiped his arm, keeping his eyes on the two men standing in front of his desk. The metal of their armbands glittered in the light from the window, making the suffused gleam of the jades look dull by comparison.

"She violated the Code, Guildmaster," said the one on the left, a pale man with straight black hair and a piercing gaze.

Oden Lan gave him a heavy stare. "You don't have to tell me about the Code, Gahang Khall. I know what must be done."

He got up from his desk and walked over to a small cabinet on the wall. Keeping his back to the two Jades, he reached for the key hanging round his neck, moving slowly so that the tremble in his fingers wouldn't be so obvious. In all his years at the Guild, his fingers had never trembled before. It was annoying to see that a simple matter of upholding the Code could bring this on.

Once the cabinet was unlocked, he reached inside and took out a throwing star from the stack at its back. His fingers traced the familiar rune even before he had a chance to read it, and each of its bends echoed in his soul. He didn't have to look to know what it said.

Black.

Oden Lan took the token over to the table and put it down. It looked so different from the *other* token that he'd held in his hands yesterday afternoon. *That* token was set with a purest white diamond, whose luster was enough to bring light into the room. The diamond set into the center of this one was black. It was cut and polished exactly like the other one, but it didn't glow. Instead, it seemed to absorb light. As Oden Lan put it on the table, it seemed for a moment as if the sun had gone behind a cloud in the clear morning sky.

The two Jades exchanged uneasy glances. Even though every ranked Majat knew about these tokens, no one among the current Guild members had ever seen one. The fact that it had to be brought out for the first time in hundreds of years because of someone Oden Lan cared for so much, made it worse.

He felt warm liquid trickle down his hand and lowered his gaze to realize he had clenched his injured fist again. He slowly unclenched it and wrapped the damp handkerchief around it.

"Choose one of your best, Gahang Khall," he said to the Jade. "And, have someone send for Master Nimos. He must be told what has happened."

The Jades saluted with fists to their chests and strode out of the room. When they were gone, Oden Lan stood for a moment longer, staring ahead with unseeing eyes. Then he reached for the bell on his desk and rang. A moment later a guard appeared noiselessly in the doorway.

"Have someone clean up this mess," Oden Lan said, looking away. "And don't disturb me until I call again."

He took a clean sheet of parchment out of the desk, careful not to touch it with the bleeding hand. Then he walked over to a small table near the window and settled down to write.

Oden Lan had just pressed his personal seal against the wax when he heard a commotion at the door. It sounded as if somebody was trying to storm his study, and the Majat guard at the door was having trouble holding them back.

Oden Lan strode to the door and flung it open. "I *said* I was not to be disturbed."

The man nearest to the door flipped off his hood to reveal a dark, bear-like face crossed by the ugliest scar Oden Lan had ever seen.

"Magister Egey Bashi," he said stiffly. "What a pleasant surprise."

"I assure you the pleasure's all mine." The Keeper's smile looked more like a scowl.

Behind him were two more shapes. One, a slim, muscular man with a ruthless look in his slanting gray eyes was the Diamond, Raishan. The other, whose long, incredibly expressive face was crossed by deep lines of age, was the old weapon keeper, Abib. They stood, shoulder to shoulder, their expressions of resolve showing the Guildmaster that they would not yield their positions even in the face of death.

"What in the hell do you want?" Oden Lan's voice rang with steel.

Abib stepped forward. "Now, Aghat," he said soothingly. "All we want to do is to talk. We didn't mean to make so much noise. It's just that the young lad here at the door wouldn't listen to reason."

"The 'young lad' had his orders."

Abib smiled and straightened out the sleeve of his robe. "And he followed them to the letter. Very commendable indeed. Now, may we come in, Aghat?"

"No." Oden Lan moved to shut the door, but Magister Egey Bashi slid forward with unexpected speed and put a foot in its way.

Oden Lan raised eyes full of surprise to the Magister. In all his years as the head of the Guild, he had never been confronted in this way. It was so unexpected that he couldn't even find room for anger.

"Is this some sort of mutiny?" he asked.

"By no means." Egey Bashi kept his foot in place to make sure that the door stayed open. "Mutiny could only be initiated by your subordinates. As it is, Aghat Raishan and Master Abib are only standing here. *I'm* the one to confront you, and I am in no way your subordinate."

Oden Lan's eyes narrowed. "I can see you have it all worked out."

Abib stepped forward to the Magister's side. "Come now, Aghat Oden Lan. We mean no disrespect. We just need to talk. Can we, please?"

Oden Lan suddenly felt very tired. He flung the door open and stood aside, letting them in.

Abib walked in first and glanced around the room. Despite his advanced years he still moved with cat-like grace and his eyes, blue and innocent, never missed a single detail. Oden Lan saw these eyes pause on a blooded chip of glass that the cleaners had missed during their hurried sweep through the Guildmaster's study. He had an uncomfortable feeling that the man knew exactly what it was, but the old weapon keeper didn't say anything. He crossed the room and settled in his favorite armchair at the side of the desk.

Oden Lan walked over and sat down in his own chair. He didn't offer seats to Raishan and the Keeper.

"What do you want to talk about?" he asked dryly, careful not to look at any one of the three men.

"We're here because of Kara," Abib said.

Oden Lan stiffened. The sound of her name made him feel as if he had been hit in the gut.

"I have a feeling," he said, "that after all this trouble of getting in, you're going to say what you came to say, whether I want to hear it or not. So, say it quickly and get out."

"If you weren't so emotional about this, Aghat," Abib said, "it would have been as obvious to you as it is to us that Aghat Kara has been set up by a very clever plot."

"*Kara*," Oden Lan said, forcing himself to pronounce it without a flinch and emphasizing by his tone the absence of a title in front of her name, "has disobeyed her orders, abandoned an assignment, and violated the Code. You know perfectly well that I have no choice in what must be done."

Raishan stepped toward the desk so fast that his shape blurred. Oden Lan blinked. Even when he felt his worst he would never stop admiring the Diamonds' quality of movement. Each Diamond was unique, a true piece of art. To think that Kara had been his best...

"The Magister and I," Raishan said, "traveled here with Kara. This man – Nimos – he went to a great deal of trouble to make himself as much of an annoyance as humanly possible. He approached us multiple times trying to bribe us so that we'd hand Prince Kythar over to his men. And, he focused a great deal of attention on Kara. He spared no effort, even risked being attacked, to throw her off balance. It all looked pretty deliberate. And, it was clear all along that he was up to something."

Oden Lan gave him a dry smile. "Of all people, I shouldn't have to say this to you, Aghat. But I'll say it anyway. No matter how *annoyed* someone makes you feel, the Code of the Guild comes first. We don't take sides because of our *personal* feelings."

"I think," Egey Bashi put in, "what Aghat Raishan and Master Abib are trying to tell you is that Master Nimos has been following some plan, and his behavior on the road, as well as his request to hire Kara, were both part of it. Don't you see that he played you? He hired Kara *knowing* she would never go with him on this assignment. He *knew* what she was going to do. He practically left her no choice."

Oden Lan measured the Keeper with his gaze. "Normally I wouldn't discuss the affairs of the Guild with an outsider. But since you obviously know more about this than you should, and since you came here in such company, Magister, I will make an exception this time. Master Nimos paid three times the price of a Diamond to hire Kara's services, by name. I accepted it and gave him her token. There was no possible excuse for her to refuse to go."

"Think about it," Egey Bashi insisted. "Why would he pay triple to hire Kara, when any other Diamond could do this job just as well?"

"My opinion about this doesn't matter," Oden Lan said. "But if you really want to know, I think Master Nimos may have had personal reasons to do this. He seemed... infatuated with her. This, however, is really beside the point. The Majat don't question our employers' motives. That's one of the reasons our services are valued so highly."

"And now," Egey Bashi pressed on, "what will happen to the money that he paid you?"

"It will be returned, of course."

"So, he actually won't be paying you anything, would he?" A strange glow lit up in the Magister's eyes.

"Since we are having such an honest conversation," Oden Lan said, "and I just happen to anticipate your next question, I'll tell you. Master Nimos also paid the price of one Diamond to ensure that no Majat could be hired to protect the boys."

"I see."

"Therefore," Oden Lan went on, "while I do agree that the way Master Nimos behaved around Kara wouldn't help to establish a good working relationship, I fail to see what he stood to gain by her actions. As of now, the boys are under her protection, which definitely makes his intentions toward them harder to fulfill. If you're right that this was part of a plot, the plot was quite badly conceived, wasn't it?"

"And what will you do now?" Egey Bashi asked.

The Majat Master glanced around the room. Abib and Raishan averted their eyes.

"That," Oden Lan said, "is none of your business, Magister."

Raishan raised his head. "Perhaps you would allow me to talk to her first, Master Oden Lan? If you send me to intercept her, maybe I could convince her to–"

Oden Lan's short glance cut him off. Raishan lifted his chin and stood to attention.

"There's one thing you didn't tell me, Aghat Raishan," the Majat Master said, "and you should have. She thinks she's in love with the boy, doesn't she? She betrayed her duty to protect him. You should know well that no matter what else happened, *that's* what really makes her actions unforgivable."

"For the Guild?" Abib asked quietly. "Or, for you?"

The silence that followed these words hit the room like a thunderbolt. Oden Lan slowly turned around to face the old man. For a moment it seemed to everyone that he was going to hit the weapon keeper, but he didn't move. His gaze became cold.

"The deed is done," he said. "Even if she decided to come back and resume the assignment, it won't change anything now." He glanced over to Raishan. The Diamond lowered his head. It suddenly seemed as if the sun had disappeared from the blazing morning sky and it had become dark and dreary in the room.

"Now, go," Oden Lan said. "There's nothing more to be said."

"Actually," Egey Bashi said, "I'm here with another business." He stepped forward and put a heavy bag of coins on the Guildmaster's desk. "I wish to hire a Diamond."

Oden Lan looked at him in surprise. "For what assignment? If this has anything to do with–"

"I assure you, it's a completely unrelated matter. I am on my way to look into certain things at the Monastery in Aknabar. I'll need a really good bodyguard."

Oden Lan leaned back in his chair. "There're not many Diamonds that are currently unassigned."

He looked over at Raishan, who stood inanimate in the way only the top gem ranks could. His slanted gray eyes were fixed impassively on the landscape outside the window.

The Magister had no way of knowing that after Oden Lan dispatched the messengers to carry the two freshly sealed packages on his desk, Raishan would be the only Diamond left who was available to go with the Keeper. At least, Oden Lan hoped that the Magister had no way of knowing it, and that this was all mere coincidence.

He paused before turning back to the Keeper.

"Aghat Raishan," he said, "is currently between assignments. He will go with you."

He reached into his desk drawer and took out Raishan's token, handing it to the Magister. He took care not to look at the gleam of the diamond, closing his fingers over it and glancing at the name rune instead. It read "hawk", but to an outsider it looked like no more than an elegant ornament at the base of the crossed blades.

"You must understand, Magister," Oden Lan said. "If I find that Aghat Raishan has interfered with Guild business in any way, with or without your orders, it will be a violation of the Majat Code. Aghat Raishan knows what that means. If he forgets his duties, even for a moment, it would be a great loss for all of us. Please make sure it doesn't happen."

The Magister nodded, putting the token away into the depths of his robe.

Oden Lan turned to Raishan. "Do you have any questions about your new assignment, Aghat?"

"No, Guildmaster," Raishan said, his eyes still fixed on the window ahead.

"You must protect the Magister," Oden Lan said, "and only him. If you get involved in the protection of the boys, or if you interfere with other Guild members doing their duty, you will suffer the same fate as *her*."

He walked to the door and held it open long after the footsteps of his unwanted visitors died out on the spiral stairway. Then he returned to his desk and rang the bell. His work for today was not done.

In less than ten minutes, two men came in. One was Gahang Khall, the head of the Jades who had been in the study earlier today when he and the gate captain, Gahang Amir, had brought the bad news. He was accompanied by a freckled young man with curly red hair. The man's light blue eyes held an expression of childlike wonder, making anyone who met him feel like smiling.

"Gahang Sharrim," Khall introduced. "He's one of my best."

Oden Lan nodded. It was difficult to imagine that this red-headed youngster would be good enough for the operation, but Khall knew his business.

A third figure appeared noiselessly in the doorway. The Jades hurriedly moved aside as he stepped in, smooth and graceful like a tiger.

"Come in, Aghat Han," Oden Lan beckoned.

The newcomer approached the desk and froze, an instant change from movement to stillness. Oden Lan looked him up and down.

Han looked like a man of Cha'ori lineage. He had dark skin, black hair, and agate eyes that were slanted much more than Raishan's, narrow slits that shot upward to the corners of his high cheekbones. Like all Diamonds, he wasn't especially big or tall, but he seemed to occupy a lot of the room with his dark, ominous presence. He and Sharrim, standing next to each other, looked like almost exact opposites, a cheerful young man who made everyone feel like smiling, and a dark, gloomy one who seemed to suck the air out of the room just by standing quietly in its corner. They made an interesting pair.

"The King and his suite are now at Illitand Hall," Oden Lan said. "You must travel by a relay, to reach them as quickly as you can. Take the fastest lizardbeasts from the stable. I'm sending messenger ravens to ensure you get fresh beasts every fifty leagues. I expect that with no delay you should get there in eight days. If anyone gets in your way, you may do whatever you need to remove them."

Oden Lan leaned forward and handed the two sealed packages to Han.

"Give this package to the King," he said, "and this one to Aghat Mai. You are to replace him as the leader of the

Pentade until he completes his mission. And you, Gahang,"
he turned to Sharrim, "will follow Aghat Mai's orders until
he releases you to return to the Guild. I trust that Gahang
Khall has briefed you on the situation and you know what
you must do?"

Sharrim nodded, his face carefully blank. Oden Lan knew
Khall must have told the Jade all the necessary details, but
he wasn't worried. Mai was one of the best, and he knew
what to do. Mai would not fail.

21
THE BLACK DIAMOND

"What will happen now?" Egey Bashi asked Raishan on the way back to the guest quarters.

Raishan walked for a while in silence, his smooth steps easily matching the Magister's purposeful stride.

"You and I," he finally said, "will travel to wherever it is you need to go, and hope that our trip doesn't bring us into conflict with the Guild."

Egey Bashi shook his head. "That's not what I asked, Aghat, and you know it."

Raishan turned his head to look directly at the Keeper.

"You're prying into Guild business, Magister. Is this mere curiosity, or do you actually think you can do something about it?"

Egey Bashi met his gaze. "Personal feelings aside, Aghat, the order of Keepers – and myself – have invested *a lot* into keeping Prince Kythar Dorn safe and out of trouble. His fate is tied to the fate of our kingdom, and what happens to Kara now will affect him directly. Simply put, I want to make sure that when it comes to action, she'll be there to protect him."

Raishan's gaze darkened. "Unfortunately, in all likelihood, she won't. Not for long."

The Magister stopped dead in his tracks. "*Tell me*, Aghat."

Raishan shrugged. "I see no reason to talk about this. There's nothing anyone can do to stop what's coming."

Egey Bashi moved his face closer to the Majat. "You want a *reason*? How about this one: I've devoted the last eighteen years of my life to keeping Kyth safe, and what happens now might well ruin all my work. That's *reason* enough for me to know, don't you think? And if no one can stop it, there's no harm in telling me, is there, Aghat?"

Raishan hesitated. It seemed to the Magister that despite the Majat's outward calmness, it was difficult for him to talk about this. Egey Bashi waited.

"As you know," Raishan said at length, "being a ranked Majat is a privilege that comes with an exceptional fighting skill. We're all proud of what we are. But this privilege also comes with a price. A ranked Majat can never leave the Guild. If this ever happens, a Majat of a higher rank is sent to track down and kill him."

Egey Bashi looked at him in disbelief. "Do you mean to tell me that your bullheaded Guildmaster would send someone to *kill* Kara?"

Raishan stiffened. "I understand you're upset, Magister. So, I'll pretend I didn't hear that first bit. And yes, that's exactly what he will do."

"But why? Why have such a rule in the first place?"

"Two reasons. First, we don't like to risk exposing the secrets of the trade. And second, it's simply too dangerous. Having a warrior of this skill on the loose could seriously disturb the balance of power. The higher the rank, the bigger the danger. It's the responsibility of the Guild to keep this danger under control."

Egey Bashi stared at him for a moment as the words settled into his head.

"But Kara's a Diamond. There's *no one* higher in rank. Who could he possibly send?"

Raishan hesitated. "There's a special mechanism in place to kill a Diamond. If such a thing is called for, the Guild sends two Majat. One – a Jade that could provide backup. And the other – the Diamond's shadow."

"Shadow?" Despite the warmth of the morning sunlight, Egey Bashi felt a chill run down his spine.

"Each Diamond," Raishan went on, "receives what we call 'shadow' training, where we're taught the exact fighting style and weaknesses of another Diamond in the Guild. In single combat, a shadow can get through the defense where other Diamonds can't. The shadow, with the help of a Jade, is the only one who could kill a Diamond."

Egey Bashi frowned. There *had* to be a flaw in this strange mechanism. "What if a Diamond you shadow doesn't have a weakness?"

Raishan shook his head. "These weaknesses aren't even known to the Diamond himself. They're identified by the Shadow Master during training and kept secret from everyone else."

"Shadow Master?"

Raishan nodded. "Everyone in the Guild secretly fears him. He knows everyone's weaknesses. We all spend time with him after the ranking, but none of us knows who we're shadowing and who's shadowing us. He's the one who does all the matching."

"He must be a great warrior," Egey Bashi said thoughtfully.

"No," Raishan said. "He's a great trainer. He doesn't fight. He watches. And then, he *tells* a ranked Diamond how to beat his counterpart."

"He's a dangerous man, your Shadow Master."

"Yes."

"But it seems to me that even if you knew another Diamond's weaknesses, the chances you could kill him are still not high enough. From what I've seen so far, a Diamond's virtually unbeatable. Even if you know his fighting style, there may not *be* enough weakness to defeat him."

Raishan nodded. "That's why a Jade is sent along. Jades are different from other gem ranks. Normally they don't go on assignments; their job is to ensure the security of the Guild itself. Their special strength is in the ranged weapons. They can't kill a Diamond, at least not one on one, but in a fight between a Diamond and his shadow they can give the shadow additional fighting advantage. The combination of a Jade and a shadow can't possibly fail."

"So, a Jade's job is to *shoot*?" Egey Bashi asked in disbelief. "What if he misses and shoots the wrong man?"

"A Jade's job is to do what the shadow tells him. To throw himself onto the Diamond's sword and die, if necessary. And, I told you, they're *good* with ranged weapons. They don't miss."

Egey Bashi paused. "So, you think Master Oden Lan will send such a pair after Kara?"

Raishan glanced at the tower behind them. "I'm sure he did it right after we left. This is high priority to the Guild and it takes precedence over everything else. Did you see the sealed packages on his desk? One of them must be the Black Diamond."

"Black Diamond?"

"It's a token," Raishan explained. "Just like any other gem token, but its stone is black. It's given to the shadow to symbolize the death contract. In exchange, the shadow brings back the Diamond's armband."

Egey Bashi shook his head. "You Majat really like tokens. So much craftsmanship, so many precious stones, just to maintain symbols."

Raishan looked at him coldly. "These tokens are issued only for Diamonds. And each of them has a name on it. This is more than a symbol, Magister. Each Black Diamond means someone's life."

Egey Bashi paused. One had to be raised a Majat to understand the significance of these tokens that meant little to everyone else except for the glitter of their stones. But Raishan's story went far beyond symbols. To think that someone with a deadly skill was being sent after Kara, and that they knew her weaknesses and was capable of killing her, was sobering.

"Who's her shadow?" Egey Bashi asked.

"No one knows, except Master Oden Lan and the Shadow Master. Just like none of us know who we're shadowing until the time comes. To my knowledge, nothing like this has happened in centuries."

Egey Bashi kept silent for a while as he resumed walking to the barracks. Raishan fell in stride with him.

"Quite a mechanism," Egey Bashi said at length.

"The Majat Guild doesn't tolerate failure."

Egey Bashi shook his head.

"Perhaps," Raishan suggested, "we should talk about my assignment? You *did* hire me for an unrelated purpose, didn't you?"

Egey Bashi turned, his thoughts slowly coming back to the present time.

"My way from here lies to Aknabar, where I must pay a visit to the monastery to find out more about Reverend Cyrros. Under the circumstances I felt that the help of a Diamond would be welcome. I couldn't afford to hire you by name, but thanks to a timely hint from Master Abib it all worked out well. You've seen these men, Aghat. Your help against them would be invaluable. We're dealing with a formidable enemy." He looked ahead and froze, his feet coming to a halt of their own accord.

A lonely figure stood at the entrance to the guest quarters. The man wore light leather armor and a hooded black cloak thrown back over the shoulders. His easy, graceful posture suggested considerable fighting skill. It took a moment to recognize his face, a short mop of brown hair standing around his head, dark eyes, sharp bird-like features that, without the ominous hood, looked almost nondescript.

Nimos.

"Magister Egey Bashi," he exclaimed with a bright smile. "Aghat Raishan. What a coincidence. Fancy meeting you here!"

"What do you want?" Egey Bashi demanded.

Nimos shrugged. "Is it a crime to want to say hello to old friends?"

"Theoretically speaking, no. But I fail to see how it's applicable here."

"You break my heart, Magister. I thought we were bonded."

"What a horrible thought."

Nimos spread his hands. "Now that the boys and Aghat Kara are gone, do we really have a quarrel, Magister?"

Egey Bashi's eyes narrowed. "Why do you look so pleased with yourself?"

"Because," Nimos said, "I'm overall an irresistible man. Don't you think so?"

Egey Bashi waited.

"And," Nimos went on, "because it all worked out so well, don't you agree?"

"What do you mean?"

"You wanted the boys to be under Kara's protection, Magister, and you got your wish."

"You seem to know a lot about this."

Nimos smiled. "Your plans, Magister, weren't hard to guess. Note that I'm not prying into where the Prince might be going so that he needs such an impressive escort."

"I wish I could say I was grateful," Egey Bashi said. "But I'm glad to see that the fact he's under the protection of someone you tried to hire makes you pleased."

Nimos's smile widened. "Aghat Kara is truly the gem of gems. I wish I could spend all my time with her. But, alas, she has two unfortunate qualities. First, she's in love with the boy, so she could never be trusted where he's involved. And second, she seems to be immune to our powers. Which really left us with only one choice."

Egey Bashi looked at him, feeling a chill creep up his spine.

"I see," Nimos said, "you're beginning to understand me, Magister. Want me to tell you all of it, or are you bright enough to guess?"

"You *bastard.*"

Nimos chuckled. "No need to be harsh, Magister. What else could we do? We can't possibly kill a Diamond who is immune to our powers. At least, not yet. But the *Majat Guild* can do it for us. Personally, I think our plan's pretty sound, don't you?"

"You *made* her disobey her orders, you son of a–"

Nimos's eyes gleamed with triumph. "Believe me, Magister. We wouldn't be having this conversation if anything could be changed. But things are in motion now. The Black Diamond's on its way. And there's no one in this kingdom with the power to stop it. The Majat Guild doesn't tolerate interference. And now, I feel I've imposed on your time far too long, Magister. Good day."

He flung the trailing end of his cloak over his shoulder and strode away.

Egey Bashi turned to Raishan, unclenching his fists and forcing the pounding in his temples to quiet down. "We must do something, Aghat!"

Raishan shook his head. "The man's right. The Black Diamond can't be stopped."

"We must see this Shadow Master. We must find out what her weakness is, and warn her."

Raishan's gaze hardened. "*No one* can see the Shadow Master. His identity is a secret. *He* sees *you*, not the other way around."

"But we have to do *something*," Egey Bashi insisted. "Can we at least find a way to warn her of what's coming?"

Raishan's lips twitched. "I assure you, Magister. She knows."

22
FOGGY MEADOWS

When the Majat Fortress was well out of sight, Kara turned her horse off the main road to a small trail running through the thick forest undergrowth. Low branches hung across, making the trail ahead hard to see. Kara rode so fast it was impossible to keep up with her and duck the branches at the same time. Kyth grabbed the reins with one hand and held out the other to protect his face.

As night deepened, fog descended on the forest around them. It hung in tiny cold droplets that had a way of penetrating every gap in their clothes, making them clammy and heavy with water. The horses' coats glistened with sweat, their vapors mixing with warm breath in the cold night air. Kara's cloaked silhouette blended with her gray mount and with the forest darkness on the trail ahead. Only the movement of disturbed branches showed where she was and how fast they had to ride not to fall behind.

Kara didn't slow until the air around them became gray with the first light of dawn. She changed to a walk and glanced back to oversee her following. Kyth's horse slowed down to keep in step, and Alder's mount almost ran into him from behind. Warning froze on Kyth's lips as he realized in amazement that Alder had dozed off while they rode. His head dipped forward and jerked up as his horse slid to a stop.

"Are we there yet?" he asked sleepily.

Kara sided off the trail, letting them level up with her. Then she raised her hand and pulled off her black mask.

Her face was drawn and determined. In the dim forest grayness it looked hollow, like a ghost's.

"There's a clearing up ahead," she said. "We can stop there for a short rest."

Kyth nodded, too tired to speak. He used his remaining strength to take off his own mask. Cold air hit his skin. He blinked, shaking off the sleepiness, and grabbed his reins in a determined hold.

The clearing was so small they probably would have missed it if Kara hadn't pointed. A pond of dark water glinted at its side. Kara stopped her horse by a gnarled tree at the edge of the pond and jumped down.

"We can rest until dawn," she said. "We move again at sunrise."

"But it's *already* nearly dawn!" Alder protested, scrambling down from his saddle onto the soft, damp turf.

She measured him with her gaze. "On this trip we do what I say. No questions asked."

"Why?"

She shrugged. "Because, I'm here to ensure your safety, and neither of you have any idea what we're up against."

"Then why don't you tell us?"

Kara didn't hurry to answer. She took her time in unsaddling her horse and set the packs and gear against a tree trunk.

"For one," she said at length, "you two are no good against orbens. If these men attack, you'd be in real trouble. Our best chance is to outrun them."

Alder looked at her in disbelief. "But you're with us. You can handle these men, no problem, right?"

This time she took so long to respond that Kyth began to doubt if she was going to speak at all. She busied herself with setting camp on the higher ground at the edge of the glade, where the grass was shorter and the earth didn't look too damp. Kyth tethered his horse to a low oak branch and joined Kara in spreading their bedrolls on the ground.

Only when they were all done and ready to sleep did Kara raise her head again. "You must learn to take care of yourselves, if need be. I may not always be here to protect you."

"What do you mean?" Kyth asked, alarm rising in his chest. There was something different in her voice, or maybe his mind was just playing tricks on him after a sleepless night?

She gave him a long look. Her eyes gleamed, but the rest of her face was barely visible in the dusk.

"Nothing," she said. "Now, get some sleep. I'll wake you up soon."

She wrapped into her cloak, stretched on the ground and went still. Kyth looked at her for a moment, but she didn't show any intention to speak again. Her eyes were closed and her breath even, as if she was fast asleep.

Kyth lay down onto his bedroll. The ground was covered with twigs and branches that dug painfully into his back. His cloak was damp and the chill crept through to his skin. He wished they could light a fire, but he knew that, with the little time they had, fire was out of the question.

Alder next to him was already asleep, his mouth half-opened and his face happy and innocent like a child's. Kyth lay there for a moment, looking at him, then closed his eyes. He was so tired his head swam and his entire body ached. It seemed as if he wasn't lying on the ground but still rocking with the measured sway of his horse's fast trot. He had time to wonder if, with such a short sleep, he would still have time for one of his nightmares. Then he remembered nothing more.

It seemed to Kyth that he had just closed his eyes when he felt somebody shaking him.

"Kyth. Wake up."

He opened his eyes to see Kara leaning over him. The beams of the rising sun lit up her golden hair, leaving her face in shadow. Her eyes were hollow, as if she'd had no rest at all. Kyth wondered if she actually slept or kept watch without telling them. But before he could ask she slid away toward their horses.

Kyth sat up, wrapped in his cloak, and looked around. Alder was still asleep. The horses wandered off to the ends of their tethering ropes, munching on the thick grass of the glade. Kara crouched on the ground, rummaging in one of her saddlebags. As he watched, she took out a small package and turned back to Kyth.

"Wake your foster brother," she said. "We must go."

Kyth struggled out of his cloak. "What is it? Why're you so…" he paused, unsure how to say it. He had never seen her so tense. It was as if her incredible inner balance was disturbed, leaving her fragile and vulnerable. It looked frightening. But how in the world could he say this to her? And, what would be the point?

She averted her eyes. "I'm fine. It's just that I'm not sure I can handle whoever's coming after us. We must do our best to beat them to the Grasslands. But since we only had a few hours' head start, I'm afraid this means lots of riding and very little sleep, at least for the next few days."

Kyth nodded. Her words made sense, but he still had an uneasy feeling she wasn't telling him something. Maybe he was too sleepy to think straight.

He shook Alder awake and went to pack his bedroll. Kara handed each of them a flask of water and a small pack.

"The Majat travel rations," she said. "Eat quickly and saddle up."

The rations were made of salted meat, mixed with dry raisins, nuts, and a strange herb with a strong, heady smell. Alder twitched his nose as he took a bite, but to Kyth anything tasted good after the crazy gallop of the previous night. Besides, the rations were surprisingly filling. After finishing his share and washing it down with water from the flask, Kyth felt refreshed and strong.

They saddled the horses and rode out onto the trail.

Kara kept the pace at a fast trot. The forest around them gave way to lower bushes, no less capable of slapping the riders in the face, but much better at letting the sunlight through. After an hour of riding their clothes had dried and Kyth finally felt warm enough to let his cloak trail behind.

By the afternoon the road began to descend downhill. The bushes ahead cascaded downward from the ridge. The slope was getting steeper as they rode, giving them an open view of the hills ahead. Below, the valley subsided into mists, bluish haze merging with the distant eastern sky. Beams of the setting sun touched the blues of the landscape with a reddish tint, blending into a deep purple haze further at the horizon.

Kyth paused at the edge of the ridge to take a full breath of the cooling air, and peered into the valley. Up ahead, the bushes opened into a winding line, running along the bottom of the deep ravine. On the southern side of the clearing a jagged line of roofs submerged into the greenery. Thin columns of smoke rose up to the sky.

Kara followed his gaze. "Foggy Meadows. The first outpost from the Majat Fortress on the road to Aknabar. There's an inn there, but we're not stopping. We still have a good five hours ahead of us before the moon sets."

Kyth nodded. He longed to ask her more about the danger they were facing and the reasons for such a rush, but he knew she would probably avoid a direct answer, just like before. Besides, with the pace she set, there was never enough time to talk.

The descent into the valley took longer than anticipated. Closer to the bottom the road became so steep that they had to dismount, leading the horses along the winding trail that creased the side of the hill. Kara's posture was tense as her eyes darted from the slippery trail down to the outskirts of the village below. A group of reddish lights flickered and moved about. Torches? They were too far away to tell.

The main road running along the bottom of the valley was wide enough for four horsemen to ride side by side, and surprisingly well maintained. The village gate ahead stood open, flanked by a tall fence of thick logs sharpened at the top, strong enough to withhold a minor siege. Sounds of voices from inside carried clearly through the damp evening air.

A crowd of men inside the gate held lit torches and bore weapons. Their faces were grim and determined as they silently watched the approaching riders.

Kara directed her horse toward the middle of the blockade and pulled to a stop a few paces away from the front line of men. "What's going on?"

A tall bearded man at the end of the line stepped forward, urged by prompting gazes of his comrades. He was wearing a blacksmith's apron and held a huge hammer in his lowered hand.

"We're under orders from the Majat Guild," he said.

Kara's face remained calm as she held the man's gaze. "Orders?"

"Yes'm. They wants ye t'return to the Guild. We was tole not ter let ye pass."

Kara turned in the saddle, her cloak folding back to reveal an array of throwing knives at her belt. The men facing her exchanged uneasy glances.

"How do you know we're the ones to look for?" she asked.

The spokesman shifted from foot to foot. "The message said: two men, one woman."

Kara laughed. "That's all? Do you know how many travelers come this way?"

"But no' many women," the man told her firmly. "Especially Olivian."

She nodded. "I can see you have it all figured out, don't you?"

The man swallowed. "Yes'm."

Kara leaned forward in the saddle. "Did they also tell you my rank?"

"Them said, 'gem'." The spokesman glanced around at the other men.

"Which gem?"

"Them didn't say."

"And my companions?"

The man's face relaxed into a smile. "Them's no Majat, only dressed like ones."

"And you think your men can take down a gem?"

Faces around her showed hesitation, but no one moved.

"There's fifty of us out 'ere," the spokesman said. "And given tha' ye gems don't kill unless you're paid fo' it—"

She sat up straight. "Did it ever occur to you men that if

I'm an outcast I may not be too keen on following the rules? Or that a 'gem' might mean something more bright and glittery than you hope?"

The men exchanged glances.

"Better ter 'ave it out with ye," the spokesman said, "than with the Majat Guild."

She shrugged. "Have it your way." She lifted her leg over the horse's neck and jumped to the ground, handing the reins to Kyth.

"Stay out of range," she told him quietly. "We don't want the horses to get hurt."

"But we can't let you fight all of them alone," Kyth protested. "There're fifty of them out there!"

She rolled her eyes. "Don't worry. There isn't going to be a fight. All they want is some bruises to show off, so that they don't get in trouble with the Guild for letting us pass without resistance."

"Maybe we could take some road around the village?" Alder suggested.

She shook her head. "The valley is narrow and steep here and the hills around it are practically impassable. Believe me, if there was another way, we wouldn't be wasting our time right now." She took off her cloak and flung it over the saddle. Then she approached the blockade and stopped.

"All right," she said. "What's the plan?"

The spokesman handed his torch to the man behind him. Then he raised his hammer and threw it from hand to hand with disquieting ease.

"We thought," he said, "with yer bein' a woman an' all, we could just knock yer out. Gentle, like."

"Fine," she said. "Go right ahead."

"Why don't yer make it easy on yerself and surrender?" he asked. "We won't molest ye or anythin'. We don't want no trouble with the Guild. We just want ter send ye back."

She laughed. "Much as I'd like to help you out, I am in a real hurry. So, why don't you men just get on with it?"

The men stood for a moment exchanging glances. Then the front line advanced, fanning out so that they could surround her on all sides.

Kyth held his breath.

Kara drew her weapon from the strap at her back, but didn't bare the blades. Sheathed, it looked like a short staff, thick enough to do serious damage, and yet small enough to wield with one hand. She held it by the end, lowered at an angle to the side of her body.

One of the men swung his club. Just as it was about to hit, she whirled around, her shape a streak of black. Her weapon thrust forward and up, catching the man's wrist in a precise blow that knocked the club right out of his hand. Another blow, and the man collapsed on the ground in a messy heap.

Five of his neighbors jumped at Kara, aiming their clubs. Kara moved between them like the wind. She swung her weapon in a figure eight, high and then low, dropping to a crouch as the clubs whizzed over her head. Her arm moved so fast it was hard to trace. There was a thud each time her staff connected, each blow sending one more man down. It took seconds for her to complete the sweep, straighten up, and go still, her weapon lowered at an angle to her body. She wasn't in the least bit out of breath.

She ran her eyes over the six bodies at her feet and turned to the remaining villagers.

"Who's next?" she asked.

There was silence.

"Come now," she said. "You do want to show the Guild some effort, don't you? Or, are you going to tell them that you gave up after losing just six men?"

The man with the blacksmith's hammer licked his lips nervously. "What's yer rank?"

She smiled. "That's the question you should've started with. And yes, it's a gem, just like you were told."

"Which gem?"

Her smile widened. "With your fighting skills, it really doesn't matter."

He eyed her with caution. "Yer no' a Jade."

"No. Not a Jade."

"Emerald?"

She laughed. "Why don't you just let us pass?"

The men exchanged glances. There was a commotion in the back rows, which suddenly looked a lot less dense than before.

"If you want it to look believable," Kara said. "I could knock out a few more of you. Any volunteers?"

The men lowered their weapons and began to move sideways, forming a corridor for them to pass. Kara took the reins from Kyth and swung into the saddle in one quick move.

"Let's go."

She kept her weapon in hand as they rode through the gauntlet. The villagers eyed them fearfully and drew back if Kara glanced their way. They rode at a walk up the street, past the inn with its brightly lit windows, and over to the other side, where a fence and a gate similar to the first one marked the edge of Foggy Meadows. The few men at the back gate hastily flung it open as soon as they saw Kara approach.

Kara flicked her weapon back into its sheath and turned to Kyth and Alder. "We must hurry. The Guild will now know which way we're headed. We must not let them catch up."

She sent her horse into a gallop and there was nothing left to do but follow.

23
CHANGE OF GUARD

Ellah woke to the sounds of banging doors and distant voices. She sat up in bed and rubbed her eyes.

It was still early. Low sunbeams crept over the azure lake surface outside the window, giving off a golden gleam in the still morning air. The room was alive with sunny reflections running around the walls and ceiling. Odara Sul's bed next to her was empty. The Keeper's white robe was neatly folded over the back of a chair, but the blanket was crumpled, indicating that Odara must have left in a hurry.

Ellah hastily got out of bed, washed in the basin in the corner of the room, and pulled on a dress, anxious to know the reason for the early turmoil. When she was fastening the last strings, the door flew open and Odara rushed in. Her hair stood like a crown of wavering snakes around her head. She ran to the chair and snatched her Keeper's robe. Her hands trembled with urgency as she unfolded it and pulled it on over her dress.

"What's happening?" Ellah asked.

Odara turned, as if only now noticing her presence. "The Majat are here! And, they're talking to the King. Hurry, if you want to learn what it's about."

"The Majat?" Ellah felt confused. The Majat were here all the time, and she had never seen Odara Sul so worked up about it.

Odara's face showed impatience as she struggled into the sleeves of her robe. "Two of them arrived from their Guild early this morning. One Diamond. And another young one of a gem rank. Let's go!"

She rushed out of the room. Intrigued, Ellah trailed behind.

When they entered the open door of the King's chambers, everyone else was already there. The action centered around King Evan who stood in the depth of the room wearing a robe over a nightgown. His long black hair flowed loosely onto his shoulders. He must have been taken straight out of bed to see the visitors, but his face showed no trace of it. He looked fresh and alert, as if he had been awake for hours spent out in the cool lakeside air.

The Rubies of the Pentade formed a row behind his back. Next to them hovered a freckled young man with curly red hair. He had an upturned nose, full childlike lips, and bright blue eyes that looked at the world with an expression of wonder, which Ellah found somewhat exaggerated. She had a distinct feeling this boyish look was just a façade, so that everyone who saw him would underestimate his true self.

It took Ellah a moment to realize that everyone's attention was focused not on this newcomer, but on the two men kneeling at King Evan's feet.

One of them was Mai. The other, a man of broader build with a dark tan and straight black hair tied back into a shoulder-length ponytail. Ellah could see his profile, a high cheekbone, wide nose, and a gleaming eye whose slanted line shot like an arrow up the side of his face. He had two curved swords strapped across his back, and a pack of throwing knives at his belt. His frightening grace, similar to Mai's, left no doubt that these two were of the same rank.

One Diamond, Odara Sul had said. *And another of a gem rank.*

Ellah crept forward and stretched her neck.

"… Guild business, Your Majesty," the dark man was saying in a low rumbling voice. "I assure you, there will be no inconvenience."

The King glanced from the newcomer to Mai. "Aghat Mai and I were just getting used to each other. Given the current circumstances, it would be highly undesirable to make a change now."

A change? Ellah moved another step forward, so as not to miss a single word.

"Aghat Han would do a better job as the Pentade leader, Your Majesty," Mai said. "He's my senior in years and is far more experienced than I am."

King Evan smiled. "Your experience is quite sufficient, Aghat Mai. I wouldn't wish for a better guard than you."

Mai bowed, his face frozen into a calm mask. "Thank you, Your Majesty. You're most kind."

Ellah's heart sank. Mai was being *replaced*? But why?

"Aghat Mai's term is not over for at least a year," Evan said to Han. "Is it common for your Guild to replace a Diamond in the middle of an assignment?"

Han's dark eyes fixed him with a heavy stare. "This is Guild business, Your Majesty. It takes precedence over everything else. However, I assure you that the Pentade will be just as efficient under my command."

Evan sighed. "I'm sure you're right, Aghat Han." He took out a throwing star with a glittering diamond set in its center and held it out to Mai. "Your token, Aghat Mai."

The Majat took it without words. The new Pentade leader, Han, handed Evan another token, which to Ellah's eye looked identical. After the solemn exchange the two Diamonds bowed and rose to their feet. Mai's observed the freckled newcomer. Then he turned and strode out of the room.

"Very well," Evan said to the room in general. "Now we all must go back to our usual routine. In my case, I'd like to finish my sleep."

He turned and walked off in the direction of his bedchamber. The new Pentade leader, Han, gestured to the Rubies, who took their place at the four corners of the space in front of the entrance. The freckled man threw a questioning glance at Han.

"You'll wait here, Gahang Sharrim," the Diamond said, "until Aghat Mai tells you what to do. From this moment on you're under his command."

He is going away with Mai? Ellah's dislike for the freckled man deepened by the minute. She felt empty. She and Mai had hardly talked in the last few days, but to imagine life in this dreary castle without him was unthinkable. The new Diamond, Han, seemed just as competent, but he was so dull, so ordinary. So wrong.

She clenched her teeth and walked out. She didn't care where she went, as long as it wasn't to her room, where Odara would see through her in a second and mock her to the end of her days. She ran along the corridor heading for the niche near the end, where a window overlooked the lake and where she could sit on the sill, invisible to the rest of the hallway, and be alone with her thoughts.

As she neared the niche, she realized that the place was already occupied. A slender shape in elegant black curled up on the windowsill, comfortable as a cat.

Mai.

He was sitting in her favorite spot. In his lowered hand was a parchment that he must have been reading just a moment ago. His other hand, resting over bent knees, held an object with sharp corners that looked like a Majat token, its stone hidden from view. His eyes were fixed unseeingly into the distance.

As he heard Ellah's approaching steps, he spun around so fast that his entire shape blurred. Ellah drew back in fright. He recognized her and relaxed back into his seat. Keeping his eyes on her face, he slowly hid the throwing star into a deep pocket inside his shirt without letting her see the stone set into its center. Then he folded the parchment he was holding and put it away.

"It's you," he said.

She nodded. "Sorry. I didn't mean to startle you."

He smiled, but his gaze remained distant. "No problem." His eyes looked past her into the hallway.

She hesitated. She was obviously intruding. Something bad must have happened at his Guild to make him look so distracted. She should just leave him alone. But she *couldn't*. Not without asking.

"Are you leaving?"

He looked at her, his gaze slowly focusing on her face. "Yes."

She swallowed. "Are you going to come back?"

The pause was longer this time. "Eventually. If I succeed."

"And if you don't?"

He smiled. "If I don't, I'll die. That's what my job is all about."

He said it casually, as if he didn't really mean it, but the mere thought of such a possibility was horrible. Ellah shivered.

"You won't die," she said quietly. "You'll succeed. And we – I mean, King Evan – will be waiting for you to return."

He paused, looking at her appraisingly.

"Want to come with me?" he asked.

Ellah's mouth fell open. She couldn't possibly have heard him right. "*What*?"

"You said you'd rather travel with Prince Kythar. As it happens, I'm going to the Grasslands. There's a high chance that our paths will cross. So, I could take you to him. If you think you can keep up."

She stared, her heart beating so fast that it threatened to jump out of her chest.

"I can keep up," she said carefully.

She was half expecting him to laugh and tell her it was all a joke. He *couldn't* be serious about this, could he? She met his eyes, preparing for the worst.

He smiled. "Go get ready then. We're leaving in half an hour."

"You're *what*?" Mother Keeper asked.

Ellah forced herself to keep calm under the older woman's gaze. "I'm going with Aghat Mai."

Mother Keeper's eyes narrowed. "Why?"

"He– he said he could take me to Kyth."

"Did he really?"

Ellah took a deep breath. "He said he's going to the Grasslands on a new assignment. He said it's very likely that he'll come across Kyth on the way. So, he could take me to him."

"And if he doesn't come across him? The Grasslands are very big, you know. They stretch from Jaimir all the way to the Eastern Mountain Crest, and to the Southern Deserts at the outskirts of Shayil Yara."

Ellah bit her lip. The possibility hadn't occurred to her.

"Then I could come back with him. He said he'll return after he completes his assignment." She didn't want to mention the *other* possibility. It wasn't going to happen. Mai could never fail an assignment, she was certain of it.

The older woman shook her head. "And you're sure you aren't being foolish? He's a killer on an assignment for his Guild. It may seem to you that he's being nice by asking you along, but do you really believe that's all there is to it? How do you know he won't take advantage of you?"

Ellah forced herself to look straight at the woman. She wished Mother Keeper would stop calling Mai a killer. Didn't she know Diamonds were trained not to kill unless they absolutely had to? On the other hand, she had to admit some of Mother Keeper's words made sense. It did seem highly unusual that Mai would risk an inconvenience on his high priority mission by bringing along someone like her. But he *had* asked her to come, hadn't he?

Maybe what he told her back on the road about his feelings was the truth.

Maybe everyone could just leave her alone and let her do what she wanted.

"He won't take advantage of me," she said with unnecessary force.

Mother Keeper stepped closer to Ellah and put a hand on her shoulder. "You can't even tell if he's lying to you."

"I can't," Ellah admitted. "But what could he possibly want from me?"

Odara Sul in her corner giggled. "Maybe your virtue? That's what you hope he wants, isn't it?"

Ellah turned, blood rushing to her cheeks. She opened her mouth for a retort, but couldn't think of anything to say.

"I feel responsible," Mother Keeper said. "I brought you along to help in your training, not to have you lose your head and run off alone with a man you know nothing about."

"We won't be alone," Ellah said. "Gahang Sharrim is coming too."

Odara Sul laughed. Curled up in an armchair, her hair wrapped into pigtails, she looked like a nasty schoolgirl. "I see, you're quite familiar with your travel companions. *Gahang Sharrim*, is it? The cute one with freckles?"

Ellah ignored her. "I *did* come with you to learn," she told Mother Keeper. "And I learned a lot already. I just... I believe my place is with Kyth. I want to travel with him."

"Are you sure that's what you want?" the older woman asked. "Or, is it Aghat Mai you want to travel with?"

Ellah stepped back, her cheeks flaring up with a deep red color.

Mother Keeper sighed. "I thought so."

"It's not like that," Ellah said quietly, but there was no conviction in her voice. She clenched her teeth and fell silent.

"How about your promise to help King Evan?" Mother Keeper asked. "If he ever again agrees to meet with our gracious host, your presence there could be quite useful."

"I don't think I could be of use to King Evan," Ellah said. "They call it diplomacy, but all they do is lie to each other. And then, just as suddenly, they all start speaking the truth and everyone gets disconcerted. I don't think they need a truthseer to tell when *that* happens. Besides, I am not a court lady, and I make a very poor sword bearer. I just... I don't belong here."

There was a pause as they looked at each other. Then Mother Keeper's gaze softened.

"Perhaps it's all for the best," the older woman said. "We could use your help to send word of our imprisonment to Magister Egey Bashi. We need *someone* to get us out of here."

Ellah nodded. "I'll do my best to get word to him." She picked up her pack and turned to go.

"Wait!" Odara Sul called out. "I want to give you something."

She reached into a pouch at her belt and brought out a small dark vial. Ellah recognized it at once. It was the magic liquid that restored Mai's face, bringing him so much pain in the process. The liquid that Odara handled with such skill and care as if it had the power to bring life.

"Don't use it on simple scratches," Odara said. "This substance is much more valuable and powerful than that. You must use it only if you ever need to heal a *really* serious wound. But whatever you do, don't let anyone's hair touch it, unless you want them to end up like me."

Ellah looked at Odara with wonder. Her moving hair. So, *that's* how it happened.

She suddenly became aware of someone standing in the doorway. She turned and saw Mai.

Her breath caught in her throat. She had no idea how long he had been standing there. If he heard what Odara and Mother Keeper said about him.

She looked at him searchingly, but his gaze was unreadable.

"It's time to go," he said.

"Aghat Mai," Mother Keeper said brightly. "So, it's true what Ellah told us just now? You're taking her along on your new assignment?"

"Yes, my lady," Mai said levelly.

Mother Keeper gave him a piercing stare, but his expression didn't change. They stood for a moment, eyes locked.

"I want your promise that you won't bring this girl to harm, Aghat," Mother Keeper said. "She's my responsibility."

"Don't worry, my lady," he said. "She'll be safe with us."

"We never doubted *that*," Odara Sul said, her eyes shining with laughter. "The question we were discussing before you arrived is whether she would be safe *from* you, Aghat."

He turned to her, the quick surprise in his eyes melting into mischief. For a moment they both looked like children playing a game.

"I think Gahang Sharrim and I can control our dangerous sides," he said, carefully keeping his face straight.

"Stop it, Odara!" Mother Keeper said. "And you, Aghat, just make sure you understand that you're taking on a responsibility. I expect you to live up to it."

He nodded, then turned to Ellah. "Let's go."

She picked up her pack and followed Mai out of the room.

There was a commotion out in the hallway. The double doors at the end that marked the boundary of the King's imprisonment stood open. The space inside was flooded with the Illitand guards, headed by the pale-faced Lord Daemur himself. The Duke's eyes were shining with anger.

Han and Sharrim stood side by side in front of the Duke. Lothar and Brannon crowded on them from behind. The other two Rubies were not in sight.

Mai strode up to the group and stopped in front of Lord Daemur, shoulder to shoulder with Han.

"Is there a problem, Your Grace?" he asked.

The Duke glared at the newcomer. Then he swallowed, struggling to control his twitching face. "It came to my attention that two Majat arrived here this morning and are now planning to leave."

Mai looked past the Duke to the guards at his back. His cold expression inadvertently brought to mind that of a butcher running his eyes over the herd of livestock brought in for the morning slaughter. The thought reflected in the faces of the guards, whose expressions rapidly changed from confidence to various degrees of unease.

"Did it also come to your attention, Lord Daemur," Mai said, "that we're in a hurry?"

Daemur looked at him in disbelief. "You *can't* leave!"

"Why not?"

"Because you're with King Evan, and he's a prisoner in my castle!"

"*Aghat Han* is with King Evan," Mai corrected. "I have a new assignment."

Daemur gaped. "Since when?"

"Since today. Now, can we stop wasting time, Your Grace?"

The Duke's pale face flushed with color. "This is my castle, Aghat Mai. And I am not allowing you to leave."

Mai shrugged. "That, Your Grace, is utterly foolish." He drew his staff from the sheath at his back with a quick fluid move. The front row of guards backed off.

"You wouldn't *dare*," Daemur said.

Mai leaned closer to the Duke. "I'm on urgent Guild business, with orders to kill anyone who stands in my way. How many men are you willing to lose, Your Grace?"

Daemur held his gaze. "Despite your exquisite skill, Aghat Mai, you're only one man. Do you think you're omnipotent?"

"By no means. But I'm also not alone. We have two Diamonds, four Rubies, and one Jade. I'd say, the odds are heavily in our favor." He nodded to Sharrim, who pulled a wide curved blade from a sheath at his back. Then he moved a hand along his staff to draw the blades out of its ends. The guards pressed backward at double speed, leaving the Duke alone in the center of the hallway, face to face with five Majat.

"You're the first in our way," Mai said. "Are you sure you won't reconsider, Your Grace?"

Daemur's gaze wavered. "You wouldn't *dare*," he repeated.

Mai's short glance made the Duke take a step back. "Watch me."

Daemur swallowed. He glanced over the blades on Mai's staff, the sword in Sharrim's hand, and the ominous presence of the other three gems, who didn't draw their weapons, but stood their ground with looks that said they would have no problem doing so in a flash. His posture deflated.

"You must swear to me that you're going on your Guild's business, Aghat, and not the King's."

"I already told you that."

The Duke's gaze wavered and lowered to the floor. "All right. You're free to go, Aghat Mai."

"There will be three of us," Mai said.

"Three?"

"Your choice is the same. You let us go or we break out by force."

The Duke looked at him for a moment. Then he turned and strode out of the hallway, guards hastily scrambling out of the way.

"I'll take that as a 'yes'," Han said.

Mai ran his hand along the staff, retracting the blades, and returned the weapon to its sheath. Then he nodded to Ellah and Sharrim. "Let's go."

They made their way out of the hallway and down the stairs to the main castle entrance. No one tried to stop them as they collected their horses from the stables and rode down the cobbled streets to the city gate. Somebody must have warned the gate guards of their arrival, because the gates rolled open as they approached. They rode through, and out of the city.

Once or twice Ellah caught Sharrim's intent gaze, but Mai never looked her way.

24

A SHORT REST

"We can sleep in the saddle," Kara said. "If we keep the horses at a walk, you two could take turns to sleep, and I'll watch."

Kyth looked at the road ahead. The shimmering moonlight painted it white, with pitch black shadows of the trees at its sides. His tired eyes couldn't distinguish any other colors.

He turned back to Kara. Her posture in the saddle was graceful and easy like always, but her face looked hollow and her eyes had a feverish glow.

"It's not just us," he said. "You need sleep too."

She held his gaze. "Sure. I can take my turn too, and you'll watch. Just make sure we don't stop."

"What about the horses?" Alder asked. "We can't drive them like this much longer. It's a wonder they've survived so far."

Kara lowered her gaze and patted her horse on the neck. Then she looked up again.

"I've been giving them goat mint," she said.

"What?"

"It's a herb that increases stamina and endurance. Very potent. It's also in the rations we've been eating."

Kyth remembered the heady taste of the herb mixed into their food rations. He always took it to be a mere flavor, to soften the strange combination of salty meat and sweet fruits.

Alder looked at Kara in disbelief. "You've been giving us a *drug*?"

She shrugged. "How else do you think we could've survived this ride?"

"An excellent question."

They glared at each other. Kyth wanted to interfere, but his tired mind couldn't come up with anything to say. *Sleep.* He gripped his reins, struggling to stay upright.

Kara's intent gaze brought him back to alertness. Her stern expression dissolved into concern.

"All right," she said. "Let's get off the road and sleep for a couple of hours."

"How about a full night of sleep this time?" Alder said. "It's been five days of crazy riding. We never stop for more than two hours at a time. Even with the drug, we can't go on like this forever."

"We only need to go on like this until we reach Aknabar," she said. "There, we'll charter a boat and sleep all we want, all the way to Jaimir."

"How far from Aknabar are we?" Alder asked.

She looked away. "At this pace – another four days."

"At this pace, we'll be dead in three."

Her eyes glinted with warning. Alder bristled, challenging her with a glance.

"Kara," Kyth said quickly. "How much have *you* slept since we left the Majat Fortress?"

She hesitated. "Enough."

"How much?"

She averted her eyes.

"Have you slept at all?" Kyth asked quietly.

She gazed at him and turned away.

Kyth rode up to her and took her hand. It was warm and light as it relaxed into his hold.

"It's not just about us," he said. "*You* can't go on like this either. You're very strong, but you're not invincible."

She shivered and drew away. "I know."

Kyth leaned closer to peer into her face, his heart seized in a tight grip of worry. In all their time together he had never seen her look so vulnerable.

"What is it? There's something you're not telling us."

She met his eyes. She suddenly looked like a child, so lost that he resisted the urge to hold and comfort her. She opened her mouth to speak, but changed her mind and subsided into silence. He waited, but she only shook her head.

"Tell us," he said quietly. "Please."

"I… I *can't*."

"Look," Alder said. "You can't ask us to follow you blindly without telling us what we're up against. This is crazy."

Her gaze swept past him, hand darting to the belt and coming up with two throwing knives. Without interrupting the movement, she flicked her wrist in the direction of the trees ahead. Then she dove off the saddle onto the road. Her hand shot up and caught something in mid air.

Kyth blinked, leaning forward in the saddle to take a look at the crossbow bolt clutched in her hand.

There was a rustle in the bushes and a dark shape fell out onto the road – a man, wearing a black hooded robe. As he fell, the hood slid off his head, revealing a closely shaved scalp that glistened in the moonlight.

Kara ran toward him and leaned over. Kyth dismounted and rushed to her side.

The man sprawled on the ground in front of them was tall, with a square jaw and a scar across his cheek. His pale eyes were open, staring into the night sky. One of his hands was still clutching a crossbow. The hilt of Kara's throwing knife was sticking out of his chest.

Kara reached forward and retrieved her knife, wiping it on the grass before she put it back into its sheath. Then she bent down and opened the man's robe, pulling something off his belt. A chain clanked as she held it up, the spiked metal ball hanging off its end.

"An orben!" Kyth's skin crept. Up close, it looked disgusting, a cross between a butcher's bone crusher and an inquisitor's tool. It was hard to imagine how one could fight against those and survive. He glanced at Kara, who stood still, facing the bushes.

"Nimos's men," she said. "They've been following us for days. It's a wonder they can keep up so well."

"But why?"

"I don't know. If they wanted to attack, they've had plenty of opportunities. It's as if they're trailing us to make sure we get to our destination." She paused, eyes wide.

"What is it?"

She looked at him, her eyes slowly losing their daze. "We must hurry."

They returned to Alder holding the horses. Kara swung into the saddle in one easy move and sent her horse into a trot along the road.

"There goes our night's sleep," Alder said, looking after her.

Kyth mounted, ignoring his protesting muscles. "I think she's in danger because of us," he said quietly. "And I think she doesn't want us to know."

Alder nodded. "Let's hope that we can really keep up. You want to try sleeping in the saddle, Kyth?"

Kyth look at Kara's rapidly retreating back.

"Why don't we catch up with her first?"

Alder nodded. They sent their horses into gallop and caught up with Kara before the next road bend. She acknowledged them with no more than a side glance as she kept her pace.

By the end of the third day Kyth was barely able to stay in the saddle. Goat mint seemed to be losing its potency, making their hasty meals less refreshing than before. The horses were also running at the end of their strength.

They didn't come across any more hooded men with orbens. As they made their regular stops to give the horses food and water, the only people they met were peasants, who looked at their weapons in fear and kept away.

Sleeping in the saddle proved easier than Kyth thought. All one had to do was find the right balance, leaning against the horse's neck and hanging the arms off each side. They also mastered the use of short feeding stops to catch bits of sleep that, for want of better rest, seemed amazingly refreshing. The only thing that really worried Kyth was Kara. She never seemed to sleep at all, and even when he insisted she lay down and close her eyes, he had the distinct feeling she was alert and ready to jump into action.

On the evening of the third day they stopped in a small secluded ravine. A spring emerged from the ground nearby and formed a pond before running off in a stream along the bottom. Its banks were covered with thick tall grass that seemed perfect for the horses to feed on. Smooth columns of beeches rose up the steep slopes, their transparent growth making it impossible to creep up unnoticed, yet hiding the entire ravine from unfriendly eyes. It seemed like an ideal resting place.

"We're about five hours away from Aknabar," Kara said. "We can sleep for four, so that we reach there early in the morning."

Kyth and Alder only nodded, too tired to discuss it. They unsaddled the horses and let them wander around the small pasture. Then they laid out their bedrolls and saddlebags. The sun set behind the treetops and the ravine submerged into shadows, making their camp all but invisible in the gathering dusk.

Alder went to sleep as soon as his head touched the ground. As Kyth prepared to lie down next to him he noticed that Kara was sitting up, staring into the forest. He rose, looking at her intently.

"Aren't you going to sleep?" he asked.

She looked at him, her face barely visible in the shadows. "In a moment."

He got up and walked over, lowering himself onto the ground next to her. The grass was dry and still warm from the afternoon sun.

"You're going to stay awake and keep watch, aren't you?" he asked quietly. "You always keep watch when we sleep, don't you?"

She hesitated.

"Why don't *you* sleep this time," he said, "and I'll keep watch?"

In the darkness he couldn't quite see her expression, but he sensed her body tense.

"I'm fine," she said. "I'm just not very tired. You must sleep while there's a chance."

He leaned over and took her hand. It seemed thinner than before, and cold. Kyth searched her gaze, alarm rising in his chest. Never before had he felt her hands cold.

"Are you all right?"

She nodded, but didn't respond.

Kyth drew closer, inhaling the faint fragrance of her skin, sweet like a forest meadow in full bloom. She went still.

"You can't do this," Kyth said quietly. "Whatever you're afraid of that's following us, you won't be able to face it if you are like this. You *can't* kill yourself protecting us."

She raised her eyes to him. "There's no other choice," she whispered.

"Yes, there is." He put an arm around her shoulders. She tensed, then slowly relaxed into his hold. Carefully, like a mother cradling a child, he lowered her onto her bedroll. Then he reached for her cloak and covered her.

"Go to sleep," he said. "And I'll sit right here next to you, and watch. I promise I won't fall asleep. But you must promise me you will."

She looked up at him but didn't move.

"Your strength is all we have," he told her. "If you lose it, we don't have a chance anymore. So, if you don't want to do this for yourself, do it for me and Alder. Please."

Her gaze wavered.

"All right," she said. "But you must promise to wake me in an hour."

"No. You'll sleep until it's time to go."

She looked at him a moment longer. Then she turned to the side and closed her eyes.

Kyth sat and watched. Her breath slowly became even, her body relaxed, and her face for the first time in days acquired a peaceful expression. She looked so beautiful as she lay there, her golden hair gleaming against her dark skin, her long eyelashes throwing off deep velvety shadows against her cheeks. He was tired, but he didn't want to go to sleep now, when he could just sit here and watch her. Despite the strain of the trip, despite the danger they were in, he felt intensely happy they were together.

Seeing her like this, so peaceful and calm, made him feel that everything was going to be all right, and that the danger they were in was exaggerated. After all, she was a Diamond Majat. There was no warrior who could better her in single combat and no force that could present a serious danger to her. As long as she was around, everything was going to be all right, and he hoped that she would stay around for a very long time. After all, she did say she wasn't planning to leave them, and she sounded like she really meant it.

He hoped it was all going to work out. He couldn't bear to lose her.

25
JADE SKILL

"There's a trail up ahead," Mai said. "We're going to take it."

They were riding abreast up the main road. Sharrim decisively kept his horse between Mai and Ellah, an arrangement that excluded her from any possible conversations. But she wasn't about to argue. Her job was to keep up, and that was taking all the effort she could spare.

At Mai's words Sharrim nodded and rose in the stirrups, peering into the roadside bushes. They were dense, a mixed growth of raspberry and wild roses that looked beautiful but none too inviting to ride between. Ahead, a gap in the intertwined branches looked as if torn through by a large animal. Mai pointed and rode into the opening, disappearing behind the wild greenery. Ellah directed her horse after him, with Sharrim in her wake.

The branches at the sides of the trail grabbed on with all their thorns, leaving long wisps stuck onto their clothes. The only comfort was that the bushes didn't rise higher than waist level, so that there was no need to protect face and neck. Ellah did her best to keep up, ignoring the stabs. She only hoped the thick cloth of her travel outfit would withstand the damage. She had a sewing kit with her, but she doubted she would have time to mend clothes on this crazy march.

Ahead, the line of roses ended abruptly, giving way to tall Lakeland ivy. As they finally cleared the bushes and rode into its welcoming shade, Mai pulled his horse to a stop.

His black outfit looked neat, as if he had just put it on. Ellah wondered how he was able to do it. She noted with some satisfaction that Sharrim's clothes looked just as bad as hers, covered by small rips and long wisps of sticky vines.

"Everyone all right?" Mai asked.

"Blasted thorns!" Sharrim exclaimed. "To think that some people actually *like* roses!" He threw an irritated glance at Ellah, as if it was she who insisted they ride through the bushes because of her love for flowers.

He doesn't like it that Mai brought me along. Too bad for him. She returned Sharrim's look, trying not to appear smug.

Mai paused, peering into the ivy growth ahead. Ellah took the time to pick the particularly long branches off her pants and the trailing end of her cloak. She left the rest for later.

"There's a small lake up ahead," Mai said at length. "We'll camp there tonight."

Sharrim nodded.

They rode on, following a trail into the deep ivy shade. Mai's black figure ahead was a focus of darkness, easy to see in the transparent greenery backlit by the late afternoon sun. Ellah did her best to keep an exact distance, not too close, and yet not too far behind. Sharrim's chestnut mare snorted in her wake, crowding onto her horse every time it slowed. She did her best to ignore it.

After a while they came to a clearing, surrounded by tall ivies on all sides. A cold fire pit in the middle indicated that the place was often used by travelers as a campsite. Off to the left the ivy growth thinned, and mirror-still waters of a small forest lake glistened through the veil of branches. Low beams of the setting sun painted the water transparent shades of pink.

They dismounted and unsaddled the horses, piling up the load under a large tree at the edge of the glade. Sharrim picked up the kettle and took off in the direction of the lake. Mai busied himself with a dry pile of branches beside the fire pit.

"You can go and take a swim while we cook," he said to Ellah.

She looked at him in surprise. Traveling with two men, she fully expected to do all the cooking. In the very least she expected to help.

"Are you sure?" she asked.

He nodded and turned his attention to starting the fire. Sharrim reappeared with a full kettle in his hand. Ellah stood for a moment undecided, then picked up her pack with spare clothes and walked off along the thin, muddy path toward the water.

The lake was dark and still. Its misty surface breathed warmth. As Ellah dipped her hand into the clear amber water, she felt the pull of the soothing undercurrents, rising in domes up to the surface. She turned back to the glade hidden behind the bushes. From here she couldn't see her traveling companions, only the thin wisp of rising smoke that told her they had started a fire. She hoped she was equally invisible to them, but just in case she moved deeper into the reed thicket. Inside their rustling mass, she pulled off her clothes and stepped into the water.

It was cooler than it seemed at first, and the bottom was very muddy. As she walked forward, her feet sunk deep into a slippery net of weeds and silt. In just a few steps the water reached all the way to her chest. She pushed off and swam, enjoying the cool feeling on her burning skin. The scratches from the afternoon tingled, soothed by the water. She dipped in her head, then turned onto her back and floated, the white of her body tanned by the amber water.

After a good swim, she made her way back to the glade, clean and refreshed, her hair dripping with water. Mai and Sharrim sat by the fire deep in conversation. As they saw Ellah they stopped, and she had a distinct feeling that whatever they discussed wasn't intended for her ears.

"How's the water?" Mai asked.

"Good," she said. "Are you going to swim too?"

"Perhaps after dinner." He took out three bowls and divided the stew into equal shares. When the kettle was empty, he took it and walked off in the direction of the lake to get water for tea. Ellah was left alone with Sharrim.

The Majat surveyed her for a while in silence. Now that Mai wasn't around, his expression changed from childlike wonder to a cold calculating look. Clearly he didn't feel the need to keep up his façade in front of Ellah. Maybe he sensed she could see through him. Or was it all in her imagination?

His intense gaze made her uncomfortable. It was nothing like the way Mai looked at her, with bold interest that made her melt inside. Sharrim's look was searching and evaluating. It was as if he was fingering through goods in a store in an attempt to find something of use. It made her feel violated.

"Why're you looking at me like that?" she demanded.

Sharrim's eyes narrowed. "Why did he bring you along?"

Ellah lifted her chin. "Why don't you ask him yourself?"

Sharrim opened his mouth to respond, but at that moment Mai reappeared with a full kettle of water. He hung it over the fire, his air of calm confidence making even the thought of an argument in his presence seem preposterous. Then he settled down by the fire and took his bowl. He didn't say anything, but his action served as an unspoken signal for everyone to start eating.

It was meat stew with some grain mixed in. The taste was a bit bland but the meal was comfortable and filling. Ellah ate her share slowly, feeling the warmth spread through her body and strength return to her tired limbs.

By the time she was done, the water in the kettle was already boiling. Mai threw in a handful of dry leaves with a heady aroma and poured the steaming brew into three mugs. Ellah picked up hers and took a careful sip. It was bitter, stronger than the tea she was used to back home.

The sun set behind the trees, its reddish glow giving way to the transparent shadows of early dusk. The glade submerged into deeper shadows, but it still wasn't dark. Looking away from the fire, one could clearly see the growth at the other end of the glade. The lake's silvery gleam lit up the forest off to the west.

Mai put aside his bowl and leaned back, keeping his eyes on Sharrim. The Jade stiffened. It seemed that something important was about to happen, something for which they had both been preparing for throughout the entire meal. Perhaps it was a continuation of their earlier conversation?

"So, tell me about yourself, Gahang," Mai said. His voice was calm, but his eyes spelled challenge.

The Jade hesitated, throwing a quick glance at Ellah. She had the distinct feeling she wasn't wanted. But she wasn't going to leave unless Mai told her to.

"I can do anything you want me to, Aghat Mai," Sharrim said. "I'm really honored to serve under your command."

Mai measured him with his eyes. Ellah had a strong sense he was purposely trying to get Sharrim disconcerted.

"That hardly tells me anything about you, does it?" he said.

"What do you want to know, Aghat?"

Mai shrugged. "The Guildmaster's letter said you're the best. Are you?"

Sharrim looked at him with uncertainty. Mai waited. His outwardly relaxed pose reminded Ellah of a cat preparing to leap on its prey.

"The Guildmaster's too kind," the Jade said at length.

Mai let out a short laugh. "One doesn't become the Majat Guildmaster for being kind, Gahang. I know Aghat Oden Lan well enough to vouch for that. But his personal qualities have nothing to do with my question. Either you're the best, or you aren't."

Sharrim shifted in his seat. "Gahang Khall thinks I'm one of the best. He's the one who recommended me for this assignment."

Mai nodded. "I heard Gahang Khall knows his job. But I can't rely on his judgment, can I? So, you'll have to convince me, Gahang."

"What do you want me to do, Aghat Mai?"

"What *can* you do that makes you the best?"

Sharrim hesitated. It was clear he had never been questioned this way before. It was also clear that behind the dog-like submissiveness he was showing Mai he was beginning to feel rebellious.

"I'm good with a bow," he said.

Mai nodded. "Let's see."

Sharrim reached for his pack, bringing out an elongated object that looked to Ellah like a sheathed lyre. He carefully pulled off the cover.

It was the strangest bow Ellah had ever seen. Unlike the tall narrow bows carried by the Lakeland archers, this one was short, wide, and very curved. A leathery cord wound around the entire length of the shaft in tight coils. The string hung loosely off one end.

Sharrim took the bow with the care of a lover. Grasping the center of the shaft with one hand and the string with the other, he rested the bow against his knee and made a quick, powerful move that inverted the curve of the weapon, clicking the string into place. Ellah blinked. It was as if he had turned the bow inside out, so that all its grotesque parts suddenly came together.

Sharrim ran his hands along the curves of the bow in a caressing move that seemed almost too intimate to watch. Then he lowered it and looked at Mai.

Mai held out a thick piece of wood of about one elbow in length. "Ready?"

The Jade flung the quiver over his shoulder and stood straight, holding the bow in a lowered hand. Then he nodded.

Without getting up, Mai swung out his arm and threw the stick high into the air. It went straight up, rotating as it rapidly ascended into the clear evening sky.

Sharrim pointed the bow upward. His hand darted to the quiver, drawing arrows one by one with dizzying speed. He shot them in a continuous movement that sent a fountain of black streaks up into the sky. Ellah tried to follow, but quickly lost count.

After a few moments the stick came down, crashing onto the ground a few feet away. It was pierced with multiple arrows, making it look like a brush.

Sharrim retrieved it and handed it to Mai. His look of quiet satisfaction dissolved into uncertainty at the sight of the Diamond's level expression.

"Seven," Mai said. "Not bad."

Sharrim kept his face steady, but Ellah could see that this casual praise meant a lot to him. He retrieved the arrows and inspected them carefully before returning them to the quiver.

"How about another test?" Mai asked. His hand slid to his belt and came up with a pack of throwing knives. He held them out to Sharrim, blades up, like a player holds his cards. Ellah counted six.

Sharrim swallowed. "I'm not sure I can do six. Not if you throw them, Aghat Mai."

Mai smiled. "This is your chance. Try."

Sharrim's hand darted to the quiver and brought out six arrows. These arrows looked different. They were slightly longer, and had no feathers on their shafts. Sharrim held the bow horizontally and placed them loosely on top, resting the ends against the string so close to each other that he could hold them all with one hand. He met Mai's eyes and nodded.

Mai's hand flew up in a short movement, whose force could be guessed only by the whistling of the knives that left his hold. Sharrim pulled the string and released all six arrows into the air, answered by a cracking sound and thuds by the tree at the other end of the glade.

Both Majat got up and peered at the tree trunk. Ellah, who was closer, could make out three knives sticking out of the wood. The rest of the knives were nowhere to be seen.

"Three," Mai said after a moment. "Not bad."

Sharrim's face lit up with a childlike smile. "Wow! Usually I can do at least four. You're so good with knives, Aghat!"

Mai glanced at him in surprise. Apparently, being praised by a subordinate wasn't something that happened to him all that often.

They searched through the grass, retrieving three throwing knives and six arrows, one of them cracked. Only then did Ellah realize the meaning of the exercise. With one shot, Sharrim was able to aim six arrows so that three of them deflected Mai's throwing knives from reaching their target. That seemed impossible. No human being could aim and shoot six arrows at once into a moving target, even if only half of them were able to hit. Ellah looked at the Jade with new wonder.

The two Majat returned to the fireside and sat for a while, sipping their tea. Ellah did her best to keep quiet. She knew she was witnessing something that wasn't normally intended for an outsider.

"How old are you, Gahang?" Mai asked.

Sharrim raised an eyebrow in surprise. Mai waited.

"Twenty-three," the Jade said at length.

"When was your ranking tournament?"

"Two years ago."

Mai slowly turned to Ellah. She sat up, as if pulled by an invisible string.

"Did he tell the truth?" Mai asked.

She called up the colors in her mind. "Yes."

Sharrim spun around, his eyes full of surprise, but Mai merely nodded as if nothing unusual was going on.

"Now, tell me, Gahang," he said. "What other weapons can you handle, and which are your worst?"

Sharrim hesitated, his look turning from surprise to anger as he continued to look at Ellah. "A *truthseer*, Aghat?"

"Answer my questions, Gahang."

Sharrim settled back into place with a defeated look. "I'm good with a crossbow," he said. His tone was earnest, but the chilling glance he threw at Ellah showed how much this honesty was costing him. "But I don't carry it. I'm much better with a bow. And, I can throw knives, but not as well as you, Aghat."

"How about that dagger on your belt? Can you use it?"

"If necessary."

Ellah sensed a change of color go through her mind as he said these words. She raised her chin. Sharrim gave her a reproachful look.

"What is it?" Mai asked Ellah.

She frowned. "I'm not sure. It's as if he carries it for a different purpose."

Sharrim shifted in his seat. "I'm not that good in a hand fight with daggers."

"Then, why do you carry one?"

Sharrim ran his eyes between Ellah and Mai with a hunted look.

Mai slowly put his mug down and leaned forward in his seat, stretching a hand out to Sharrim. "May I see it?"

The Jade hesitated. For a moment it seemed to Ellah that he was going to refuse. But then he slowly reached to his belt and drew the dagger, handing it to Mai, hilt forward.

"Don't touch the blade," he warned.

Mai took the weapon and turned it in his hands. He carefully studied the blade, then brought it closer to his face and sniffed.

"Black Death," he said. "A strange choice of poison, Gahang."

Sharrim shrugged. "It's slow, but certain. And, there's no known antidote. I also use it on some of my arrows."

Mai's eyes narrowed. "*Not* on this assignment, Gahang."

"Whatever you say, Aghat Mai." Sharrim threw a nervous look around.

Mai handed back the knife and winked to Ellah across the fire. She smiled.

"I know it's not my place to ask, Aghat," Sharrim said, "but why's *she* here?"

Mai gave him a calm stare. "You're right, Gahang. It's not your place to ask. *Ellah* is here because I asked her to come with us. That's all you need to know." He held Sharrim's gaze until the Jade sank back into his seat. Then, he got up and collected the dishes into the empty kettle.

"I'm going for a swim," he said. "Want to come along, Gahang?"

Sharrim hesitated, then nodded.

"We'll be right back," Mai told Ellah. "You should sleep. We start early tomorrow."

He walked away along the trail to the lake, Sharrim hurrying in his wake. Before disappearing behind the bushes, the Jade turned back and gave Ellah such a bloodcurdling glance that she felt her hair stand on end.

26
THE ROAD TO JAIMIR

Morning mists hung low over the Holy City of Aknabar, mixing with thick wisps of smoke. Slow gusts of wind carried odors of refuse and rot, blending with heady aromas of incense and the stale smell of the river water. To their left Kyth could see the ominous star-shaped building of the Great Shal Addim Temple looming over the top of the West Hill. The monastery wall ran from the temple all the way through the city, enclosing a large chunk of the hillside and the area beyond. The Dwelling of the Holy Maidens crowned the distant East Hill, its smoothly polished stones glowing in the sun. Ahead, the oily gleam of the River Elligar showed in patches through the gaps in the stone maze of buildings that ran in cascades down to its turbid waters.

At this early hour the streets were empty. Regular citizens were just waking up, throwing open heavy window shutters and bathing their sleepy faces in early sunbeams. As for the pilgrims, Kyth was fairly sure that all of them were gathered at the river bank, prostrating on the stone steps that lined the entire Aknabar riverfront, in the holy ceremony of greeting the sun.

"We should go straight to the port," Kara said. "By the time we get there, the morning rituals should be over. That's the time the boats start to Jaimir."

Kyth nodded. She looked refreshed after her night's sleep. The feverish gleam in her eyes was gone, and her posture in the saddle had become more relaxed. Her quick smile made him feel warm inside.

They made their way down the street maze, maneuvering around the burnt heaps of trash. Closer to the port the streets became more busy, people hurrying around on early morning chores. Aromas of baked bread and roasting meat joined the bouquet of other smells, creating a dizzying combination that made Kyth's mouth water. All they had eaten for the past ten days were the rations Kara brought from the Majat Fortress. Meat and bread seemed unattainable – like heaven.

"Nimos's men didn't bother us much on the road," he said. "You must've scared him off."

Kara shook her head. "They've been following us all the way. Even through the city."

"They have?" Kyth glanced over his shoulder to the empty street behind.

"Yes."

"But why?"

She shrugged. "There's only one explanation. Their purpose is not to stop us, but to make sure we get to our destination."

"They *want* us to reach the Grasslands?"

"Whatever they want is not important anymore."

"Why?"

"I can't tell you. Sorry."

Kyth recognized the determined expression on her face that made it useless to question her further. She rode on ahead and there was nothing left but to follow.

The maze of streets became denser as they approached the port. As they cleared the last stone archway, the market plaza opened ahead of them wide and long, running in cascaded stone terraces all the way down to the docks.

Even this early, the place buzzed with activity. In the semicircle adjacent to the front row of buildings, merchants were setting up their stalls, preparing for a big market day. Further on, the docks gave way to a network of floating platforms that connected to each other and to the shore, creating a labyrinth of pathways and streets that extended almost to the middle of the river. Boats of all sizes and shapes towered among the platforms, rocking with the flow of the Elligar waters.

The morning bathing ritual was over. Scantily clad people made their way out of the river, dripping wet, emanating a faint smell of mud and decay. Holy books taught that the waters of Elligar had the power to purify, but it took a real fanatic to ignore the fact that this river also served as the sewerage for the entire city, as well as the burial place for the holy pilgrims, whose rotting corpses were often seen floating up from the river's turbid gut. Kyth shivered, pulling his horse to a stop next to Kara, who was peering through the sunlit morning haze toward the docks.

"There're many boats about to leave," she said. "Let's go."

She dismounted and led her horse toward the water. Kyth and Alder followed, trying not to fall behind.

It wasn't easy to maneuver in the thickening crowd. The pilgrims streamed the other way, their enlightened faces turned up to the looming shape of the Great Temple that loomed over the city from the top of the Western Hill. They showed no awareness of the three travelers struggling to pick their way through.

Kara headed toward a large freight barge at end of the boat row. Something about it was familiar. Its upper deck was piled with crates, and the lower deck had a row of openings, with oars sticking out halfway like a set of short, thick bristles. A name was written on its side in large bold letters. Kyth was almost sure he knew what it said, even before they got close enough to read it.

"*Lady of Fortune*," Alder said.

Kyth nodded. A few months ago, he took this barge upriver with Alder, Ellah and Kara, on their way to Tandar. He wasn't looking forward to repeating the experience.

"Imagine that," he murmured. "Captain Beater'd be thrilled to see us."

"Not *us*," Alder corrected.

Kyth looked ahead with a sinking heart.

Kara stood beside the boat talking to a short, bald man, whose sturdy build suggested a considerable physical force. His yellow beard stuck out over the bushy growth on his chest, visible through the open collar of his linen shirt. He held a polished wooden stick, tapping it on the open palm of his other hand. His beady eyes misted as they rested on Kara, his tongue licking his lips in such a meaningful way that Kyth's stomach turned. He hurried to catch up.

As the foster brothers approached, Captain Beater tore his eyes away from Kara and gave her companions a disappointed look. "So, the boys're still tagging along with you, my pretty? Eh?"

"We're traveling together, yes," Kara said. "And I'm not 'your pretty'."

He measured her with a slow, sticky glance that stopped just short of reaching her face. "Not yet. But if we're to spend all this time together on the boat, there's no reason to get lonely, eh?"

"I won't be lonely, thanks."

Captain Beater winked. "Neither will I, I hope. 'specially with you on board."

Kyth grasped the reins of his horse. "We're wasting time. Let's go find another boat."

The captain laughed. "Moody, eh? Do you want passage to Jaimir or not?"

"It depends," Kara said, "on when you're planning to leave."

He gave her a meaningful smile. "When do you *want* to leave?"

Kyth bit his lip. The barge was one of the very few boats in this port capable of carrying horses. They needed it badly, but the idea of watching this man undress Kara with his eyes for the entire trip was too much to think of. He opened his mouth to refuse, but Kara's look stopped him.

"We'd like to leave right now," she said. "We're in a hurry."

The captain held his stick to the side and gave her an elaborate bow. "Anything you say, my beauty. Captain Beater and his boat are at your service."

She paused, giving him an appraising glance of her own. "The pay's six silvers. This covers myself, my companions, and our horses."

Captain Beater smacked his lips, holding her gaze. "You drive a hard bargain, girl. How about somethin' extra? Such as you, warming up my bed on a cold night, eh?"

She moved her face closer to him. "Only in your dreams. And this had better be the last time I hear about them, Captain Beater, or else the nights you mention might become a lot colder than they already are."

The captain swallowed and took a careful step back. "There's no need to get touchy. I was just suggestin' we get to know each other better, that's all."

She smiled. "That, we certainly will. Now, here's another silver for the horse feed. Have your men get some hay. We're in a *real* hurry."

Captain Beater's misty expression made Kyth wonder if he really took Kara's warning seriously.

"Don't you worry, my beauty," he said. "It goes fast when you travel downstream. You and your lads'll be in Jaimir in no more'n ten days."

"At this speed," Mai said, "we'll be in Jaimir in about ten days."

Ellah leaned closer to the fire. She felt sore after a long day's ride, but she wasn't about to show it. She bit her lip as she reached over to take a mug of tea from Sharrim's hands, her muscles screaming in protest at her every move.

The forest darkness was alive with sounds. A distant howling, answered by barking in the depth of the trees around the camp, made Ellah's skin creep. At times the sounds seemed to get closer, as if some large dog-like beasts circled the camp, having an invisible conversation.

Sharrim shifted nervously in his seat.

"They say these woods run south all the way to the Forestlands," he said, "and the wolves that live here are descended from the ancient breed of dogs that went astray after the first Holy Wars. They're huge and vicious, and they're not afraid of people."

Mai sat for a while looking at the fire.

"They say a lot of things, Gahang," he said. "But we don't have to listen to all 'they' say, do we?"

Sharrim glanced at him sidelong. "But it's true, Aghat. I've seen one myself. It was as big as a bear, and its fur was pale like–"

"Like a ghost," Mai said slowly, looking past him into the darkness.

Ellah turned, a chill running down her spine.

A large animal stood at the edge of the trees, barely visible against the light. It resembled a very big wolf, with fur so pale it made the creature seem transparent in the wavering shadows. Firelight reflected in its eyes with a deep greenish glow. Behind it, more eyes glowed in the forest darkness like eerie swamp lights. Ellah suddenly realized how still it was, and how the howling had stopped right at the moment the beast appeared in the glade.

Sharrim slowly reached for his sheathed bow, but Mai's hand stopped him.

"You can't hope to shoot all of them, Gahang," he said quietly. "There are too many out there."

Sharrim gave him a helpless glance. "But we can't just let them attack us, Aghat, can we?"

"No."

Mai rose to his feet and walked toward the beast, so fluidly that his movements were hard to trace in the gathering darkness. Ellah's breath caught in her throat, her heart pounding.

"What is he going to do?" Sharrim whispered by her ear.

Mai stopped five paces away from the beast, keeping his hands loosely by his sides, so that they were in plain sight. His still shape blended with the shadows, and Ellah had to blink to see him. The man and the wolf stood, staring at each other. After a while the large beast started to look restless, as if it was having trouble keeping its eyes focused. It growled, turning its head from side to side. Then it lowered its eyes and crept forward, sniffing the air.

When the wolf came within touching distance, Mai slowly reached forward and put a hand onto its forehead.

The beast became very still as Mai ran his hand along its fur. Then it crept another step and leaned its head against Mai's knees. The movement was so forceful that Mai's body shook with the impact. He kept one hand on the beast's forehead, his stillness blending with the wolf's so that both of them had become barely visible in the darkness.

After a while, the wolf raised its head. It gave Mai a long look, then turned and padded away into the forest.

The greenish lights of the eyes went out one by one. The howling stopped. The forest turned dark and still again.

Mai came back to the fire. He looked calm, as if nothing had happened.

Sharrim slowly opened his mouth, struggling to produce a sound. Ellah could only stare.

"What– what did you just do, Aghat?" Sharrim managed.

Mai shrugged. "You said they were descended from dogs, didn't you?"

"Yes, but–"

"I took your word for it." Mai leaned back against a tree and subsided into silence. Ellah couldn't help noticing that after his encounter he continued to emanate calmness, so that just by sitting next to him she felt relaxed and sleepy.

"Are you really an animal whisperer, Aghat?" Sharrim asked quietly.

Mai laughed. "Is that what they say about me?"

"I never believed it. But how else could you–"

Mai shook his head. "I assure you, Gahang, I possess no such power. What I did was just common sense."

"What's an animal whisperer?" Ellah asked.

"It's a power," Sharrim told her. "An ability to talk to animals and understand what they say. An animal whisperer can tame any animal, even a raging tiger leaping to attack."

Mai laughed. "You don't really believe this nonsense, Gahang, do you?"

"I didn't, Aghat Mai, until I saw what you did just now. If it wasn't a special power, how did you do it?"

Mai looked at him, laughter dancing in his eyes. "Simple. I was calm as I approached, and the beast sensed it. Dogs always do. They only attack someone who's out of balance inside."

Sharrim shivered.

"I suggest," Mai went on, "that we go to sleep now. We need to move on at dawn. I'll stay up for a while and keep the fire going."

He wrapped himself in his cloak and leaned against a tree. As Ellah settled down on the other side of the fire, she watched his still shape illuminated by the firelight. He was so perfect as he sat there, his pose graceful and easy, his golden hair resting against the smooth skin of his muscular neck. His eyes were open, looking absently into the darkness. He still emanated that special feeling of calmness which made his closeness, even from across the fire, so soothing.

Ellah felt so happy she was traveling with him, even if Sharrim was constantly nearby and clearly didn't like her. She had thought before that she wanted to find Kyth and help him on his quest, but now she was beginning to realize all she wished was for this trip never to end so that she could always be by Mai's side.

She was sure he cared for her – the way he cut off Sharrim when the Jade asked about her on their previous stop, the way he was so attentive to her needs and comforts. She was sure the only reason he could have asked her to come along was so that they could be together for longer, even if his duties prevented him from taking any further steps. She felt lightheaded from his closeness, from the way he sat there looking so handsome, so that she could just lie quietly and enjoy the incredible force and calmness that he emanated.

He said they would be in Jaimir in ten days. She wished the next ten days could last forever.

27

THE HOLY MONASTERY

"Do you think Kyth and Kara are still in Aknabar?" Egey Bashi asked.

Raishan shook his head. "Kara would move as fast as possible. The only way we could have caught them would have been by a lizardbeast relay."

"Lizardbeast relay? What's that?"

"When the need is urgent," Raishan said, "the Guildmaster sends ravens out to ensure that the Majat messengers get fresh lizardbeasts every fifty miles. If you don't stop to sleep you can travel two hundred miles a day, a lot faster than with horses."

"Yes," Egey Bashi told him, "the Keepers do that too. We call it 'breakneck run'. Except, we can rarely afford to change mounts every fifty miles. Not lizardbeasts, for sure."

"It's a considerable expense," Raishan agreed, "but seeing how Master Oden Lan was all worked up about this one, I'm certain he sent the Black Diamond by relay. If Kara's shadow was at the Fortress when that happened, she would be dead already. But since Master Abib was kind enough to tell us that the only available Diamond other than me was Han, I'm fairly sure it didn't happen. Let's hope she still has some time."

Egey Bashi looked grim as he rode for a while in silence.

"We need to leave our mounts," he finally said, "and get the necessary gear, so that we can pay a visit to the Monastery. There's an inn in the city, run by a man who is loyal to the Order of Keepers and could probably help us, but it's all the way on the other side of the Holy Hills. Ideally, we should find something a bit closer to the Monastery. Any thoughts, Aghat?"

Raishan glanced at him, sidelong.

"There's an inn fairly close by that's paid for by the Majat Guild. You remember it, don't you?"

Egey Bashi nodded. "You mean the one run by that good woman who looks more like a troll?"

Raishan smiled. "Mistress Yba. Her inn may not be that cozy, but it's served the Guild well for over twenty years. I'm sure she'll have what we need."

They navigated through the narrow streets drowned in the afternoon smoke of burning trash. By the time Raishan pulled his horse to a stop in front of a beaten sign with a picture of a white mountain flower, Egey Bashi felt that his face had become as soot-stained as the words, barely visible underneath.

"'Wild Aemrock'," he read. "So, your Mistress Yba has a feminine side after all. At least, she likes flowers."

"It was named by me father," came a low, thick voice from the inn's doorway. "They call it 'Emrock' down south. Never liked the name meself. Most of me customers can't even say it right."

Mistress Yba emerged through the doorway, coming into full view. She was large and chubby, with knobby elbows, a pudding-like torso, and bold features that didn't provide any clues about the gender of their owner. The only feminine thing about her was the fact that she wore a dress, a misshapen woolen garment that fit over her like an oversized sack.

Egey Bashi dismounted and looked her up and down.

"Of course not, Mistress Yba," he said. "Forgive the suggestion."

She narrowed her eyes. "Do I know you?"

"He's with me," Raishan said, stepping up to the Keeper's side.

Mistress Yba's face dawned with recognition, her irritated expression dissolving into a grimace she probably considered to be a smile.

"Aghat Raishan," she said, her thick voice sweet and sticky like treacle. "What an honor. Please come this way."

She threw open a small side gate and led them into a narrow back yard. The stench of manure hit the nostrils with eye-opening force. Egey Bashi twitched his nose as he followed Raishan to a stall at the back, covered by a piece of sail cloth stretched overhead to protect from the rain. They left their mounts in the care of a thin, nervous stable boy and entered a small back door into the inn's main room.

"Now," Mistress Yba said, folding her large hands over her chest. "I assume you'll need room and board for you and your companion, Aghat. How else may I be of service?"

Raishan pointed to the Keeper rummaging in his pack.

"I have a priest's robe," Egey Bashi said, bringing a folded bundle out into the open. "But you'll need one too, Aghat. I also suggest you take a less conspicuous weapon. Your sword would be difficult to conceal."

"Let me worry about my sword, Magister." Raishan turned to the innkeeper, who was watching him with reverence. "Do you think you can get me a black hooded robe, Mistress Yba?"

Her lips stretched into another smile-like grimace. "Of course, Aghat. When do you need it by?"

"After sunset," Egey Bashi said. "That's always a good time to venture into the Holy Monastery."

The sharp crescent of the new moon shimmered just above the horizon as they entered the stone maze around the main temple. Keeping to the shadows of the columns surrounding each of the endless monastery courtyards, they crept deeper and deeper into the compound. Every time Egey Bashi glanced at Raishan, he couldn't help envying the Majat's stealth. The Magister felt like a trampling bull next to a sleek Grassland antelope.

They passed through a low archway that, by Egey Bashi's calculations, should have led to the Reverend's inner sanctum. The stone courtyard in front of them, awash with moonlight, led straight to the next archway. The shadows beyond gaped at them like a dark eye, daring the intruders to move even deeper into the heart of the monastery.

Egey Bashi started toward it, but Raishan's hand shot up, freezing him in his tracks. They stood still, listening. It took the Keeper several moments to catch what Raishan, with his sharp Majat senses, must have heard right away. The sounds of a quiet conversation from ahead. Now that he knew where to look, Egey Bashi also spotted a faint flicker of light, a reddish glow through the opening of a narrow passage ahead.

Raishan lowered his hand and slid along the wall, his cloaked shape blending with the shadows. Egey Bashi followed. They passed through the arched gate into a vaulted passage that ended in a doorway. The voices were coming from inside.

They crept closer. From here they could clearly make out two voices. One was low and rich, its rumbling undertones reverberating with a dark, unsettling timbre. The other was soft. It seemed vaguely familiar.

"...to the Grasslands," the deep voice was saying. "Thanks to your careful planning, Kaddim Nimos, they'll all arrive there at about the same time to take care of our little problem once and for all."

Kaddim Nimos? Egey Bashi suppressed a shiver, stretching his neck to see through the cracks of the half-opened door. The man the speaker was addressing had his back turned, but his slight shape looked familiar indeed.

A chill ran down Egey Bashi's spine. He should have made the connection when Nimos was gloating back in the Majat Guild about the way he had managed to take care of Kara because she was immune to their powers. While this, and the fact that Nimos's companions carried orbens, suggested a parallel with the man who had attacked Prince Kythar back in the Crown City, hearing this title, cursed and forgotten centuries ago, was bad news all over again. Was the ancient Kaddim brotherhood truly on the rise? And if so, what were its members doing here in the heart of the Holy Monastery?

"We have very little time," Nimos said. "We must follow the Black Diamond very closely and capture Prince Kythar as soon as Aghat Kara is out of the way. We must not lose a moment. There's no way of telling how much the boy can figure out about his gift, and we can't afford to allow him to learn enough to resist us. Even the Reincarnate himself doesn't know what the boy is truly capable of."

Reincarnate. Egey Bashi held his breath. Supreme Grandmaster of the Kaddim order had gone by this title in the old days to reflect his origins. Reincarnation of Ghaz Kadan, the Cursed Destroyer in the flesh. *Blast it.*

How could the Keepers have possibly missed this coming?

"The boy is that powerful?" Nimos's companion asked doubtfully.

"If we capture his power and find a key to his gift, there'll be no stopping the Brotherhood."

"Your plan is brilliant indeed, Kaddim Nimos," the other man said. "And it's working well. But it seems a waste to kill that woman, Kara. We could have used her to get insights into the special talents of a Diamond Majat. Perhaps their gift could be captured as well? It would help us immensely in the training of the Warriors of Kadan."

Nimos shifted in place, his robe rustling against the cold stone floor. "Not Kara. As much as I regret having someone like her put to waste, we have no choice. With her ability to resist us, we have no means to deal with her. But if things stay on schedule, we can take the one the Guild sent after her."

The other man nodded. "He will do. The Reincarnate will be pleased."

Nimos looked up. His hood folded away, letting the torchlight lick his hollow cheek. It painted his pale skin with a reddish glow, stopping just short of the dark eye sockets.

"Since we began our attempts to capture Prince Kythar," he said, "the Reincarnate has also expressed a particular interest in his foster brother, Alder. Apparently, he is the latest consort of the Forest Mother."

The other man hesitated. "But he has no gift. What use could he possibly be to us?"

"He has something that made the Forest Mother choose him for a mate. The Reincarnate wishes to study him further. Given the opportunity, we should capture both boys." He turned, giving Egey Bashi a full view of his hooded face, the dark pits of his eyes gleaming with a deep fire. It seemed that these eyes could penetrate the shadows behind the doorway, to see him and Raishan pressed against the wall. But before the Keeper could wonder, a chuckle behind him rang clearly through the stone gallery.

Egey Bashi froze and slowly turned around.

A robed figure took shape against the darkness of the column vault and came out into the patch of moonlight.

"Magister Egey Bashi. Aghat Raishan. What a surprise." The newcomer's soft, insinuating voice crept straight into the gut, making the hair on the back of the Magister's neck stand on end.

"Reverend *Haghos*?" he asked slowly.

The former Reverend of the Church, displaced from his high post by an impressive showdown that also put King Evan on the throne and restored Kyth's position as his rightful heir. Didn't the Keepers expel the man for good?

Haghos chuckled. "I'm so glad you recognize me, Magister. And it's Kaddim Haghos, thank you very much."

Of course. How silly of me not to guess. Egey Bashi narrowed his eyes. Was Haghos a Kaddim Brother all along? Or did his exile, after a failed attempt to usurp the throne, drive him to the Brotherhood?

"What're you doing here?" he asked.

Haghos's smile widened. "You'd really like to know, wouldn't you, Magister? No wonder you're snooping around. And speaking of that, did you really think a Diamond Majat could protect you within our walls?"

Our walls. With the ancient brotherhood infesting the Monastery things were much worse than he thought. *Does the new Reverend Cyrros know?*

Is he one of them?

The thought was too disturbing to dwell on.

"I was under the impression I was venturing into holy grounds," Egey Bashi said. "If I'd known I was walking into a lair of Ghaz Kadan worshippers–"

"Don't speak the sacred name in vain." Haghos threw his hood off, revealing a tonsured head and a pale bony face.

His eyes gleamed with a feverish glow. Behind, Nimos and his companion emerged from the open doorway, blocking the way to escape.

"You have no idea what you're up against, do you, Magister?" Haghos said. "How about a small demonstration? Kaddim Farros?" He nodded to Nimos's companion.

The hooded man nodded and stretched out his palms, parallel to the ground. A silent thunder shook the air, pressing on the eardrums with an invisible force. The blast brushed past the Magister and hit Raishan full in the face. The Diamond swayed. His face became deadly pale. A thin streak of blood appeared from his nostril. He struggled to keep upright, then, after a terrifyingly long moment, he sank down to his knees onto the stones of the courtyard.

The hooded man lowered his hands. The pressure subsided, but Raishan did not rise. Egey Bashi resisted the urge to help him up as he watched the deadliest fighter that ever walked the earth grovel on the ground like a drunken man. His heart quivered.

A smile twitched Haghos's pale lips. "That blast would have killed you, Magister."

Egey Bashi met his gaze. "Let him go. You don't want to quarrel with the Majat, do you?"

Haghos shook his head. "When we are done, the Majat won't matter anymore. But…" he looked past Egey Bashi to the silent shapes of Nimos and his companion, "as much as I'd like to continue this demonstration, we are in a hurry. Our little session with you will have to wait. In the meantime, you can perhaps provide some company for our poor old Reverend Boydos. Ex-reverend, I should say." He laughed, then clapped his hands. Hooded figures appeared from the shadows at his back, surrounding Egey Bashi and Raishan. The Magister's arms were grabbed from behind and a bond that felt like wet leather pulled his wrists together, making his hands go numb.

As the men approached Raishan, the Diamond pushed off, sliding behind a stone column. A blast from the hooded Kaddim Brother shook the air, but missed its target. Before Raishan could make his way across the yard, all three Kaddim Brothers rushed forward, stretching out their palms. Force reverberated in the narrow space between the columns. Raishan fell on the cobbles face-down, twitched, and went still.

Egey Bashi watched with a sinking heart. Up until now he hoped against hope that other Diamonds, like Kara, could develop immunity to the Kaddim. But, as he looked at Raishan's limp shape sprawled on the cobblestones, he was fighting a feeling of helplessness. With Raishan disabled and Kara about to be assassinated by her own kind, what hope could they possibly have?

Their captors tied Raishan's hands behind his back with force that seemed enough to dislocate his shoulders. The Kaddim Brothers' faces showed relief. Despite his sorry condition, Egey Bashi made a mental note of it. Something in this short scene troubled them, and the source of that trouble might well hold the key to their escape. The Keeper just had to find out what it was.

"It has been a pleasure, Magister," Haghos said. "Perhaps we'll see each other again, but I can't guarantee that you will still know who I am. Our inquisitors know their job."

He nodded, the three Kaddim Brothers brushing past toward the exit at the end of the gallery. Robes rustled on the cold stone and the three figures blended with the shadows, melting away into the distance of the monastery courtyards.

Hands grasped Egey Bashi from behind with such severe deliberation that there was no use in fighting. He relaxed against their hold, concentrating his efforts on making himself as much of a burden as possible. His mind raced.

Raishan seemed badly hurt. When the robed men pulled him upright, the Majat's head lolled and Egey Bashi noticed a smear of blood on his face. It was clear that Raishan was in no position to offer any help. He was the one that needed saving.

The men turned Egey Bashi toward the side courtyard exit, where a gaping doorway led into a darker passage. From his previous assignments he knew his way around the monastery pretty well, but this part was unfamiliar. By the position of the moon he was guessing they were facing the northeast corner of the compound, housing the deep dungeons and the inquisitors' grounds. They were going to be tortured and mutilated. And then, they were going to be left to rot until the Kaddim Brothers returned from their hunt for Kyth.

Egey Bashi couldn't allow this to happen. He had to get out and find his way to the Grasslands in time. Except, what could he possibly do against men who could disable a Diamond Majat so easily?

A commotion around Raishan drew his attention. The robed men were having trouble keeping the Majat upright. His injuries were apparently far worse than any of his captors imagined. As the Keeper watched in a horrified silence, Raishan fell sideways, collapsing against the man next to him. The man cursed, struggling to keep the limp body of his captive from sinking to the ground. Another hooded man hurried to help.

As they steadied Raishan, he suddenly came to life, pushing against his captors' arms. As they stumbled back, overbalanced, he sprung forward, his momentum carrying him onto the other captors with dizzying speed. His knee shot up and caught the man in front right below the belt. The man doubled over with a satisfying grunt. Raishan continued his movement, landing on one foot and swinging out the other so fast that the air around him whistled. Bones cracked, followed by short screams as two men at his back collapsed, grasping their legs. The last man backed off toward Egey Bashi's group, but he wasn't fast enough. Raishan completed the spin, his heel catching the man on the chin. The man fell backward onto the stones of the courtyard, splattering blood.

Egey Bashi let out a breath, watching the men crouched on the ground with horrible injuries that had taken Raishan seconds to inflict. One of them was clutching at his groin. Two others lay flat on their backs, whimpering, their out-turned knees suggesting really bad breaks. The fourth one was still.

A blade pressed against Egey Bashi's neck.

"Tell your friend to stop, Magister," said a voice by his ear.

Egey Bashi took a breath. "Aghat Raishan," he said quickly. "If they kill me, you must go and help Kyth. This is my dying wish." He gasped as the blade pierced the skin. But it didn't go any deeper. The events in front of them unraveled too fast.

Raishan's muscles rippled. A dark blade slid out of his sleeve into his hands, tied behind his back. Steel glinted in the moonlight and the tight ropes holding his arms together up to the elbows snapped loose. Raishan shook his hands, flicking them to the sides as he faced the remaining enemies. His eyes had a ruthless, frightening glint that echoed in the set of his features. A long, dark stiletto geamed in his hand.

The men around Egey Bashi backed off, holding the Keeper in front like a shield. Raishan leapt forward, his blade sweeping by so fast that it blurred. Egey Bashi felt the hold on him released as the body by his side sunk to the ground like a deflating sack. He stumbled and Raishan caught him by the shoulder and pulled him over to his side, cutting the ropes around the Keeper's wrists in one short move.

Egey Bashi flexed his fingers, feeling slowly returning to his numb hands.

"Are you hurt, Magister?" Raishan asked.

"I'm fine."

"Then let's get the hell out of here."

They turned and ran.

The sounds of pursuit grew fainter as they sped through the stone courtyards like two dark shadows. They didn't stop as they saw the wall ahead of them, whipping out their grappler hooks as they ran. In no time they were over, running along the cobbled street on the other side into the maze of alleys leading down the Holy Hills toward the port.

After the monastery wall was out of sight, Egey Bashi paused to catch his breath. Raishan waited. They eyed each other in silence, then started down the street at a fast walk.

"Couldn't you have given me a sign or something?" Egey Bashi asked after they turned the corner.

"Why?"

The Keeper opened his mouth to speak his mind, but decided against it. Tempers aside, Raishan was right. There was probably no reason to let Egey Bashi know that the Majat was actually all right, and that his near-death state was no more than pretense, aimed to give him advantage in a fight.

"I thought you were really hurt," the Keeper said. "What the Kaddim Brothers did to you looked bad."

"It felt bad," Raishan confessed. "I thought it was going to kill me. What the hell was that power?"

Egey Bashi frowned. "When the Kaddim's mind control is focused onto one person, it becomes so intense that it can make a man's heart explode. Used like that, it is called Power to Kill. One needs a great command of power to be able to do that."

"That man – Kaddim Farros, was it?"

Egey Bashi nodded. "He's very powerful. If Nimos brings him along in his hunt for Kyth, there's no telling what they can do."

They turned onto the familiar street with the battered sign showing a blackened picture of a wild mountain aemrock.

"We must go to the Grasslands at once," Egey Bashi said. "I don't care what your Guildmaster says, but we must help Kyth. We can't allow him to fall into these men's hands."

Raishan glanced at him but said nothing.

"We must leave right away," Egey Bashi went on. "We must beat the Kaddim Brothers to it, if we can."

"I doubt it's possible," Raishan said. "They'll probably use a lizardbeast relay, or something. But we can certainly make good speed if we hurry."

28

ON THE RIVER

Kyth dreamed.

He was standing in a large field, facing three robed figures. The hoods were pushed back, but their faces shifted features, making it hard to see what they really looked like. Waves of force emanated from their outstretched palms. Three streams of force joined into one, an overwhelming torrent too strong to oppose.

People crouched on the ground at Kyth's feet, covering their ears against the pressure. Their faces were pale and blood trickled from their nostrils. Kyth knew they were about to die, crushed by the hooded men's power.

He had to stop it.

The pressure of the force was enormous. While Kyth didn't seem to be affected as much as the others, he was weakening under the flow. Soon he would be overpowered, and then nobody could save them anymore.

He raised his head, searching for anything to aid him.

The wind.

He had to relax and let in the wind. But if he did, he would also let in the power of the strange men. He would no longer be able to resist it.

He had no other choice.

He relaxed, letting go. The wind filled him, mixing with another type of power, darker and heavier, but still adding to the flow. In his mind, he gathered it into a single point, shaping it into an invisible spearhead. He held it out toward his enemies and moved it, cutting through the blanket of power.

The pressure subsided. The hooded men looked at him in surprise. Then they changed, focusing their entire blast on the people dying at Kyth's feet.

I have to save them.

He focused his spearhead into a large streak of light, sharp like the finest blade he had ever wielded. He made it wider, cutting through the power that enfolded each of the people in turn. He watched them lift their heads, one by one. Their agonized faces relaxed, making them once again recognizable: Alder; his foster father, the Forestland blacksmith; Garnald the Mirewalker; Ellah; Magister Egey Bashi…

They were all getting to their feet, smiling. He had saved them from certain death. But just as he was about to rush to them and embrace them, a terrible blast of power sent him tumbling over the ground. His spearhead shattered into a thousand pieces.

He screamed and woke up.

It took Kyth a moment to realize where he was. He sat up in bed, slowly recognizing his surroundings. He was in the crew tent, in the bow section of the upper deck of the barge they were traveling on. He was lying on a low wooden bed nailed to the deck. Water splashed overboard, and low gusts of the cool night breeze touched his skin.

He took a deep breath, the nightmare slowly releasing its hold. Then he saw a dark, still shape at the tent's entrance, watching.

Kara.

When she realized he had noticed her, she turned and walked out of the tent. Kyth hastily scrambled out of bed and followed.

The deck was awash with moonlight. The lonely crewman on duty quietly dozed at the wheel. Kara made her way past him to the aft section, through a narrow winding passage between the barricades of crates piled on deck to a small, secluded space at the stern. Kyth hurried to catch up.

She stopped at the rail, looking at the river whose majestically flowing waters glimmered in the light of the moon high overhead. Kyth came over and stood by her side.

"It seemed like a bad nightmare," she said.

He nodded. "Some are worse than others. I hope I didn't scream and wake you."

She shook her head. "I wasn't sleeping."

"Why not?"

She smiled. "Maybe because I've had enough? Ever since we came on board, all we do is sleep."

"We have a lot to catch up for," he said, "after our ride to Aknabar."

They stood side by side, looking at the low bushes passing by on the distant shore, painted into silvers and blacks by the streaming moonlight.

"We're making good speed," Kara said. "We should arrive in Jaimir tomorrow morning. With luck, we'll cross over to the Grasslands right away."

Her voice sounded calm, but, knowing her well, Kyth could tell she was holding something back. He turned and peered into her face, trying to see her expression. She averted her gaze. It seemed she was deliberately trying to keep her face in the shadows.

"What is it that you're not telling me?" Kyth asked quietly.

She turned her face into the stream of moonlight and closed her eyes, a silvery gleam washing over her face. She looked so beautiful that Kyth's breath caught in his throat. He could just stand like this forever, watching her.

"Remember," she said, "when I told you I wasn't sure I could handle whoever's coming after us?"

"Yes," Kyth said slowly.

"After we meet with the Cha'ori," she said, "you'll be under the protection of their hort. You must promise that whatever happens, you'll think only of your mission. You won't try to do anything foolish."

Kyth gave her a searching look. The feverish gleam was back in her eyes, just like before, when she didn't sleep for eight straight days. Standing next to her, he could feel how tense she was. He had never seen her this way before.

"You *know* what's coming, don't you?" he asked quietly. "You've known all along."

"Yes."

"Then, *tell me*."

She raised her eyes and finally met his gaze. "The Majat Guild. They… they'll try to capture me and bring me back. They won't do anything to harm me, but they'd likely have orders to kill anyone who stands in their way. I want you to remember that and not interfere, however bad it looks. Can you promise me that?"

"You want me to stand by and watch you get captured?"

Her face was desperate. "There's nothing you can do. Believe me. I can handle them. If you interfere, you'll get yourself killed for nothing."

"*Can* you handle them?"

"Yes." She looked away, watching the shore slowly moving by.

Kyth reached over and put an arm around her. She turned and hid her face on his chest. He held her, gently stroking her hair, resting his cheek against the side of her head. He had never seen her like this. Something was terribly wrong, and she wasn't going to tell him what it was. He stroked her until she quieted, her tense muscles relaxing under his hands.

After a while, she raised her face to him and put her arms around his neck, drawing him toward her. Lightheaded with her closeness, he brushed his cheek against hers. She turned and met his lips.

The kiss echoed through his body like thunder, overpowering his weakening mind. He stroked her and she responded, shivering and clinging to him as if her life depended on it. A light moan escaped her lips as his hands found the right spots, evoking a response that surged through, forcing out the last bits of reason. All that remained was raw senses, taking over all possible control.

Kyth didn't remember when he suddenly felt that, instead of the shirt, he was touching her bare skin, smooth and firm under his hands, and so hot it burned his fingers. He wasn't sure how the cloth that separated them disappeared, their contact so sensational that for a blissfully long moment it seemed too overwhelming to bear. He could no longer tell up from down, but it seemed that instead of standing they were lying on a heap of clothes, the rough boards of the deck underneath soft and smooth like the finest bed. His entire being focused on their contact, deeper than one could experience in a lifetime.

He was so strong he could lift mountains. If he let his strength loose, he would crush her with his passion. He tried to hold back, but her arms grasped him with the force that left no way for gentleness anymore. His body moved of its own accord, driven by a force more primitive, more powerful than the conscious mind.

She opened up and yielded to him so completely that he could no longer tell them apart. Each of his senses echoed in her, as they moved against each other, infinitely close, and yet urging for even more closeness. He gave her all his incredible strength, filling her like a vessel so that she could in turn give him the strength of her own. Their bodies, their senses became one, raising them both to heights of passion too big for one person to hold. There couldn't possibly be anything more in the world Kyth could want, and if he were to die right now, he would die the happiest man that ever lived. He was never going to be afraid of anything anymore. He was invincible. He was immortal.

He was complete.

Afterward, they put their clothes back on and sat close together on the deck, shivering and weak, unable to draw away from each other even for a moment. It felt to Kyth that if he ever let go of her, he'd die, a feeling that echoed in the way she clung to him, as if grasping a lifeline. He held her, immersed in her faint flowery scent, in the warmth of her body against his, hiding his face in her silky golden hair. Through its soft glow he watched the dawn of a new day, its beams illuminating the most beautiful river that ever existed.

They didn't get up until they heard voices on the deck behind the crates, people moving in a hurry that exceeded the usual everyday routine. Oars banged below deck, rowing against the current to bring the barge to a stop.

Ashore, a jagged roofline emerged from around the river bend, marking the first outskirts of a giant city, bathed in the morning mists, waiting for their arrival.

They had reached Jaimir.

29
THE GRASSLANDS

Captain Beater's eyes were misty with lust as he watched Kara emerge from the bow section of the barge, leading her horse. He opened his mouth to speak, but she fixed him with a short glance that made the captain subside back into silence. He turned to Kyth and Alder waiting to follow Kara down the wide ladder onto the docks.

"Plannin' to come back this way soon, eh?" Captain Beater asked.

"We're not sure," Alder said politely.

Captain Beater's expression as he glanced over Kara's back view made Kyth shudder.

"Well," he said with a meaningful wink. "Make sure if ye do, ye'll think of the old *Lady of Fortune*, eh?"

"We will, thanks," Kyth told him stiffly and followed Alder ashore.

Kara stopped at the bottom of the ladder and surveyed the crowd milling by the docks. Kyth followed her gaze, half-expecting to see a row of hooded figures with orbens lined up to greet them. But nobody seemed to pay them any special attention as they walked off the boat. A couple of men in the vicinity glanced at Kara, but as far as Kyth could tell they weren't even looking at her face.

"Stay close behind me," Kara told them. "And watch out. We're headed for the ferry. Let's hope we can reach it without trouble."

It was early, but the Jaimir's giant market plaza was already full. Rows of stalls ran almost all the way to the water, so rich in colorful displays that one couldn't help but gape. Ornate Harnarian rugs hung next to the impressive displays of Bengaw weapons and the garlands of peppers and dates from the southern lands. Aromatic oils and spices from Tahr Abad filled the air with their heady, exotic flavors. As they pushed their way through the crowds heading for the place where two thick cables running across the river marked the site of the ferry, Kyth felt dizzy from the rich bouquet of smells of spices, roasting meat, cheap perfume, manure, smoke, and sweat.

Everything in sight boiled with activity. A fat man in a dirty apron was fishing golden balls of dough out of a vat of bubbling oil and laying them out on a tray, then sprinkling them with powdered sugar and cinnamon whose sweet smell spread around in mouthwatering waves. An old woman next to him hung out garlands of dried figs, wrinkled like the skin on her gnarled hands. A weapons merchant scurried around a richly clad customer, balancing a dark curved blade over his arm. Kyth could see from here that the balance wasn't all that great, but the buyer didn't seem to notice, nodding with the air of self-importance at the merchant's explanations. Further away, a young girl was balancing a pile of stacked crates, each containing a wildly clucking chicken. Under a canopy stretched between sturdy wooden poles, a blacksmith was hitting an anvil with a rhythmical sound, his glistening skin blackened by the smoke from the forge.

Pushing through the crowd with horses in tow proved to be more and more difficult. Kyth stretched his head not to lose sight of Alder's towering figure up ahead. He couldn't see Kara at all. He hurried on, doing his best to squeeze through the dense rows of bodies.

Somebody caught him by the arm. He turned and came face to face with a large man in a leather apron over a baggy outfit. He had a big, unshaved face and a gap between his front teeth, wide enough to fit a finger.

Kyth raised his chin, his arm slowly going numb in the man's grip.

"How much for the horse, boy?" The man's thunderous voice made people in the vicinity turn their heads.

"It's not for sale." Kyth glanced at his horse, whose eye darted sideways betraying its fear of the thick, noisy crowd.

The man's grin widened. "Come now, boy. Don't think ye can drive a hard bargain. I've been bargainin' in this market when you still didn't know how to wear yer pants the right way up. Five silvers, that's me offer."

Kyth reached over and took the man's hand off his arm with a slow, deliberate gesture.

"I *said*, my horse's not for sale. Thanks all the same."

He turned to leave but the man stepped forward and planted himself across Kyth's path.

"Nobody walks away from Big Ronan, boy." The man's face drew so close that Kyth caught the stench of his breath – a mix of beer, onion, and rot. "I *said* I wanted yer horse. Six silvers, but that's really as high as I can go."

"Get out of my way." Kyth tried to side-step the man, but the crowd around them was too dense.

The man smiled. "Me thinks ye're in bad need of a lesson, boy. Or, would ye rather just sell me yer horse? Last chance, while I'm still askin' nicely."

Kyth clenched the reins and measured the man with an appraising glance. He was twice as wide as Kyth and almost a head taller. Kyth wasn't sure if he could stand up to such a man in a fist fight, but there seemed to be no other choice.

"Let me pass," he said. "Unless you *really* want to fight."

The man threw his head back and roared with laughter. Then he addressed the thickening crowd of spectators, like an actor addresses an audience waiting for a show.

"Did ye hear it? The little puppy's trying to bite. Come, show me your teeth, puppy."

He beckoned with his left hand, gathering his right into a fist the size of a child's head. Kyth searched for a place to hook up the reins, so that he could free both hands. But at that moment his horse whinnied loudly and reared, tearing free from Kyth's hand.

A blade whistled by. A hooded man at the edge of the crowd swayed and collapsed. Kyth spun around and saw two more figures disappearing into the crowd behind.

A hand touched his shoulder. He turned, fist at the ready, and came face to face with Kara.

"Are you all right?" she asked.

He nodded and turned to catch the reins. His horse shied sideways, but after recognizing Kyth it calmed down enough for him to regain hold. Kyth gathered the reins and patted the horse's steaming neck. Kara pushed past him and leaned over the fallen man.

"Ye killed him!" a voice from the crowd said in disbelief.

The man groaned and rolled over. Kara picked up her throwing dagger, which she must have used to knock the man out, and reached for a small object lying on the ground next to the man's outstretched hand.

It was a metal dart. She turned it in his fingers, then sniffed it and frowned.

"What is it?" Kyth asked.

"Wartbane."

"What?"

Kyth knew the plant with silvery leaves and small yellow flowers that grew back by the tool shed in the corner of the castle's gardens. Common folk used this plant to brew potions against warts and calluses, but apart from its questionable medicinal properties, Kyth had always considered it to be quite harmless.

She gave him a square look. "It's poisonous to horses."

With a sinking heart Kyth turned to his horse, its head high, eyes rolling nervously around.

"I don't think he had time to do it," Kara said. "But you should really watch out when you go through a crowd like that."

"But why would someone attack my horse?"

"Someone's trying to slow us down. Where's that man you were talking to?"

They turned around, but Big Ronan was nowhere to be seen. Kyth saw Alder at the edge of the crowd holding the reins of two horses, and exchanged a glance with his foster brother.

"I didn't see him leave," Alder said. "There was too much going on."

"He wanted to buy my horse," Kyth said in a shaky voice. He realized how stupid he had been. Ronan was an obvious decoy, meant to distract him while the real action was going on behind. Why would anyone in this busy marketplace want to pay him six silvers for a horse?

"It's all right," Kara said. "We'll question this one." She nodded to the man on the ground. "Who sent you?"

The man's hand darted to his mouth with surprising speed. Kara rushed forward, but it was too late. The man gasped, then shook and went still.

"Poison!" Someone shouted from the crowd. "The witch poisoned him!" People around them backed off, eyeing Kara with fear.

Kara clenched her teeth as she turned and took her reins from Alder.

"Let's move on," she said. "We surely learned one thing: we're making good speed. Let's keep it up." She turned and walked on through the rapidly parting crowd. Kyth followed, trying to ignore the rising buzz behind them, like that of a disturbed beehive.

The ferryman, a large man with an eyepatch, whose chest and stomach, exposed by an open leather vest, resembled a hard iron washboard, looked them up and down in recognition.

"I remember you," he said slowly. "You were here a couple of months ago crossing over from the Grasslands, weren't you?"

"Yes," Kyth said carefully.

The ferryman shifted from foot to foot, but before he could say anything else, Kara reached over and handed him a coin. The stern look on her face discouraged further questions.

The man took the coin, bringing it closer to his eyes for a short glance. Then he rolled his tongue and spat on the boardwalk at his feet.

"The pay's a silver," he said.

"Since when?"

"Since I saw the trouble you stirred up at the market plaza."

Kara leaned closer. "If you really saw it all, you wouldn't want to make me angry right now. Trust me."

He crossed his arms on his immense chest. "If you do one of your tricks on me, who's going to take you across the river? D'you think one of these boys could pull all of you, including three horses? Or, do you plan to do it yourself?"

He looked at Kyth and Alder with calm satisfaction. Kyth had to admit the man had a point. The pulley mechanism that drove the ferry across the river required a great deal of force. Even Alder, by far the largest in their group, didn't seem up to the task.

Kara clasped the hilt of her dagger, but Kyth put a hand on her arm.

"It doesn't matter," he said quietly.

She looked at him, anger in her eyes slowly subsiding. Kyth took a silver coin out of his purse and handed it to the ferryman.

"For this price," he said. "We expect you to make it quick."

The man nodded, meeting Kyth's eyes. A smirk passed over his face as he hid the coin inside his vest. Then he stepped aside and gestured them aboard.

Kyth could indeed see the extra effort as the man rotated the huge handle that connected to the rusty pulley mechanism, driving the floating platform across the water. Kyth suspected, however, that the effort was necessary not because of anything he said to the man, but because of the extra weight of four people and three horses that the ferryman had to pull across the river by working his impressive muscles.

As they neared the other shore, Kyth saw a group of riders up on the hill. They stood still, watching the three travelers get off the ferry and walk their horses up the tall bank.

When they got closer, Kyth started to make out the faces. They all looked familiar. His heart leapt with joy as they came up close enough to recognize them.

The two on the outside, dark men with slanted eyes and waist-length braids, were Cha'ori warriors. The one on the left was very young, no older than Kyth and Alder. He kept his face straight as he eyed the approaching newcomers, but there was laughter in his gaze. Kyth smiled back. Adhim had been a great friend back during their ride through the Or'hallas a few months ago. It was great to see him in the greeting party.

Kyth also knew the man on the right, an older warrior whose skin stretched over his high cheekbones like dry parchment, his hair heavily stained with gray. Khamal, the Warrior Elder.

Kyth turned to the woman in the center, riding a sleek sand-colored mare. Dagmara, the woman who gave him the medallion last time they traveled with her hort. A foreteller of incredible powers, who foresaw the dangers on Kyth's path, and the importance of his mission. The look in her eyes told him that it was no coincidence that she and her hort came here to meet them. Their mission was going to succeed. Or so he hoped.

Kyth was overjoyed to see another rider emerge in the wake of the Cha'ori greeting party. A sturdy middle-aged man with brown skin, shiny dark eyes, and a mop of unruly hair, in which dark and blond strands were mixed, as if having trouble deciding on the man's true lineage. Unlike the Cha'ori, he sat in the saddle awkwardly. His broad-featured face melted into a smile as he saw Kyth and Alder, but the quick glance he threw at Kara was full of suspicion.

"Garnald!" Kyth and Alder rushed up to the man. The Mirewalker was the closest thing to family, a man from the Forestlands where Kyth and Alder grew up. Seeing him made Kyth feel homesick.

The Mirewalker dismounted and gave each of them in turn a long embrace. "You boys grew up! You look like men now. Your father, the blacksmith, will be pleased."

"How is father?" Alder asked.

The Mirewalker smiled. "He's well," he said. "Worried sick about you two. Where's Ellah, by the way? Her grandma was askin' about her."

Kyth and Alder exchanged glances.

"Ellah stayed behind in Tandar," Kyth said. "She's fine." He had many more questions, but Dagmara's raised hand stopped the conversation.

"We have very little time," she said. Her voice was low and soft, but it carried around their group without effort. "We must move."

"Did you know we were coming?" Alder asked.

She only smiled. Then she turned her horse, signaling for them to mount.

"We can talk on the way," Garnald said. "If that beast of a horse cooperates. He gave me a hell of a time on the way here, I can tell you."

Kyth smiled, watching the older man struggle with his mount. Garnald's home was in the forest, in thickets so deep that no horse could ever make it through. He seemed out of place in the open Or'halla plains. Yet, it was so good to see him.

"Why are you here, so far out of the Forestlands?" he asked, matching his horse's trot to keep up with Garnald.

The Mirewalker looked at him sideways and took a firmer grip on the reins. "There's trouble brewing up in our parts. A dark order or something. They're invading the Grasslands and were even seen going through the Hedge."

"Through the Hedge?" Kyth and Alder looked at the Mirewalker in shock.

"Down by the Hazel Grove. They've some strange power that can make people do what they want. From the look of it, they were just testin' if it'd work on the villagers, but it wasn't pretty, I can tell you."

Kyth and Alder shook their heads. The Forestlands had always been a haven of safety. True, there were plenty of dangers in there, like Twilight Moths, Rock Monsters, snakewood trees, and Ayalla the Forest Woman with her deadly spider-guardians and the frightening powers that controlled the forest itself; but one could learn to get by and avoid them without problem. To think that somebody could have come to one of the Grove villages and force its inhabitants into something unpleasant was horrifying.

"Dagmara," Garnald went on, "was on her way to meet with Ayalla. She summoned us to prepare the meeting when news of your arrival came."

"News?"

The Mirewalker shrugged. "Some of her foretellings. Not sure how she does it. Anyway, she foresaw you coming, and Alder, and Ellah."

"Ellah?"

The Mirewalker made a move to spread his hands, but a side step of his horse made him grasp the reins with new force.

"Dagmara was anxious to meet you herself," he went on. "She kept talking about some danger or something, days before you arrived."

He gave Kyth one of his penetrating looks that made Kyth feel that the old Mirewalker understood a lot more than he cared to show.

Ahead, they could now see the familiar shapes of tents rising out of the grass. The horses sped up, sensing familiar ground. Garnald was suddenly a lot more busy trying to stay in the saddle, and Kyth and Alder left the Mirewalker behind. Their horses leveled up with Kara, riding in front with the three Cha'ori.

Kyth couldn't help noticing a special detached look about Kara. Something had changed in her after they had met up with Dagmara. She looked calm, but something in her gaze, directed ahead with an absentminded expression, alarmed Kyth.

She turned and gave him a brief smile. Then she glanced back to where the Trade City of Jaimir was barely visible in the distant haze. She narrowed her eyes, as if trying to make out somebody in the city crowd on the market plaza, but from this distance it was, of course, impossible. After a moment, she turned and fixed her gaze on the Grassland plain ahead.

30
PURSUIT

Mai kept such a fast pace that at the end of each day Ellah could barely stay in the saddle. She had given up any attempts to help with everyday chores, letting the Majat set camp, cook, clean and, on occasion, even spread out her bedroll. By the end of the tenth day she almost welcomed the sight of the wide ocean of houses that opened up to them from the hilltop, marking the outer boundary of the Trade City of Jaimir.

During the trip Mai had been calm and friendly, but he never let down his guard to allow her a glimpse of any emotion. At any other time she would have regretted it, but now, after the exhausting ride, she was so tired she had no strength to wonder anymore. She was quite content with staying in the saddle all day and still being able to walk after getting off the horse.

The ride through Jaimir was uneventful. Mai easily navigated through a maze of narrow streets, leading them straight to the port where the huge market plaza opened up in front of them all at once with an explosion of sights, shapes, colors and smells.

The late afternoon crowd in the marketplace was too dense to stay on horseback. They dismounted and continued on foot toward the ferry dock. Mai led the way, with Ellah and Sharrim in his wake. At the sight of the two heavily armed Majat, the crowd parted hastily to let them through.

The ferryman towered nearly a head over Mai, twice as broad in any dimension. Yet, as his single pale eye fell on the Diamond, there was a glint of respect in his gaze. He actually straightened up, waiting for Mai to approach.

Mai handed him a coin and the man put it away with a nod, surveying their group.

"By the time you get across, it'll be near sunset," he said to Mai. "Are you sure you wouldn't rather stay in the city? I open early tomorrow and can take you across at first light."

Mai shook his head. "We're in a hurry."

Ellah's heart beat faster at the thought that she would soon see Kyth again. She missed him and was worried about his mission. But she was also aware that after she met him, her trip with Mai would come to an end.

Mai pulled his horse to a stop and peered into a large trail of hoof prints running off into the distance.

"They're surely in a hurry," he said. "In the past day, we haven't closed in on them all that much."

Sharrim nodded. "I heard the Cha'ori can make a hundred miles a day on heavy marches. Our horses can't do much better, Aghat."

Mai shrugged. "We're about five hours apart. And, they're probably going to camp for the night. If we sleep for a few hours and then ride the rest of the night, we should catch them in the morning."

Sharrim nodded, directing his horse to a small group of trees. Ellah dropped the reins, letting her horse follow. She was too tired to do anything. She wanted to tell Mai that there was no need to hurry so much on her account and that she could well wait a couple of days longer to be reunited with her friends, but talking required strength and she was much too exhausted. Besides, if Mai thought it necessary to keep this pace, she wasn't going to be the one to drag behind. She had promised him she could keep up, hadn't she?

She rode over to where Sharrim had tied his horse to a low branch and stopped, too tired even to get down from the saddle. As she sat there, gathering the strength to move, Mai appeared by her side.

"Are you all right?"

Ellah tried to smile. "I'm fine. Just a little tired."

He reached up and helped her out of the saddle. When her feet touched the ground, her legs gave way and she almost fell. Mai steadied her, holding her in a half-embrace. His closeness gave her strength. Even in her tired state her heart beat faster as she felt his warmth against her and inhaled his faint smell of fresh water and pine.

"I'm fine," she said. "I can keep up. Really."

Mai nodded. He put an arm around her waist and led her toward the place where Sharrim had already started a small fire.

"We'll eat rations tonight," he said to Sharrim. "We must use all the time we have to rest."

Sharrim walked over to his saddle bags and fished out three small packets. Mai took two, and came back to Ellah. Crouching on the ground in front of her, he unwrapped one of the packets and held it out to her.

"Eat this. And drink some water. Then you must sleep."

She nodded and took the packet, too tired to speak. It was a strange blend of salted meat, dry sweet fruits, and a herb she didn't know that gave it all a strong, heady flavor. It didn't seem like much food, but after eating it, Ellah felt better. She took a flask out of Mai's hand and drank some water, watching Sharrim in the distance spread out the bedrolls.

When she was done, Mai pulled her up to her feet and led her to her bedroll. He helped her down, covering her with a cloak. Then he sat next to her and put a hand over her forehead, resting his fingertips over her eyelids that fell closed under his touch.

A calm feeling emanated from him, just like the time he confronted the wild dogs.

"Sleep," he said, and she felt the warmth from his hand spread along her body, making her feel heavy and relaxed. Despite her tiredness, she was acutely aware of his closeness, of his hand touching her. She wanted to wait longer and enjoy this feeling, but his calmness drew her into a void and she remembered nothing more.

Ellah awoke because somebody touched her shoulder. She opened her eyes. It was still dark. She sat up and peered at the figure kneeling in front of her. His face was in shadow, but his golden hair, backlit by the pale moonlight, was easy to recognize.

Mai.

"Get up," he said. "It's time to go."

He stepped over to Sharrim's just-visible, crouching shape next to the glowing embers in the fire pit. Ellah got up and straightened out her clothes. She was afraid she wouldn't be able to move after the way she felt the previous night, but she felt surprisingly refreshed. She combed her hair and washed her face with water from her flask. Then she walked over to sit with the Majat.

The night was chilly, but the embers emanated warmth. When she sat down next to Mai, he handed her another ration and a warm mug of brew. It was even stronger than the tea they usually made, and had the same heady flavor as the food.

Having learned a bit about herbs from her grandmother, Ellah could tell that this new flavor, present in the food and drink, came from a herb that was making her feel so refreshed after such a short sleep. She finished her tea and felt full of energy, almost eager for another day in the saddle.

They quickly packed up the camp and set out on their ride across the plain.

By the time the eastern sky lit up with a glow, the landscape had changed. The trail of hoof prints they were following kept close to the river. On their right, along the tall bank, groups of trees grew so close to each other that they looked like the outskirts of a small forest. If one kept riding south, these small groups would eventually give way to the tall haven elms of the Forestland Hedge. By Ellah's estimation it was about ten days away. Her heart raced at the thought of being so close to home.

The sun was already in the sky by the time they saw the distant shapes of the Cha'ori tents. Thin wisps of rising smoke indicated that the camp was occupied. Ellah felt her heart beat faster at the thought that she would soon see Kyth and Alder. If this was Dagmara's hort, she would also see other people she had bonded with during their travel together just a few months ago. She let her horse run ahead, and Mai and Sharrim closed in behind her.

As they approached the low hill that separated them from the camp, five riders rode up to block their way. Their pointed helmets bore the sign of an eye, the sight that made Ellah's heart leap. *The Overseer Hort.* Dagmara must be here, and Kyth and Alder were probably with her.

The leader of the patrol was a young man of about Ellah's age, with a waist-length braid. Behind him rode two more warriors and two archers, resting arrows against the strings of their bows as they galloped to intercept the intruders.

Out of the corner of her eye Ellah saw Sharrim's hand dart to his own bow. Mai stopped him with a short gesture and the two Majat rode up either side of Ellah. Their postures became calm and relaxed. Only by having traveled with them for a long time did Ellah know that behind the calmness they were alert and ready to spring into action.

The Cha'ori warrior addressed Ellah as the leader of the group.

"State your business."

"I'm here to meet with my friends." Ellah peered into the face of the young warrior. His face, half-covered by a stiff leather flap that protruded from the forehead downward over the nose, looked familiar. He was young, not much older than her. "Kyth, Adler, and Kara. Are they here?"

"Our foreteller," the man said, "didn't mention anything about Prince Kythar's friends coming this way." He glanced at the archers, who raised their bows.

Prince Kythar. He's here then. Ellah's heart raced. She looked at her companions, but their relaxed postures didn't change, as they calmly stared ahead, waiting for her to continue the conversation. Ellah couldn't figure out why they weren't trying to help her talk their way through, but there was no other choice but to proceed.

"Kyth is here to meet with Dagmara," she said. "Is she your foreteller, warrior?"

The riders leaned forward in their saddles, peering into her face. "You know a lot about us, stranger."

Ellah let out a sigh. She never anticipated it would be so difficult to gain passage into the Cha'ori camp.

If this was indeed Dagmara's hort, she should know this man. She narrowed her eyes, trying to see under the helmet. As if in response, he rode closer and lifted his strange visor.

"Ellah?" he asked slowly.

"Adhim?" A smile spread over Ellah's face. She couldn't believe it had taken her so long to recognize him. Adhim had been a great friend to them all on their march with the Cha'ori.

"You cut your hair," Adhim said. "And changed clothes. It looked… unusual. I thought I knew you, but I wasn't sure. I'm sorry I didn't recognize you sooner."

She nodded, relief washing over her. After traveling with the Cha'ori she had cut off her long braid, which Adhim must have remembered, and learned to ride like a man. So long ago. And yet now, after meeting with Adhim, it seemed just like yesterday.

"I'm here to see Kyth and Alder," she said. "They're with you, aren't they?"

Adhim nodded. "Yes. And Kara. She's also here. It's the three of them that Dagmara told us to protect."

Ellah smiled. "Don't worry, Adhim. We bring them no danger."

She turned and looked at Mai. Adhim followed her glance, but saw no threat in Ellah's silent companions. She wondered briefly why it was that Mai and Sharrim hadn't said a word during the entire encounter, but there seemed to be no reason for them to speak. She had handled things well, hadn't she?

They gathered the reins and followed Adhim and his party downslope into the Cha'ori camp.

31
SHOWDOWN

"If we're to speak of reclaiming our seat on your council," Dagmara said, "we must have the Forest Mother on our side."

"I have great respect for Ayalla," Kyth said. "But why must we seek her help?"

Dagmara exchanged a glance with Garnald standing by her side. "Lady Ayalla is the most powerful being in existence, the one whose magic brought about the world as we know it today. Of course," she glanced humorlessly at Kyth, "you're too young to know that."

And you're not. Kyth knew that Dagmara, a woman of incredible powers, was a lot older than a normal human should be, but to hear her talking of bringing about the world…

Having grown up in the Forestlands, he knew a lot of tales about the Forest Mother, and had even met her once when he ventured into the Dark Mire where she lived. Her shroud of magic, powerful and ancient, was all about the forest and its secret life. Little else seemed to interest this strange woman, and if anything could ever catch her fancy, kingdoms and laws seemed to be as far from it as Kyth could imagine.

"Ayalla could never be persuaded to leave the forest," he said.

Dagmara smiled. "Don't underestimate her, Prince Kythar. She's already agreed to come here to meet with the Cha'ori, and we aren't in the forest, are we?"

"No," Kyth admitted.

"Trust me on this, Your Highness," Dagmara said, pronouncing the foreign title with care.

Kyth sighed. "Does Alder have to go across the river to meet her?"

Dagmara glanced at Garnald. "I am told your foster brother shares a special bond with her."

Alder blushed and lowered his head. The Mirewalkers around him exchanged meaningful looks. Kyth felt like an intruder prying into something that was none of his business.

He hesitated. There shouldn't be any reason why Alder couldn't take the trip across the river with the Mirewalkers to meet Ayalla and escort her back to the Grasslands. Yet, Kyth couldn't escape a heavy feeling that something was about to go wrong. He glanced at Dagmara, standing motionlessly by his side, but the foreteller's gaze was unreadable.

"We'll be back soon," Garnald told Kyth. "The day after tomorrow, at the latest."

Kyth nodded. He looked at Kara watching Alder with a detached expression that made Kyth uneasy. It was as if Alder was leaving forever, as if she was never going to see him again. Kyth forced himself to relax. Dagmara's gift of foretelling should warn her of any danger. She wouldn't send Alder into peril, would she? Not when she had already expressed interest in an alliance with the King.

"Be careful," Kyth told his foster brother.

Alder laughed. "We'll only be gone a couple of days. What could possibly happen in such a short time? Besides, I'll be well protected. No one messes with the Mirewalkers."

He said it with pride, as if he was talking about his kin, and the men around nodded their acknowledgment as if accepting it. Kyth studied them with curiosity.

It was the first time he had seen so many of the Mirewalkers together. Some of them were familiar from his childhood in the Forestlands, but most of the faces were new. Watching them closely, Kyth realized with surprise that whenever their eyes turned to Alder their expressions changed. There was a strange mix of surprise and reverence in the way they studied Kyth's foster brother. It was as if Alder was special, as if his trip across the river to meet with Ayalla meant more than a simple detour.

"We must go," Garnald said. "The Forest Mother is waiting."

Dagmara nodded.

Kyth watched the Mirewalkers approach the river and descend down its tall bank, his foster brother in their midst. Before disappearing from view, Alder glanced back and gave Kyth a reassuring smile.

When they were gone, Dagmara turned to Kara, her strong-featured face set into a calm mask. "Danger's close on your heels, Olivian. And I am not sure my hort can protect you."

Kara nodded. "It's not your battle. Your people should stay out of it, Dagmara. I just hope if something happens to me you can keep Prince Kythar out of danger."

Kyth opened his mouth to protest but words froze on his lips as he heard the neighs of horses and raised voices at the edge of the camp. A distant group of riders was approaching at a fast walk. Their silhouettes, outlined against the blaze of the morning sky, seemed familiar.

"*Ellah*?" Kyth stared.

She looked thinner, prettier and more mature than when they last saw each other in the King's castle before departure. Her confident posture in the saddle spoke of the many days she must have spent on horseback. She smiled and waved to Kyth, urging her horse into a trot.

Kyth frowned in surprise at the sight of Ellah's companions. Mai was the last person he expected to see here, but there was no mistaking the youthful, arrogant look and the easy grace of the Pentade leader that made even the Cha'ori riding next to him look clumsy by comparison. Men bristled up as Mai rode by.

Kyth's heart raced. Mai wasn't supposed to leave his father's side. *Is father all right?* But if not, Ellah wouldn't be smiling as she rode beside Mai, would she?

Her other companion was also a Majat, judging by his graceful movements and abundance of weapons, but clearly of a lower rank. Kyth had never seen this man before.

He turned to Kara and realized that she was no longer by his side. He searched around and saw her, a distance away, on a small hilltop. She had drawn her swords, watching the approaching riders.

When Mai's eyes fell on her, he drew his weapon and threw his horse into gallop. As he approached Kara at breakneck speed, he rose in his stirrups and leapt off the saddle, somersaulting in the air to crash onto her, showering blows with his staff.

Kyth gasped.

Kara met the attack on her blades and pushed Mai back by throwing her weight against him. She spun out of the deadlock and edged away. The moment their bodies separated, a string of arrows whizzed through the air. Kara fended them off with a sword, but as soon as her attention was diverted, Mai thrust forward, the tip of his staff coming through the brief opening in her defense. She jumped sideways and put a blade in his way, but Kyth could see how close Mai's weapon came.

Where the hell are the arrows coming from? Forcing his eyes away from the battle, Kyth saw the other Majat who had arrived with Ellah and Mai. He had dismounted and planted himself onto a flat space fifty paces away, keeping the two fighters in a clear line of sight. An arrow rested on top of his bow, but he wasn't releasing it yet, his eyes fixed on the fight.

Ellah dismounted and ran up to Kyth, panting. "What happened? Why did Kara–"

"I thought you knew! They came with *you*, didn't they?" Kyth met her bewildered eyes. Then the clash of battle drew him and he forgot all else.

Mai and Kara moved so fast it was difficult to follow. Kara's blades blended into two fans of air. Mai's staff was a blur between them, going for every gap and met with a matching blow. He jumped sideways, forcing her to follow. She resisted, trying to draw him back to the original position. It was hard to understand the purpose of the maneuver, until Mai completed the switch and attacked her from the side. As she faced him, her unprotected back came into the full view of the archer. He used the moment to shoot a string of arrows that fountained off his bow as he drew them from his quiver with dizzying speed.

Kyth's heart raced. *They won't do anything to harm me*, Kara had told him before. *Don't try to interfere, however bad it looks.*

This looked *really* bad.

As the arrows approached, Kara dropped to a crouch, leaving Mai in the line of fire. He leaned away to let the arrows pass. She used the delay to thrust upward at his chest. One of her blades ripped through his shirt. For a moment it seemed as if the blade had hit flesh. But Mai recovered, stepped aside and parried, showering blows onto her from above. She cushioned the attack by falling back, and bounced off the ground, rebounding to meet his blow midway. The force of his staff made her stumble.

286 BLADES OF THE OLD EMPIRE

Mai pressed on, landing several more blows she was forced to parry head-on. She edged back to absorb the impact. She was panting, sweat caking her hair, but Mai looked no better. The deadly dance was costing both of them a lot of strength.

I can handle them, she had said. But it didn't seem true anymore.

As Kara and Mai separated after another exchange, the Majat with a bow fired a new string of arrows. Kara turned to deflect them, but as soon as she did, Mai attacked her from the other side. She used her blades to fend off both attacks, but this time she wasn't fast enough. One of the arrows came through and hit her in the forearm.

As soon as it happened, the archer lowered his bow with the air of a man who had done his job.

Kara struggled to regain balance against a renewed attack Mai launched from the side of her injured arm. There was a screech and one of her swords slid out of her hand. Mai pressed on. She backed away, her remaining blade moving with the speed and precision that matched his weapon precisely. Yet it was clear that with her wound and having lost one sword, she wouldn't be able to hold off much longer.

However bad it looks.

Kyth shook off his stupor. Despite what Kara told him back on the boat, he wasn't going to just stand here and watch. He drew his sword, vaguely aware of Ellah shouting in his ears, of hands grasping him. He relaxed against the grip and let go, taking in the entire force of the wind roaming through the Grasslands. A powerful surge flowed into his body, filling him with strength far greater than any of them could possibly imagine. An entire Cha'ori hort couldn't stop him now. He easily shook off their hold and rushed off in the direction of the fighting Diamonds.

When he was almost upon them, Mai's body unfolded like a whip, knocking Kara's blade aside with a blow of such vicious force that her entire body shook from the impact. As she fought for balance, the tip of his staff came from the top, aiming straight at the unprotected spot at the base of her neck, where the two collarbones met. His hands slid along the staff. Too late, Kyth recognized the move that set in motion the secret blades, making them spring out of the tips of the deadly weapon.

A click of the released spring rang terrifyingly loud to Kyth's sharpened senses. The blade hit, thrusting deep into the flesh. It tore through with a ripping sound and withdrew, as Mai flicked his hands again to retract the blades back into the wood.

In the stillness that had descended onto the grass plain, Kara's body folded backwards, arms out, sword sliding out of her unresisting hand. She fell flat on her back. Blood gushed out of the wound in a few strong pulses and subsided.

With a scream, Kyth raised his sword and leapt, covering the last few paces that separated him from Mai. He let the entire force of the Grassland wind focus into the tip of the blade, aiming it to hit, to kill this man who had just shattered his world. He held nothing back.

Mai knocked Kyth's blade aside with a careless gesture, as if waving away a fly trying to get to his food. But Kyth's hand didn't waver. His blade slid forward along the staff in a sneaky attack that came straight through Mai's defenses.

The Majat parried just before the blade reached his skin. His eyes widened in surprise. He leapt backward and gripped his staff into a battle hold.

Kyth clenched his teeth and attacked with all his might, showering blows onto his opponent. Mai's eyes became empty, a ruthless glow in their depths showing Kyth that if he was defeated there would be no mercy. But Kyth didn't care. All he wanted was to hurt, to kill this man who had just won what had to be the most unfair fight in the world.

They circled around each other and clashed in a face-on attack. It was hard to imagine how someone of Mai's slight build was capable of such force, but there was no time to wonder. The Diamond advanced, his movements becoming so fast that his entire shape blurred. Kyth could no longer focus on his face. He concentrated on the staff, trying to match its dizzying movements.

The rage building up inside him was overwhelming. He wavered under its strength, the wind filling him with a force too great for him to control. He kept up the melee, but his attack and defense were no longer balanced. Mai's staff came through, hitting his shoulder. Kyth stumbled under the impact, but recovered to meet the next blow. The staff swept low, aiming to knock him off his feet. He jumped over, looking for a gap to attack. But just as he landed, Mai's hand unexpectedly swept back.

It came so fast it was hard to see. The blow, aimed higher than before, caught Kyth right below the knees, knocking his legs from underneath him. As he fell, Kyth kept his sword in front, ready to spring back. But the moment he touched the ground, Mai's staff was already there, thrusting forward in a rotating movement. Kyth's sword flew out of his hand and landed way out of reach. He pushed off, trying to jump back up to his feet and rush for his weapon, but a blow to his chest sent him back to the ground.

It seemed to Kyth that his heart exploded. As he struggled to recover his breath, he felt the wood at his throat, the end of Mai's staff pressing hard against his windpipe. Kyth gasped.

Mai's face appeared over him. It was calm, but his eyes gleamed with anger.

"If you move," the Majat said distinctly, "you die."

"Fine." Kyth clenched his teeth. His eyes darted sideways to where his sword lay, just a few yards away. He focused his strength, trying to twist from underneath the staff point pressing on his throat. If he could just reach his sword...

Mai's eyes flashed. He changed the grip on his weapon and Kyth recognized the movement that switched on the mechanism to control the retractable blades. In a moment, a sharp steel point would spring out of the end of the staff pressing against his throat. The blow would probably be strong enough to sever his head.

He was out of time.

He didn't care.

"Do it!" he rasped. "Kill me! Murderer!"

Mai's hand wavered. His eyes fixing on Kyth slowly acquired a shade of reason. He hesitated and withdrew his weapon.

Kyth grasped his throat with both hands, fighting for breath. His left arm was numb from the earlier blow to his shoulder. His chest hurt where Mai's staff hit him square in the center, and his lungs burned with lack of air. He wondered if his windpipe was actually broken.

Mai's face appeared right above him, and Kyth felt a hand at his throat. He tried to fight back, but he had no breath left.

"Lie still," Mai said through clenched teeth.

Before Kyth could react, the Majat's fingers hit his neck in a precise blow. Pain shot through Kyth's body. He gasped and coughed as the flow of air poured into his lungs, sweet like nothing he had ever tasted before.

Mai put a hand behind his back and helped him sit up. Kyth had no strength left to fight. He leaned heavily on Mai's arm, struggling to stay upright.

"Now," Mai said. "For your own good, stay out of this."

Kyth clenched his teeth. He didn't care about himself anymore, and he certainly wasn't going to listen to whatever this man told him. But he was too weak to move. Fighting the feeling of helplessness, he watched Mai get to his feet and walk over to where Kara's body lay sprawled on the grass a few paces away. The other Majat – the archer – was already kneeling over her.

Phrases of their conversation floated in through the mist in Kyth's ears.

"Is she dead?" Mai asked.

"Yes, Aghat. That blow… it was brilliant. You–"

Mai's glance stopped him. "Go find her armband, Gahang. You must return to the Guild as soon as possible to deliver the news."

The Jade sprung to his feet with dog-like obedience, but as he turned to go, he hesitated.

"What about her weapons, Aghat?"

"I'll take care of them. Go!"

The Jade turned and ran off in the direction of the camp.

When he was away, Mai leaned over Kara and quickly pressed several points at the base of her neck and in the center of her chest. Her head rolled sideways, and for the first time since the encounter Kyth saw her face. It was pale, her dark skin a lifeless gray. Her eyes were closed, her features hollow, devoid of the vivid glow that always made her so fascinating to watch. Kyth's eyes veiled with tears. He angrily blinked them away.

Mai got up to his feet and headed back to the Cha'ori camp. As he walked past Kyth, the Diamond turned and met his eyes.

"Stay with her," he said, without breaking stride.

Kyth found his strength, scrambled to his feet and

slowly approached Kara. He wasn't sure why Mai said this to him, and he didn't care. The man was a killer who fought without rules. Whatever he said couldn't possibly be important. And yet…

Kyth lowered himself on the ground next to Kara. She was still, eyes closed, face ghostly gray, almost transparent. He carefully reached over and touched her hand. It was cold.

Stay with her.

He carefully put his arms around her and lifted her up, resting her weight against him so that her head lay on his shoulder and she was curled in his lap like a sleeping child. From this angle it really seemed as if she was asleep, her long eyelashes a shadow against the cheeks, her full mouth set into a quiet expression that looked almost like a smile. It was so easy to imagine she was alive, curled in his arms just like the time they were together back on the boat. Except that now her body, relaxed against him, didn't emanate any warmth.

Carefully supporting her, Kyth used his other hand to spread his cloak around both of them, so that her body would be protected from the wind. Then, he put both arms around her, holding her like a mother cradles a child, gently rocking it to sleep.

Sleep, he thought. *She's asleep. And when she wakes up, everything will be fine.*

Around them the gusts of the Grassland wind ripped through the terrain. But Kyth didn't feel it. Inside his cloak, it was warm. It had to be. He had to keep Kara warm, so that she could finally have her rest.

He hid his face in her hair and closed his eyes.

32

MENACE

Ellah felt numb as she stood next to Dagmara. She couldn't take her eyes off Kyth's still shape, so small in the giant grass plain as he sat crouched on the ground, cradling Kara in his arms.

It didn't make sense. It couldn't be happening. Why would Mai and Sharrim do such a terrible thing to one of their own?

She woke from her trance as she realized that someone was standing in front of her. She raised her gaze and saw Sharrim. His freckled face folded into a smug expression. It didn't go well with his usual look of childlike wonder, but he probably didn't think it necessary to pretend when no one of importance to him was around.

"*Now* I know why Aghat Mai brought you along," the Jade said. "If it wasn't for you, we would never have gotten so close without raising an alarm. He's just so brilliant, isn't he?" He glanced at Mai walking toward them.

Ellah's hands balled into fists. Her eyes filled with tears and she angrily shook them away.

How could she have been such a fool? How could she have thought that Mai really liked her, that he had asked her along on the trip so that they could be together? He had been *using* her all along, and she had followed him, like a blind, trusting dog!

"Get lost!" she snapped.

The Jade chuckled. "It's all right. You're not the first one to be deceived by his looks."

Ellah's hand twitched, but before she could slap him Dagmara caught her by the wrist. Her expression made the Jade step back.

"You heard Ellah," the foreteller said. "Go."

Sharrim's eyes narrowed. He eyed Dagmara for a long moment. Then he turned and strode away in the direction of the Cha'ori camp. Ellah watched his retreating back, hatred boiling in her chest. *Why* would Mai and Sharrim turn against Kara? How could Mai, who had always avoided killing, go and do such a horrible thing?

"It wasn't your fault," Dagmara said quietly. "They would have done it anyway, with or without you."

Ellah clenched her teeth, but a treacherous tear escaped from the corner of her eye and rolled down her cheek.

"I made it bloody easy for them, didn't I?"

Dagmara shook her head. "There are things at play here bigger than you or me. Or them, for that matter. At times, we become no more than toys in the hands of destiny, and there's nothing we can do about that."

Ellah fell silent as Mai approached and stopped in front of her. He looked bad. His shirt, ripped from the collar down, exposed an oozing streak of red across his chest. Sweat and dirt caked his face, his hair matted with grass. Ellah had never seen him look so disheveled. Not that she cared anymore *what* he looked like.

"Stay away from me!" Her lips trembled. "Don't you dare." A lump rose in her throat and the tears she couldn't hold back any longer rolled down her cheeks. She wanted to run away, but Dagmara's hand held her in place. She struggled for a moment and gave up, looking at Mai through the veil of tears.

She hated him. And yet, she couldn't draw away from the look in his eyes, so bold and intense as if he was able to see through her. Against reason, she felt warmth inside her as she held his gaze, anger in her chest slowly subsiding to give way to new floods of tears. She stood in front of him and sobbed, like a little girl.

"How *could* you?" she whispered. "How could you do such a horrible thing?"

A shadow ran over his face.

"I had no choice," he said.

She clenched her teeth, fighting back the tears. "And what do you want from me *now*?"

His eyes flicked to a pouch at her belt. "Odara Sul gave you her elixir, didn't she?"

"What?" She stared. This was the last thing she expected him to say.

His gaze showed urgency. "Do you have it?"

"Yes," Ellah said slowly.

"Go and use it on Kara's wound. *Now*."

"What?" Ellah still couldn't believe her ears. "Why?"

He drew closer, his voice dropping to a near-whisper. "Because you wish you could make it all go away, don't you?"

Ellah continued to stare, but he had already turned to Dagmara.

"Gahang Sharrim needs to find something in Kara's things and take it back to the Majat Guild as soon as possible," he said. "It's very important that he leaves right away."

The foreteller nodded. "Go, help him," she said to the Cha'ori warriors lingering nearby.

Two young men peeled off from the group and followed Mai to the tents.

Dagmara turned to Ellah. "I think you'd better go and do what he said."

Ellah stared. She felt like she was having serious trouble catching on. "But Kara's dead. What good could it possibly do to treat her wound?"

"If she's dead, it certainly wouldn't do any harm, would it?"

Ellah threw a hesitant glance at Kyth's distant shape. It didn't seem that he was aware of his surroundings. He was so still among the wavering grass that he looked inanimate. It was painful to watch.

"I'll come with you," Dagmara said quietly.

Ellah nodded.

When they approached, Kyth showed no awareness of their presence. He sat still, his face buried in Kara's hair. They stopped a few paces away, waiting.

After a long moment, he raised his eyes. They were dry, their expression so empty that Ellah's heart wavered. In all the years she had known Kyth she had never seen him like that.

She swallowed a lump and threw a brief glance at Dagmara.

"Kyth…" she began.

His eyes narrowed, as if he had just recognized her. His lips twitched but he didn't speak.

"I have an elixir that comes from the Keepers," Ellah said. "For treating wounds. Very serious wounds. I… I want to use it on Kara."

"Why?" His voice was hollow, his face still like a mask. A frightening emptiness in his gaze.

Ellah hesitated. "I think it could help."

His lips twitched again. As he tried to control them, his whole face contorted into a grimace. "You already *helped*. You brought them here, didn't you?"

It took a moment for his words to sink in. It felt as if he had hit her in the stomach. Her eyes welled with tears. She clasped a hand over her mouth, fighting back a sob.

Dagmara stepped forward and kneeled in the grass by Kyth's side.

"Neither you nor Ellah could have changed what happened," she said. "It's useless to think of the past. And even more useless to blame those who bring help." She reached out to Kara's body, but he drew back, closing in his protective embrace.

"Stay away from her!"

Dagmara's hand dropped away. "I understand your grief. Believe me, I do. But however shattering it is, you can't let it stand in the way of her only chance."

His face contorted into a mask. His lips trembled. "Her *chance*?"

There was a pause.

"I don't know for certain," Dagmara said. "But if she's really dead, whatever we do to her can't bring any harm. And if, by a very small chance, she is still alive and we can save her, you'll never forgive yourself if you stand in our way. Would you?"

The silence seemed to last forever. Then Kyth drew back and opened his cloak to expose Kara's body resting against him.

She curled in his lap, with her head on his shoulder. She would have looked asleep if it wasn't for the ashen gray color of her skin and the gaping hole at the base of her neck. It was caked with blood, black against the dark skin.

Weakness rose in Ellah's stomach as she stepped forward and knelt on the grass next to Kyth. She wasn't good enough to do this. Yet, both Kyth and Dagmara watched her expectantly, as if she was a skilled healer summoned to the deathbed of a very sick patient.

She reached out and pulled the wet, sticky cloth of Kara's shirt away from the wound.

"We need water," she told Dagmara. "Lots of water. The wound must be very clean before we do anything."

Dagmara nodded and gestured to the Cha'ori standing in the distance. One of them approached her at a fast run.

"Bring us five skins of water," she said. "And some clean cloth. And, tell the man who did this to come here as soon as his companion's off."

Kyth's hand clenched into a fist. "No! Not *him*."

"He made this wound," Dagmara persuaded. "He's the only one who knows exactly where it goes and how deep it is. We can probably do this without him, but he can help us avoid a fatal mistake."

Kyth looked back at her, his face showing so much hatred that Ellah's heart ached. It was so unlike Kyth to be like that. She considered telling him that it was Mai who first suggested for her to treat the wound, but decided against it. Seeing the look on Kyth's face, she felt that this information might actually make Kyth go back on his decision to go along with the treatment.

The Cha'ori arrived at a run, bringing waterskins and enough cloth to wrap a horse. Ellah took out her dagger and cut away the blood-soaked folds of Kara's shirt, leaving the top of her chest bare. As she cleaned the skin around the wound, bloodied water streamed down, soaking Kyth's clothes, but he didn't seem to notice. His eyes focused on Kara, his face so still Ellah wasn't even sure he was aware of his surroundings.

Every time she glanced at him her eyes filled with tears. She had never seen so much grief. It was worse because he didn't cry, or seek any comfort from those around him. It was as if all this enormous grief was trapped inside him, tearing him apart.

Ellah wasn't sure how long he would be able to hold on. She forced the thought away, focusing on her task.

When the wound was clean and dry, she took out the small vial from the pouch at her belt and looked at it with hesitation. She still remembered how much pain it caused when Mai's wound was treated, and how incredible was the healing power of the substance. She doubted Kara would be able to feel the pain, even if by some miracle she was still alive, but she was deeply aware that a single mistake could ruin everything. She wished that she had asked Odara Sul more about how the substance worked, or that somebody more experienced was at her side. She raised her hesitant gaze to Dagmara. As she did, she caught a movement further away and saw Mai coming up to them.

Kyth raised his head when Mai approached, his eyes so hateful that the Majat stopped dead in his tracks.

"Stay away."

"I can help," Mai said.

"I won't let you touch her!"

Mai reached up and drew his weapon, sliding his hand along its length to draw the blades from its ends.

33

DEVIL'S SQUADRON

The Cha'ori closed in, shielding Dagmara with their bodies. But Mai didn't look like he was about to fight. He held the staff out, showing Ellah one of the blades.

It was covered with dry blood to about two thirds of the length.

"That's how deep it went in," he said, seemingly ignorant to the reaction he caused. "You'll have to make sure the substance reaches all the way to the bottom of the wound."

Ellah glanced at the dark vial in her hands. "But how?"

Mai looked at Kyth. "You'll have to convince your friend to let me approach."

Ellah nodded and turned her pleading gaze to Kyth.

"Please," she urged. "Let him help. I'm not sure I can do it on my own."

Kyth's cold gaze made her shiver. "Then," he said distinctly, "you and your *friend* can get out. I don't need your help."

Mai moved another step forward. "*You* don't," he said quietly. "But *she* does."

"*Not* from you."

299

Mai held Kyth's gaze. "You do want her to live, don't you?"

Kyth went so still that for a moment he appeared inanimate. Then he lowered his eyes.

Mai approached the rest of the way and knelt on the ground next to Ellah. He took out a narrow dagger and measured it against the blood-stained blade at the end of his staff. Then he stuck it, hilt-first, into the ground, so that it stood in front of him with the blade up. He unfastened a small flat flask from his belt and carefully spread some of its contents over the blade. Finally, he took out a flintstone and struck a spark. To Ellah's surprise the blade sprung into a blue flame. The Cha'ori, watching Mai's movements in an entranced silence, drew back in fright, but the Diamond sat still, keeping an eye on the flame as it burned for a minute or two and slowly died out. Then he turned back to Ellah.

"I didn't see what Odara Sul did to my face," he said. "But from the way it felt I believe she put the substance on the inside of the wound, right?"

Ellah nodded.

"We need to coat the blade of this dagger with the substance," Mai told her, "and put it in."

"In *where*?"

He met her gaze. "Just spread your substance over it, and give it to me."

Ellah carefully opened the vial. There was a small brush inside, the one she saw Odara Sul use on Mai's wound. It was attached to the lid, so that one could use it without touching the sticky liquid.

Mai took the dagger by the hilt and held it out to her. She leaned over and carefully spread the glistening paste along the entire blade. When it was done, she sat back and looked at the Diamond.

"Be careful it doesn't touch the hair," she said. "Or it will start moving, just like Odara's does."

He nodded, his gaze reflecting a brief wonder. Then he turned to Kyth. "We have to do it quickly. Lift her up and hold her very still. Her body must not move when I'm doing this, do you understand?"

Kyth carefully lifted Kara to a sitting position. Her head fell back against his shoulder, so that the gaping wound at the base of her neck came into full view. It looked awful. Seeing it, Ellah finally realized how futile their attempts to help were. *Why does Mai insist on this cruel charade?* she wondered. Yet, for Kyth's sake, she couldn't refuse to play along.

Mai knelt in front and slid his hand inside Kyth's embrace, giving additional support to the top of Kara's body. Then, in a smooth, deft movement, he thrust the dagger into the wound all the way to the hilt. There was a collective gasp from the spectators as he held the blade for a moment, then withdrew it and handed it back to Ellah. She took it, looking at the blood-stained steel. It didn't seem like a proper way to heal a serious wound. Fortunately, like Dagmara said, they were unlikely to do any harm.

Mai pressed his free hand against Kara's chest. The movement was smooth like a caress, but by the way her body shuddered under the pressure, Ellah could guess how much force he was applying. When his hand was all the way up at her throat, he moved it down again, holding a closed palm against her skin.

"We need more," he told Ellah over his shoulder.

She leaned over to him, the vial in hand.

"I'll hold her," he said, "and you put it into the wound."

She nodded and started unscrewing the cap. At that moment they all heard a chuckle.

Ellah raised her head and gasped.

A row of hooded figures stood shoulder to shoulder just a few paces away. Behind them loomed the riders, wearing similar robes but with the hoods thrown back. They looked just like the strange men that had attacked Kyth back in Tandar and had accompanied the mysterious Kaddim Tolos in Castle Illitand, except that this time there were a lot more of them.

The man in the center slowly removed his hood, revealing a sharp-featured face framed by short brown hair. His eyes were very dark and seemed to have no irises. They looked like the eyes of an owl.

"Nimos!" Kyth gasped.

"Long time, no see, my prince." He cast his eyes over Kara's lifeless body. It seemed to Ellah that she saw regret in the owl-like gaze. Then he raised his face back to Kyth, a triumphant smile creasing his thin lips. "We've all been waiting for this, Highness. Now that your pretty little friend is dead, there's nothing to stop us from developing our relationship further, is there?"

Kyth carefully eased Kara's body down to the grass. "Don't take another step." His hand darted to his sword.

Nimos smiled. "Don't be so melodramatic, Your Highness. I brought enough men to make sure we could match your fighting skills. They're considerable, I'm sure, but still—"

Mai stepped up to Kyth's side. He held his staff in a lowered hand, face calm as he surveyed the enemy rows. The Cha'ori warriors slowly gathered behind, their faces grim, curved sabers at the ready. More were hurrying downhill from the direction of the camp.

Nimos watched the activity, his face spreading into a wide smile. "Aghat Mai, if I'm not mistaken."

Mai kept his silence.

"Allow me to congratulate you on a successfully accomplished mission, Aghat," Nimos went on. "A brilliant blow, if I may say." He glanced at Kara's body again.

Mai raised the staff.

Nimos chuckled. "I'm glad you are trying to resist us, Aghat. I thought all our preparations were useless. For a moment there, it looked too easy."

Two men next to him removed their hoods. Their confident postures suggested they shared the same command privileges as Nimos. The one on the left looked familiar. *Reverend Haghos?* Ellah had no time to wonder.

She moved sideways, shielding Kara's body from the attackers. Who knew what could happen to someone near-dead if these men started using their powers?

The three men drew themselves up and spread out their palms. A collective force blast swept over the grass and hit everyone in sight. Ellah shuddered and covered her ears, sinking to the ground. The Cha'ori swayed and went down one by one. Through the mist in her eyes Ellah saw Mai raise his staff, but his movements were not nearly as fast or confident as usual. Half a dozen of the attackers fanned around him, spinning their orbens. He thrust against the nearest one, but his staff wavered, knocked by a sideways blow. A chain hooked around it and tore the weapon out of his hands. He staggered. An attacker in front released an orben straight at his chest. The blow connected with a thud, sending Mai backward to the ground.

As he landed, one of the riders in the back line lashed out with a whip, hooking it around Mai's ankles, and tugged, sending his horse into gallop. Mai tried to lift up, but one of the attack leaders stretched his arms, forcing the Majat down. His head hit a boulder. Blood gushed out of the cut at his temple and his body went limp, like a rag doll.

As his captor urged the horse along the plain, Mai's body bumped against another boulder on the way, bouncing off and folding away, as if devoid of bones. Then the rider who captured him disappeared behind a low hill, Mai's body dragging in his wake.

Tears rolled down Ellah's face. It was horrifying to see a Diamond of Mai's skill defeated so easily by just a handful of men. It was also clear that no one could possibly survive being dragged behind a galloping horse through the rough Grassland terrain. If Mai wasn't dead yet, he was unlikely to live much longer.

Nimos turned to Kyth and studied him with his dark, owl-like eyes.

"That was fun," he said. "And quite easy, as you may see. Now, would you like to surrender, Your Highness?"

"In your dreams!" Kyth lashed out with his sword, but Nimos leaned out of the way.

"Why don't you use your power, Prince Kythar?" he suggested.

Kyth rushed at him. Nimos evaded the blows with snake-like speed as he backed off, luring Kyth deeper into the enemy's line. The hooded men surrounded him. An orben hit his blade and Kyth swayed, twisting his weapon out of the lock. He dodged another blow and darted to the edge of the attackers' circle. The air around him filled with spinning orbens. One of them brushed Kyth's shoulder, throwing him off balance. Another one hit the back of his head. He shuddered, sword sliding out of his hand, and collapsed face-down onto the grass.

Ellah screamed and rushed to his aid, but a blast of force sent her down to her knees. As if in a nightmare she watched the hooded men bend over Kyth, deftly tying his ankles and wrists with wet straps of leather. They threw a cloak around him and wrapped it with a length of rope on the outside.

Lifting him like a sack, they flung him over the back of a spare horse and tied him to the saddle with a couple of quick knots.

Through her tears, Ellah could see another packhorse with a similar bundle flung over the saddle. Strands of dirt-stained blond hair were visible at one end. *Mai.* She hoped he was still alive, but after the way she saw them drag him over the ground it seemed hard to imagine.

The attackers mounted and rode off, their large group slowly subsiding into a cloud of dust in the distance.

Ellah painfully struggled to her feet. Dagmara crouched on the grass next to Kara's body, a thin streak of blood running down from her nostril. Ellah and the Cha'ori hastened to help her up.

Dagmara's smile was strained as she leaned heavily on Ellah's arm. "I'm too old for this. Their powers are indeed enormous. And it seems that Kyth is the only one capable of withstanding them."

Ellah nodded, looking into the distance. "Kara was immune to them too," she said in a hollow voice.

They looked down at Kara's body. It was still, and, to Ellah's relief, appeared undisturbed. When she leaned closer to inspect the wound, she realized that it had actually closed, and only a deep scar remained at the base of the neck where the gash had been just a short while ago.

"Are you sure this liquid only works on living flesh?" Dagmara asked.

Ellah hesitated. "No. I'm still not sure why Mai told me to do it."

"Asking him about it might prove difficult."

They stared at the distant cloud of dust. Elah felt empty inside. It was true that Mai had shamelessly played with her feelings to get his way, but she found herself intensely wishing she could see him again.

34

THE FOREST MOTHER

The road from the Cha'ori camp descended steeply down to the water. Alder threw his pack higher onto his shoulder and hurried to catch up with Garnald at the front of the line.

"How are we going to cross the river?" he asked. "The current's too strong to swim over. And the ferry's more than a day's travel upstream." He looked down to the water, words freezing on his lips.

A raft was waiting for them down by the shore. It was a flat platform composed of intertwined leathery branches of snakewood trees, the kind that to Alder's knowledge grew only very deep inside the Mire, in the heart of the Forestlands. As they approached, he could make out several trees, complete with roots and earth stuck in between, huddled together inside the woven leathery mass. Looking down at them, he had an uncomfortable feeling the trees were watching him. He forced the thought away as he followed Garnald on board.

As soon as the last man was on the raft, it pushed off the shore without any visible help. The river Elligar was wide in this place, and the current powerful, but the raft headed to the other shore in a straight line, toward a spot almost exactly opposite to where it had started. Alder tried to imagine what this strange contraption could possibly use to propel itself, but the thoughts were too uncomfortable to dwell on.

As soon as the raft touched the riverbank, the roots of the snakewoods dug into the earth. As Alder watched in stunned silence, they took hold with the comfortable look of something that had been growing there all along.

Unlike the steep slope of the left Elligar bank, the ground on this side of the river was low. Thick grass pasture stretched from the veil of the weeping willows lining the waterfront all the way to the main road, and the forest beyond. They made their way toward it, and in less than two hours entered the protective shade of tall white birches with thick hazel undergrowth.

A trail ran off the main road into the forest, wide enough for two men to walk side by side. As they stepped into the tree shade, Alder couldn't help noticing that the trail had no footprints on it. It seemed as if it had been made especially for their group, so that they could enter the forest in this particular spot, level with the raft's landing. Looking behind, Alder saw a dense wall of trees with no clearing in between. The trail was closing as soon as they passed.

He hurried ahead and fell into step with Garnald. For a while they walked in silence. Alder considered bringing up the subject of the trail, but eventually decided against it. He knew Ayalla the Forest Woman was capable of ordering trees to move, opening and closing paths at her will. It seemed quite logical to imagine she had the same power here, in the airy growth of hazel and birch, hundreds of miles to the north.

He threw another glance at Garnald walking by his side. He was dying to know more about why all the Mirewalkers were looking at him with such strange expressions, and why they thought it was so important for him to leave the Cha'ori camp and come out to meet Ayalla.

Garnald understood the unspoken question. "You're wondering, aren't you?"

Alder nodded. Now that he saw Garnald's eyes on him, he suddenly had a suspicion where this conversation was going. Back in the Forestland, Ayalla had once taken him for a mate, a privilege also extended to the Mirewalkers and some of the more adventurous villagers. She was a beautiful woman and she had made him very happy that day. But it didn't make him different from any of these men, did it? He held Garnald's gaze, feeling the color creep into his cheeks.

Garnald smiled.

"She's never been the same since the time she was with you," he said. "She's more... sane, if you will. And the trees in the Mire – they're becoming different now. Tall and straight, with airy crowns that reach far into the sky. We all think they're yours."

Alder's blush deepened. He had heard Garnald say such things before, but it just didn't fit into his head. "Forest Mother" was a name woodsfolk had called her in their fireside tales, nothing more. No living woman could possibly give birth to trees. Especially not after being with a normal man. And yet...

"I know exactly how you feel," the Mirewalker said. "When it first happened to me, I was like that too. These things just blew my mind. And, in a way, even the fact that you get to be with the most beautiful woman in existence doesn't make the rest of it any easier to accept."

Alder didn't respond. It *did* blow his mind, even to consider the possibility that Garnald was right. He hadn't stopped thinking about Ayalla since the brief time he had spent with her, but he never thought she'd want to see him again. She was not only beautiful beyond reason, but also powerful and ancient, more so than Alder could ever comprehend. She could have any man she wanted.

"When you think of it," Garnald went on, "you must always remember one thing. One doesn't choose to become a Mirewalker. The Mire chooses you, and all you can do is follow its call. Don't resist it, boy."

A Mirewalker? The question froze on Alder's lips as the path in front of them suddenly opened into a glade surrounded by tall birches. Thick grass covering its floor looked as if no foot had ever walked upon it.

In the middle of the glade stood a tall, slender woman. She had a perfect oval face and deep indigo eyes. Alder shivered as he met her gaze.

Seeing Ayalla in the flesh made his memories of her beauty seem pale by comparison. She was perfect down to a single touch. Her face, as if carved out of a precious gem; her soft skin, whiter than birch bark and smoother than the silky grass under her feet; her body, slim and tall like a young pine singing to the sky.

When she saw him, her full lips folded into a smile. She beckoned.

"Welcome, Alder." Her soft, deep voice reached down to his very soul.

Her skin had a faint smell of honeyed ivy buds and river water. As he approached, it made his head swim. He reached over to take her hand and drew back as he caught the movement on the bodice of her dark velvety dress that traced all the curves of her tall, slender figure down to her feet.

In horror, Alder realized that this dress was not made of any cloth he had ever seen. It was made of live spiders that clung to her, covering every inch of her skin. Each was large and hairy, creating the soft velvety look of the garment woven of their creeping mass. As Alder watched in fascination, one of the spiders moved over, opening a glimpse of her bare skin underneath. Then its place was taken by another, closing in the gap.

The Guardians.

Alder edged back. He couldn't stand spiders, even ordinary ones. But these, almost as big as a man's hand, were not only horrifying to look at, but also deadly. To imagine anyone walking around wrapped in *spiders*…

She laughed. "Don't worry, sweet one. The Guardians won't harm you. You are at one with the forest." She lowered herself down to the grass, the spiders hurrying to spread around her legs like the hem of a real dress. Then she signaled for the Mirewalkers to join her. They settled around her, forming a circle in the center of the secluded glade.

"Before I come out to meet with the grass people," Ayalla said, "you must tell me what you learned when you were out there."

"The Wanderers are disturbed by the dark order," Garnald said. "The trouble we had – that's nothing compared to what they did in the Grasslands. They attack the Cha'ori horts and take their horses. They bend people to their will. They kill. They're a threat to everyone. The Cha'ori say they come from an outpost in the south, at the outskirts of the Bengaw Crest."

Ayalla looked past him into the forest. "Why should we be concerned about them? My children can protect themselves. Those that came through the Hedge will never do it again." She looked around the group, a chill in the depths of her indigo eyes. Alder shivered. He could only guess what had become of the intruders that crossed the Hedge. The forest was a peaceful place, but it had ways to protect itself.

He realized everyone was looking at him.

"Tell me, Alder," Ayalla said in her deep, melodious voice. "You have been to the north, all the way across the lakes. What goes on there?"

Alder cleared his throat. "What do you want to know?"

Ayalla smiled. "Tell me about your foster brother. Son of a king, is he?"

Alder nodded, unsure of what answers she was looking for.

"His gift is so strong it echoes all the way through the realm," Ayalla said. "It shouldn't be possible, but I saw this with my own eyes. Did his father pierce him with a sword?"

Alder swallowed. The royal succession ceremony, where a father had to run a sword through his son, was difficult to forget. "Yes."

Ayalla nodded, her eyes aglow with a strange light. "Then, it's time for a change. It's time for your priests to reconsider their ways."

"I think," Alder said, hoping that it was the right thing to say, "that's exactly why the King sent Kyth and me here. He wants to ally with the Cha'ori and change the Ghaz Shalan law."

"A noble cause. Is your foster brother the one who is going to bring this about?"

Alder thought about it. He hoped it was going to happen this way, but too many things were going wrong. He couldn't stop thinking of Nimos and his men who had followed them all the way from Tandar. He suddenly had an urge to go back right now, to make sure Kyth was all right.

Ayalla watched him with an intent gaze that seemed to penetrate his thoughts.

"Your foster brother is in trouble," she said quietly.

How could she possibly know? Alder's heart raced. Somehow, he didn't doubt Ayalla knew what she was talking about.

"I summoned you here," she went on, "because I couldn't allow you to share his fate. You weren't meant for it."

"Meant for what?"

She rose to her feet in a quick, powerful move. The spiders crawled around, quickly rearranging themselves back into a long narrow dress but, for a brief moment, Alder could see her bare leg, slender and tall, all the way up to the hip.

"You're anxious to go back, aren't you?" she asked.

Alder nodded.

"Then, let's go. It's safe now." She led the way in the direction they had just come from.

Safe? Is he safe now? Alder wanted to scream, but the words froze on his lips under Garnald's heavy gaze. He picked up his pack and followed.

The path opened in front of Ayalla with a rustle, trees moving aside with nearly visible speed. It looked as if a gust of wind blew into the airy mass of birch crowns, pushing them to a standstill a small distance away from their original spot. It was dizzying to watch but Alder was too preoccupied.

Something horrible had happened in the Cha'ori camp. Ayalla had known about it and summoned him here so that he could avoid that fate. But Kyth…

Alder's hands balled into fists. He wasn't going to let anyone mess with his foster brother. Whatever danger Kyth was in, Alder was going to do everything in his power to save him.

35
NEWCOMERS

"We should move Kara to my tent," Dagmara said. "At least there we can keep her warm. She'll need that, if she's really alive."

Ellah nodded, too tired to talk. She reached over and touched Kara's hand. It was cold. As far as she could tell, there was no pulse and her chest wasn't moving. She saw no chance that Kara was still alive. No one could possibly survive such a blow.

At Dagmara's signal Cha'ori warriors came over and carefully picked up Kara's body to carry it back to the camp. Dagmara followed, and Ellah fell into stride by her side.

When they were halfway there, Ellah saw movement on the other side of the camp. A group of riders milled behind the main tent, with more Cha'ori hurrying toward them. From this distance she couldn't tell what it was all about, but she saw glints of drawn weapons and heard voices raised in heated argument.

"Take Kara to my tent," Dagmara said to her escort. "I'll go look what's going on." She peeled off from the procession at a fast walk. Ellah hurried to catch up.

When they approached, the fight was about to start. In the center were two newcomers, the apparent focus of the turmoil. Ellah recognized them at once. Magister Egey Bashi's scarred face flared with anger, his whip-like weapon ready in his lowered hand. Raishan looked calm, but the tense set of his muscular body showed that he was about to charge.

Dagmara's raised hand froze the action as she strode through the parting crowd toward the newcomers. Ellah did her best to stay close behind.

"Who are you, and what do you want?" Dagmara demanded.

"Who wants to know?" Egey Bashi asked, his voice on edge.

Dagmara's hand wavered, ready to signal the attack.

Ellah took a breath. "Wait! I know these men!"

All heads turned to her.

"They're friends," Ellah said. "This is Magister Egey Bashi from the Order of Keepers."

"*Your* friends, you mean? Just like the other ones?" The young Cha'ori who spoke was one of the archers that had escorted Ellah, Mai and Sharrim into the camp. Only yesterday, but it seemed like an eternity ago.

"Are you also going to say they bring no danger, just like the men that came with you?" another voice shouted from further away.

"Maybe she's at one with them?"

The crowd rippled, voices rising in anger. But Dagmara's hand stopped them.

"Go on," she told Ellah.

Ellah met Egey Bashi's gaze.

"Magister Egey Bashi risked his life for Kyth's sake," she said. "And Raishan used to be Kyth's bodyguard. Last time I saw them, a few weeks ago, they were traveling with Kyth and Kara. I don't know why they're here, but they deserve to be heard, Dagmara."

"Dagmara?" Egey Bashi's dark eyes lit up with a deep glow.

The foreteller gave him a calm look. "You've heard about me?"

"Yes. You're the one they call Cha'ori Overseer."

Her eyes narrowed. "Very few know of that. How did you come upon such knowledge, Keeper?"

"I have my ways."

They looked at each other in tense silence. Then Egey Bashi broke the contact and turned to Ellah.

"What danger are they talking about? Where are Kyth and Alder?"

Ellah shivered as she kept her eyes on him. "Kyth's been captured."

Egey Bashi's gaze wavered, his eyes reflecting both shock and acknowledgment at the same time. He didn't look surprised. "Then Kara's dead?"

Ellah lowered her head, aware of the sudden silence around her.

"Who was the one that came after her?" Raishan asked.

Ellah looked at him, trying to control her trembling lips. "Mai."

"I thought so." Raishan exchanged a glance with Egey Bashi.

"Can you ask your men to stand down so that we can talk?" Egey Bashi asked Dagmara.

She hesitated, then raised her hand and held it up in the air with an open palm. Weapons lowered everywhere in sight.

"You must surrender your horses," she said.

Egey Bashi nodded. At Dagmara's signal, their horses were taken away. The Cha'ori crowd dissipated, leaving a few warriors that formed a semicircle, showing firm intention to follow the newcomers everywhere they went.

Dagmara led the way to the center of the camp. Ellah and Egey Bashi followed side by side, with Raishan close on their heels. As soon as they started moving, Egey Bashi turned to Ellah, his scarred face holding concern.

"Tell me what happened."

Ellah tried to recall the horrible events of the past few hours. She wasn't sure where to start.

"These men – they appeared out of nowhere, only a short time after Kara was down. They blasted everyone in sight with some horrible power. Kyth was immune to it, but he couldn't fight all of them. Mai tried to stand up to them, but they–" she swallowed, forcing herself to go on. "They hurt him really bad. And then, they took both of them away."

"Both Kyth and Alder?"

Ellah gave him a blank stare. It took her a moment to realize what he meant.

"Both Kyth and Mai," she said.

A gleam lit up in Egey Bashi's gaze. "What happened to Alder?"

She shrugged, unsure of why he was so insistent on changing the subject after the horrible things she had told him. "Alder wasn't here. I think he went across the river to meet with the Forest Mother."

Egey Bashi nodded. "At least we have one less person to worry about now. And, if Mai was captured with Kyth, they would have more hope of escaping, wouldn't they?"

Ellah continued to stare. How could he not understand? "I *told* you. When they captured Mai they hurt him really bad. I'm not sure he's still alive." She paused, struggling to continue. She was certain he couldn't possibly be alive, but there was no way she was going to say it. She couldn't. She couldn't even *think* that way. Ellah lowered her head, unable to hold back her tears anymore.

The Keeper reached over and patted her shoulder. His hand was so rough she could feel the callouses through the cloth of her sleeve, and so warm it burned against the chill of the Grassland wind. His touch was also soothing. After a few moments her tears subsided. She sniffled and raised her face to him.

"We'll go after them," the Keeper said quietly.

She nodded. She wished his words could comfort her, but after seeing Mai dragged over the rocks behind a galloping horse, she couldn't find any room for hope. She was too old to believe in miracles. Yet, she didn't want to voice the thought. She forced a smile, brushing the tears off her cheeks with the back of her hand.

Dagmara stopped, halting the procession. With a start, Ellah realized that they had reached the center of the camp and were standing in front of the Foreteller's tent.

"What did you want to talk about, Keeper?" the Cha'ori woman asked.

"I came here to try to prevent what happened," Egey Bashi said gravely. "I can see I am too late."

A dry smile passed through Dagmara's lips. "The men who attacked us have a power that's unheard of. They knocked down everyone in sight. The only one who could resist them was Prince Kythar, but his skill was not sufficient to defeat so many men. If you were here, Keeper, you would have suffered the same fate. And if by some chance you could resist their power, I doubt you could have defeated them either. There were lots of them. Each was an incredible fighter and they wielded weapons we haven't seen before."

Egey Bashi nodded. "Orbens. They're quite exotic, and they do require a lot of skill. You are most likely right, Dagmara, that if I was here I would have suffered the same fate. But your gift must have also told you how important it is to rescue Kyth from these men. They threaten our entire existence, and his gift is the only hope we have of ever defeating them. Even though I know I would probably fail, I have to try to save him."

She lowered her gaze. "I know how important he is. But I don't see what any of us can do. I can't send my men to certain death. The Cha'ori will not help you, Keeper."

He studied her face. "A pity. But if this is your decision, Dagmara, then I must go on alone."

Dagmara's eyes flicked to Raishan. "You have a warrior with you, whose skill is evident in his every move. He will probably be useless against those men, but he should provide more protection than my people ever could."

Egey Bashi shook his head. "Aghat Raishan is bound by a word to his Guild not to interfere with Kyth's fate. However much it pains me, I'll have to leave him behind."

"Actually," Raishan said, "this is not exactly true, Magister. These men have also captured a member of my Guild. I can't help you with Kyth, but it's definitely my duty to do everything in my power to rescue Aghat Mai."

Egey Bashi grinned. "I'll be damned. Why didn't I think of that, Aghat?"

"You're quite inexperienced with the Majat Code, Magister, aren't you?"

"Apparently so. But now that you made it clear to me, Aghat, we must go without delay."

A shadow ran over Raishan's his face. "Before we go, I would like to see Kara." He looked at Dagmara. The Cha'ori woman nodded. She turned and led the way into the tent.

In the semidarkness, Kara's skin looked even paler than before. Her body, laid out on a cloak, was relaxed, but she no longer seemed asleep. Maybe it was the pose, with her face up and her hands folded over her chest, that made her look dead. Or the way two Cha'ori warriors sat beside her in solemn stillness, keeping vigil. Ellah's eyes filled with tears at the sight. She didn't bother to blink them away.

Raishan slowly approached and lowered to the ground at Kara's side. He folded away the cloak that covered her, looking at the bloodstained shirt, whose front had been cut off to expose the chest, and the forearm where the arrow had gone through, leaving a ragged wound that nobody had bothered to treat. He moved his gaze down her body and back to Ellah and Dagmara, standing on the other side.

"Where did he hit her?" the Majat asked quietly.

Ellah cleared her throat. "On the base of the neck over there. It was very bad. But Odara Sul gave me a healing elixir, and Mai told me to use it on Kara, so the wound – it's not there anymore."

There was a stillness of an indrawn breath in the quiet air of the tent as Raishan and Egey Bashi slowly raised their faces and stared at her. Then the two men spoke at once.

"He did *what*?"

"She did *what*?"

Their intensity forced Ellah to step back.

"*Odara Sul*, gave me an elixir, and *Mai* told me to use it on Kara's wound," she explained carefully.

The two men exchanged a glance.

"Do you know at what angle the blade went in?" Raishan asked.

Ellah hesitated. The question was strange, but there was so much urgency in his gaze that she got caught in it. She tried to remember the way Mai had put in the dagger coated with the healing substance.

"Straight down. Like this." She moved her hand, imitating the direction.

"Are you sure?"

"Yes."

Raishan bent over Kara. His hands moved so quickly that they blurred as he ran his fingers along her neck, pressing against hidden points that made her body shudder. After a moment the Majat raised his face to Dagmara.

"You must keep her very warm. Wrap her up in blankets. Start a fire. Have somebody stay with her all the time. It's very important."

Dagmara looked at him for a moment. Then she nodded and rushed out of the tent to give orders. Raishan turned to Ellah, who was staring at him in an entranced silence.

"You can save her life," he said. "If you keep her warm."

"Save her life? But–"

Raishan's gaze became impatient. "Do you think Aghat Mai would have asked you to treat a dead body with a precious healing elixir? How stupid is that?"

Ellah blinked. Stupid wasn't the word that had originally come to her mind. But with all the recent events she just didn't have time to give it serious thought.

"Do what you can for her," Raishan went on. "Treat that wound on her forearm, too. And be sure someone's with her, day and night. If she gets worse, here's what you should do."

He moved two fingers along Kara's neck, pressing symmetric points in the center of the chest and another two, just above the collarbones. Then he rose and touched similar spots on Ellah's neck. His fingers were hard like steel. For a moment she was scared he'd choke her. She drew back, grasping her throat.

"Just quick pressure," he told her. "Don't hold it any longer than this."

"But– How would I know if Kara gets worse?"

Raishan shrugged. "Use your judgment."

Ellah glanced around helplessly.

"If Odara Sul gave you this elixir," Egey Bashi said, "she must have thought you have great potential as a healer. She doesn't just give it to anyone, believe me. And if you're as good as she thought, you'll have no trouble with this."

He turned and walked out of the tent. Raishan followed, just as Dagmara came in with two women carrying a heap of blankets and a pan filled with hot coals. In a very short time the air in the tent became so warm that Ellah felt overdressed.

She took off her cloak and sat on the floor looking at Kara. There was no color at all in her ghostly pale cheeks. Her face looked hollow and still. And yet, now that Raishan said there was hope, Ellah started to realize something. Kara's body wasn't getting stiff. She was cold, but she still seemed warmer than the outside air. And now, in the glow of the hot coals, her skin started to warm up. Ellah wrapped the blankets tighter around her.

She suddenly remembered what Mai said to her, just a short while ago. *'You wish it could all go away.'* She realized how much she wished it right now – that none of this had ever happened, that Kara was alive, that Kyth and Mai were here so that they could all laugh about their fears and enjoy a moment of peace. But wishing was useless. Wishing never did any good.

She prayed Egey Bashi and Raishan would succeed in their task. And yet, after what they had done to Mai, she was very sure it was impossible. What could anyone do against men who could easily disable a Diamond Majat?

How could she ever hope to see any of them alive?

36
THE THREE KADDIM

When Kyth opened his eyes, he had trouble understanding where he was. His head pounded, dark mist swimming in front of his eyes. The base of his neck felt as if it was about to disconnect from the skull. To make things worse, someone was shaking him, so that his head rhythmically bounced against something not hard enough to break the bones, but definitely harder than comfortable.

He tried to move, but after an effort realized that all he could move was his fingers, and even those moved with difficulty, as if not entirely under his control. He couldn't feel his feet at all.

Kyth concentrated, trying to recall what had happened. He vaguely remembered being hit on the head with a hard metal object. That must be where the pain at the base of his neck was coming from. After a moment's concentration, he realized his shoulder and chest were also aching, suggesting that there must have been more blows he had withstood before ending up in his present position. But how did it all happen?

He strained his ears to catch any sounds that could give him a clue to his whereabouts. The rhythmic pounding that coincided with the frequent bangs to his head sounded like the hooves of galloping horses.

Horses. Was he with the Cha'ori?

But if so, why was he traveling in such an uncomfortable way?

He concentrated, forcing bits of memory back into his aching head. They had found Dagmara and her hort and traveled with them for one day. They had spent a night in a Cha'ori camp. Then he saw Ellah riding downhill. But what happened next?

He strained his mind to remember more, but just as he seemed to be getting a grip on it, he heard voices and the horse he was traveling on came to a jarring stop. After a while hands took him off the saddle and lowered him to the ground with a certain degree of care. He felt the pressure ease around the middle of his body as someone must have untied some of the ropes holding him. The cloth wrapped around him fell away. Light hit his face.

"This one's conscious," a voice said above him.

"Tie him to a tree," another voice responded from a distance.

Kyth lay on his back, staring into the deep greenery of the tree crowns overhead. Judging by the light it was early evening, right around sunset. The wavering leaves overhead allowed glimpses of the sky, suggesting that this place wasn't a real forest. More likely, they were stopping to set camp in one of the small groves lining the riverbanks at the edge of...

The Grassland plains.

And then, suddenly, he remembered everything.

Kara.

Memories hit him with such strength that he shut his eyes, unable to face it. His chest felt so empty he wanted to wail. He clenched his teeth, shutting it away.

Hands lifted him to a sitting position. After a moment he forced himself to open his eyes. The pain in his chest slowly unfolded, taking over his body so that it felt empty and numb. He didn't care where he was and what his captors were going to do to him. He didn't care if he lived or died. He *couldn't* face his life anymore.

A man appeared in front of him and he recognized Nimos. He remembered that just a short while ago, during his capture, he still cared. He even attacked this man with a sword. Now, he couldn't care less. Whatever this man's intentions toward him, it didn't matter anymore.

"Change his bonds to the regular rope," Nimos ordered. "Or he'll lose his hands and feet really soon."

Kyth was curious enough to try to move his fingers and realized that by now he couldn't feel them at all. The wet leather they had used as a bond when they captured him must have dried during the day, becoming so tight that it had cut off the circulation. For all he knew, his hands and feet were dead already. But he didn't care.

Men leaned over him, cutting his bonds and putting new, looser ones in their place. Then they tied him to a tree, coiling a rope around his waist. He winced as the pounding in his temples resumed, echoing with the hollowness in his chest.

Kyth's captors untied another bundle, revealing a limp shape of a man. His clothes were so torn and dusty and his face so matted with blood and dirt that Kyth had trouble making out his features. The captive lay very still while the robed men bustled around him, changing leather bonds to regular rope, just like they had for Kyth. Nimos stood over them, watching.

"Are you sure he's alive?" he asked.

"Gortos was a bit rough on him," one of the men admitted. "But how were we to know he'd be so fragile? He seemed unbeatable without your power, Kaddim."

Kaddim. So, Nimos had this title just like Tolos. The attacks on Kyth by these two men were obviously connected, but now Kyth didn't care anymore. Back in the castle, Kara had defeated these men easily. And now...

He looked at the still shape on the ground, suddenly realizing who it was. Mai.

Kyth's hatred boiled anew as he looked at the Diamond. Not only had Mai killed Kara and almost killed him, he had also made a mockery of trying to heal her afterwards. The hope he'd stirred up made the pain of the disappointment even worse when it became clear that the pretended healing, done undoubtedly to win the Cha'ori's trust, hadn't worked. Whatever their captors had in mind for Mai, he deserved it ten times over. If, of course, he was still alive.

Kyth rolled his head to the side and watched one of the men bring a bucket of river water and splash it into Mai's face. The Majat stirred, a barely perceptible twitch that didn't say anything about whether or not he was conscious.

Nimos nodded. "Good. He's alive. Tie him up to a tree over there. And, make sure his hands are where we can see them. There's no way of telling what he's capable of."

The men lifted Mai to a sitting position, hanging his tied wrists by a rope flung over a thick branch overhead. Mai looked badly hurt. His face, underneath the mask of blood and dirt, was deadly pale. Blood oozed from a cut at his temple and a black bruise covered his eye and cheek. His shirt hung in rags and a nasty orben wound gaped in the center of his chest. His head lolled when the men leaned him against the tree.

Nimos stood for another moment surveying his prisoners. The other two leaders joined him.

"Do you think the Prince needs to be watched, Kaddim Nimos?" one of them asked.

Nimos's pale face folded into a smirk. "He's too weak to do anything, Kaddim Haghos. Ropes should hold him just fine."

Kaddim Haghos. The former Reverend of the Church, a Kaddim. In some other life Kyth might have cared. He watched the familiar face with disinterest.

The Kaddim Brothers headed to where the others had already started a fire. They sat in a triangle, so that at least one of the three could always keep the prisoners in the line of sight.

Sometime during the evening a man with a closely shaved head, square jaw and bulging muscles, brought Kyth a cup of water and a small bowl of watery grain stew. Kyth didn't care one way or the other, so he ate it, just so that the man would leave. After he was done, the man brought another share for Mai. He had to hold the Majat's head up to pour water into his mouth. A lot of it escaped, running down Mai's neck in a small bloodied stream. The Diamond didn't take any food.

Kyth spent the night dozing against the tree trunk. He couldn't fall asleep, because every time his head dipped forward a sharp pain in his neck woke him up. He was almost grateful for that, because the only thing he could see when he closed his eyes was Kara, her body falling back, arms out, blood gushing out of the fresh wound at the base of her neck. In the end he couldn't take it anymore. He kept his eyes open, so dry that they hurt, and sat through the rest of the night staring into the wavering shadows, trying his best not to think of anything at all.

In the morning another man brought him breakfast, which seemed to be leftovers from the previous night. Kyth ate it, keeping his eyes on Mai. Two men were bustling around him with Nimos watching.

It must have been bad, because they actually cleaned and treated Mai's wound, dressing it with a crude bandage across his chest. Then one man held his head up while the other fed him the watery meal. Kyth could see that the swelling on Mai's face had subsided a little. His eyes were closed, but after watching intently it seemed to Kyth that he saw a glint from underneath a lowered eyelid. Kyth narrowed his eyes to see better, but it was gone. He wasn't sure why he was paying so much attention to the murderer who didn't deserve to live after what he'd done. It must be boredom, he decided. He couldn't care less what happened to Mai. He just had nothing better to do.

They spent another day wrapped in cloaks and flung across the saddles, but the horses traveled mostly at a walk, making the bouncing a bit more bearable. The pain in Kyth's head subsided and the swelling in the places where Mai had hit him with the staff reduced to simple bruises, painful to the touch but no longer making him feel as if his chest and shoulder were about to explode. By the evening, when Kyth was once again tied in a sitting position against a tree, he felt almost refreshed. He watched them take Mai off the saddle and unwrap the cloak around him with all three Kaddim Brothers in attendance. It wasn't clear whether these men were more afraid of Mai dying, or being well enough to fight.

This time they camped in a deeper forest. By Kyth's calculation they were getting closer to the Forestland Hedge, and the growth of willows and birches became more and more familiar. Here and there, they could see an oak, or even a patch of crawling tentacle bushes, shy and uncertain so far away from the protective shade of the Forestland thickets.

The tree they tied Mai up to was close to Kyth's. A thick branch protruded from it at the height of about eight feet, several heads taller than an average man. They flung the rope holding Mai's tied wrists over it, stretching it tighter than before and securing it around the trunk of the neighboring tree. They tied his ankles with another rope, and left to attend to their camp duties.

Kyth couldn't tell if the Majat was conscious, but his face looked much better than the previous night. There was no more swelling, and apart from the black bruise over the left eye and cheekbone, he no longer looked deformed. His eyes were closed, but once again Kyth had a distinct feeling that Mai was alert.

After a while the robed men brought them food and drink. They fed Kyth his usual fare and gathered around Mai. Nimos stood at the side, watching.

"How is he?"

"He's recovering well, Kaddim Nimos," one of the men said with satisfaction.

Nimos peered into the Majat's face. "Is he well enough to fight if we let him loose?"

The spokesman hesitated. "Probably. He's still bleeding here and there, and his chest wound doesn't look too good, but I don't think there's any permanent damage."

"Cut off his arms," Nimos said.

"What?" The men backed off, expressions ranging from hesitation to shock.

Nimos shrugged. "If he recovers any more, we won't be able to keep him captive unless a Kaddim Brother is watching him day and night. Yet, if we beat him again, we aren't sure he'd survive. But if we mutilate him, he'll still be alive, but he won't be able to fight, will he?"

The men nodded. Some still looked shocked, others relaxed into smiles.

Nimos glanced at the tallest and strongest man in the group. "Go, bring a cleaver. And call in Kaddims Haghos and Farros. I'll stay here and make sure he doesn't attempt anything foolish."

He planted himself in front of Mai, surveying him with cold satisfaction. Pulsing force emanated from his still figure. He wasn't using full power, but from where he sat Kyth could see Mai's face go pale. The Diamond was definitely alert and knew exactly what was going to happen to him. He could probably defend himself if Nimos wasn't using the power to suppress his strength. Kyth was sure that, given a chance, Mai would do anything possible to save himself, but Nimos's power robbed him of this chance.

Kyth's mind raced. This didn't seem fair. *No one* deserved to end up like this, not even the worst villain in the world. He would never be able to forgive Mai for what he had done, but he couldn't just sit here and watch this incredible fighter get mutilated like an animal, tied and helpless, without a chance to stand up for himself. Not even animals deserved to be treated like this. He had to do something.

Could he help Mai resist these men?

He was sure that back in the castle he helped Kara gain resistance by sending his emotions to her. Could he do it again? He thought of his recent nightmare, where he was able to protect people from the Kaddim by wielding an invisible spearhead. He wasn't sure it would work in real life, but he had to try.

The night was calm and quiet. A slow breeze crept through the terrain, making the tree crowns above their heads rustle as if having a whispered conversation. Kyth opened up his senses and let the breeze in, gathering its combined power over a great distance of the Grassland plains beyond. He focused the force in the calm center of his body, shaping it into a spearhead that cut through the descending power like a sharp blade cuts through a soft smothering blanket. He directed his spearhead toward Mai. With his inner vision he could actually *see* Nimos's power, a cocoon enfolding Mai like a fly trapped in a web.

He was vaguely aware of more shapes coming over. Haghos and Farros stopped by Nimos's sides, the three Kaddim Brothers combining their powers to enfold Mai. Another one, a huge man whose rolled-up sleeves exposed hairy muscular arms, held a butcher's cleaver large enough to decapitate a horse.

"Do it," Nimos said. "Chop off his arms at the shoulders. We want to make sure he'll never be able to hold a weapon again."

Kyth was out of time.

37
BREAKOUT

The man with the cleaver took aim and raised his weapon. Kyth concentrated. Praying that Mai's injuries were not too grave and he was still able to fight, he sent over his spearhead, cutting through the cocoon around the Majat. It struck like lightning, ragged bits of the invisible blanket falling away like dust.

"Mai!" Kyth shouted at the top of his lungs. "Defend yourself!"

Mai's eyes flashed, his body coming to life with the speed that made time around him momentarily stand still. Grasping the rope that hooked his hands to the tree branch, he pulled himself up, swinging his tied feet straight at the man with the cleaver. The blow caught the man on the chin and he fell backwards, blood splattering out of his mouth.

Without interrupting the movement, Mai pulled up his feet, so that for a very brief moment he was hanging in a crouched position upside down. A streak of steel slid out of the boot into his hand. Then Mai gave the rope a sharp tug, sending his body up onto the branch above his head. He landed on his feet, throwing off the cut pieces of rope, and looked down on his attackers. His posture was easy and balanced. His ankles and wrists were no longer bound. He held a long narrow dagger.

Several orben-bearers rushed forward, aiming their weapons at Mai's feet, within easy reach on the low branch. Mai danced between them, so fast that his shape was hard to trace against the dark tree crown. When one of the orbens shot up higher, he leapt with his feet forward in a move that was surely going to knock him off his perch. His attackers on the ground leered, waiting for him to fall, but at the last moment he put out his hands, landing on the branch in a sitting position. His feet closed on the orben chain, catching the spiked metal sphere at the base. He gave it a sharp tug. The orben holder swayed and let go. Mai reached out and caught the flying chain with a free hand, then pushed off and dropped down to the ground. He had an orben in his right hand and a dagger in his left. Kyth couldn't see his face, but he could clearly see the faces of his attackers, who edged back from him with expressions ranging from surprise to fear.

The three Kaddim brothers stepped forward, eyes shining with anger, hands outstretched. Kyth could sense how much force they were sending at the Majat, but now that he had the hang of it, he had no trouble cutting through with his invisible spearhead, keeping Mai clear of the pressure.

When the Kaddim realized their power wasn't working, they lowered their hands.

"You think you can fight us all?" Nimos asked Mai.

Mai flicked his wrist, sending his orben into a spin. He kept a short leeway, not letting the chain out too far, so that its major length was wrapped around his forearm.

"I don't have to," he said. "You can just let me go."

"Attack!" Nimos commanded.

Mai's hand moved faster. He swept the orben, his unfolding body briefly blending into a streak of black. A man at the end of the line collapsed. The rest of the attackers backed off.

The Majat moved like the wind. The orben in his hand spun so fast it wasn't visible anymore. The entire group of their captors fanned around him, their faces determined as they lashed out with forceful orben blows. Mai was picking them off like flies, dodging the orbens with a speed and precision that made everyone around him seem clumsy and slow.

As he spun around, Kyth could finally see his face. His heart wavered. Mai didn't look well at all. He was deadly pale, a streak of blood running down his face. The bandage on his chest was soaked through. It was clear that, despite his incredible skill, he would not last much longer.

"Get him!" Nimos urged. "He's badly hurt!"

The men hesitated, throwing glances at each other and at the fallen comrades at their feet. No one seemed to be willing to make the first move.

Nimos threw off his cloak and strode forward, drawing two curved sabers out of the sheath at his back. His confident, graceful posture reminded Kyth that none of them had ever had a chance to appraise his sword skill. His heart sank as he looked at Mai's pale, bloodstained face. *Is he well enough to face this?*

The two opponents stood still for a moment, looking at each other with charged intensity.

"Let's see how badly we hurt you," Nimos said.

Mai smiled, his eyes lighting up with a devilish gleam.

"I don't normally feel this way," he said, "but I think I'm going to enjoy this."

He flicked his orben at one of the blades in Nimos's hands. The Kaddim darted to the side, avoiding the blow, but the metal orb moved in a sneaky spin, coiling around the blade very close to the hilt. Mai gave it a sharp tug, but Nimos held on. For a moment, they stood opposite each other, tugging at the chain. Then Mai threw the dagger, aiming for the hand holding the blade. Nimos let go, sweeping his hand out of the way. Mai tugged the chain and caught the saber with his free hand.

He kept the orben in his right hand, using it as a shield as he launched a left-handed attack with the saber. He was perhaps moving slower than usual, so that spectators could fully appreciate the quality of his movements, so smooth and precise that they seemed like a dance. Nimos parried each of the blows, but from the start of the melee he never had a chance to launch an attack, forced to stay firmly on the defense. His face was composed, but Kyth sensed concern behind the calm mask. He was clearly having trouble fencing with one saber against a highly skilled left-handed opponent. The fight wasn't going the way he anticipated.

As Mai thrust his blade forward, his orben hand unfolded, sending the metal sphere straight at Nimos's chest. It came so fast that even Kyth, having a good side view, had trouble catching on. The Kaddim saw the orb too late. He tried to jump out of the way, but the metal spikes caught him on the shoulder. He dropped the saber. The tip of Mai's blade touched his throat.

Kaddim Farros rushed toward them, stretching his hands to launch a terrible blast of power at the Majat, but Kyth held his invisible spear at the ready, cutting the power away like soft butter with a hot knife. Haghos stood back, hesitant to join the fight.

Nimos's eyes showed panic. He glanced around and fixed his gaze on Kyth.

"Get the boy!" he shouted. "He's the one doing this!"

The Kaddim Brothers regrouped toward the new target, but Mai was faster. He dove forward and rolled over the ground, coming up to his feet beside Kyth. With a quick move he cut through the ropes, then turned, shielding Kyth against the advancing Kaddim. Kyth shook off the ropes and jumped to his feet.

"We have to get out of here," Mai said. "Can you do this thing you're doing and run at the same time?"

"I think so."

Mai flicked the orben at one of the attackers, sending him rolling on the ground. The Kaddim Brothers backed off, avoiding the sweep of the spiked metal ball.

"Get to the horses," Mai ordered.

They turned and ran. Barked orders, cursing, and cracking echoed behind. Kyth kept all the distractions at the back of his mind, concentrating on holding his invisible spear above Mai's head.

As they emerged from the protective shade of the trees, they saw horses gathered in the field. Each horse was tied to a short pole, with sufficient rope to wander around the pasture.

"We'll have to ride bareback," Mai said. "No time to saddle up."

Kyth nodded. He could hear the rapidly approaching sounds of pursuit behind them.

"Get those two." Mai pointed. "Ride out and wait for me. *Now!*"

Kyth rushed toward the chestnut and the bay at the edge of the field. As he unfastened the ropes, he saw Mai glide in between the horses, moving very fast, in what looked like some sort of dance. The saber glittered in the moonlight, a streak of light in the Majat's hands.

Kyth mounted just as the first of their pursuers emerged from the deep tree shade. A dark shape flew by, and Mai jumped onto the horse next to Kyth.

"Move!" Mai threw his face up and produced a long, shrill whistle between his teeth, answered by an erupting stampede behind. Amidst the whinnying, shouting and cursing, they threw their horses into gallop. Kyth kept his invisible spear at the ready, but no one behind them was trying to use any power. A quick glance back told him that the pursuers had other things on their hands. The chaos of horses running off in all directions and men trying to catch them left no room for any other action.

"What happened?" Kyth shouted to Mai above the wind.

"The Cha'ori battle signal. I ordered the horses to retreat."

"How do you know–" Kyth stopped himself. It didn't matter, as long as they were away. He sensed a wisp of power sent in their wake and focused to counter it. Then he glanced at Mai.

The Majat looked very pale. It clearly took effort for him to stay on horseback. In the glistening moonlight, Kyth thought he saw a streak of blood running out of the corner of his mouth. Mai caught Kyth's gaze and wiped it off with the back of his hand.

They rode on through the night, first at a gallop then at a fast trot, until the sky in the east became gray, foreshadowing the arrival of a new day. Every once in a while Kyth threw glances behind them, but there was no pursuit.

After a while Mai slowed his horse to a walk and Kyth followed. As he looked at the Majat in the dawning light, he realized with horror that Mai was barely holding on, and that the reason his horse had slowed to a walk was because it was getting no more signals from its rider. As he watched, Mai swayed, his head dipped forward and he slid off the horse onto the ground.

Kyth dismounted and ran toward him. The Majat lay very still, his body turned in an unnatural way. Kyth carefully took him by the shoulder and rolled him onto his back.

Mai's eyelids trembled and slowly opened. He seemed to have trouble focusing.

"Ride on," he whispered, his words barely audible above the rustling breeze. "Leave me."

Kyth glanced around. They were alone in the middle of nowhere. The only company they could expect in the near future was that of their pursuers. They *had to* move on.

"Are you badly hurt?" he asked. The question seemed redundant, but he just wasn't sure what to do. It was so frightening to see Mai in such a state that Kyth couldn't even hate him anymore. Against reason, his heart quivered with worry as he looked searchingly into the Majat's face.

Mai turned his head with visible effort. "I'm… fine. Just need a little rest, that's all." He closed his eyes and went still.

Fighting rising panic, Kyth reached to the Majat's neck to feel the pulse. It was there, but very weak and irregular. A streak of blood appeared from the corner of his mouth, dark against the ghostly white skin. Kyth didn't know much about healing, but he knew enough to understand that such insistent bleeding without an obvious wound couldn't be good. Mai was bleeding inside, and that meant trouble.

It was clear that the Majat wouldn't be able to ride further on his own. Yet, leaving him here as suggested would mean certain death. Kyth had no doubt their captors would eventually recover their lost mounts. The ride through the night had given Kyth and Mai a few hours' head start, but their pursuers couldn't be far behind.

True, only a short while ago the only thing Kyth wanted was to see Mai dead. He tried to tell himself it was still what he wanted, but seeing the Majat so helpless was too much.

He wanted to defeat Mai in a fight, to make him suffer for everything he did. But to let him die like this, wounded and helpless, after saving Kyth from his captors, was wrong.

He carefully leaned down and put his arms around Mai's torso, trying not to touch the chest wound oozing though its crude bandage. He lifted the unconscious body and slowly rose to his feet, supporting Mai's weight against him.

The Majat was surprisingly light. He was about the same height as Kyth and his entire body was sculpted of muscle, toned even in his unconscious state. It took Kyth much less effort than he imagined to walk Mai back to his horse that was fortunately standing still, calmly watching the action.

Kyth crouched and hooked his arm around Mai's knees, lifting him up onto the horse. Then he mounted, careful not to disturb the body. Firmly settled, he pulled Mai higher up, easing him into a sitting position in front and using one hand to hold him around the waist. It was awkward, but after a moment Kyth was able to find the right balance. He urged the horse on at a walk, focusing on keeping Mai upright and cushioning the movement so that the ride wouldn't cause any more damage.

The second horse followed. Kyth had no free hand to lead it by the rope, but the horse seemed intent on keeping up on its own. They rode on, the sun slowly rising from behind the Eastern Mountain Crest, lighting up the wavering grass with the pinks and blues of the early dawn.

A movement off to the left drew Kyth's eye. Two riders had emerged from the line of bushes by the river and directed their horses toward him at a gallop.

Kyth's mind raced. He had no means to defend himself. He didn't even have time to lower Mai off the horse so that he could free his hands. And, he couldn't afford to let go. In Mai's fragile state, a fall like that might well kill him.

His eyes darted around, searching for possible help.

The riders were approaching fast. From this distance he started to make out their features. They looked familiar. He narrowed his eyes, heart pounding in his chest. Could it be?

The rider in front was middle-aged, with a huge, ugly scar crossing his face. Behind him rode a lean, graceful man whose quality of movement left no doubt he was an unmatched fighter.

Egey Bashi and Raishan!

Kyth pulled his horse to a stop, feeling the deadly strain in his exhausted body give way to an overwhelming wave of relief.

38

VIPER'S KISS

Kyth sat on horseback, waiting for his rescuers to approach.

"Thank Shal Addim!" Egey Bashi exclaimed, pulling his horse to a stop.

Raishan dismounted and rushed up to Kyth's horse, eyes fixed on Mai's lifeless shape.

"He broke us out," Kyth said. "But he's very badly hurt. I think he's bleeding inside."

Raishan's hand shot up to Mai's neck to feel the pulse. His eyes locked with the Keeper's.

"I believe I have something that might help," Egey Bashi said, "but it'll take some time. Why don't we get back to our camp?"

Raishan looked back across the Grassland plain. "They might be followed, Magister. If we camp and they catch up with us, I'm not sure I can deal with the Kaddim any better than last time."

"If we don't treat these injuries right away, Aghat Mai will die. It may be too late already, but if you want him to have a chance, there's no other alternative."

Raishan's frown deepened as he appeared to consider the options.

"We'll have to stop anyway," Egey Bashi pointed out. "If not now then later on. We can't ride on forever. And from what we've seen so far, an entire Cha'ori hort is just as useless against these men as you and I, Aghat."

"I think," Kyth said slowly, "I can protect at least one of you from their power. If I do this, do you think you can handle them, Raishan?"

"How many are there?" the Majat asked. "Back in the Cha'ori camp I heard different numbers, from fifty to several hundred."

"It was about three dozen or so to start with. During our escape Mai took down at least ten, maybe more. He also scared away their horses."

Raishan nodded. "Should be manageable. If you're sure you can really do what you say."

"That's how we broke out," Kyth said. "Mai did all the fighting, I just kept their power off him."

Raishan nodded. His face was grave as he carefully lifted Mai off Kyth's horse into his own saddle. He rode at a walk, forcing Kyth and Egey Bashi to slow down as they made way to the line of bushes by the river.

The cozy campsite was surrounded by bushes on three sides and open to the river on the fourth. The dying embers emanated warmth, a kettle and two empty bowls scattered around as if abandoned in a hurry. Matted grass marked the places where Raishan and Egey Bashi must have slept, only a short time before spotting Kyth and Mai down on the plains. The sight made Kyth's tired muscles ache with desire to lie down and rest. He suppressed it. He had to be awake if the pursuit came. Raishan needed him if they hoped to fend off an attack.

Raishan spread his cloak and lay Mai on top of it. After a short survey he took off his belt knife and cut away the remaining strips of the ragged shirt. Then he removed the bandage from Mai's chest, exposing the ugly wound that looked even worse than Kyth remembered on their first day of captivity. Its leaden color suggested that it was beginning to become infected.

Raishan shook his head as he peeled away the last pieces of pus-soaked cloth. "These men really spared no effort on him, did they?"

Egey Bashi crouched on the ground next to Raishan, taking a small vial from a pouch at his belt.

"The internal bleeding is what's going to kill him first, unless we do something about it," he said. "This liquid should help, but he needs to drink it. I can't just pour it down his throat while he's unconscious."

Raishan nodded. He took out a small flask and forced several drops of the substance between Mai's lips.

After a long moment Mai coughed and opened his eyes. He looked at the faces bent over him, recognition slowly stirring in his gaze. A streak of blood appeared in the corner of his mouth.

"Aghat Raishan," he whispered, his lips twitching into a ghostly smile. "How the hell–"

"We'll discuss that later, Aghat. First, Magister Egey Bashi wants you to drink something."

"It's going to hurt," the Keeper warned.

Raishan frowned. "From what I know about injuries this looks bad. He's had a nasty blow to the head and this wound on his chest is about to poison his blood. Are you sure he can take this treatment of yours?"

"It's rough, Aghat, I know. But I see no other choice." Egey Bashi leaned over Mai, holding the vial in his hand.

"You're bleeding inside," he told Mai. "This liquid can stop it, but it's going to hurt. Bad. You must drink it in one gulp."

Mai met his gaze. He looked very weak, but his eyes still gleamed with mischief.

"Another one of the Keepers' cures, is it?" He moved to raise up on his elbow, but Raishan held him down.

"Don't," he warned. "Or you'll make it worse."

Mai lay back and allowed Raishan to lift up his head. But when Egey Bashi put the vial to his lips, he reached out and took it with a weak hand.

"I'll do it myself, thanks." He lifted the vial and drank it.

He was still for a moment. Then his body twitched and he collapsed into Raishan's arms, shaking with seizures. His head fell back. Muscles bulged on his neck, blood running down the side of his face as he thrashed against Raishan's hold. His eyes rolled, so that only the whites showed through. Kyth could tell it was costing Raishan a lot of strength to hold Mai down.

After a while the shaking stopped and Mai went still.

Raishan removed his hands. "Now what?"

"Now," Egey Bashi said, "we must wait. In a few hours we'll know if it worked."

"*If* it worked, Magister?"

Egey Bashi met his gaze. "Yes. *If.*"

"I *thought* you told me it *was* going to work."

"I *thought* I told you it might help, Aghat."

The two men glared at each other. Then Raishan strode over to his horse, took out a blanket and spread it over Mai. Egey Bashi busied himself with starting the fire.

Kyth sat on the ground, looking at Mai's face. It was pale and hollow. The bruise on his face blackened against the white skin. The bleeding had stopped, which meant that either the Keeper's substance was working, or Mai was very close to death.

Raishan brought over a kettle of water and carefully cleaned Mai's chest wound. He used some liquid from another flask at his belt that made the infected flesh flake off in thin white streaks, and spread some gray powder over it that bubbled as it touched the oozing pulp. Mai didn't seem to feel it, so deeply unconscious it wasn't even clear if he was breathing.

With deft movements, Raishan dressed the wound with fresh bandages and used another piece of wet cloth and more of his liquid to clean up the cuts on Mai's face and the gash at his left temple, where his head must have hit a boulder during his violent capture. He spread a different type of powder over those. It was white and soaked right in, stopping the bleeding. His movements were confident and precise, as if he had done such things many times before. His face was calm, but when he finally covered Mai with the blanket and turned back to his companions, Kyth noticed a vertical line across Raishan's forehead.

"Now," he said to Kyth. "Let's look at your wounds."

Kyth hesitated. "I think I have mostly bruises. They weren't as rough on me as they were on him."

"I'll be the judge of that." The edge in Raishan's voice left no room for argument.

Kyth winced as Raishan helped him out of his shirt. For the first time since his fight with Mai two days ago he had a chance to look at his own body to survey the damage. A large bruise blackened in the center of his chest where the point of Mai's staff hit him. Another one colored his left shoulder and the side of his torso into deep blue and purple shades. Raishan frowned over those, and spent another length of time inspecting the base of his throat where Mai's staff had almost choked him to death. Then he moved around and pulled up Kyth's hair to examine the wound at the back of his head, where an orben blow had hit him to unconsciousness. Kyth felt a wet cloth on his neck, and then another liquid, light and cool, that stung as it touched the injured skin.

Raishan finished and sat back, looking at him thoughtfully.

"That blow to the back of your head's healing well. Your hair must've cushioned it when the orben hit. But these other bruises – they don't look like orben blows. How did you get them?"

Kyth's mouth twitched as he glanced at Mai's still shape. Memories came back with renewed clarity, making him feel so empty inside that it hurt.

"I… I fought Mai before we got captured. He knocked me down with his staff."

Raishan's eyes narrowed into slits. "You did *what*?"

Kyth held his gaze in silence.

"You aren't joking, are you?"

"No."

"*Of course* he knocked you down. What were you thinking, fighting a Diamond?"

Kyth clenched his teeth, forcing himself to keep Raishan's gaze. "I wasn't thinking anything. I wanted to kill him."

"To kill him."

"Yes."

"Of all the stupid things…" Raishan paused, studying Kyth intently. "I guess it doesn't matter now, since you're obviously still alive. Just tell me one thing. If you wanted him dead so much that you risked your life for it, you could've just left him back there in the Grasslands to die, couldn't you?"

"I could have," Kyth admitted.

"Yet, you carried him on your horse and risked being caught by your pursuers. So?" Raishan waited, his eyes fixed on Kyth's face.

"It just… it seemed wrong for him to die like that," Kyth said. "Not when I could do something about it. We can settle the score later, when he's well."

"Settle the *score*?"

"Yes."

Raishan leaned closer. "Before you set out to do a foolish thing like that, perhaps there's something you should know about him first. He's a legend in our Guild. To my knowledge, there's no living man who could settle any kind of *score* with him in an equal fight. I'm sure he wouldn't fight you again, but if he did, he'd squash you like a fly."

"In that case," Kyth said slowly, "I'd die knowing that I tried. There's no other choice."

Raishan continued to study his face. "You attacked him because of Kara, didn't you?"

Kyth's mouth twitched. A lump in his throat warned him against trying to speak. He glared at Raishan from across the fire.

"Then, you don't know?"

"Know what?" Kyth's voice came out hoarse. "He and his accomplice *murdered* her. What else is there to know?"

Raishan let out a sigh. "Mai saved her life. He risked everything to make sure she survived. If our Guildmaster ever finds out what he did–"

"*Survived*?" Kyth's breath faltered. He stared at Raishan in entranced silence.

"That blow he struck her with – it's called 'viper's kiss'. It looks deadly, but when treated in time the wound can heal without a trace. It touches no vital organs, but disconnects the reflexes, so that the breathing and the heartbeat become very slow, almost undetectable. Do you know how much skill it takes to deliver such a blow against an equal opponent?"

Kyth continued to stare. "But his companion, the archer, checked that she was dead."

Raishan nodded. "And afterwards, did Mai come and do something to her?"

Kyth thought about it. He remembered how, after the Jade was gone, Mai leaned over Kara and hit her in several spots at the chest and neck. He slowly raised his gaze and looked into Raishan's face.

"If you had delayed him any longer," the Diamond said, "you could have ruined everything. No wonder he hit you so hard. If I was in his place, I might've done worse."

Kyth looked down at the black bruises covering his body. He remembered the empty look in Mai's eyes, the speed of his movements, the strength of the blows that seemed way too much for a man to be capable of. He shivered. To think that he could have ruined everything.

"But why did he have to do this in the first place? Why not just let her go?"

"Because, if his companion – the Jade – had suspected that Mai hadn't done his job to the end, it wouldn't have helped Kara. The Guild would have sent Diamonds after both of them. They wouldn't have given up until the job was done. The Majat Guild doesn't tolerate disobedience. And, they never give up. They only thing Mai could do was to make the Guild believe she was really dead."

"But…" Kyth was still trying to make sense of it. "Kara said if they defeated her, they were going to take her back to her Guild. She told me they weren't going to harm her."

Raishan looked at him with pity. "If she had told you the truth, would you have been able to stand back as long as you did and not interfere?"

"No," Kyth said quietly.

Raishan nodded. "If you tried to defend her, you would've

been killed. Mai had his orders, and Kara knew them well. She wanted to make sure you didn't die needlessly, that's all."

Kyth suddenly felt very weak. "Is she really alive?" he whispered.

Raishan held his gaze. "She needs care. But with proper treatment, she'll survive. It would be good, though, if we manage to get Mai there in one piece before it's too late. He struck the blow. I did what I could for her, but he's the only one who can revive her."

Kyth sat back. Tears he had not been able to shed before filled his eyes. He wasn't able to say anything. He just sat there, looking at Mai's face, so pale and still in the flickering firelight.

He had been hating this man with all his heart. He had wished him dead. If he'd only known what Mai had done.

"Will he be all right?" he asked in a trembling voice.

Raishan followed his gaze, the vertical line back on his forehead. "We'll see. Even if the Keepers' cure is as good as the Magister makes us believe, we still have his wound to deal with. It doesn't look good, I can tell you. What did these men do to him?"

"During our capture, they hit him with an orben, and dragged him behind a galloping horse. I think he almost died. And then, last night, he had to fight all of them to break us out. I'm sure it made things worse."

Raishan looked at Kyth in grim silence. Then he turned to help Egey Bashi with the fire.

As the water in the kettle started boiling, they heard the sound of galloping hooves, approaching them across the plain. Raishan carefully set down the pouch with tea leaves and drew his sword.

"You're on, Kyth," he said.

Kyth raised his head and saw Nimos ride toward them across the field, with a dozen men in his wake.

39

BLACK DEATH

Nimos's gaze narrowed as he saw Raishan and Egey Bashi. "*You.*"

"How did you two escape?" Haghos demanded, pulling up by Nimos's side.

Egey Bashi smiled. "I guess you'll never find out."

"You just don't give up, do you?" the ex-reverend's voice rang with anger.

"No."

"And you, Aghat," Haghos turned to Raishan. "I thought you'd had enough. I guess we should have killed you after all."

Raishan remained still, but his sword arm tensed.

Kyth took care to stay behind and remain as inconspicuous as he could. He was tired and weak, but he pushed the weakness away and focused on the wind. He opened up and let it in, enjoying the sense of lightness it gave to his body, the strength it filled him with. The feeling came easier this time. Kyth balanced it, shaping it into a focus of power that hung in front of him like an invisible spearhead.

Nimos's eyes flashed toward Mai's still shape, stretched on the ground on the other side of the fire. His dark gaze lit up with triumph. "He was one of your best, wasn't he?"

"He still is," Raishan said calmly.

"Perhaps," Nimos agreed. "But not for long. I've seen his injuries, Aghat. There's no need to bluff. He is dying because he couldn't stand up to us. One minor blow would kill him, and I don't think even the Keepers' cures could save his life. Do you want to end up the same?"

Raishan measured him with a quick glance, then looked further at the men behind him. Kyth couldn't help noticing that the row of hooded figures looked sparse compared to the impressive force that had attacked and captured them two days ago. Raishan was clearly of the same opinion.

"Are these all of your men still able to stay in the saddle?" he asked.

"These are all the horses we could catch at short notice," Nimos replied, "but more are coming. Rest assured, Aghat Raishan, we are well prepared."

"I doubt it."

Nimos drew himself up, but his posture looked just a touch less confident than before.

"By the way," he said. "I distinctly remember that your Guildmaster gave us his word, backed by a considerable sum of gold, that no Majat would interfere with our mission to capture Prince Kythar. Aren't you violating your orders by standing up to us?"

"This has nothing to do with Prince Kythar," Raishan said. "I am protecting a Guild member."

Nimos smiled. "No problem then. You give us Prince Kythar, and we won't touch your Guild member, how about that? With the condition he's in, I doubt he'd be of any value to us anyway."

Raishan shook his head. "As it happens, I wouldn't be able to stand up to you without Prince Kythar's help. So, I'm afraid I can't oblige."

"Are you sure you can stand up to us *with* his help?"

Raishan shrugged. "I see only one way to find out."

Nimos turned back to his men. "Get the boy!" he ordered.

The riders raised their bows, aiming them at Kyth. The three Kaddim Brothers in front stretched their hands, sending a blast of power toward Raishan.

Kyth tried to ignore the approaching arrows, a dark cloud closing in too fast to focus on. Balancing his invisible spear over Raishan's head, he met the blast of Kaddim power head-on. The spearhead cut through it, peeling the sticky folds away from the Majat.

Raishan's sword swept across, cutting the arrows in mid air. His free hand darted to the belt and came up with a pack of throwing knives. He released them one by one, a continuous streak of steel flying off his palm. Through the waves of the force Kyth could see men swaying in their saddles, grasping at wounded arms, or doubling over with more serious injuries, as Raishan's knives reached their targets. In one sweep, the line of the combat-effective attackers was reduced by half. The few that remained looked hesitant.

Nimos uttered a short curse and released the pressure, looking at his disabled bowmen. Before he could say a command, Raishan leapt forward. The tip of his sword skimmed along the line of horses with a long, smooth movement. His hand darted to his belt again and came up with a short whip. He lashed it at Haghos. The Kaddim's horse reared, and the other two shied sideways, scrambling to get out of the way.

Nimos was the fastest to react, jumping down before his gear slid off, dangling with the cut saddle straps. Farros followed, steadying himself against the horse's side. But Haghos wasn't able to recover the fall. He went straight down onto his back with the saddle and gear landing on top. The uninjured men at the back rushed to his aid.

Nimos and Farros drew curved sabers from the sheaths at their backs and fanned out, advancing on Raishan. They were moving at a slight crouch, fast and graceful like the best swordsmen Kyth had ever seen. He prayed that the combined skill of the two of them together wasn't a match for a Diamond.

The Majat's face showed nothing but calm concentration. Fending off Nimos on one side, he lashed out his whip in Farros's direction. The force of it flattened the front of Farros's robe before the tip came through and hit him on the cheek. The Kaddim gasped, clasping a hand to his face.

Orbens swept at Raishan from all sides as the other attackers recovered. He slid between the weapons, crowding on Farros who was clearly having trouble keeping up. Raishan seemed so intent on finishing the job that for a moment it looked as if he had forgotten all about the attackers at his back. Nimos saw the opportunity at once. He leapt forward, launching a powerful thrust.

Just as the blade was about to hit, Raishan stepped out of the way with dizzying speed. The blade continued on without resistance, and hit Farros in the chest.

There was a collective gasp as the wounded Kaddim stumbled backward, clasping hands to his chest. Nimos's eyes flared with anger. But Raishan didn't slow down. His blade snaked around Nimos's sabers, coming through at an impossible speed. There was a screech and both blades flew out of Nimos's hands. The man edged back, Raishan's sword point touching his throat.

In the ensuing silence, weapons lowered everywhere in sight. The men watched the scene in horror.

"We give up," Nimos said.

"Kill him, Aghat Raishan!" Egey Bashi shouted. "This is no time for chivalry."

Raishan hesitated. Nimos used that moment to move toward his unsaddled horse. He mounted it in a frantic leap and steadied himself with visible difficulty. His men followed the unspoken signal, helping their injured comrades onto the horses.

"You don't understand, Magister, do you?" Nimos said. "You can't kill a servant of Ghaz Kadan. We'll come back more powerful than you ever imagine."

He turned his horse and threw it into a gallop. The others followed. Soon their shapes turned into a cloud of dust on the horizon.

Raishan lowered his sword, watching. Then he turned back to the camp. The Majat's breath was uneven, suggesting that the fight wasn't as easy as it had looked. Kyth relaxed, laying down the invisible spearhead, letting the power out of his body to be replaced by weakness. Raishan met his eyes with a nod of acknowledgment.

"Why didn't you kill him, Aghat?" Egey Bashi demanded. "You had a chance and you–"

"He was unarmed," Raishan said, a touch more forcefully than necessary. "And he surrendered."

"This man's scheming has almost killed the two best Diamonds of your Guild, Aghat! One is now an outcast, and either of them might still die."

Raishan paused.

"He did something to you, didn't he?" Egey Bashi said. "He used some other power, something Prince Kythar missed, to stay your hand."

Raishan shrugged. "I'm not sure. You have to understand, Magister. We must avoid killing at all cost, unless it's a part of an assignment."

"But–"

"That said," Raishan went on, "I did feel strange for a moment. When he said he surrendered, I–"

Egey Bashi studied him intently. "Some of the Kaddim were rumored to have a rarer power, one that clouded people's judgment so subtly it was hard to detect. It is rumored that this power – an extremely difficult one to wield – is nearly impossible to resist." He glanced at Kyth.

"Perhaps," Raishan said. "But if so, it was very subtle indeed. It just made sense to spare his life. In any case, it doesn't matter now, they're gone. And I don't think we should expect them back any time soon. Not while Kyth's with us." He bent down to collect his throwing knives.

"I believe," Egey Bashi said, "we were about to have some tea."

He threw a handful of leaves into the boiling kettle and poured out three mugs, handing them around. Kyth sipped the tart, heady liquid that rolled through his body with pleasant warmth. He felt so weak even sitting straight was an effort, but he forced himself to stay upright, chewing on the dry meat ration that Raishan took out of his bag. This one didn't have any unusual herbs in it, bringing no relief for his fatigue, only heaviness to his tired limbs.

Kyth was about to lie down when Mai stirred and opened his eyes. He struggled to rise on his elbow and moved his gaze around the group, his eyes aglow with a feverish gleam.

"What did I miss?" he asked. He spoke slowly, as if he was about to fall asleep.

Raishan turned to face him. The vertical line was back on his forehead.

"Some of your friends came by, Aghat. But they're gone now. I don't think they'll be bothering us for a while."

Mai nodded, his expression making Kyth doubt he was really aware of his surroundings. Raishan put a hand on his forehead. He paused for a second, the line between his eyebrows becoming deeper. Then he turned to Egey Bashi.

"It's starting," he said quietly.

He carefully folded away the blanket covering Mai. The bandage on his chest had soaked through. Redness was spreading around the wound, lashing out along the skin in thin, narrow tongues.

"Lie back, Aghat," Raishan said. "Let me take a look at your wound."

Mai obeyed. His eyes had an absent expression. It wasn't clear if he was aware of what was going on. Egey Bashi moved over and sat on the other side, watching Raishan peel off the bandage to expose the injured flesh. Its deadly leaden color was back. As far as Kyth could tell, it wasn't healing at all.

"Do the Keepers have any remedy for *that*?" Raishan asked.

The Magister hesitated. "One. But you're not going to like it." He reached into his medicine pouch, took out a small flat vial and handed it to Raishan. The Majat took it and unscrewed the lid, carefully smelling the contents. Then he closed it and stared at the Keeper with a shocked expression.

"*Black Death?* Are you out of your mind, Magister?"

"I'm afraid we don't have much choice, Aghat."

Raishan shook his head. "This poison's not only deadly, but there's no antidote to it. If you want to kill him, why not just stab him through the heart to spare him the agony?"

Egey Bashi smiled. "What you say is true, Aghat, but there's one thing about this poison, not commonly known. Taken in small doses, it counters the effects of severe infections. It's rough, but given Aghat Mai's injuries, I'd say we have nothing to lose. He'll die for certain if we don't do anything. But if we get the dose right, he might survive."

"*Might*?"

"It's the best I can offer, Aghat. Believe me, I understand how precious his life is to your Guild. This is exactly why I think we should try."

"It's not about his worth to the Guild. He's one of the best fighters in existence. We can't afford to gamble with his life!"

Mai woke up from his daze and pushed Raishan's hands away, struggling to sit upright. Raishan moved to stop him, but Egey Bashi held him back. He reached over and handed Mai a mug of tea.

The Majat took it and drank. Then he lowered it and looked at the Keeper. He seemed unsure of where he was.

"How are you feeling, Aghat?" Egey Bashi asked.

Mai appeared to consider it. "Hot. I think."

"Your wound is infected," the Keeper told him. "It's poisoning your blood. You know what this means, don't you, Aghat?"

Mai looked down to his chest. His hollow cheeks burned with feverish color.

"I bet even the Keepers have no cure for this one." He sounded almost sane as he said it, but in a moment his gaze became absent again. He looked around for the blanket and pulled it over himself, shivering.

"You bet wrong," Egey Bashi told him. "We do."

He showed Mai a small vial. The Majat looked at it absently. He clearly had difficulty concentrating.

"My cure," Egey Bashi said, "is Black Death."

Mai seemed to have lost track of the conversation. He stared at the vial in the Keeper's hand, then looked away toward the fire.

"It will make you sick for a while," Egey Bashi went on. "You may not survive. But as far as I know it's your best chance. What do you say, Aghat?"

Mai smiled. His eyes gleamed, and for a moment he looked alert, almost normal. "I feel lucky. Why not?" He wrapped the blanket tighter around himself and lay back.

Raishan gave the Keeper a dark look. "He's delirious. I don't think he really understood you."

Egey Bashi shrugged. "You can't make this decision for him, Aghat Raishan. And neither can I. Like you said, none of us has the right to gamble with his life. His word is all we have to go on. Chances are low either way, but at least if we follow his wish, we'd be doing *something*."

Raishan hesitated, but Kyth could tell he was giving in.

Egey Bashi poured new tea into the mug, filling it halfway, and opened his vial. He added one very small drop and mixed it carefully into the liquid. Then he leaned over Mai.

"Can you understand me, Aghat?" he asked.

Mai's eyes searched around and fixed on his face. "What do you want?"

The Keeper held the mug out to him. "You must drink this all the way to the bottom."

Mai struggled and pulled himself up, but the effort was clearly costing him a lot of strength. Raishan hurried to support him. Kyth watched, mesmerized. It was frightening to see Mai in such a state. In a way it was more frightening than seeing him unconscious.

Mai took the mug and stared into it. Then he sniffed it.

"Drink it," Egey Bashi prompted.

Mai met his gaze. "Is it going to hurt?"

"Not right away."

Mai nodded. "Come to think of it, it really doesn't matter." He raised the mug to his lips and drank. As he did, Raishan moved to interfere, but stopped halfway and sat back, watching. The vertical line was back on his forehead, so clear it threatened to become permanent.

Mai drank up and lay back on the cloak, staring into the sky. Egey Bashi carefully took the mug from his hand and looked back at Raishan.

"You can treat his wound now," he said. "He will be calm for a while, but afterwards he'll become delirious. We'll have to keep watch over him."

"How long?"

"His fever should break by dawn. After that, we'll know if it has worked. Either way, tomorrow morning we should start back to the Cha'ori camp. There's nothing more we can do."

Raishan didn't respond. He turned and busied himself with the wound. Mai looked awake, but he lay still, showing no reaction to what was being done to him. His breath became shallow and even from where he sat Kyth could feel the heat emanating from his body.

Raishan dressed the wound with a fresh bandage and examined the other cuts that still needed attention. Kyth was amazed to see that the bruise on Mai's face was almost gone, leaving no more than a shadow under the eye. The other cuts had healed, except for the deeper one at the left temple that was still visible but no longer bleeding.

It was still broad daylight by the time Raishan was done, but everyone felt exhausted. Kyth had trouble holding his eyes open. He dozed off and woke up, catching Egey Bashi's gaze.

"Why don't we all get some sleep," the Keeper suggested. "We might be in for a rough night."

40

HIGH TREASON

Evan looked up as he heard voices at the entrance to the hallway, the boundary of his imprisonment. He almost welcomed the interruption of his daily routine, which consisted mostly of staring out the window onto the lake or listening to Odara Sul and Mother Keeper arguing about the subtleties of the Keepers' Order operations. For the past three weeks he had had no other company.

The new Diamond of the Pentade, Han, was a man of very few words. Under his command the elite Kingsguard turned into little more than silent statues, always present but never offering any variation to the daily boredom. Evan found himself missing Mai, whose natural glamour had a way of keeping everyone on their toes.

The doors to the chamber swayed open, revealing the commotion outside.

The Rubies had their backs to Evan, weapons out, shielding the doorway. Han raced past them into the chamber, giving fast hand signs as he rushed by. He took his place by the King's side and drew swords from the sheaths at his back.

The intruders halted behind the line of the Rubies. In the lead was the Olivian ambassador Tanad Eli Faruh, his scarlet and blue robes an assault to the eye in the tranquil grays of the castle's decorations. Next to him walked a lean, graceful man with a gaunt face and striking pale eyes that looked yellow in the bright sunlight streaming through the windows. Twelve men formed a line behind them, orbens at the ready. A group of Illitand guards brought up the rear, their faces bearing expressions of uncertainty as they kept glancing at the doors behind.

"What is the meaning of this?" Evan demanded. He threw a curious glance at the Tanad's yellow-eyed companion. It could only be the mysterious Kaddim Tolos, the man who led the attack on Kyth back in Tadar and whose strange power got Mai into an ordeal down in the Illitand Castle hallway.

The Olivian ambassador stepped forward. "Forgive the intrusion, Your Majesty, but I believe it's time that you and Lord Daemur talked. You can't just stay in this castle and refuse to see him forever."

"Of course I can," Evan said. "And it's exactly what I intend to do until the Duke ends this outrage and lets me go."

"Come now, Sire," Eli Faruh persuaded. "All anyone wants to do is talk. What harm could there be in that?"

Evan turned and walked back to his chair, taking time to settle in and arrange the folds of his cloak around him. "Is Daemur willing to apologize, then?"

The Tanad spread his hands. "Aren't you taking this a little bit too far, Your Majesty? Lord Daemur and you played together as children. What's a few harsh words between old friends?"

Evan shrugged. "I don't think you could possibly understand, Tanad. So it's obviously a waste of time for me to try to explain. I regret you had to come all the way to my chambers just for this."

The hesitant glance Eli Faruh threw at his companion confirmed Evan's suspicion that the real conversation was just about to start. He surveyed his bodyguards. Han by his side looked easy and confident. He seemed like adequate protection, but Evan couldn't help thinking that the rest of the Pentade was too far away, so that in case of a fight they could be easily separated from their leader.

He remembered what Daemur Illitand had said about the Pentade leaders' styles, after his pathetic attempt to ambush Evan during their previous meeting. If Mai was still in charge, he would be out in the front now, and the Rubies would be spaced in the way that left Evan protected from all sides.

Kaddim Tolos stepped forward. Evan's skin crept as he watched the man approach the Rubies, who closed in their shoulders to block him.

"You will come with us, Your Majesty," Tolos said in a low, deep voice. He drew himself up and spread out his hands. A surge of power swept through the room, smothering all sounds as it pressed on the ears with a silencing pulse. The Rubies dropped their weapons, sinking onto the floor. Han stepped forward and raised his swords, but his movements were slow and uncertain, as if he wasn't sure what he was doing.

The Kaddim gave a short command and his men fanned out, side-stepping the Rubies crouched at their feet. Han stood in their way, but despite his high ranking he suddenly didn't seem like adequate protection anymore. His body shuddered as the Kaddim's power hit him, and Evan had a distinct feeling that while the Diamond still managed to stay on his feet, he was having trouble holding on to his weapons. He reached inside his cloak and drew his own sword, struggling against the pulses of power emanating from the Kaddim's outstretched palms.

The men spun their orbens, lashing them at Han. The Diamond advanced, his swords cutting the air. He moved with difficulty, as if trying to run through a thick layer of treacle. His thrust blocked one of the orbens, tearing it from the attacker's hand. His other blade hacked through a chain and a spiked metal ball flew off, spinning through the room and landing with a thud against the wall. He slid forward, but his movements had none of the speed or precision Evan knew him to be capable of.

An orben came through, sweeping Han's shoulder and leaving a dark streak of blood on his torn sleeve. Han wavered, too slow to dodge another orben coming at him at full speed. The weapon hit him on the side of the head. Han stumbled.

Orbens were coming from all sides, too many to dodge. One hit him on the shoulder, making him waver and lose his balance. Another crashed into his skull from the back. The ugly cracking sound echoed through the hall, blood splattering out of the wound. The impact sent Han flying. He folded as he fell, as if suddenly devoid of bones. Swords flew out of his hands, leaving bloody trails as they skidded along the polished stone floor.

As if in a nightmare, Evan watched his top-ranked elite guard roll to a standstill at his feet. The Majat was no longer bleeding. His eyes stared unseeingly at the ceiling, head tilted at an angle that indicated a broken neck.

Tolos lowered his hands. "As you see, Your Majesty, this wasn't even much of a fight."

Evan's skin crept with terror he hadn't experienced in a very long time. He wanted to respond, but his voice failed him.

This wasn't possible. It simply couldn't be happening. *No one* was capable of killing a Diamond Majat. Not like this, without even much of a fight.

It *couldn't* be true.

A door opened and closed, footsteps echoing through the hallway. Daemur Illitand strode in and stopped dead in his tracks, color draining from his pale cheeks.

"What happened here, Kaddim Tolos?" he demanded.

"They tried to resist us," Tolos said. "But we have everything under control, Your Grace."

Illitand's lowered hand trembled. "You and your men just *killed* a *Diamond Majat*!"

Tolos nodded with satisfaction. "Yes. And now the King is much less protected than before. We can easily control his guards. He's all yours, to do with as you please."

"*Are you out of your mind?*"

Tolos shrugged. "You took King Evan prisoner, so that you could make him agree to our terms. But it has become all but impossible with the way he spends all his time in his chamber, locked away with his unbeatable guards, refusing to see anyone. We helped you to break the stalemate, that's all. Your Grace should be thanking my men and me."

Illitand stared at him with the chilling expression of a snakecharmer. "Get out. Whatever it was you wanted from me, the deal's off. I want nothing more to do with you."

Tolos's lips folded into a smile. "I'm afraid, Your Grace, it's a bit too late for that. My men and I are here, and as you see, quite capable of getting our way by any necessary means. We have your entire household, as well as the key to your southern sovereign, little Princess Aljbeda, under our control. You'll *have* to deal with us, whether you like it or not."

The Duke abruptly lifted his chin, his face showing a mixture of shock and surprise as if he had just been slapped by a wordless servant. He stared at the Kaddim, then turned to Evan who was watching the scene with a carefully arranged expression of calmness.

"This wasn't our deal," the Duke said quietly. "You promised me–"

The Kaddim laughed. "I thought our deal was off. Didn't you just say so, Duke?"

"But–" The stare of the Kaddim's yellow eyes froze the words on the Duke's lips.

Tolos's smile became triumphant. "There are times, Duke, when you simply can't get what you want. At such times, you must learn to settle for what you're offered. I suggest you take it before the offer gets worse."

He turned and strode out of the room. His men followed. In the shocked silence that followed, the Rubies recovered their weapons and slowly gathered around Han's body. Illitand guards in their green and gold livery stood still, their faces contorted with horror. Mother Keeper and Odara Sul appeared in the doorway behind them with grave expressions.

Evan turned to Daemur and the Tanad. "What was the deal he offered the two of you?"

"It doesn't matter anymore," Daemur said. "Whatever his deal, I'm no longer interested. The man's *out of his mind!*"

Evan smiled. "I wouldn't be so sure, Duke. He looked quite sane to me. In fact, he may have been the only man in this room with a firm grip on reality. He played you, and if you want a chance to save yourself, you'd do well to admit it."

Daemur's gaze flared with defiance, but he controlled it and lowered his head.

"No need to dwell on past mistakes, Sire," he said. "I regret what happened. All of it."

"Is this an apology?"

The Duke met his gaze. There was a long pause.

"I am sorry for keeping you prisoner," he said. "And, I'm sorry for what happened here today. But I will never apologize for what I said. Not before you do."

Evan smiled. "Fair enough. Neither will I."

"Perhaps, my lords," Tanad Eli Faruh offered, "these matters can wait until a more appropriate time. The *real* question is, what are we going to do now?"

Evan shrugged. "Not my problem. You and Daemur are the ones who got yourselves into this mess. The only thing I can do is to order my Majat guard to detain both of you for high treason. We could all be prisoners in these chambers. But I won't do it. Personally, I don't care for the company. And it seems this wouldn't make your situation any different, would it?"

Illitand walked forward and stood over Han's body. He was shaking. Evan doubted the Duke had even heard what he'd said.

"I must send him to the Majat Guild," Daemur said quietly. "With my deepest regrets, and an honorary guard fit for royalty. I must make them realize this wasn't my fault."

Evan's smile widened. "Good luck with that. I heard the Majat Guildmaster is a kind, understanding man. I have no doubt he'll see it your way."

Daemur looked up, his eyes so empty that against reason Evan felt sorry for the man. Then the Duke turned and strode out of the room.

Tanad Eli Faruh shifted uncomfortably from foot to foot. "You're completely right, Sire. Kaddim Tolos has the entire household in his power. His men are everywhere. And he's keeping Princess Aljbeda under lock and key. Even I can't see her." He looked at Evan pleadingly. "We have to do something, Your Majesty. Our only chance is to stay united."

Evan scoffed in disbelief. "*United*, Tanad? Isn't it a bit too late for warmth and friendship? The best you and Daemur can do now is let me out of here. If you still can."

The Olivian shook his head. "The castle's under their control. We are prisoners here, Sire, just like you."

Evan laughed. "And you still came here to offer me your terms, Tanad? Politics isn't a card game, you know. Even if you bluff, you have to have something up your sleeve in case things get out of hand."

The Olivian stepped forward and knelt at Evan's feet. He looked repentant, but Evan noticed how he took care to avoid splotches of blood on the floor that could stain his expensive silk robe.

"Please forgive me, Your Majesty," the Olivian said. "I was blind. This man did something to my mind. I wasn't acting on my own will. If we ever get out of this, I will be, to the end of my days, your loyal and devoted servant."

Evan shook his head. "If we ever get out of this, you'll be in a lot of trouble, Tanad. Now, get out."

Eli Faruh raised his face to Evan with the disbelieving expression of a dog who had been hit by its master after showing obedience.

"*Out*," Evan said.

The Olivian scrambled to his feet and rushed out of the room, leaving Evan to stare at Han's body. This wasn't happening. It *couldn't* be. The Majat were a formidable power that kept kingdoms on their toes. *No one* killed a Diamond for sport and hoped to get away with it.

How powerful had the Kaddim Brotherhood really become?

A rustle of robes on stone startled Evan out of his thoughts. The Keepers swept through the room and knelt on the floor to examine Han's body.

"Blessed Shal Addim," Odara Sul whispered. "He's really dead."

Hair snaked around her head and settled into a twisted knot. She made no attempt to straighten it out. She just sat there, staring.

It was indeed a frightening sight. The blow had come from the back, leaving Han's face undisturbed except for the blood splatters. His slanted black eyes were half-open, staring at the ceiling with an expression of surprise. The left side of his skull was crushed in. Wounds gaped on his chest and shoulders, where the other orbens had hit him during the attack. Many of them showed no sign of bleeding. The weapons had connected after the Diamond was already dead.

Evan didn't have a chance to know Han well, but looking at the broken body he felt a lump rise in his throat. His eyes itched with unshed tears, absolutely unbefitting a king. The Pentade duty took into account the possibility that a Majat could die defending him, but such a thing certainly hadn't happened in the written history of Tallan Dar. The Pentade had been historically considered more of an honorary assignment, intended to maintain the wealth of the Guild and its presence at the King's court, with no real action involved.

To Evan's knowledge, Diamonds rarely got killed at all, as no other warriors came close to being their match. He didn't envy Daemur Illitand for having to explain the incident to the Majat Guildmaster, who was bound to take this very personally.

He was startled from his thoughts again when he realized everyone in the room was looking at him. There was a general air of expectation, reminding Evan that now, more than ever, he was the one in charge.

He looked at the Rubies kneeling on the floor, singling out a strongly built man with sunburnt skin and pale blond hair.

"Jeih Lothar," he said. "You're in charge of the Pentade until the time we can have another Diamond to replace Aghat Han."

The Ruby got up to his feet and stood to attention. Evan fumbled in the folds of his robe and produced a glittering Diamond token. He handed it over to Lothar.

"This is Aghat Han's. I assume it must be sent back to your Guild with the body."

Lothar bowed his head, his lips pursed into a straight line. He reached out and took the token with a stiff hand.

"The Duke of Illitand," Evan continued, "will send his men to prepare the body and take it away. You are free to do what you will, according to the Majat ways. I suggest that you cooperate if your customs permit it, for the Duke's intentions in this matter are well placed. You may also take time to perform any rituals that your Guild demands before sending Aghat Han on his last way."

"There are no rituals, Your Majesty," Lothar said. "Aghat Han died defending you. It's an honor for a member of the Pentade to die in your service."

Evan nodded. Honor was very far from his mind, but he wasn't about to bring it up at such a solemn moment.

A group of Illitand guards came in with a stretcher and a large quantity of rags and buckets. They stopped in the doorway, keeping their eyes on Evan.

"Do what you must," Evan said.

He strode past them out of the room to a private niche at the end of the hallway. Settling on the windowsill, he looked into the distant haze over the glimmering waters of the lake.

41
A MOONLIGHT SWIM

Kyth woke after dark. He felt refreshed. His chest and shoulder didn't seem as sore as before, and his limbs were filled with new strength, making him feel much more fit than he had been in the morning. The idea of riding for another day back to the Cha'ori camp didn't seem horrifying anymore. He sat up, looking around.

Egey Bashi sat by the fire sipping his tea, the two Majat stretched out next to him. Raishan, wrapped in his cloak, looked fast asleep. Mai lay flat on his back, covered with a blanket up to the chin. Kyth couldn't tell if he was conscious.

When Egey Bashi saw that Kyth was awake, he leaned forward and handed him a small bowl of stew and a mug of tea. The meal was cold, suggesting that it had been cooked some time ago, but Kyth took it with gratitude, suddenly realizing how hungry he was. All he had eaten for the past three days was the watery grain soup his captors had fed him, and the dry meat that he'd had in the morning.

The stew was made of meat and bread, mixed with a herb that gave this filling meal a faint, refreshing flavor. Kyth ate everything and sat back, sipping his tea under the Keeper's intent gaze.

"How's Mai?" he asked.

Egey Bashi shot a quick glance at the Majat's still shape. "His fever's high. But the worst is still to come. Are you well enough to keep watch?"

Kyth nodded.

"If he wakes up and starts moving around," the Keeper said, "the poison will spread too fast and things might get out of hand. You must get him to stay lying down. He'll probably be delirious, so it may not be easy. If you feel like you can't handle him by yourself, wake us up. Can you do that?"

Kyth hesitated. Mai looked so sick that he couldn't imagine it would be hard to keep him down. Yet, the edge in Egey Bashi's voice suggested there was more to it than he realized. He looked at the Keeper with question.

"It shouldn't really start until after midnight," Egey Bashi said. "Just make sure you wake up Raishan before then." He wrapped into his cloak and lay back. It seemed like only a moment before his breath became even, showing that the Keeper was asleep.

The moon loomed high above the horizon, a full crescent pouring silvery light onto the landscape. Chilly night air crept through the gaps in his clothes straight under the skin. Kyth sat closer to the fire, watching the still shapes of his sleeping companions. Everything was quiet, except for the barking of the coyotes and the distant boom of a bittern in the reeds downstream.

Kyth was beginning to doze off when Mai suddenly sat up and looked around. His eyes shone brighter than usual on his drawn face, but he seemed alert and quite aware of his surroundings. He didn't look delirious at all. In fact, he seemed almost recovered, so that looking at him Kyth felt relieved. The Keepers' cure must have worked after all, and the worst was behind them.

Mai caught Kyth's gaze and winked. Then he got up and walked toward the river.

At first Kyth thought he was just following nature's call, but when Mai went without stopping all the way to the bank and leaned over the water, Kyth suspected something was wrong. He hastily got up and ran over to where Mai was standing, dangerously close to the edge.

"Mai!" he called out. "What are you doing?"

The Majat turned and gave him a long look. From up close, Kyth could sense the heat emanating from his body and see the feverish chills that rippled the muscles of his bare torso. He paused, alarm stirring in his chest as he belatedly remembered Egey Bashi's warning.

"I'm hot," Mai said. "I need to go for a swim." He leaned forward, balancing precariously over the water. It seemed to Kyth he was about to fall in.

"You can't go in there!" Kyth reached out and caught Mai by the elbow.

The Majat's body tensed up. He spun around so fast that his shape blurred, and grabbed Kyth's wrist. Kyth's fingers unclenched of their own accord. His hand was slowly going numb, but Mai still held on until Kyth couldn't feel his fingers anymore.

The Majat's face filled Kyth's vision, the heat he emanated warming the air around them. Mai was shivering, but his hand was steady like iron. It was hard to imagine such a sick man could still be so strong.

"Let me go," Kyth said.

Mai hesitated, a shade of doubt appearing in his gaze. After a long moment he released his hold and turned back to the water.

"Don't touch me again," he said.

"But–" Kyth began, but at that moment Mai stepped

forward, right off the shore. Kyth reached over and grabbed him with both arms around the waist, throwing his weight back to keep Mai from falling into the water.

The Majat turned in his arms with dizzying speed and Kyth felt a hand on his throat.

"I warned you not to touch me again."

Before he closed the grip, Kyth took in a full breath of air and shouted at the top of his lungs:

"Raishaaaaaan!"

Then they swayed and tumbled over, straight into the turbid Elligar waters.

The water was deep right near the shore, and much too cold. Kyth gasped, struggling against Mai's grip. He wasn't a good swimmer, and without the ability to fully use his body he was having trouble keeping his head above the water.

"Mai!" he gasped. "Let me g–"

The Majat twisted against his grip and came up on top, pushing Kyth's head down. Water filled his mouth. He grasped Mai trying to tear him off, but it was as useless as wrestling with a rock. Mai's arms were steady, his muscle harder than seemed possible for living flesh. His eyes had an empty look. Kyth wasn't sure the Majat could understand what he was doing. He grasped on tighter, but his fingers kept sliding and he couldn't get a good grip. His vision darkened. He saw the moon above his head getting dimmer through the thickening layer of water.

He was going to drown.

Use… your gift.

Use… the water…

… or die.

With the last of his weakening senses, he relaxed against Mai's hold and opened up his mind to let in the water.

A powerful surge flowed into his body. It overwhelmed his senses, his body shuddering with strength he couldn't control. Then he got a hold on it. He tore off Mai's grasping hands and held him back, their bodies tumbling over in the turbid flow.

Air.

Need… air…

The strength filling him was enormous, but his mind was darkening, his lungs burning from lack of air. They were still going down, tumbling, so that he could no longer tell where "up" was. He was losing hold, Mai's body heavy against him as the river grasped both of them into its arms.

Air.

His feet touched the bottom, but he no longer had the strength to push off. He held onto Mai, both of them dragged along the muddy rived bed.

He had to… take… a breath.

He had to…

Give in.

He gave in, letting the river fill up his body with no resistance at all. He only had moments left to live, but those moments made him strong beyond anything he could ever imagine. He let the water carry him, curving into a powerful wave that reached all the way to the bottom, bringing precious air along with it. He inhaled, and the water carried him up to the surface and higher on to the shore, pushing off to bring him all the way upstream, back to their camp.

Kyth was only vaguely aware he was still clutching Mai's body, and of Raishan's arms pulling them both out onto the delightfully dry ground. They lay side by side, coughing and spluttering water. They were breathing. They were alive. Kyth looked into the sky at the bright crescent of the moon, whose glow seemed like the most beautiful thing he had ever seen.

Raishan's stern face appeared above him. "What in the hell happened?"

Kyth took a breath, enjoying the absence of pressure on his throat and the abundance of fresh air around him. It seemed like he had wasted a lot of his life without appreciating these things before.

"Mai…" he managed, "he wanted to go for a swim. I tried to stop him. I didn't realize he was still so strong."

Raishan gave him a strange look. "By the amount of time you spent in the water, you should have come up way downstream. But there was this big wave that just brought you back here. Care to tell me anything about it?"

Kyth looked away. He wasn't sure what had happened, and he didn't feel like talking about it.

Raishan gave him another look, then turned to Mai crouching on the ground. Egey Bashi took his place.

"I thought I told you to keep him from moving around!"

Kyth shot him a glance. "It got out of hand."

"Why didn't you wake Raishan?"

Kyth shrugged. He *did* wake Raishan, just not right away. But it was useless to argue now.

"Is it going to make him worse?" Kyth asked.

Egey Bashi glanced over to where Mai sat on the grass, doubled over, coughing.

"What's done is done," the Keeper said quietly. "It's all up to how strong he is now."

It seemed as if Mai heard these words. He raised his head and looked straight at the Keeper, his eyes shining with such a ruthless gleam that Kyth shivered. Mai slowly got to his feet and made an unsteady step in their direction. Egey Bashi backed off.

"That's what I was afraid of," he said quietly. "The Black Death driving him."

"*Now* you're telling us," Raishan grumbled.

He slowly straightened out and stepped into Mai's path. The Majat looked at him with an empty gaze. He stood still for a moment. Then he leapt forward without warning, throwing his weight against Raishan. The two Diamonds rolled on the ground. Mai went straight for the throat, the force of his grip making Raishan's face go red. He clutched at Mai's hands, pressing on the points at the base of the wrists. Mai eased the hold and Raishan knocked his hands off. They struggled, moving so fast it was dizzying to watch.

"Don't hurt him, Aghat Raishan," Egey Bashi warned.

"This isn't exactly my concern at the moment," Raishan rasped. Mai was on top, the strength of his grasp visible in the way Raishan's arms shuddered under the strain.

Raishan twisted out of the lock and threw his weight sideways, rolling over and throwing Mai onto his back. Before Mai could recover, Raishan pinned his wrists to the ground. He threw his entire weight against the hold. He was taller and heavier built, but it clearly took all he had to keep Mai down.

"I'm afraid," Raishan said with difficulty, "I might have to knock him out."

"Wait!" Egey Bashi reached over and put his hand onto Mai's forehead. Mai threw him a murderous look and twisted in Raishan's grip, but Raishan held on with what looked like the last of his strength.

"Whatever you're doing, Magister," Raishan said through clenched teeth, "do it fast."

Egey Bashi closed his eyes. Kyth sensed waves of calmness emanating from his still shape. It was subtle, nothing like the smothering feeling emanated by the Kaddim Brothers. *Can the Keepers control minds too?*

After a long moment Mai's arms relaxed and his gaze become absent again, just like it had been earlier in the day.

"You may let go now, Aghat Raishan," Egey Bashi said.

"Are you sure?"

Egey Bashi nodded and stood up. Raishan slowly disengaged himself and rolled off, sitting on the ground and massaging his wrists. Mai lay still, staring into the sky.

"I'll be damned," Raishan said. "I kind of assumed he'd be weaker by now."

"Perhaps it's all for the best," Egey Bashi said. "He'll need all his strength to deal with what's coming."

Raishan's eyes widened. "Do you mean to say after all this there's something else *coming*?"

The Keeper shook his head. "Let's just get back to camp, Aghat. Kyth needs to get dried off. And I think all of us could use more rest."

Raishan looked down at Mai, who hadn't moved since their fight. Then he leaned down and touched his neck.

"He's cold," he said after a pause, "and his pulse is very weak. What did you do to him, Magister?"

"I don't think it was me. Things just went a bit faster than they should have. There's nothing else we can do for him anymore, so let's just get back to the fire before anyone catches cold. Whatever happens now, we must ride out at dawn. Staying here any longer won't help."

"You mean, we just leave him here for the rest of the night?"

"Believe me, Aghat," Egey Bashi said. "That's the best we can do."

"But he's soaking wet. It's a damn cold night. And his wound needs a fresh bandage."

Egey Bashi's gaze didn't waver. "In this particular case, cold's exactly what he needs. As for his wound, it can certainly wait a couple of hours."

Raishan hesitated, looking down at Mai. Kyth came over and stood by his side.

Mai's face was pale and drawn. He lay on his back, arms out. Finger-shaped bruises marked his wrists, similar to those darkening on Kyth's own skin. He lay very still, and it looked like he wasn't breathing.

"Are you sure he's... all right?" Kyth asked in a trembling voice.

The other two men gave him a strange look. Then they turned and walked toward the fire.

They spent the rest of the night in preparations for the early start. Raishan picked up the saddles lost by their attackers and repaired the straps, fitting them onto the two horses that Kyth and Mai had used to escape. Egey Bashi built up the fire and Kyth huddled closer to dry off. They put on the kettle, warming up the remainder of the previous day's meals.

Every once in a while each of them threw glances at Mai, stretched a small distance away on the riverbank. He was very still. Kyth was sure he didn't stir or change position even once. Clearly the Majat was either deeply unconscious, or...?

Kyth didn't want to think of any other possibilities. After the last two days he felt a strong bond with the Majat. This man had risked his life to save Kara. And Kyth, not knowing that, almost let his hatred bring Mai to irreversible harm. It would be unthinkable if Mai died now, when they were safe, Kara was alive, and they were going back to the Cha'ori camp to set things right.

Kyth sat, looking that way until the sky became gray. He watched the golden glow at the horizon paint the scarce clouds yellow and pink and shoot long arrow-like shadows off every rock and bush in sight. They all pointed toward the river, where Mai lay on the tall, flat bank, very still among the wavering grass.

Kyth couldn't take it anymore. When Egey Bashi and Raishan turned away to tend to the horses, he hurried over and knelt beside the outstretched body.

Mai's face was so pale it was hard to imagine it belonged to a living man. His bare torso was stained with dirt and grass, the bandage on his chest hanging in rags, soaked with blood and pus from the wound. He lay in the same position he was the previous night, arms out, head turned to the side, just the way Raishan and Egey Bashi left him after the fight. He hadn't moved all night.

"Mai," Kyth called softly. "Wake up. It's time to go."

There was no response. Kyth leaned over and touched Mai's face. It was cold and still wet from their swim in the river.

He *couldn't* be dead.

That would be just too unfair.

Kyth leaned closer.

"Mai," he called. "Wake up, Mai!"

It seemed that there was a movement, a barely perceptible ripple of the muscle on Mai's outturned arm. Kyth sat back on his heels, watching.

Mai's eyelids trembled and slowly opened. He met Kyth's gaze with strange recognition. For the first time in the past few days, Mai's eyes looked sane and normal, the way Kyth remembered them back at the King's castle. There was laughter in their blue-gray depths, and just a touch of arrogance that made men around him bristle up.

"What did I miss?" Mai asked weakly.

Relief washed over Kyth, his face relaxing into a smile. He was only vaguely aware of Raishan and Egey Bashi who approached and stood on the other side, watching.

He looked down into Mai's eyes.

"Not much," he said wholeheartedly. "Really not much."

42
THE PLEDGE OF A MIREWALKER

The snakewood raft waiting for them at the shore was bigger than than last time. Alder counted at least twelve leathery logs, forming a structure strong enough to hold their entire group and comfortable enough for them to space out as it steadily propelled itself against the powerful flow of the Elligar waters.

Alder stood next to Garnald, conscious to keep a clear distance from the creeping spiders of Ayalla's dress. He was amazed to see that the other Mirewalkers didn't seem in the least disturbed by it. They stood close, some within touching range, so that the hairy bodies swept against them as the Guardians moved around in constant turmoil. Alder wondered what kind of training it took to stand next to the deadly spiders, almost as big as a man's hand and capable of dissolving an entire body with a single sting, and not to be bothered at all.

When the raft reached the bank, the snakewoods took hold like last time, by digging their roots into the wet earth next to the water. But they didn't stop at that. As Ayalla and her suite stepped ashore, the trees pulled themselves upright. Glancing back as he walked up the steep path toward the Cha'ori camp, Alder saw a small snakewood grove that wasn't there when they came. It *moved* as they walked, following Ayalla and her suite at a steady distance.

A welcoming party gathered in the Cha'ori camp to meet them. Dagmara's neat shape made an unquestionable center of the group. Her deep amber eyes met the indigo of Ayalla's in a long, private glance.

"Welcome, Forest Mother," she said solemnly. "It's an honor of a lifetime to greet you here in our camp."

Ayalla merely nodded, running a slow glance around the gathered men and women.

"Please make yourself at home," Dagmara said. "We'll have our council later in the day."

She beckoned to Ayalla and her suite, but before anyone could move, Alder pushed forward to Ayalla's side.

"Where's Kyth?" he demanded.

Dagmara's eyes widened in anger, but a glance at Ayalla froze the words on her lips.

"He's worried about his brother," the Forest Woman said with an indulgent smile, the kind a mother reserves for her favorite child.

Dagmara let out a sigh, her shoulders relaxing as she gave Alder a reproachful look. "Go to my tent. Your friend Ellah's there. She'll tell you everything."

"*Ellah*?" Alder stared.

She couldn't mean *Ellah*. Ellah was miles away, with the King and the Mother Keeper. He opened his mouth to question it, but Dagmara's look warned him off.

Better to find out for myself. He brushed past the Cha'ori group, heading for Dagmara's tent that stood aside from the others on the higher ground.

Hot air enfolded him as he pulled aside the door curtain and stepped inside. He wiped his sweating brow, waiting for his eyes to adjust to the semidarkness.

A lone figure crouched in the far corner, next to the glowing coal pans.

Ellah.

Alder gaped. Despite Dagmara's words he simply couldn't believe his eyes. There was no way Ellah could be here, when they'd left her back in Tandar weeks ago to follow quite another path. Yet, there was no mistaking her thin angular shape, her short brown hair that draped around her face and neck making her look a little like a boy.

Alder smiled and rushed to greet her, but her look warned him off. He paused a few steps short, his skin creeping with horror as he realized that Ellah wasn't alone.

A body stretched on the floor beside her.

Kyth? Alder leapt forward, covering the remaining distance to sink down by Ellah's side. Relief mixed with horror as he recognized the short golden hair, the dark Olivian skin, the face, barely familiar in its deadly stillness…

Kara.

He meant to say it aloud, but his voice caught, his lips moving mutely as he stared at her with stinging eyes.

During their mad rush to the Grasslands she had tried to warn them of the danger close on their heels, but Alder never listened. She seemed invincible with her Diamond ranking and her amazing skill. He couldn't bring himself to believe that any enemy could possibly defeat her. And now…

"Who did this?" he asked hoarsely.

Ellah didn't respond. She turned away abruptly, dipped a cloth into a pail by her side, and wiped Kara's forehead. Then she reached over and covered the body with a blanket up to the chin.

"Where's Kyth?" Alder insisted.

Ellah kept her silence. *Has she gone deaf? Is she–*

Leaning closer, Alder realized her lips were trembling and she was pursing them closed, trying to control her contorting face. He reached over and put an arm around her shoulders, pulling her close. She held back for a moment, then relaxed against him, dissolving into sobs.

"Kyth's been captured," she cried. "After you left... they... they..."

He held her, fighting a sinking feeling in his gut. Back in the forest, Ayalla had told him it was safe to go back. While he never had a chance to question her, he had assumed she meant the danger was over and Kyth was safe. But now he realized with renewed strength that she had never said anything of the kind.

Was Kyth–

He bit back the thought, cradling Ellah in his arms. After a long moment, she pulled away and sat up, brushing the tears away.

"We were attacked," she said. "By Reverend Haghos, and some man called Nimos, and another one with strange powers."

Nimos? Reverend Haghos? Alder stared. Was Ellah delirious? But if so, how could she know about Nimos? And if the man did indeed attack Kyth, why didn't Kara interfere?

"Did they do this?" He nodded at Kara's body.

Ellah shook his head. "No. This happened before they arrived."

This made no sense at all.

"Who did this?" Alder insisted.

Her eyes fluttered, meeting his gaze with a helpless expression.

"Mai. The Majat Guild sent him after her."

Alder sighed. She had to be out of her mind. "*Mai?* The King's bodyguard?"

Ellah held his gaze. "Not anymore. He…" Her lips trembled. "He tried to defend Kyth and they captured him too." She covered her face with her hands and broke into sobs again.

Alder put both arms around her, gently stroking her hair. He held her until her shivering died down and she drew away, looking at him in the semidarkness of the tent.

"You don't believe me, do you?" she said quietly. "You think I'm out of my mind."

He hesitated. "I think you're in shock."

She shook her head. "I came here with Mai, and another Majat, all the way from the Illitand Hall." She paused, controlling a twitch in her mouth. "They made me believe they wanted to help me find you and Kyth. But in truth they were after Kara. They *used* me to get to her. And they *killed* her. As soon as they did, those men came and took Kyth and Mai away. Without Kara, no one here could really resist them."

She bit her lip, giving Alder a challenging look he knew so well since they were little. He held her gaze, realization dawning. It all made sense now. Her drawn, determined face as she kept vigil over Kara's body as if her life depended on it. Her defensiveness as she told him what had happened. Her tears. She felt guilty about what had happened, and this guilt was eating her from the inside.

Alder reached over and took her hand.

"It's not your fault," he said quietly.

She went stiff and slowly drew her hand away. "How do you know?"

The way she said it sounded so much like the Ellah he knew, a girl who wouldn't admit her fault even if it screamed at her from the nearest tree branch. She could be stubborn as a rock when she was like this, and ever since childhood Alder knew of only one way to deal with this kind of mood. He had to carry on the conversation as if he was oblivious to it, if he wanted to find out what happened.

"How many men were there?" he asked.

"It seemed like hundreds. But I think in reality it was not that many. Dozens."

"Did anyone go after them?"

She nodded. "Magister Egey Bashi and Aghat Raishan. They arrived very soon after it happened. The Magister was confident they could catch up with them. If only…" She hesitated.

"What?"

"I don't think a Diamond can do anything against them."

Alder shook his head. "Of course he can. You saw how Kara took down those men, didn't you?"

Her eyes lit up with a strange gleam.

"You don't get it, do you? Kara was special, and now she's gone. When they attacked us, *Mai* was trying to fight them, and they took him down in moments. Raishan's no different. They're so powerful, they can *kill* a Diamond. I think they did." She covered her face again, shaking with sobs.

Alder put a comforting arm around her and drew her close again, stroking her hair. He finally caught the special way she said it. *Mai.* Was *he* the real reason she was so flustered? Had she developed an attachment to that strange man?

Alder searched his feelings, trying to understand how he felt about it. He and Ellah had always been close, and everyone in the Forestlands where they grew up assumed they were sweethearts. He always thought that one day, after their adventures were over, they could consider settling down together. She was a girl any man would be happy to have. But did he truly feel this way about her?

As he thought about it he suddenly realized that nothing really stirred his soul. Ellah was a good friend. No matter what happened, they would always be friends. But when he thought of more, Ellah was not the one that came to mind. Her image was overpowered by another, perfect in its ageless beauty. He was Ayalla's man. There couldn't be anyone else.

"I'll talk to Ayalla," he said quietly after Ellah's sobs had died down. "If anything can be done about this, she's the one to do it. I'm sure she can. She'll find a way to bring them back safely. Both of them."

She met his gaze and Alder saw deep gratitude in her eyes. She gave him a hug. Then she sat back and watched as he got up and walked out of the tent.

The outside air seemed much too cold after the blazing heat of the tent. Alder shivered as he stood for a moment looking around the camp.

The council seemed to be over and the Cha'ori had resumed their usual activity. Off in the distance the Mirewalkers were setting up camp. Beyond stood a small snakewood grove that wasn't there before. As Alder looked closer, he realized the grove actually looked more like a hut. The trees formed a circle folding their intertwined branches into a roof and walls, leaving a small gaping doorway covered by the drooping branches in the likeness of a curtain.

Alder made his cautious way toward it. As he approached, the leathery branches moved away, inviting him inside. He entered and stood, his eyes adjusting to the semidarkness.

Ayalla was sitting on the floor in the center of the small space, the crawling mass of spiders draping around her like the skirt of a real dress. They covered up her breasts, but left the shoulders bare, making the outfit seem like some of the less modest dresses Alder had seen at the King's court.

He stood, looking down at her, unsure of what to do. He was intruding. He should probably leave. Except that he simply had to talk to her.

He took a deep breath. "Kyth has been captured. You knew about it, didn't you?"

Her large indigo eyes beckoned like two bottomless pools. "Yes."

He hesitated. "We have to do something to rescue him."

Ayalla bent her head to the side, as if listening to something inaudible to Alder.

"He has it within him to defeat these men," she said quietly. "It's up to him now. There's nothing any of us can do for him beyond that, but I believe he'll manage. Your brother is very powerful, Alder. These men are no match for him."

"What do you mean?"

She smiled. "Do you trust me?"

"Yes," he said even before he had time to think. With surprise he realized that he had spoken the truth. Despite how absentminded she seemed, despite how frightening her powers were, he *did* trust her. He knew she would never bring him or his loved ones to harm. He knew that if she said Kyth could defeat these men, he would.

Ayalla held his gaze. Then she brushed a hand against the grass beside her, swiping a large group of spiders out of the way to make room next to her on the tent floor. It looked natural, as if she was moving the fold of a skirt out of the way.

She beckoned. "Come, sit with me."

Alder hesitated, looking at the crawling spiders of her dress. Even from where he stood, he imagined he could hear the faint crackling as their hairy legs touched each other.

Ayalla followed his gaze. "You're afraid of the Guardians."

Alder swallowed a lump. He knew he wasn't supposed to be afraid of them. But seeing the mass of them crawling around so close to his feet was simply too much.

"It's all right," she told him. "They don't have to be here."

She looked down to her living dress. There was a short pause. Then the spiders streamed down her body and out of the tent. In a few moments there wasn't a single one in sight. She sat back, stark naked, and looked up at him.

"Is this better?" she asked.

Alder gaped. Her pose was easy as she curled on the floor, hugging her knees with her slender arms. Her long hair streamed down her back in smooth, silky waves. She looked so natural as if there was nothing out of the ordinary in being naked in front of a man. And she was so beautiful it was almost painful to watch.

She met his dumbfounded gaze and laughed.

"You are afraid of me," she said. "Aren't you?"

"No," he said, hoping that he was telling the truth.

"Then, you can come and sit next to me. Can't you?"

Alder slowly walked over and lowered himself by her side. He felt hot. He tried to look away from the slender curves of her body, from her full breasts, but his eyes kept coming back. She was perfect beyond reason. There wasn't a single flaw in her graceful, strong body.

Her look made him blush to the roots of his hair.

"You're hot," she observed.

Alder made an effort to keep her gaze. "I am."

She smiled. "If you're uncomfortable, you're free to leave. But I'd much rather you stayed and kept me company."

He nodded. He *did* feel uncomfortable. But as he thought about it, he realized that he would never trade his current place for anywhere else in the world. He sat still, aware of her eyes studying him, trying very hard to suppress a blush. It didn't quite work.

"You still think I'm scary?" she asked.

He shifted in his seat and slowly raised his gaze to her.

"I think you're beautiful," he said quietly. "You're the most beautiful woman in the world."

She smiled, a simple acknowledgment of a simple fact.

"Then, why do you feel so uncomfortable around me, Alder?"

He hesitated. Come to think of it, the question made sense.

"I…" he took a breath. "I can't possibly imagine how a woman as perfect as you would want to have anything to do with someone like me."

"You really can't, can you?" She reached out and touched his hand. Her skin was warm and soft, her touch echoing in his body with a shiver he couldn't control. Without letting go, she moved her face closer to him. Her indigo eyes filled his vision and he inhaled her maddening smell, honeyed ivy buds and fresh river water.

"Take off your clothes," she whispered.

He obeyed, only vaguely aware of what he was doing. Her closeness was so overpowering that he felt his body slowly lose control. He didn't remember how he found himself naked next to her, her hands moving along his skin, her body slipping into his waiting arms, her warmth against him, her overwhelmingly sensual smell. Her lips were hot as she met his, drinking of him with the need of a traveler dying of thirst in a hot desert. She was so close he could feel her with every inch of his body. His body responded to her urge, filling him with the power to match.

He lifted her up and lay her down onto the soft grass, moving on top of her, driven by the primal knowledge that bypassed his conscious mind. She drew him in, so hot inside that he shuddered from the contact. Her need made it impossible to hold anything back. He gave her everything he had, so that he could meet her desire and exceed it with the desire of his own.

In the semidarkness of her earthen tent, time stood still. They moved outside it, driven by the powers of life, of creation more ancient than the world. Her thirst was enormous, but he was up to it, and more. She gasped in his arms, clinging to him, and pushing him away, and clinging to him again with more fierceness than before. They soared, one single being that spent its entire life force in the sweet agony that seemed to last forever. And then they descended back to the real world, weak and breathless, with no strength left for anything but to lie down side by side, helpless like babies first brought into the world.

After a long while she stirred in his arms and raised her face to him.

"Are you still afraid of me?" she whispered.

He cupped her face and drew it close, searching for her lips. Her kiss was sweet like honey. She yielded to his touch, her hand moving down his body so that his skin tingled in response to her caress.

"How could I ever be afraid of you?"

She smiled and drew away, her face leaning over him.

"I don't force myself on anyone," she said quietly. "But when you're with me, I want all of you."

He held her, the heat of her slender body against him filling him up with new strength. He was drunk with her scent, the silky touch of her hair streaming down his side in a smooth wave, her body warm and relaxed against his. All he ever wanted was to hold her in his arms, to make this wonderful, overwhelming feeling last forever.

"I'm yours, Ayalla," he whispered. "All of me."

She grasped him and rolled over, drawing him on top. Then she wrapped her legs around him, pulling him even closer. He yielded, his body under her touch filling up with a passion that matched hers.

He was hers, body and soul. He never wanted it to stop.

43
OLD WOUNDS

Ellah sat in the tent by Kara's side when she heard the shouting outside. She looked at her patient, just as still and cold as she was two days ago when Raishan had told her to keep her warm. She doubted this vigil with coal pans that made the entire tent hotter than a baker's kitchen was doing anything good. Yet, she promised herself she wouldn't leave Kara's side until Raishan, or Mai, came back and told her what to do.

By now she didn't believe that would ever happen. But if there was one thing in her life she knew how to do well, it was being stubborn. She took all her meals by Kara's side and dozed off only when Dagmara and her little daughter Chaille were in the tent and could raise the alarm if there was any change in Kara's condition.

She wasn't planning to go outside and check on the source of the noise. It was probably something unimportant, like the Cha'ori returning from a hunt, or the Forest Woman walking through the camp in her horrible spider dress. She nestled further away from the coal pan, pulling up the sleeves of her dress to cool off. She knew that when the sun reached its zenith, the air in the tent would be steaming. She hoped this was what Raishan wanted her to do.

The shouting and noise outside was insistent. It didn't dissipate like it usually did after a regular disturbance in the camp. It fact, it was getting stronger. It also seemed to be getting closer to Dagmara's tent.

Ellah was still debating with herself whether she should go to take a peek, when Ohdi, a young Cha'ori girl of about Ellah's age, ran in and stopped in the doorway, panting.

"Come!" she shouted. "Quick!"

Ellah shrugged and slowly rose to her feet. She didn't believe whatever was happening out there was important enough to see, but before she could reason with herself, her feet carried her out through the door into the open air. The outside seemed much too cold after the stuffy air in the tent. She stood, shivering, shielding her eyes against the bright sunlight.

Four riders were approaching at a slow walk. As she recognized them, her knees felt weak and her stomach tied into a knot. She grasped a tent pole for support and stood, watching.

Raishan and Egey Bashi sat straight in their saddles, with the satisfied air of men who had done their job. Riding beside Raishan was Kyth, shaken but overall unharmed. At his side. Ellah paused, trying to control her trembling lips.

Mai.

Ellah was so relieved to see him alive that it took her a second look to realize that he wasn't well. His face was pale and drawn, with dark circles under the eyes, and a deep cut on his left temple. He slumped in the saddle, grasping the reins as if it was costing him effort even to sit upright. As he dismounted, he swayed and steadied himself against the horse's side.

Ellah rushed toward them.

"Thank Shal Addim!" she breathed out. "How did you–"

The urgency in Mai's gaze stopped her.

"How's Kara?" he asked.

Ellah hesitated. "Her wound's healed. And, we're keeping her warm. But I'm not sure that she–" She stopped. She *couldn't* say it. Not with Kyth looking at her, his eyes filled with such hope it made her heart waver.

"Where is she?" Mai asked.

Ellah gave him a strange look. This was for Kyth's benefit, she decided. There was no way Mai, or anyone else, could bring Kara back after three days in this near-death state.

"Follow me." She turned and led the way, with everyone close on her heels.

They stepped into Dagmara's tent.

"That's *warm*," Mai said after a moment, wiping his forehead.

"Like hellfire," Raishan agreed.

"Um, that's what you wanted me to do, wasn't it?" Ellah asked just a touch defensively.

"Yes, but," Raishan glanced around with a quick frown, "she'll need fresh air when she wakes up. Why don't we take her outside?"

He pushed past Ellah, carefully picked up Kara and carried her out into the open.

They made their way to the outskirts of the camp, where Raishan found a flat grassy patch behind a large kiuri bush, whose wide leaves provided good shelter from the wind. Mai took off his cloak and threw it on the ground, and Raishan carefully placed Kara on top. A group of Cha'ori youngsters gathered at a safe distance, stretching their heads and chattering among themselves in their guttural tongue.

Mai knelt beside Kara and slid one hand behind her back, supporting the upper part of her body to keep it off the ground. He used the other hand to measure up a distance about a palm down from her throat, resting two fingers against the spot. Then he flicked his hand in a precise blow that made her entire body shudder with its force.

Kara gasped and opened her eyes, grabbing Mai's wrist with dizzying speed. Her body shook from head to toe and she fell back against his hold, grasping him until her knuckles went white. Her grip must have hurt, but Mai kept very still, supporting her in his arms like a precious fragile vase. His eyes lit up with concern as he watched her gasp, struggling to steady herself against him.

After a while her breathing calmed. She pulled herself upright in his embrace. Her eyes widened as she recognized him. She made a move to draw away, but there was nowhere to go.

"Aghat Mai?"

"Try to relax," he said. "You need a little bit more time."

Her face slowly lost its dazed expression as she looked in turn at his arm around her waist and at her hand clutching his wrist. Carefully, as if she was touching a dangerous weapon, she released the hold. He dropped his hands away.

She raised her eyebrows, looking into his face. "But you–"

He smiled. "It's a long story. Just take it easy for now." He threw a quick glance at Kyth and nodded. Then he got to his feet and stepped away.

Following the unspoken signal, Kyth crept forward and sat on the ground next to Kara, his eyes filled with such happiness that Ellah's eyes misted with tears. Watching him felt like an intrusion. She turned away to the group of men standing at her side.

"That was amazing, Aghat Mai," Egey Bashi said. "To be honest, I never believed that could actually work."

Mai opened his mouth to respond, but Raishan's short glance silenced him. "You need rest, Aghat," he said. "And your wound needs a fresh bandage. We must find a good spot to treat it."

Mai hesitated as if he was going to object, but obviously changed his mind. He merely nodded, then turned and made his unsteady way to the other side of the camp.

A grip of worry seized Ellah's heart as she hurried to catch up, falling in pace with Raishan and Egey Bashi. She was aware no one had asked her to tag along, but she simply couldn't stay away. Besides, she still had Odara Sul's elixir. Maybe, just maybe, she could actually help?

They found a secluded spot behind a large boulder at the edge of the camp. Mai winced as Raishan helped him out of his shirt and peeled off the bandage, revealing an oozing gash across his chest, filled with pus and gore. It looked much worse than Ellah had imagined.

"I still have some of Odara Sul's elixir," she said. "Would it help?"

Egey Bashi shook his head. "Let me first take a look at the wound."

His frown deepened as he took his time to feel around the wound. Mai endured it with outward calmness, but his face became so pale it was nearly transparent. Knowing him well, Ellah was aware of how much pain he felt. She clenched her fingers, forcing herself not to look away.

"I have to clean the wound if we want to try the elixir on it," Egey Bashi finally said. "I'd have to cut away all the infected flesh. I'm not sure in your condition, after everything you'd been through, you can take this kind of pain, Aghat Mai."

"I'm fine," Mai said through clenched teeth. "Just get on with it, Magister."

Egey Bashi dug around in his pack, taking out a set of small blades and tweezers, the mere sight of which made Ellah's stomach twist into knots. He started a small fire and carefully heated them one by one, laying them out on the flat edge of the boulder so that their thin curved edges wouldn't touch the stone. Then he sat back on his heels, looking at Mai with doubt.

"I still don't think–" he began.

"I've been through worse," Mai said.

"Not in your condition, Aghat."

Mai glanced at the tools, then at the oozing wound on his chest. "From what I know about wounds, this one has very little chance to heal on its own. Not for a long time."

Egey Bashi also looked at his tools. "True. Yet, with everything you've just been through, Aghat Mai…" He hesitated.

"Just do it, Magister."

"I can knock him unconscious," Raishan offered.

Mai shot him a warning glance, his muscle tensing. "Don't bet on it, Aghat."

"But you are in no shape to–"

"I'm in better shape than last time you tried, Aghat Raishan."

Egey Bashi raised his hands. "Please stop, both of you. I don't think any of us here care for the excitement of seeing you two fight. It was quite enough the first time around."

Ellah followed Raishan's glance to his bruised wrist, but the question froze on her lips as she saw three figures appear from the direction of the Mirewalkers' tents and make their way toward them. There was no mistaking the tall, stately woman walking in front, clad in a long narrow dress that from this distance seemed to be made of exquisite dark velvet, its soft folds shimmering in the sun.

Ayalla.

Alder and Garnald strode in her wake, both wrapped in long cloaks in the style common to the Mirewalkers. It didn't escape Ellah how familiar Alder looked in these surroundings, as if finding a place where he belonged.

His glance thrown at Ellah was full of happiness and embarrassment that made her wonder. But any questions would have to wait for later.

Ayalla looked cheerful and carefree, like a young village maid. Ellah didn't like the Forest Woman, but even she noticed a special air of radiance that made her seem even more flawless than she already was.

The trio approached them and stopped. Ayalla peered at Egey Bashi, then moved her eyes to Mai.

"You are hurt," she said. "I can help."

"I don't think—" Egey Bashi began.

Ayalla's glance stopped him. She slowly reached forward and covered Egey Bashi's scarred face with her palm. Her face acquired an absentminded expression. The spiders of her dress became more active, running around to expose random glimpses of the skin underneath. The air around her crackled as she held still for several long moments. Then she removed her hand and turned to Mai, who was watching her in guarded silence.

"Your wound's new," she said. "Who hurt you?"

"Does it matter?"

She smiled. "You're not like the others. You don't respect me as much as they do."

"I respect you," Mai said. "I just don't see how you could possibly help."

Her smile widened. "You really don't, do you?"

Mai kept his silence.

"You're one of the killers from the North, are you?" she asked.

"You could call me that, yes."

She stepped forward and knelt by his side. His eyes darted to the crawling spiders of her dress, his muscles knotting under the bare skin of his chest and torso.

"The Guardians won't harm you," she said. "Just hold still."

"But–"

Ayalla reached over and put her palm across the wound. Mai shuddered and bit his lip, color draining out of his face. Spiders streamed forward along Ayalla's arm and covered his chest with a velvety mass that hid the wound from view.

Ellah shivered, looked at Egey Bashi, and gasped.

The ugly, deforming scar across the Magister's face was gone. In its place was a thin line, defining the place where the scar had been, but no longer disfiguring his features. For the first time Ellah could see what he really looked like underneath the injury. His strong face was carved with bold strokes, irregular but very expressive. He must have been quite handsome in his youth. He was still handsome, in a rugged sort of way.

"What happened to you, Magister?" she whispered.

He was about to speak, but at that moment Ayalla straightened out and broke the contact. The crackling force around her subsided. The spiders rushed along her arm to resume their places on her bare shoulders.

Mai shivered and drew back with a short gasp. They all stared at his chest.

The wound was completely gone. There was no trace of the ugly, infected flesh torn beyond recognition that had been there only moments ago. All that was left in its place was a white star-shaped scar, no more than an inch in width. It was barely visible on his pale skin, as if the wound that left it healed ages ago.

Ayalla ran her eyes around the group. She rested her eyes on Mai and gave him a small nod of acknowledgment. Then she looked at Egey Bashi with the expression of an artist surveying a finished painting.

"Anyone else need healing?" she asked.

Egey Bashi's fingers traced the remainder of his scar. "I don't think so," he managed.

Ayalla nodded. Her eyes met Alder's. She paused for a moment, then turned and walked away toward the Mirewalkers' camp.

"I'll be damned," Raishan said. "Of all the miraculous cures I've seen—"

"No miracle at all," Garnald said, throwing a strange glance at Alder. "Ayalla's in a good mood, that's all. Just be thankful you two happened to be in her path." He turned and strode away in Ayalla's wake.

Alder stayed behind, his blush deepening as he met Ellah's gaze. "I think… um… I'll go check on Kyth."

He hurriedly turned away and Ellah had a distinct impression he was trying to avoid any possibility of being questioned about this further. She watched his retreating back, then looked at Mai, who sat still with a dumbfounded expression.

"How do you feel?" she asked.

He hesitated. "Fine. I think."

They all looked at the distant figure of Ayalla, who had reached the Mirewalkers' tents and disappeared into a small grove of snakewoods growing in their center.

Egey Bashi ran his fingers along the thin line, barely visible on his restored face. "Good mood, eh?"

"You'd wonder," Raishan agreed.

"It must have been one hell of a good mood," the Keeper said. "This scar came from the Holy Wars. It's hundreds of years old."

Ellah's mouth fell open at this confession. She knew by the steady green color in her mind that he was telling the truth. But it didn't make sense. He looked no older than forty, a man full of vigor, whose age could be guessed mostly by the scarce touch of gray in his thick dark hair. He couldn't *possibly* be old enough to have fought in the Holy Wars.

Were the rumors true? Did the Keepers really harbor the secret of immortality?

At that moment she finally remembered something she should have said a long time ago. She turned to Egey Bashi with urgency.

"I have a message for you, Magister," she said. "From Mother Keeper. She and King Evan are prisoners in the Illitand Castle. She said if you knew that, you'd help her to get out."

Egey Bashi stared, his expression of wonder slowly giving way to shock.

"Illitand Castle? Is the Duke out of his mind?"

Ellah opened her mouth to respond, but Mai spoke first.

"The Duke seems to have formed an unfortunate alliance with the Kaddim," he said. "I'd say he's in as much trouble as the King, even if he doesn't realize it yet. We must conclude our business here and get back to Castle Illitand before things get out of hand."

Egey Bashi nodded. "You're right, Aghat. We must hold our council and head back without delay."

44
VIPER

Kyth stayed with Kara until the Cha'ori women came over and took her away to wash and change her. Relief at seeing her alive was so overwhelming it made him weak. He strode unseeingly through the camp until he found himself at the pasture, where their horses roamed freely among the large herd of Cha'ori mounts. Kara's gray mare stood munching grass at the side, next to Mai's black stallion. Kyth's horse was nowhere to be seen.

Kyth paused, taking a full breath of the cool evening air. Too many things had happened to him in the last few days. He couldn't believe that the worst was over and everything was all right again. With Kara back from the dead nothing bad could possibly happen to them anymore.

He sensed a movement beside him and turned to meet Mai's gaze.

The Majat was back in his own clothes, neat and elegant as if the last few days hadn't happened. He was still pale, and the dark circles under his eyes were still prominent, but the easy grace of his movements was back, making him look strong and confident just like before.

Seeing his master, Mai's stallion snorted and made its way toward them. He pressed his muzzle against Mai's shoulder with a force that made him stumble back to keep his balance. Mai patted the shiny, raven-black coat, his expression tender as he ran his hand along the stallion's neck in a slow caress.

Kyth hesitated. He wanted to say so much, but he didn't know where to begin.

Mai spoke first. "I never had a chance to thank you for saving me from a fate far worse than death."

Kyth looked into his eyes, blue and tranquil like the summer sky.

"I didn't do much. You're the one who saved yourself. And me. I just gave you a chance."

Mai held his gaze. A shadow fell over his face.

"I'm trained to fight," he said, "and I'm prepared to die in battle, if it ever comes to that. But to lose my arms and never be able to hold a weapon…" He paused. For a moment he looked almost vulnerable. Then the impression was gone.

"I know you also saved my life more than once when I was unconscious or didn't know what I was doing," Mai went on. "I'm in your debt for those times as well. I hope I can repay it some day."

Kyth lowered his gaze and raised it steadily back to Mai's face. "No. You don't owe me a thing. What you did for Kara…" He stopped, unable to go on.

Mai's gaze became distant. "It's not your score to settle. I didn't do it for you."

"I know."

They stood for a long moment looking at each other.

"Fine," Mai said. "If this is the way you want it to be."

Kyth hesitated. "When I used my gift to shield you from their power, I didn't do it for you either. I really hated you at the time."

"Why did you do it then?"

"I felt that if I let them do this to you, I'd be no better than them. Not if I just stood by and watched, when there was something I could do about it. So, in a way, I did it for myself."

Mai gave him a long look.

"Fair enough," he said. "But if I were you, I wouldn't be so quick to reject favors. I don't owe them to many people."

He turned to his stallion and whispered in its ear. Then he patted the horse one last time, released the hold and turned to go back to camp. After a few paces, he stopped and looked at Kyth.

"If you follow my horse," he said, "you'll find the one you're looking for. He's on the other side of the field."

Kyth stood for a moment, hesitating. Then he turned and followed the elegant shape of Mai's black stallion into the dense herd.

Mai stopped at the edge of the camp and glanced around, his eyes taking in all the activity of a busy evening. His gaze hovered over a distant figure, slim and elegant in her neat black clothes as she sat on the far side polishing a narrow dark blade. He paused, then made a decisive way over to her.

When Kara saw him approach, her eyes widened and she tensed up, the violet of her gaze meeting his blue with an almost audible clash. She kept her face blank as he came up to her and stopped.

"Mind if I join you?" Mai asked.

Without saying a word, she moved over to make room for him. He lowered down by her side, but didn't draw his weapon from its sheath to join the polishing ritual. Instead he sat still, watching her. She made an attempt to resume her task, but soon gave up and lowered her sword.

They sat for a long moment looking at each other.

"It was 'viper's kiss', wasn't it?" she asked at length.

A shadow moved in the depth of his eyes. "Yes."

"Why did you do it?"

A brief smile touched the corners of his mouth, but it never made its way to his eyes that remained in shadow as he looked at her.

"Does it really matter?"

She hesitated. "No."

He nodded, their gazes locked so tightly as if an invisible thread held them together.

"That blow," she said. "Is it true that you invented it, Aghat?"

He laughed. "Is that what they say about me?"

"Among other things. They talk a lot about you in the Inner Fortress."

His eyes lit up with laughter, but there was something else behind it that she couldn't quite catch.

"Strange that you should mention it," he said. "When I was still around, all they did was talk about you."

She looked searchingly into his face. "Really?"

"Really."

She shrugged, trying to relax and not quite succeeding. "I can't imagine any of it could be half as impressive as what they say about you."

He continued to hold her gaze with an unsettling mixture of seriousness and laughter.

"It was impressive enough," he assured. "But none of these rumors do you justice."

She smiled, searching for laughter in his eyes, but it was suddenly gone and only the seriousness remained. His look was so intense that it caught her like a bond. She sat back, her dark cheeks slowly lighting up with color.

He held a pause. Then, without taking his eyes off her, he slowly reached into his pocket and took out a small object.

"I have something for you." He held it out in an open palm.

It was a Majat token, a throwing star, but the stone in the middle of it was black. Instead of radiating light, like a regular Diamond token, this one seemed to absorb it.

"*Kar'Aghat*," he said. "The Black Diamond. I believe that now it belongs to you."

She hesitated. "As far as the Guild is concerned, I'm supposed to be dead."

He shrugged. "As far as the Guild is concerned, you are. At least for the moment."

"They'll find out. Sooner or later they will, Aghat."

He smiled. "I believe in living dangerously. Don't you?"

She gave him a searching look.

"You put your life on the line for me," she said quietly. "I'm not worth it."

His gaze became tranquil. "It was my call to make. Not yours."

"Why did you do it?"

"I thought you told me it didn't really matter to you."

Her gaze wavered. "It shouldn't," she admitted.

"But it does. Or else, you wouldn't be asking again."

"Can't you just tell me?"

He laughed. "You don't actually think I will, do you?"

"Why not?"

"Because," he said, "it would make this conversation far too personal. And I've already made you uncomfortable."

He watched the blush rise to her cheeks.

"You're good at it," she admitted.

He paused a moment longer, then lowered his eyes. There was a shudder of released tension as he sat back and relaxed, his gaze once again becoming distant and tranquil.

"I did it," he said quietly, "because I believed it was the right thing to do."

There was a long pause. Then she carefully reached out and took the black diamond token from his hand. She put it into her open palm. Her gaze became thoughtful as she traced the smooth curves of the name rune with her thumb.

"So, that's what it looks like," she said.

"Yes. And since I know your name rune now, I believe it would be fair that I showed you mine."

He held out another token. This one had a white diamond in its center, throwing its glimmering light all around.

She looked at it and raised her face to him, eyes wide.

"Viper," she whispered.

He held her gaze. "Perhaps it answers your earlier question about rumors. This one happens to be true. I did invent that blow. But I didn't name it. To be honest, I don't really know who did."

Her lips twitched. "There's also 'viper's sting'. It's almost indistinguishable from the outside."

He nodded. "Same spot. Different angle. Death's instant. I've only used it once in my life."

"So, the rumors are true after all."

He shrugged. "This one's an exception. If you ever hear them talk about me again, don't believe anything they say, Aghat."

A shadow ran across her face.

"Don't call me that," she said quietly. "I'm not a Diamond anymore."

He reached forward and gently cupped her hand, closing her fingers over the black diamond token resting in her palm, so that the stone was no longer visible.

"It's a diamond," he said, "no matter what the color. No one can change what you are. Never forget that, Aghat."

He sat for a moment, holding her hand between his. Then he dropped his hands away and got to his feet in a single fluid move.

"Wait!" she called out.

He paused looking down at her. His face was calm, but in the depths of his eyes was a strain. It stayed there for a brief moment and was gone, giving way to a smile.

"If they send a Black Diamond after you," she said quietly, "I'll fight by your side."

He smiled and bowed his head in acknowledgment. Then he turned and walked away.

Raishan was waiting a small distance away. As Mai walked past, he turned and fell into stride. They walked for a while in silence, Raishan's eyes fixed on Mai's face.

"Something you wanted to say to me, Aghat Raishan?" Mai asked after a pause. There was an edge in his voice, but Raishan didn't waver.

"Yes," he said.

Mai stopped abruptly in his tracks and turned to face him. "Make it quick."

"It wasn't a regular 'viper's kiss', was it?" Raishan asked. "If it was, I should've been able to revive her myself. But I tried and it didn't work."

Mai smiled. "I had a hard time with this one. It didn't go exactly right. She's too good a fighter to hit with a perfect blow."

Raishan nodded. "It took a hell of a lot of skill to do what you did, Aghat."

Mai didn't respond.

"Why *did* you put your life on the line for her, Aghat?" Raishan asked eventually.

"I can't imagine, Aghat Raishan, why it would possibly matter to you."

Raishan's eyes narrowed. "It matters, Aghat Mai, because it closely concerns the affairs of our Guild. When Master

Oden Lan asks me why I stood aside and did nothing when I learned about this violation of the Code, when he sends Black Diamonds after both of you and I will have to stay back and pray I'm not your shadow, I'd want to know why I had to do all these things. It's best if you told me now, so I can be prepared."

"There will be no Black Diamond for her," Mai said. "It's already out."

"Yes," Raishan agreed. "But yours isn't. So, just this once, why don't you tell me what's on your mind, Aghat?"

Mai met his gaze. There was a long pause. Raishan waited, a glow lighting up in the depths of his slanted gray eyes.

"She's the most amazing fighter I've ever seen," Mai said at length. "Her life's too precious. It wasn't up to me to take it. And it's not up to Aghat Oden Lan to decide her fate."

Raishan shook his head. "You know well that it's not up to you to question the Guildmaster's orders. You staked out your life – for her."

Mai looked away. "She's barely nineteen. When I was her age, I wasn't even ranked yet. None of us were. I had the best Jade they could find for the task. We fought against her, two to one, and she still came through and left a mark on me. In fact, she almost gave me a mortal wound. Her skill is incredible, Aghat. It's like nothing I've ever seen before." He paused and gave Raishan a long look. "I simply couldn't do it," he added quietly. "Her life's more precious than mine."

Raishan studied his face. "Master Oden Lan feels very personally about this one. It won't be long before he learns what you've done. It will be bad. For both of you."

"She has a way to make everyone feel personal about her, doesn't she?"

Raishan shook his head. "It's a dangerous game to play. When I say personal, I mean it. I was there when he gave the order."

"I know how he feels about her," Mai said quietly. "I was trained in the Inner Fortress. I was around when it started."

"What do you mean?"

Mai smiled. "He never let her see it, of course, but he has felt this way since she was ten. By the time I left to join the Pentade, she was fifteen, and gorgeous. I can only imagine what it's like for him now."

Raishan stared. "You knew, and you *still* disobeyed his order?"

Mai shrugged. "I'm fairly sure he couldn't possibly have been thinking straight when he gave it."

"I can't presume to get into Master Oden Lan's head," Raishan said. "But one thing's for certain. She was set up. This man, Nimos, went to a lot of trouble to make sure Kara abandoned her assignment and Master Oden Lan knew why. Nimos showed rare knowledge of the Majat Code and the Guildmaster's character in getting it to work, which *had* to involve help on the inside. It worked exactly as he planned, too. Master Abib and I tried to stand up for her, but the Guildmaster wouldn't even listen."

"Nimos." A ruthless glow lit up in Mai's eyes.

Raishan nodded. "He played our Guildmaster like a well tuned lute."

"I think," Mai said, "when Aghat Oden Lan learns what happened, he'll be grateful to me."

"Perhaps. But he'll never forgive you anyway."

Mai shrugged.

"Then," he said, "I'll be the second Diamond in two hundred years to meet my shadow. But if worst comes to worst, I'll die knowing I did the right thing."

45
WAR COUNCIL

It was getting dark when Kyth returned from the horse pasture to the Cha'ori camp. He paused at the edge, looking for Kara, but she was nowhere to be seen. As he was about to move deeper into the circle of tents, someone stepped out of the shadows and blocked his path.

It was Dagmara. Her dark, strong face was calm, but her amber eyes gleamed in the light of the rising moon.

"Come with me," she said.

Intrigued, Kyth followed her to a smaller tent set aside from the main camp. She raised the door curtain and led him inside.

Two figures sat on the pillows around a small table in the center of the tent. One was Ayalla, her living dress covering her just below the shoulders, leaving her arms and the top of her breasts bare. When Kyth walked in, her dark blue eyes lit up with interest that made him feel uneasy. He looked away to her table companion.

It was Egey Bashi. Or, Kyth thought it was.

He stared.

"What happened to your face?" he demanded, so surprised he forgot to be polite.

Egey Bashi glanced at Ayalla.

"You might want to ask your foster brother about it some day," he said.

Alder? Kyth's eyebrows rose as he turned to the Forest Woman. She responded with an absentminded smile, the air of detachment around her cautioning against further questions. Kyth sat down, keeping clear of her spider dress.

They sipped dark, tart tea from small cups – a Cha'ori ritual that always preceded any serious conversation.

"Our enemies are stronger than we imagined," Dagmara finally said. "We were meant to hold this council days ago. But things got out of hand. We were fortunate that the major forces to be accounted for in our lands could be gathered here for this council." She ran her eyes around her table guests and turned to Kyth. "Why don't you begin, Prince Kythar? Tell us what the King has to offer."

Kyth slowly reached up and took off Dagmara's medallion hanging around his neck. He laid it out on the table for them to see, a black stone disk with an amber inlay in the shape of an eye.

"When I last traveled with your hort and you aided me," Kyth said, "you told me that this medallion would make any Cha'ori give anything to me. Including their lives."

Her gaze hovered over the medallion; her expression softened as she raised her eyes back to his face.

"I came to call it in," Kyth went on. "We need you, Dagmara. We need the Cha'ori back on the High Council."

She shook her head. "When our alliance with your kingdom was broken hundreds of years ago, it was not meant to be restored. We will never obey your rules. Our children cannot be tested by your church."

"This law is about to change," Kyth said. "And it can only happen if we all stand for it. This is your chance to do something about it, Dagmara. The Cha'ori seat on the council is still there. All you need is to take it. Don't you want the feud between our people to end?"

She shook her head again, her expression so distant that Kyth felt a shiver run down his spine. Did he make this trip, did everyone risk their lives for him in vain?

"You know it's important, Dagmara," he persuaded. "You're a Foreteller. You know more than I do."

She straightened out.

"Don't presume to tell me about my gift," she said. "You cannot possibly know anything about it, Shandorian royal."

Kyth sat back, suddenly sensing something he almost missed before. There was a strain in her that was so unlike her usual calm composure. It was as if she was not telling him something important, and this lack of exchange made their conversation go the wrong way. He looked searchingly into her eyes, but her gaze became stern as she looked back at him.

"You are right," Kyth said at length. "I can't presume to tell you about your gift. But back when we traveled with your hort, you believed I was important enough to make a difference some day."

She hesitated. "You *are* important. And this may, or may not be the day when you make a difference. My gift told me nothing about this."

Something about the way she said it made Kyth wonder. He searched for her gaze, but she looked away.

"Is there something wrong with your gift?" he asked quietly.

The silence in the tent suddenly seemed too loud. Dagmara looked at him in pain, as if he had struck her. There was also wonder in the depths of her amber gaze.

In the stillness, the rustle of Ayalla's living dress became audible. The Forest Woman spoke, her voice deep and caressing like a whisper.

"It's the Dark Order. It's affecting your power of foretelling. It will affect everyone's power if you allow them to do what they are set out to do. Kyth is the only one whose power can grow into a force to resist them." Her deep eyes rested on Kyth with an unsettling expression, as if she was trying to probe into his soul. He paused, unsure what to say.

"You should listen to this boy, Dagmara," the Forest Mother went on. "He may be much too young to bring wisdom, but what he says is true. It's not about your quarrel with kings long dead, nor about the priests and their petty laws that are long due for a change. This is about the new enemy we all have, the one that none of you can conquer on your own. If you don't unite, the Dark Order will destroy you."

"What do you know about the Dark Order, Ayalla?" Egey Bashi asked carefully.

She gave him a long look. "They saw your book, didn't they?"

The Keeper stared at her, dumbfounded. "How do you know about that?"

Her eyes became darker, shadows moving in their depths.

"They learned things from it they're not supposed to know. They wanted to use Kyth as a key to unlock that knowledge. You must resist them at all cost. But you, who call yourselves Keepers, won't be able to do it on your own. The enemy's too strong. And they're getting stronger." She turned to Dagmara. Her gaze became piercing.

"Your gift may be weak at the moment, Grassland Woman," she said, "but I know it had already told you enough about this boy's ability and how important it is. His gift, Ghaz Alim, as your priests call it, is the only thing that can save you. All of you. If he offers you an alliance, you should follow him without question."

They all were staring at her now. The tent suddenly seemed brighter, the flame of a single candle in the center of the table rising taller in the still air.

"What do you know about my gift?" Kyth asked slowly.

Ayalla smiled. "It's for you to discover. I cannot teach you how to use it. My gift is different from yours."

"But you know something about it, don't you? Why don't you tell me?"

She held his gaze. "I know what you know. You can resist their power to command. You can use the forces around you to fill you with strength beyond anyone's control. You can command the elements, and protect others from the enemy's power. Your gift doesn't end there, Kyth, but this should be enough for a start, shouldn't it?"

Kyth thought about it. She was right. But somehow when he actually used his Ghaz Alim, it didn't seem quite so impressive. He could be a decent fighter when he used the wind, but he couldn't maintain this ability for long. He could resist the Kaddim's power and protect one person from their control, but he never really tried to split this protection to affect more people. As for commanding the elements...

He suddenly remembered the wave that reached down to the bottom of the river when he and Mai were drowning and brought them back ashore, far upstream from where they were supposed to be. He hesitated.

"It sounds more impressive than it is," he said truthfully. "I can only do these things on a very small scale. Because of that, I can't really make my power, whatever it is, a bargaining chip to forge an alliance. It would be wrong to give anyone this false hope. I want the Cha'ori to join us, but not because they believe that my gift could protect them from anything."

Ayalla shook her head. "So noble. So foolish. You should be able to realize that if you can do these things on a small scale, all you need is to expand the boundary of your mind. It's only a matter of time. But if you insist on doing this your way, there is only one other thing the Forest Mother can do for you. I will follow you to the Crown City and take a seat on your council."

Everyone stared.

"You?" Kyth asked in disbelief.

She returned his gaze calmly.

"There was a seat on this council once," she said, "for an emissary from the Forestlands. It's time to get it restored."

"That was more than a thousand years ago," Egey Bashi protested. "In the days of the old empire. I don't think that–"

Ayalla's look cut him off. "It was *my* seat. I held it, and now I will go back to reclaim it. Changes are coming. It's time for the Forestlands to return. If the Dark Order takes over, the Forest will suffer. I will not be able to protect my children." Her gaze became sad. She lowered her eyes and sat back. There was silence as everyone stared at her.

Kyth knew that she was very old. But to think that a thousand years ago, in the days of the old empire, Ayalla had a seat on the High Council…

He cleared his throat.

"It may not be my place to speak for everyone," he said, "but I think it is a great idea. I believe that your alliance, Lady Ayalla, will be invaluable."

She smiled. "They are children, too busy with their petty quarrels to pay attention to the important things. I will be glad to have your support, Prince Kythar, and that of others, but you don't need to worry. No one in that council chamber will challenge my claim."

She sat back, the spiders of her dress rearranging themselves in a turmoil that made Kyth blush. He saw Egey Bashi hastily look away. The Magister's transformation was striking. Without his scar, he looked like a completely different man, younger and stronger than before.

Ayalla reached down to push the last couple of spiders into their places, with the absentminded gesture of a woman smoothing out a fold of her dress. Then she sat up and ran a glance around the room, fixing her eyes on Dagmara.

"What do you say, Grassland Woman?" she asked. "You and I go back hundreds of years. I know, gift or not, you are capable of making the right choice. Will you go with me and Prince Kythar to the Crown City?"

Dagmara sat up straight.

"If the Forest Mother herself is asking me to go, I cannot possibly stay behind. We invited you here for a council, Ayalla, and I will follow your lead. The enemy is too powerful to face on our own. And you are right, Kyth. Some day this feud between our people has to stop."

"There's one more thing," Egey Bashi put in. "As I learned today, King Evan and Mother Keeper are prisoners in Castle Illitand. Before any of the things you mention can be done, they must be rescued."

Dagmara frowned. "If your King can be held prisoner by one of his vassals, what power does he really have?"

"He's not held by one of his vassals," Egey Bashi said, "His imprisonment has been cleverly arranged by the Kaddim Brothers of the Dark Order. They also hold the Duke of Illitand himself, as well as the Princess of Shayil Yara."

Kyth looked at him in shock. He heard bits of it from Ellah in the short time they had to catch up on all the events, but he never realized things were this bad.

"What are we going to do?" he asked.

Egey Bashi shrugged. "I see only one way. We must go to Castle Illitand without delay and break them out."

Ayalla nodded. "We must not delay. My children will take everyone across the water. They will also make a path through the forest, straight to Illitand Hall."

46
EMISSARIES OF THE EMPIRE

Evan had been avoiding the room where Han was killed. Even though the castle servants spent long hours and what seemed like barrels of water scrubbing the floor clean, he still imagined he could sense the tart smell of blood every time he walked into the chamber. He knew it wasn't possible, but the smell in his mind simply wouldn't go away.

The only alternative that allowed him to stay as far as possible from the place was the company of the Keepers, whose incessant ability to discuss the details of their order seemed admirable under the circumstances. It was as if there was nothing more important than to make an immediate decision on how many members of the Inner Circle should be allowed to vote on promoting new initiates, or whether the distribution of the founder substances, whatever they were, should be restricted only to the scholars. Getting into these detailed discussions that could last for hours, Odara Sul and Mother Keeper seemed to become oblivious to their imprisonment, as if the only thing keeping them away from their Order was the fact that they couldn't come to an agreement on these important matters.

Evan wished he could have something like that to occupy his mind. He tried to think past the situation he was

418   BLADES OF THE OLD EMPIRE

in, but despite all his efforts, he couldn't escape the feeling of helplessness that had became more prominent as the days went by. At times he was actually starting to doubt if they were ever going to get out of the castle alive. Daemur's promise that Evan would rot in these walls seemed to be coming true, even if not yet in the literal sense.

The Majat were around him all the time. While Lothar seemed to be doing an adequate job as their leader, Evan couldn't help sensing the general atmosphere of defeat that prevailed in the small enclosure of their imprisonment. It was disheartening to watch.

Days came and went without bringing much variation in daily routine until Evan stopped counting them anymore. From a corner window with a limited view of the castle's front entrance, he watched the impressive funeral procession that had set out to the Majat Guild to escort Han's body, led by Daemur Illitand's own nephew from the lesser house Ilmareil. The golden embroidery of the cover draping over the casket weighted down the thick wheels of the funeral cart, pulled by a magnificent train of eight snow-white horses. The guards of Lord Ilmareil's suite wore white plumes in sign of mourning, and the young noble himself had his head bare, a waterfall of auburn hair cascading down his shoulders.

Evan didn't envy the Duke the position he had got himself into. He doubted that even such a lavish display was going to impress the Majat Guildmaster enough to forget the incident, but he couldn't blame Daemur for trying.

Watching out of the window, Evan could also see Kaddim Tolos, who stood beside Daemur watching the procession take off and followed the Duke inside with the air of a man in control. Nobody bothered the King for many days after, except the servants who brought food, changed linens, and took care of the daily chores. They all looked alike, silent men dressed in green tunics with sparse yellow trim, meant to represent the Illitand gold without the expense, their faces bearing fish-like expressions of silent obedience. After a while Evan stopped noticing them.

One day, when Evan was making his way to the Keepers' quarters for his daily lesson in the affairs of the Outer Circle, he heard footsteps and metal clanking outside. The doors flung open, letting in Kaddim Tolos with twelve hooded men close on his heels.

The Majat surrounded the King in a protective ring and drew their swords, but Evan saw hesitation on their faces that echoed in his own heart. They all knew how useless they were against the frightening power commanded by this slim, yellow-eyed man.

The Kaddim came within twenty paces of Evan and stopped. Despite the dramatic entrance, he seemed in no hurry to start the conversation, surveying the King and his sparse suite with a cold expression.

"I trust you find your accommodations comfortable, Your Majesty?" he asked at length.

Evan held a pause, measuring the man up and down with a cold gaze. "Where's Lord Daemur?"

Tolos spread his hands. "I thought you didn't want to speak to him again, Your Majesty."

"True. But given the choice, I'd rather speak to him than to you."

The Kaddim smiled. "I thought you might feel that way. This is why I'm not here to talk. I came to take you with me, so that you can speak to my brothers instead. Kaddim Nimos, Haghos, and Farros have just arrived in the castle, and they all are eager to meet you, Sire."

Evan stood up straight. Having more Kaddim Brothers around wasn't welcome news.

"I have no knowledge of the men you are speaking about," he said. "But it seems that if they're as eager to meet me as you say, they would have had no trouble coming here. These chambers have become less private than a city tavern on a busy night. Everyone feels free to come and go as they please."

"Except you," Tolos pointed out with just a touch of smugness. "And Mother Keeper."

"What is it you really want?" Evan asked. "You can't keep us here forever, you know."

"Nor do I intend to, Majesty. I was only waiting for my brothers to get here. And now, we are planning a council. Yours and Lord Daemur's presence would make the highlight of it. Mother Keeper and Tanad Eli Faruh are also invited, of course."

He nodded and two of his men brushed past, flinging open the door to the Keepers' quarters without ceremony.

"I'm not coming," Evan said. "I'm certain you and your brothers can hold your little council without me."

Tolos smiled. "And how do you propose to resist us, Your Majesty?"

Evan glanced at the Majat, tense and ready with swords in hand. He knew they would fight for him to the death. He also knew they would lose.

"Stand down your men, Jeih Lothar," he said. "There's no use in fighting when you don't have a chance."

The Majat looked at him with hesitation.

"It's an order." Evan raised his voice just a tone higher, so that it rang clearly through the hall.

"The Majat don't obey the King, Your Majesty," Lothar responded. "Regardless of your orders, it's our duty to our Guild to protect you with our lives." His gaze was firm, but there was no conviction in his voice.

"The Pentade would serve me better by staying alive. *Not* by getting themselves killed and leaving me entirely without protection. Didn't they teach you that in your training, Jeih?"

Lothar kept Evan's gaze a moment longer, then stepped back and lowered his sword. The rest of the Majat followed.

"A wise decision, Your Majesty," Tolos said. "Your guards may stay here and wait for your return. It won't be long if you cooperate."

Mother Keeper appeared from the inner chambers, escorted by two robed men. She was wearing her Keeper's garb, a white cloak with an embroidery of a lock and key on the left shoulder. Its hood was thrown back, revealing smoothly arranged hair. As she stepped out of the chambers, she met Evan's gaze and gave him an encouraging nod.

Tolos led the way through the numerous castle corridors with the look of a man who knew his way well. As they walked, Evan strained to remember the hallways and passages, familiar to him from his childhood visits to Illitand Hall. From the looks of it they were headed for the large audience chamber downstairs, which members of the Illitand family fondly referred to as the throne room. As he walked, Evan did his best not to show excitement at leaving behind the enclosure of his involuntary dwelling.

Tolos's men flung open the large double doors and led the way inside. A small circle of chairs was set in the middle of the giant room. Most of them were occupied. The pale and disheveled Daemur Illitand sat in his chair with the look of a man past caring what was going on around him. Tanad Eli Faruh on his left was dressed as richly and colorfully as always, but his dark Olivian skin had a grayish tint, and the circles under his eyes were definitely darker than the rest of his face.

Evan looked further, to the other participants in the gathering. Seated across Daemur were three men, whose draping robes and the cold, creeping quality of their gazes were eerily similar to Tolos's. Evan's skin prickled as he walked toward them, careful to keep his face calm.

He approached the indicated chair and lowered onto the hard wooden seat, watching Tolos unhurriedly take a place next to the man whose dark eyes didn't seem to have any irises, making his sharp-featured face look almost inhuman. Next to him sat a thin man with a tonsured head and speckled brown-and-gray eyes, and another, with thin hair and bird-like features. Evan stared.

"Reverend Haghos?"

The man's thin lips twitched. "*Kaddim* Haghos, Your Majesty."

Evan could only gape as the man calmly introduced his companions. "Kaddim Nimos, Sire. And, over here, Kaddim Farros."

Evan forced himself to relax under the heavy stares of the Kaddim Brothers. He felt too tired to be surprised. If the former reverend of the Church chose to ally himself with the Kaddim, there seemed nothing more to be said.

"Now," Tolos said, "since we're all gathered here, my lords and ladies, it's time to discuss our plans. Kaddim Nimos?" He turned to the man with dark irisless eyes.

"Our plan is very simple, my lords and ladies," Nimos said. "We want to restore the old Shandorian Empire."

In the pause that followed everyone looked at him in disbelief.

Evan recovered first. "You *can't* be serious."

Nimos's dark eyes bore into him with feverish intensity. "Oh, but I am, Your Majesty."

"You are talking about vast territories, inhabited by people so different that they would never–"

"I'm talking about everyone on our side of the Eastern Mountain Range." Nimos glanced at his companions. "The old empire stretched from the Ridges all the way to the Southern Marshes – a peaceful union, where everyone coexisted in harmony, under one rule."

"Peaceful?" Evan began, and bit his lip. There was no need for a political argument. He was certain the preposterous suggestion to restore the bloody rule of the raging maniacs that called themselves emperors did not come from ignorance.

Nimos shrugged. "It's understandable that Your Majesty would feel somewhat emotional about our plan. But a good emperor–"

Evan smiled. "I can see we're finally coming to the point. Who do you have in mind?"

Nimos held a pause, running his eyes around the entranced group. "A highly worthy man, I can assure you, Sire."

"You mean, one of your brothers?"

Nimos gave Evan a pitiful look. "Your vision is so limited, if I may be so bold. Our true master is the only one worthy of ruling the empire. We're here as his emissaries, no more."

It seemed that the room had become darker as he said these words. Evan felt a chill pass over the stone floor and resisted the urge to pull his cloak tighter around himself.

He remembered a strange sign burned into the shoulder of the man they'd captured in the castle courtyard, after the attack on Kyth back in Tadar. The sign of Ghaz Kadan. When these men referred to their master, could they really mean…?

Evan took a breath. "This is insane. You can't mean your master, as in Ghaz Ka–"

"*Silence!*" Tolos rose up from his seat. "Don't speak the sacred name in vain!"

Evan receded back into his chair. "If your plans are as grand as all this, why play this charade and go to such lengths to gather us all here?"

"Simple," Nimos said. "The old empire has been divided into the kingdoms of Tandar and Shayil Yara, as well as the Bengaw Province, the Order of Keepers, the Wanderer people, and the Majat Guild. These are all independent forces not to be ignored, but only the two kingdoms and the Order of Keepers by now constitute real power. We gathered you here so that you could sign a treaty indicating your voluntary decision to join the empire."

Evan smiled. "Lord Daemur and I speak for Tandar," he said. "But whatever the Tanad signs for Shayil Yara couldn't be held as a true document. He's an ambassador, no more."

Nimos nodded. "Of course. The signature has to come from Princess Aljbeda. We know that the Tanad advises Her Highness, so we took the liberty of bringing him here to ensure her cooperation."

"But the Princess is only five years old! She can't be held accountable!"

"She is the heiress to the Southern Throne. As such, her word means a lot. She is five, true, but I assure Your Majesty that she realizes the responsibility. Her cooperation would mean as much as yours."

Evan hesitated. It was true. Ridiculous as it was, if Princess Aljbeda signed the document it would be binding under the circumstances. Even her mother, Queen Rajmella of Shayil Yara, wouldn't be able to annul it without risking a war.

"Where's the Princess?" he asked slowly.

Nimos smiled. "Don't be concerned, Your Majesty. The Princess is safely in our care. Her ladies in waiting have been most gracious in allowing us to set our own guard around Her Highness. In fact, despite the late hour, the Princess will be brought here as soon as we are ready. I'd like to remind you that her wellbeing is not only the Tanad's, but your responsibility to your southern sovereign. If Her Highness were to suffer an unfortunate incident in your kingdom, Queen Rajmella would be quite unlikely to ever forgive you. Personally, I'd hate to see a war started over something as small as this."

There was another long pause.

Evan took a deep breath, steadying his voice. "You know very well that none of us would ever sign such a document. If this is your worst threat–"

"It isn't," Nimos said calmly. "We can do better. Consider this, Your Majesty. If you don't sign this document, none of you will ever leave this chamber alive."

Evan ran his eyes around the pale faces of his companions. They were alone here, with more than a dozen deadly warriors and four men who possessed the power to control people's minds.

"You'll never get away with it," he said quietly.

Nimos smiled. "And who do you think would oppose us, Sire?"

"How about the Majat? You've discounted them from your treaty, but it seems to me they're a considerable force that could bring you down."

Nimos waved his hands in a dismissive gesture.

"Your information is outdated," he said. "The Majat are formidable warriors, but without their skill they are just as helpless as anyone. Their best are the Diamonds, and I'm told you had a chance to see how easy they are to deal with. In fact, there are only twelve Diamonds that are currently in top shape for active assignments, and by our reckoning three of them should be dead by now. Including, I might say, your former Pentade leader."

"Aghat Han," Evan said quietly.

"Yes. Him too. But I was actually referring to Aghat Mai. He and Aghat Kara are both dead."

Evan raised his face to the man, feeling a chill creep up his spine. What he said wasn't true. It simply *couldn't* be.

"Now, Your Majesty," Nimos said. "Will you sign the document?"

47

A NEW ALLY

Kyth found Kara at the edge of the camp polishing her weapon. He knew this was a time she preferred not to be disturbed, but during their strenuous march he had become all but desperate to catch her alone. After her recovery she spent all her time with Mai and Raishan, receding into their company like a shelter. Kyth understood she needed time. She had come out the other side of death, an outcast chased by her own kind, all because of him. Her future, as far as the Majat Guild was concerned, was uncertain and he couldn't offer nearly as much comfort in dealing with it as people of her upbringing. Kyth had been careful to stay away during the entire trip but now, as they neared Illitand Hall and their plans were about to be set into motion, he had to talk to her.

She raised her head as he approached and silently moved sideways to make room for him on the dry patch of grass. Kyth sat down, taking a moment to enjoy her closeness and the warmth of her shoulder next to him. There was so much he wanted to say to her. But he wasn't going to.

"It's today, isn't it?" he asked.

She nodded.

"I hope you're planning to bring me along," he went on.

"We're debating it," she said. "I, for one, think it's much too dangerous."

"But I can protect at least one of you from their power!"

She shrugged. "I'm still immune. This should be enough in a tight spot. If I can take out the Kaddim Brothers–"

"You haven't seen them fight! Nimos was able to stand up to Mai for quite some time."

"Mai was badly wounded at the time."

Kyth paused. She had a point, but he simply couldn't accept it. To sit back and do nothing when Kara was risking her life against impossible odds to save his father…

"I want to come," he said. "If you're against it, I hope Mai and Raishan would see it my way."

She looked at him, suddenly serious. "I don't want anything to happen to you."

Did her voice really waver, or was it his imagination?

"Nothing will happen to me," he said. "Not while I'm with three Diamonds."

She looked past him into the forest shadows. Kyth turned.

The blackness behind him shaped up to become Mai.

"It's time," the Diamond said.

"I'm coming with you," Kyth said. "My power can be of use to you."

Mai gave him a long look, then nodded. Kara's eyes darted between them, but she said nothing as she sheathed her weapon and sprang to her feet.

Raishan and Egey Bashi materialized from the shadows behind them.

"Aghat Mai wants to bring Ellah with us," Raishan said to Kara. "But I'm not sure it's a good idea."

"Ellah?" Kyth looked at Mai in surprise.

The Diamond's expression was impenetrable. "Her gift could be of use to us. Just like yours."

"How?"

Mai shrugged. "I believe there're people in the castle who'd actually be willing to help. Knowing who they are would eliminate a lot of unnecessary killing. But we can't trust any of them unless we have a truthseer with us."

"But she can't even fight!" Kyth protested.

Mai measured him up and down with his gaze. "No offense, Your Highness, but for the task we're facing, neither can you."

Kyth bit his tongue. He wanted to remind Mai how for a short time back in the Grasslands they fought as equals, and how his gift gave him powers Mai could never dream of. But now didn't seem to be the time.

"It's her *life* you are risking," he said instead.

"I think this one's not for you to decide, is it?" Mai held Kyth's gaze for a moment. Then he turned and walked off into the darkness.

"Since when is *he* in charge around here?" Kyth wondered.

Egey Bashi patted him on the shoulder. "I hate it myself when they get like that," he said. "But Aghat Mai's right. Ellah's gift can be of use to us. And, she's free to refuse if she isn't up to it."

"But she…" Kyth looked to make sure Kara and Raishan were out of earshot. "She'll come just because of Mai."

Egey Bashi squeezed his arm. "I fail to see the difference, lad," he said. "If you know what I mean."

Kyth lowered his eyes. *Kara didn't ask me. I insisted on coming myself.* But deep inside he knew the Keeper had a point.

Through the intertwining branches of the forest thicket he threw a last glance at the camp. Most of the people were asleep. Alder and Garnald sat beside Ayalla's snakewood hut, deep in conversation. A few Cha'ori from Dagmara's escort were tending to their horses. Mai and Ellah stood at the side of the dying campfire. They exchanged a few words, then turned and disappeared into the bushes. A few moments later Kyth heard the approaching rustle of their footsteps. Ellah met Kyth's gaze and gave him a brief nod.

"Let's move," Kara said from the shadows ahead.

They moved in a single file along a barely perceptible trail that led off through the trees to the distant glimmer of the Illitand Lake. Kyth was careful to keep up behind Kara, straining his eyes to see her in the forest darkness. Her slim shape, draped in a dark cloak, blended with the shadows. She moved so smoothly that she was almost invisible.

After half an hour of fast walking they came to the edge of the forest. The open glade in front ran into the shimmering water of the lake. The city of Illitand Hall rose in its center, straight out of the water. Scattered night light reflecting off the lake surface coated the ornate stone lace with a sparse glint of tarnished silver, making the entire city look like an object of ancient craftsmanship. Its dark outline loomed against the low clouds, a powerful, ominous beauty warning intruders against any attempts to penetrate its walls.

"How do you propose to storm this?" Egey Bashi asked.

The Majat exchanged glances.

"There are two ways," Raishan said. "The easy way would be to get close to the walls without being noticed."

"What's the other way?"

Raishan calmly returned his look. "The *other's* the hard way." He turned to move on.

"Wait!" Egey Bashi called out.

All three Diamonds turned to him.

"There's something I need to tell all of you about the Kaddim Brothers," Egey Bashi said. "Their power only acts within visual range. If you're behind a wall, or a very thick door, they can't affect you."

"How do you know this?" Raishan demanded.

Egey Bashi looked him straight in the face. "It has been bothering me for a while, but I've just realized. That time in the monastery, when they tried to blast you – you got behind a pillar and they missed you. Remember, Aghat Raishan?"

Raishan hesitated, then nodded.

"Let's move." He turned back to the silent shape of the fortress.

They crept low along the ground, moving as smoothly as they could and keeping to the natural shadows of the landscape. The wall loomed ahead, a rough stone structure that rose to the height of at least three houses and ran all the way around the city. Kyth noticed how the Majat kept their eyes on the narrow slits along the top of the wall, and how their postures were very alert, as if waiting for an attack. But no one tried to stop them as they made their way across the stone bridge to the bottom of the wall.

Kara and Mai were in the lead. When they reached the massive city gate, they stopped, bringing the entire party to a halt in their wake. The two of them exchanged short phrases, indistinct to the rest of the group. Then Kara stood back and ran her eyes up the roughly hewn stones.

Kyth crept closer, so that he could hear what was going on.

"I'll cover you," Mai said. He took out a crossbow and drew it with a smooth wrist movement, placing a bolt against the string.

Kara nodded. Kyth had no idea what they were going to do, but it didn't seem to be a good time to ask. He crouched against the wall, watching.

Kara threw off her cloak and took out a small grappler hook. Her arm flew back in a powerful sway. A thin metal streak darted through the air and they heard a click high above. She tugged at the rope, so thin that it was hard to see in the darkness. Then she nodded to Mai and pushed off the ground, sliding up the rope quickly as if someone from above was pulling her up. Mai stood back, crossbow at the ready.

Raishan swept past him to a small door, sharply outlined within the massive gate.

"Stay close, everyone," he said. "Be ready to get inside."

A thud echoed above, followed by metal clanking. Mai's crossbow hand flew up and the bolt went off, whistling as it cut through the still night air. There was a gasp and a large bulky shape disengaged from the top of the wall and tumbled down onto the ground at their feet. It bounced as it landed, and rolled to a standstill right beside Kyth.

It was a man in leather armor covered by a green and yellow Illitand cloak. His helmet slid off after the fall, revealing a young face, barely older than Kyth's. His head turned to the side, unseeing eyes staring into the sky. A crossbow bolt protruded from his chest.

Ellah gasped and hid her face on Kyth's shoulder. Kyth looked past her to Mai, who calmly reloaded his crossbow and looked up the wall. There seemed to be no more activity above. After a long moment Mai lowered his weapon.

"Clear," he said. He unloaded the crossbow with a quick move, and put it away. Then he bent down and picked up Kara's cloak.

There was more clanking and the small door within the gate swung open. Kara stood on the other side, her face calm and composed. Behind her, lifeless shapes sprawled on the cobbled stone pavement. Kyth counted five, all of them wearing outfits of the Illitand city guard. From this distance he couldn't tell if they were alive.

They stepped inside. Raishan, walking last, closed the door behind them. Kara took her cloak from Mai and wrapped into it, once again blending with the shadows of the gray stone walls.

They made their way uphill, past rows of houses lining the street that ascended from the gate at a steep angle toward the distant shape of the castle. The city looked fast asleep. There was nothing in the streets except occasional stray cats that shied away at their approach and surveyed them from the shadows of side alleys with huge glowing eyes. A dog barked at them from one of the enclosed yards, but stopped abruptly as Mai walked by, throwing a short glance through the thick wooden fence. They waited a moment to see if the incident had raised an alarm, but the streets seemed to be as quiet as before.

By the time they reached the upper city, Kyth was out of breath. Ellah and Egey Bashi also looked winded, but the three Diamonds were calm and fresh, as if they spent the entire time resting, not ascending the mountain at a fast pace.

They stopped in front of the castle gate, the carved ornaments along its top clearly outlined against the night sky. This wall was not as tall as the one down below, but it was hewn much smoother, making it harder to climb. Just like at the city entrance, there was a small door at the base of the gate, tightly shut.

"Shouldn't be a problem," Kara said after a pause. "Unless, of course, there's a large force waiting for us on the other side."

"The way to scale this one is on the side, over there." Mai pointed. "The wall's lower in that place, even if it doesn't seem that way. Once you're up there, you'll get a good view of the entire yard before they have a chance to see you."

Kara nodded and took out her grappler hook again. But before she had time to do anything, the door at the base of the gate screeched and slowly swung open.

Mai and Raishan closed in, shielding Kyth and Ellah with their bodies. Kara, in front, tensed up for action.

A lonely figure came into view, clearly outlined against the doorway. A young woman with pale skin and flaming red hair, dressed in a deeply cut green dress with a golden trim.

They all stared.

"Lady Celana Illitand?" Egey Bashi asked.

The royal lady nodded as she ran her eyes around the group, pausing in turn on each of the faces. Then she walked forward and stopped in front of Kyth, dropping a deep curtsey.

"Prince Kythar." Her voice was clear, and its ringing timbre had a way to reach its listeners without obvious effort on her part. "I'm so glad you are finally here. I was waiting, so that I could be the first in this castle to offer help in setting King Evan free."

Kyth stared. "Why?"

Lady Celana straightened out and gave him a look, in which the outward shyness of a young maid was greatly outweighed by a chilling intelligence that made Kyth feel instantly alert.

"I am afraid, my lord," she said, "that both our fathers have fallen victim to a very powerful enemy. While I know the impressive force you bring would normally be sufficient to break the King out, this time we are dealing with something out of the ordinary. These men can kill a Diamond Majat. They've killed Aghat Han."

There was a shocked silence.

"*What* did you say?" Egey Bashi demanded.

She shook her head. "It was an unfortunate incident, for which I am afraid my lord father will be blamed, even though he had nothing to do with it. We sent off a funeral procession to the Majat Guild days ago. But since then Kaddim Tolos and his men have taken over the castle."

"Kaddim Tolos?" Kyth echoed.

Lady Celana met his gaze. In the darkness her green eyes acquired a velvety touch that made them look like two bottomless pools of water.

"He is a powerful man, who bent my lord father to his will and made him do things that, to my regret, may challenge the good standing of our house. That's why I am here, Prince Kythar. I wish to redeem my family's honor as much as possible under the circumstances. I will do whatever is in my power to aid you. I will give you my life, if need be. I am yours to command, my lord." She bent down in another deep curtsey and stayed, head lowered.

Kyth gave her an uncomfortable glance. "Rise, my lady," he said.

She straightened out and stood, holding his gaze. Her face was calm, but Kyth had a feeling that she had more control of the situation than he did. He threw a hesitant glance at Egey Bashi.

The Keeper nodded, taking the cue. "From what I heard, my lady, your house and especially your lord father, have done a lot of harm to the King. Why should Prince Kythar believe you?"

Lady Celana moved her gaze around their group and fixed it on Ellah. "You are a truthseer, aren't you?"

"Yes," Ellah said slowly.

"Tell the Magister – do I speak the truth?"

Ellah held a pause, then nodded.

"All of it?" Egey Bashi demanded.

Ellah slowly turned to him. "Since the lady met us here, she hasn't told a single lie."

Lady Celana's face remained calm, but Kyth noticed a brief expression of relief that echoed in his own heart. She *was* being sincere. She was really here to help.

He took a breath. "Thank you, my lady. We will gladly accept your help."

She smiled, her porcelain face for a moment acquiring a glimpse of warmth. "We must move. We have very little time."

She turned and walked back inside the courtyard. Kyth wanted to follow, but Raishan blocked him and moved in first, Kara after him and Mai, beside the doorway, kept his hand up, signaling for the rest of them to pause. After a moment, he lowered his hand and stood back, letting everyone through.

Lady Celana led the way to a small group of Illitand guards gathered in the center of the courtyard.

"The prisoners are kept in the throne room under heavy guard," she said. "They've been there for hours. And worse, they've just sent for Princess Aljbeda. I am afraid it will all end badly if we don't do something right away."

The three Diamonds exchanged glances and Kyth saw quick hand signs go between them.

"We must split up," Raishan said. "Ellah. You'll go with Kara to the Princess's quarters."

"I'll send a guard to show you the way," Lady Celana said. "If you hurry you can probably get there before they do."

Kara nodded. Ellah glanced at Mai, who wasn't paying any attention to her. Kyth could well relate to her fear. He didn't like the idea of being separated from Kara any more than Ellah from Mai. But he wasn't about to interfere in the Majat's plan. He reached forward and patted the girl's arm.

"Be safe," he said quietly.

Ellah gave him a quick nod and hurried to catch up with Kara and one of the guards, already halfway up the stairs to the castle. Kyth watched them go, praying they were going to be safe.

"The four of us are going in together," Raishan went on. "Prince Kythar, you're covering me. If I get wounded or disabled, you must immediately switch to protect Aghat Mai. One of us must be able to fight at all times."

Kyth hesitated. "If you get wounded and I stop protecting you, they'll kill you."

Raishan's gaze became cold. "This isn't about me. We're here to rescue the King. If some of us die in the process, this is the way it has to be. Let's keep our goals clear, shall we?"

Kyth turned away. He didn't like this, but he had to admit that Raishan was right.

"You should stay behind, my lady," Raishan said to Lady Celana. "It's not safe for you to come."

She nodded. "My guards will show you the way. May Lord Shal Addim protect us all."

48

A VISION IN LILAC

Evan peered into the faces of their captors. In the past hour they had barely said a word to each other, but there was considerable movement in the room as more hooded men streamed into the chamber, flooding the space around the prisoners. Each had a weapon in hand, a spiked metal orb hanging off a chain.

When the movement in the room ceased, Kaddim Tolos addressed the assembled troops. "I think it's time to invite Her Royal Highness to join our gathering."

Evan looked up. He was tired of the pointless argument with their captors, but he also had a strong sense that *someone* had to offer resistance, and none of his fellow prisoners seemed eager to do it. Daemur and the Tanad had fallen into apathy more than two hours ago, and Mother Keeper was exhausted after a long and intimidating exchange with Kaddim Farros, who turned out to be more proficient in politics than his looks suggested.

"There seems to be no point in bringing the Princess here," Evan said. "None of us have signed your document."

Tolos smiled. "Exactly, Majesty. Somebody has to start, don't you think? I am sure Her Highness would be just the right one to help all of you to overcome your fits of stubbornness."

At his signal a large group exited through the back doors of the chamber, the sound of footsteps receding down the hallway.

"There's hardly any glory," Evan said, "in bending a five year-old child to your will."

Tolos's smile became wider. "I admire you, Sire, for your incessant courage. You find it worth your while to fight even the losing battles, don't you?"

Evan didn't feel the need to respond as he calmly held the man's yellow gaze.

"As for your question," Tolos went on, "this isn't about glory at all."

"Actually," Evan said, "it wasn't a question. Merely an observation."

Tolos glared. Evan calmly returned his gaze. He was past caring what would happen to him, and he wasn't about to give in to the man's intimidation tactics.

After a while they heard footsteps at the back door and a group of people entered the hall. The little princess walked between the robed guards with a dazed expression of a child taken out of bed past her usual sleeping hour. Her pale golden hair looked like it was combed and arranged in a hurry, leaving small wisps sticking out of the loose knot at the back of her head. Her chocolate skin was paler than usual, and her bright violet eyes shone like gems, surveying the large gathering around her with wonder.

Her soft purple dress accented her eye color, not as elaborate as what she usually wore to court, but undoubtedly chosen with care to make the Princess look fragile and adorable. Such a trick would have possibly worked to soften the hearts of their captors, had they happened to be normal people and not obsessed maniacs that worshipped the Cursed Destroyer, but Evan still

admired the Princess's caretakers who hadn't spared any
effort to give the child her best chance.

The usual Princess's retinue of twelve Olivian ladies, which
Evan had come to think of as a natural addition to her wardrobe,
was absent. Only two ladies walked beside the child, both
dressed in lavish silk gowns whose lilac color provided a proper
accent to the rich shade of the Princess's garb. Apparently the
ladies didn't have a chance to think carefully about their own
appearance, directing all their creativity to the Princess's outfit.
Their dresses seemed much more fit for an intimate candlelight
evening than for an armed gathering in a gloomy stone hall.
Low cuts left the necks and shoulders bare, exposing enough
cleavage to make a focal point for all gazes thrown in their
direction. To ward against the night chill, they also wore light
silk cloaks with hoods on, clipped at the neck in a way that,
instead of covering up the exposed flesh, made it even more
obvious. The effect was compelling. Even in his sad situation,
Evan couldn't help but stare.

He knew that one of the privileges of the Olivian ambassador
consisted of hand-picking the ladies for the Princess's suite, and
that Tanad Eli Faruh exercised this privilege to the full. It was
clear from the display in front of them that he had spared no
effort in choosing the best the entire kingdom of Shayil Yara
had to offer.

Both ladies looked familiar. Evan was fairly sure that the one
with a sensationally tall neck, whose full breasts threatened to
escape from the low opening of her dress, was Lady Lavinia. Her
delicate oval face, partly hidden by the folds of the hood, was
framed by luscious golden hair, cascading in carefully arranged
ringlets down one side of her neck onto her bare shoulder.

The other lady was slimmer, and her breasts were a bit
too small for what Evan believed to be the Tanad's taste.
The dress she wore was perfectly designed to expose them

just enough to make one wonder if the rest was as gorgeous as the small bit visible to the eye. She had a special refined quality of movement, so that as she walked across the floor, holding the hand of Princess Aljbeda who seemed anxious to keep by her side, Evan found it difficult to look away. He peered at her face, but the deep folds of her light hood made it hard to see. He had surely seen her at court, but he couldn't recall her name.

Evan glanced at their captors, wondering if they were also impressed by this display of Olivian beauty, but the four Kaddim Brothers remained calm. Nimos's dark eyes glinted as he watched the newcomers, stopping just short of the ladies' faces and lowering down to the Princess.

The child stopped before the circle of chairs, clutching the hand of the lady by her side.

"Welcome, Your Highness," Tolos said. "Won't you join us?"

The Princess drew closer to her lady in waiting.

"I already joined you, sir," she said in a clear voice that carried easily through the hall. She spoke without any of the speech impediments of a small child, or the southern accent that dominated the speech of some of her countrymen, including Tanad Eli Faruh.

The child and the Kaddim stood for a moment facing each other.

"I don't think I know you," Princess Aljbeda said. "If you wish to talk to me further, you must first introduce yourself."

Evan was amused to see Tolos's eyebrows rise as he stared at the Princess with a bewildered expression.

"I am Kaddim Tolos," he said.

"Kad-dim?" The princess stretched the word as if trying to feel its taste. "This title is unfamiliar to us."

Tolos exchanged hesitant glances with his companions. Evan silently cheered the Princess on, but he knew that despite the admirable way she held herself there was no possibility of a good outcome to this conversation.

Nimos stepped up to Tolos's side. His gaze was cold.

"We summoned you here, Princess," he said, "to sign a very important document. Perhaps we should stop wasting time and get down to business, shall we?"

The child grasped the lady's hand tighter. "I don't sign very important documents, unless I have first had a chance to discuss them with the Lord Ambassador." She looked at Tanad Eli Faruh for support, but her trusted advisor didn't offer any. He sat very still, eyes darting between the Princess and their captors.

"If you really must, Highness," Nimos said. "Just be quick about it."

The Tanad shrunk away under Nimos's gaze. If the Ambassador had a chance to discuss anything with the Princess, Evan had no doubt about the advice he would give. But the Kaddim obviously didn't have a big discussion in mind. They waited, staring the child down with their cold, unblinking eyes.

Lady Lavinia stepped forward. "I don't think it's wise to frighten Her Royal Highness, my lord," she said in a deep velvety voice, as luscious as her skin that gave off a warm glint in the flickering torchlight. "Her age is quite delicate, and if I may say so, it's long past her bedtime."

Nimos gave her a cold look. "If you speak again, I'll give you to my men waiting outside, to handle as they please. Think of it, my lady, before you decide to open your pretty little mouth."

She looked at him in stunned silence. Then she stepped back and lowered her gaze. Evan noticed a quick glance that went between the two Olivian ladies before both of them receded into stillness, looming protectively over their young ward.

"That wasn't very nice, sir," the Princess said. "I'm sure you meant well, but I think you have upset Lady Lavinia.

You must apologize at once."

Nimos held her gaze. "I don't think so. But I could act on my threat, if Your Highness continues to be stubborn. My men are rough at times, but I'm certain your lady can keep them quite entertained before they finally do away with her."

Evan was sure the child didn't understand what he meant, but the threat in his voice was obvious. Princess Aljbeda's face twitched as if she was about to cry.

"It seems that everyone here is afraid of you, sir," she said. "I don't think you are up to any good. I wish to go back to my quarters."

"You're not leaving, Princess, until you sign the document." Nimos stepped forward and stretched out a hand. "Come here, Highness, I'll show you what to do."

The princess threw a helpless glance at the lady holding her hand and received an encouraging nod in return.

"I will not go to you, sir," she said. "You have evil eyes. I wish to stay with *her*." She raised her gaze to the lady. "Except," she added quietly, "we left my quarters so suddenly I didn't have time to catch your name."

The Olivian lady raised her hand and threw the hood off her face.

"My name's Kara, your Highness," she said.

Evan's astonishment echoed the gasps from around the hall. He stared. In all the times he saw her in a Majat outfit, he never imagined she would look like *that* in a dress.

The Kaddim Brothers went very still as they surveyed the new menace. Kara used the pause to bend down and pick up the Princess. The child threw her arms around Kara's neck and hid her face on the Majat's shoulder.

"You're *dead*," Nimos whispered.

Kara measured him up and down with her eyes.

"Strange, I haven't noticed."

"*Get her*!"

The men with orbens fanned around Kara. Evan's heart sank. He knew how good she was, but she was also unarmed, with a child in her arms, facing a roomful of deadly warriors. His hand darted to his sword, but the two men next to his chair reacted faster. A hand grasped Evan's shoulder and he felt steel at his throat. He eased back into his seat, the sharp metal tip pressing so hard he was sure it drew blood.

Kara used her free hand to pull off her cloak, flinging it into the way of the orbens. Her arm moved so fast it blurred. There was a metal screech as a chain twisted around the cloth, the spiked metal sphere stopping just short of reaching her hand. She dodged an orben coming from the back and continued the wrist movement, giving the cloak a sharp tug. Cloth ripped. The attacker stumbled, overbalanced, and released the chain. She caught it, flicking it into a spin with a very short leeway.

"Give me the Princess!" Lady Lavinia shouted.

One of the men swept past, dragging her out of the way and leaving Kara alone with the Princess in the ring of enemies.

"Hold on tight," Kara told the child. "And don't look."

Princess Aljbeda dutifully clasped on, burying her face deeper in Kara's shoulder.

Kara swayed the orben in a wide arch. The man at the end of the line stumbled and fell, blood gushing out of his torn neck. Kara edged back toward the door they came in from, but her way to safety was firmly blocked. She spun the orben, eyes darting between the men surrounding her. They looked determined, but no one seemed willing to attack first.

Nimos and Tolos threw off their cloaks and strode forward, each drawing a pair of curved sabers from the sheaths at their backs.

"I'm actually glad you survived," Nimos said. "You and I are *destined* to have some fun together."

He ran an oily glance that reached deep into the low cut of her dress. Evan shuddered, marveling in the way she deflected it, without even a flinch. Her face showed concentration as she spun the orben in front of her like a shield, eyes darting between her opponents.

The two Kaddim Brothers fanned out and crouched to attack.

Evan's heart wavered. This didn't look good. She didn't stand a chance with one orben against four blades. In addition to all the other handicaps, he could only imagine how hard it was to move around in a dress that was designed for an entirely different kind of activity.

The doors at the other side of the hall flung open, revealing a battle going on behind. All heads turned to watch four men rush in. Evan's heart washed with relief as he recognized them. In front were Mai and Raishan, weapons drawn. Kyth and Egey Bashi came up behind. Blood smeared the Prince's cheek, but otherwise he seemed unharmed. As Evan watched, Egey Bashi leaned forward and said something into Kyth's ear, receiving a nod in response.

Haghos and Farros stretched out their hands, directing a joint blast of power toward the newcomers. Before it hit, Egey Bashi and Mai drew back behind the doorway. Kyth's expression became detached as if he was wielding some sort of power.

Raishan raised his sword and advanced. The Kaddim's blast didn't seem to affect him at all. He made his steady way into the center of the room. His blade moved like a streak, men collapsing around him, but with the amount of enemies he was facing it was clear that it would take a while to reach the prisoners. Evan's eyes inadvertently went back to the action close by.

50
ROYAL BONDS

Evan looked at the approaching group, feeling the deadly strain of the past few hours slowly release its grip, giving way to fatigue. Kyth was in the lead, closely followed by Raishan and Egey Bashi. Watching him, Evan reflected that he would never again think of his son as a boy who needed guidance to understand the ways of the royals. Kyth was a man, his equal, the rightful heir to the throne.

His eyes itched. But kings didn't cry or rush forward to embrace anyone, even their only sons returning from a deadly battle. He smiled instead.

"Well done, son."

Kyth nodded. Their eyes locked, blue on blue, and a long private look passed between them.

Evan looked further to Raishan and Egey Bashi, his gaze inadvertently pausing on the Keeper's face. Staring closer, Evan realized he wasn't sure if it was the same man he knew.

"Magister Egey Bashi?" he asked. "What the hell happened to your face?"

The Keeper gave him a dark look. "It's a long story, Your Majesty."

Mother Keeper brushed past Evan, stopping in front of the

Magister. She reached out and touched his face, running her fingers along the barely visible line where the scar had been. For a moment she looked fragile and vulnerable like a little girl.

"I, for one, look forward to hearing this remarkable story, Magister," she said. "And I'm so glad to see you."

"Likewise." Egey Bashi gave her a slight bow, his eyes burning with an intensity that made Evan feel he was prying just by witnessing it. He looked away to Mai, who stood at the back holding little Princess Aljbeda in his arms.

"Aghat Mai," he said. "I was beginning to feel concerned about you."

The Majat bowed. He looked like he was about to say something, but at that moment Princess Aljbeda lifted her head.

She was pale, but seemed unharmed. Her eyes shone with bright curiosity as she surveyed Mai's face, first from up close, then drawing further away to see him better.

"I know who you are," she said. "You're Aghat Mai. The King's bodyguard. My ladies talk about you a lot." Her gaze became thoughtful, as if she was trying to recall the words. "They say things about your body. They like it, I think. They call you... dashing and dangerous, I believe. But I think they only mean to say that you are attractive and handsome. They say that too, sometimes. They also say you look good enough to eat." She gave him an appraising glance. "I don't think they really mean this last bit," she added.

There was an awkward silence.

"I think they do," Egey Bashi said under his breath.

Evan suppressed a smile, watching Lady Lavinia step forward and take the child from Mai's arms. As she did, she gave him a meaningful glance. "You're very good with children, Aghat."

Mai bowed. "You're very kind, my lady."

She smiled and measured him with another long look before receding to the back of the group.

Evan's gaze moved to Kara, who had kept very quiet during the entire exchange. Even after her ordeal, wounded and disheveled, she still looked stunning. The lilac silk brought out the deep shine in her violet eyes and accented her dark smooth skin, so that it gave off a faint suffused glow. The lines of her shoulders and breasts, carefully emphasized by the low cut of the dress, were so perfect that Evan found it difficult not to stare. It took a second look to notice the deep crimson streaks staining the precious cloth, and a rip in front that exposed the bare skin underneath. He hoped that some of this blood belonged to her enemies and that she wasn't hurt as badly as the state of her dress suggested.

"Are you all right, Aghat?" he asked. "You gave us quite a fright."

She smiled. "Sorry, Your Majesty. It was too late to devise a better plan for saving the Princess. Getting into her retinue was the only thing I could do."

Evan nodded. "It was a very clever disguise. You had everyone's attention completely distracted. You looked so–"

She stiffened. Mai and Raishan by her sides stood up straight, fixing their eyes firmly ahead.

Evan took the hint.

"–so much in control," he finished smoothly.

The tension in her neck relaxed. "My disguise was Lady Lavinia's idea. She's really good at such things." She turned to the Olivian, who stood calmly by her side, holding the Princess in her arms.

Lady Lavinia's smile held the approval of a teacher looking at a very talented student.

"You're kind, my lady," she said, "but I really didn't do much. With your looks, I didn't need to."

"I am afraid I ruined this beautiful gown, Lady Lavinia."

The Olivian lady smiled. "You did it credit, my lady. It

was as if this gown was made for you. You should always wear dresses."

"Regretfully, it's not my style, my lady."

Lavinia shook her head, the golden ringlets of her hair scattering seductively over her bare shoulder. "Of course it is, my lady. You have a beautiful body. You shouldn't be shy to show it."

Kara went very still. Her eyes darted to the two Majat, who stared ahead, their faces so straight that they seemed wooden.

"Not if I can help it," she said through clenched teeth.

Daemur Illitand approached, his eyes darting between Evan and Kyth with an expression of uncertainty.

Evan smiled. "You're under arrest, Lord Daemur. For high treason. As well as you, Tanad," he turned to Eli Faruh, who trailed behind the Duke, trying hard to blend into the background.

Daemur lifted his chin. "You're still in my castle, Your Majesty. I regret what happened between us, and I no longer intend to keep you here against your will, but on this soil I command a greater force than you. None of your guards are even here. You can't hope to apprehend me all by yourself, can you?"

Evan looked past him, meeting Mai's gaze. The Diamond stepped forward and lowered on one knee in front of the King.

"Your Majesty," he said. "With your permission, I'm here to resume my duty on the Pentade." He held out his Diamond token. Evan reached forward and took it.

"Welcome back, Aghat Mai," he said.

A look passed between them. Then Mai's hand shot up, drawing his weapon from the sheath at his back. As he rose to his feet, the tip of his staff touched Daemur's throat.

"I probably *could* apprehend you all by myself, Lord Daemur," Evan said. "I've always been a better swordsman than you. But since Aghat Mai is here, it won't be necessary."

Daemur's eyes darted between Evan and Mai with the look of a trapped animal. Before he could speak, the door at the back of the room flung open, letting in a procession led by a slight, elegant figure in a green dress with a golden trim.

Lady Celana crossed the hall toward them. Her heart-shaped face, red hair, and porcelain skin were no less striking than Lady Lavinia's features, but instead of drawing gazes she reflected them like a polished mirror as she walked, her steps so smooth that she seemed to be gliding over the floor. Her deep green eyes shone with a chilling intelligence far beyond her age, which Evan believed to be sixteen.

Two dozen Illitand guards followed in her wake, along with Ellah, Odara Sul and the Rubies of the Pentade. They caught Mai's gaze and stood to attention, their faces reflecting carefully disguised relief.

Lady Celana knelt on the floor in front of the King.

Evan hesitated. He couldn't help feeling uneasy about this sudden display of loyalty from someone who had been a party to keeping him prisoner for the past few weeks.

"Rise, my lady," he said.

She remained kneeling. "I beg for mercy, Your Majesty."

"If you beg for your father, my lady, it's not up to you to decide his fate. His crime's too grave."

She raised her face to him. "My lord father was influenced by an evil man. You know this man's power, Your Majesty. You know he can control minds and bend people to his will. My father fell victim to him, just like you."

Evan looked at Daemur who stood very still, with the tip of Mai's staff at his throat. He knew the Duke too well to fully believe Lady Celana. Yet, there was sense in it. He and Daemur had grown up together. When Evan came to this castle in disguise, he hadn't anticipated being held captive. It would have been utterly stupid for the Duke of Illitand to think he could get away with it. Only Kaddim Tolos could have thought...

He stopped himself. Whatever the Duke's reasons, he would never trust this family again.

"Rise, my lady," he said again. "It's not up to you to decide your father's fate."

Her eyes searched out Kyth, prompting.

He stepped forward. "Lady Celana helped us, father. She led us into the castle and sent her guards to aid us, so that we could reach you in time. On behalf of her family, she pledged loyalty to our house. And, since Ellah was with us, we know she was speaking the truth."

Daemur looked up. "She did *what*?"

Lady Celana glanced at her father calmly and turned back to Evan.

"Our house is loyal to the King," she said. "Prince Kythar was kind enough to accept my pledge. I am, forever, loyal to him. And to you, Your Majesty."

Evan looked at her in surprise, catching a reflection of his thoughts in Daemur's gaze. The Duke of Illitand had called Kyth an abomination and offered his daughter to Evan as a bride. Yet now, when Kyth singlehandedly drove away the deadly force that had attacked this castle and nearly destroyed the entire monarchy in Tallan Dar, the tables turned. Evan could see the thought process going on behind the smooth white skin of the Duke's forehead.

Daemur Illitant paused, then slowly lowered to his knees in front of Evan. "I join my daughter in begging your forgiveness, Your Majesty. I have been led astray by a powerful enemy. I wasn't acting of my own will."

"While I was here," Evan said, "things have been said between us that would be hard to redeem, Duke."

"I regret everything that I said, Sire," Daemur said

quietly. "I wasn't in control of my mind. If you can't find it in your heart to forgive me, I'll gladly pay for my mistakes."

Evan gave him an appraising look. He didn't believe any of it, but now wasn't the time to find out the truth. They had more urgent business to attend to.

"Rise, Lord and Lady of Illitand," he said. "You will come with me to the Crown City. There, your fate will be decided."

Father and daughter slowly rose to their feet. It didn't escape Evan how Lady Celana chose a place very close to Kyth, giving him a private glance that Kyth returned with polite indifference.

Despite everything that had happened, Evan couldn't help thinking how good the two of them looked together, two royal children of the rival houses. They were a match, both in age and in looks, a handsome heir to the ancient Dorn line, and a beautiful, smart lady, fit to rule the lands by his side. The children of their union would bear the bloodlines of the two royal families, ending centuries of rivalry between the Dorns and the Illitands. These children would be undisputed rulers of the kingdom of Tallan Dar.

Evan knew that Kyth was in love with Kara, but there was nothing good that could come of this unnatural affection of a crown prince for an elite warrior of the Diamond rank. One day, she could perhaps become the leader of his Pentade. But she could never be a queen to rule by his side.

Evan met Daemur's eyes.

"We must travel back as soon as we can," he said. "We have a High Council to hold."

51

FOCUS

Kyth made his way across the camp to Alder, sitting alone at the edge of the glade. It was dark, but his foster brother's gaze, directed into the bushes, was alert, as if watching intense activity. Three large spiders perched on his left shoulder. Kyth's skin crept as he settled on the log next to his foster brother.

They sat for a moment in silence. Then Alder spoke.

"I heard what you did back at the castle. Amazing."

Kyth smiled. "I keep hearing some amazing things about you. Can you really talk to trees?"

Alder's gaze became distant.

"They're my kin," he said quietly.

Kyth hesitated. It was the first time that Alder hadn't included him when talking about anything that concerned him closely. He looked searchingly into his foster brother's eyes.

"Garnald says you're a Mirewalker now," he said.

Alder nodded. "Yes. But that name doesn't really mean much. It's not about the Mire at all."

"What *is* it about, then?"

Alder met his gaze, but didn't speak.

"It's about Ayalla, isn't it?" Kyth asked quietly.

Alder's eyes became dreamy. "Yes. But not in the way you think. At least, not *only* that way." He paused, color slowly rising to his cheeks. Kyth waited.

"She's not just a beautiful woman," Alder went on after a moment. "She's the mother of the forest."

Kyth hesitated. He knew what she was. And yet, the way Alder said it made him wonder if he really did.

"You mean," he said carefully, "the trees are her *real* children."

Alder looked at him in exasperation.

"Not just the trees. The *forest*. Life. All of it."

Kyth still didn't understand. He felt as if he was falling into an abyss, too big for him to comprehend. Perhaps he wasn't really meant to know a truth so important that catching a glimpse of it had made Alder so mature and so different in such a short time. Perhaps Kyth simply wasn't ready for it.

"So, what happens now?" he asked quietly.

Alder smiled. "Life. Ayalla says we all have a chance, because of your gift."

"A chance?"

"Our enemies serve the Cursed Destroyer. They're against life, against everything Ayalla stands for. It will get worse before it gets better, but Ayalla says there's hope."

Kyth continued to hold his gaze. He still didn't understand, but again, he had a feeling that perhaps he wasn't meant to.

"What'll happen to you?" he asked. "After the council's over, will you go back with Ayalla?"

Alder hesitated. "She says you need me"

"I do," Kyth said. "I always feel better with you by my side. But it's not about me. You must follow your heart. I'll never ask you to stay with me if it isn't what you want to do."

Their eyes met. Just like in the old times, a private exchange that only the two of them could understand. "All is well," their eyes said. They smiled, sitting next to each other, looking into the dark forest.

Egey Bashi looked around the camp. Everyone was settling down to sleep. In the distance, four large tents rose out of the grass, housing King Evan, the Olivians, and the Duke of Illitand with his daughter and servants. Setting the tents up every night was a waste of time. But matters of etiquette demanded that the royal ladies, including little Princess Aljbeda, remained hidden from the men's eyes during such intimate times as sleep, and the King couldn't possibly be extended less courtesy than his highborn guests. Needless to say, the Duke of Illitand, despite being the King's prisoner, couldn't settle for anything less than his royal counterpart. Things tended to get out of proportion where royals were concerned.

It would have been better if they had stayed at the inns, plentiful along the main road. But there were no inns large enough to accommodate their entire party that, with the Cha'ori, the Illitand guards and the Olivian ladies came close to six dozen people. Besides, Mai had insisted that it would be safer to camp, so that the King's deadly escort of seven gem-ranked Majat could maintain a safe perimeter around the entire group by spacing themselves evenly on the outside of the tent circle. Evan was eager to go along with it. After recent events, he seemed to trust his bodyguard unconditionally.

He glanced around the camp again and finally spotted the man he was looking for. Mai was sitting alone at the edge of the shadows, his black-clad shape blending with the darkness of the forest behind. His position gave him the best view of the King's tent. The Diamond was relaxed, graceful like a cat curled up after a successful hunt. His staff lay next to him on the ground, its polished wood reflecting the light of the distant campfire.

Egey Bashi made his way over, and lowered to the ground next to the Majat. Mai turned and gave him a calm look.

"So," the Keeper said. "How did you do it, Aghat?"

"Do what?"

"Break out of their power. You're the second Diamond who was able to resist them. I want to know how."

Mai smiled. "Why don't you ask Kara? She was the first, right?"

"I'm asking *you*," Egey Bashi said, "because I saw you do it, Aghat. They had disabled you before. They almost killed you this time, but you still didn't hesitate."

"How do you know I didn't?"

Egey Bashi didn't respond. In the ensuing pause, he started to wonder if Mai was going to speak again.

"You said it yourself, once," Mai said at length. "The key to resisting their power is focus. I focused, that's all."

Egey Bashi continued to look at him. "It's hardly that simple, Aghat. You *knew* what you were up against. You stepped into that room *knowing* what they were going to do to you. The only thing you didn't know was whether or not you could overcome it, did you?"

Mai's gaze wavered. "No."

"And yet, you still went out there. Why?"

Mai smiled, but his eyes were in shadow. "I thought I told you. I had no choice. There was no one else in that room who could get to her on time." His words died out into stillness as he sat, looking into the distance.

The Keeper peered searchingly into his face, but he couldn't read anything behind the calmness.

"From what I heard about the Majat," he said, "I know that to get your high ranking you must have a very focused mind."

"Among other things."

Egey Bashi nodded. "A Diamond Majat can offer more resistance to the Kaddim Brothers than anyone else. I've seen it myself when they tried to disable Aghat Raishan. And yet, his incredible training still wasn't enough. It takes additional focus to overcome their power."

Mai leaned against a tree. "Is there a point?"

Egey Bashi looked into his eyes, trying to force his way past the tranquil expression, smooth like a mirror surface of the water.

"It's because of the way you feel about her, isn't it?" he said quietly.

Mai kept his silence.

"Your focus," the Keeper insisted. "It has to come from a very deep feeling that goes far beyond your training. You knew you had to overcome their power to save her, just like she, before, knew that she must resist them to save Kyth. Only this urge, on top of your training, could have made each of you immune to their powers. A Diamond in love."

Mai's gaze glinted like a steel blade flicked out of its sheath. The change was so sudden that even though the Majat didn't move a muscle, Egey Bashi backed off, words freezing on his lips.

"Did it ever occur to you, Magister," Mai said, "that some things in this world are simply none of your business?"

Egey Bashi smiled. "Occasionally, Aghat. But not this time."

Ellah sat alone by the fire looking at Mai's distant shape. He was sitting on the ground at the edge of the camp, talking to Egey Bashi. The conversation lasted a while. Then the Keeper got up and walked off, leaving the Majat all by himself.

She hadn't spoken to Mai since they caught up with Kyth and Kara in the Or'halla Grasslands. Back then, he had been so attentive to her that she believed against hope that he really cared for her. But since that time they had never been alone again. With all the things that had happened, there was little chance for it, but she also sensed a change, as if he was no longer seeking her company. It was as if a page in his life had turned, leaving her behind. It hurt to think like this, but how else could she explain the way he was of late, friendly but distant, never approaching her without reason or spending enough time with her to have a conversation.

She heard a rustle and raised her gaze to see Odara Sul. The Keeper came up and lowered herself on the ground.

They sat for a while, staring into the fire. Odara's dark eyes studied her intently.

"So," she said at length. "He doesn't play with you anymore, does he?"

Ellah turned to her as suddenly as if she had been slapped. The look in Odara's eyes was so unsettling that the harsh words she was about to utter froze on her lips. She wanted to get up and run away, but Odara's knowing expression told her this was exactly what the Keeper expected her to do. She forced herself to keep her ground, giving Odara a challenging look in return. After a moment, the Keeper's gaze softened.

"You don't have to act tough with me," she said. "I'm not trying to hurt you."

"Why did you say it then?"

"I'm trying to teach you not to fool yourself. This is the first thing a Keeper needs to learn."

"I am not a Keeper," Ellah retorted.

Odara shrugged. "True. Even the Initiates of the Outer Circle are smarter than you."

Ellah measured her up and down with her eyes. "What do you want from me?"

Odara smiled. "Mother Keeper wants to know if you have decided to continue your training. I believe it's a waste of time to train you, but she seems to think you have potential."

Ellah hesitated. Something in this woman's pale, beautiful face, in these dark, almond-shaped eyes that looked at her with such an unsettling expression, continued to hold her, despite the insulting things the Keeper had said.

"Why do you think it's a waste of time?" she asked.

Odara moved her face closer to Ellah's. "Because you can't control your gift unless you first learn to control yourself."

Ellah raised her eyebrows in a silent question.

"Mother Keeper and I both told you what we think about Aghat Mai," Odara went on. "We told you that he can't possibly be interested in you. But you didn't believe us. You thought you knew better. And now, you sit here torturing yourself with doubts, when all you have to do is simply go and find out."

"Find out? How?"

Odara smiled. "Easy. You can *ask* him. A Keeper would do just that."

Ellah stared. What Odara Sul was suggesting was impossible. A girl didn't just go and *ask* such things of a man.

"I'm not a Keeper," she said again, trying to hide the indecision in her voice.

"Not yet."

Odara's eyes taunted her. They also beckoned. Ellah had never noticed before how deep they were, their bottomless glow opening up such an abyss of knowledge that she felt her head spin just by taking a glimpse.

She hesitated. "I don't think he'll tell me."

Odara's full lips folded into a mocking expression. "I think you're afraid."

Ellah held another pause, then slowly got to her feet.

Mai smiled, watching her approach. She felt naked under his gaze, a feeling made worse by the way Odara Sul's eyes bore into her from behind, with such intensity that she could feel it from all the way across the camp. She did her best to look relaxed.

"May I sit down?" she asked.

He nodded. She lowered herself in front of him, so that their faces were level.

"So," she said after a pause, her voice just a touch higher than normal. "You're really twenty-four, aren't you?"

He looked at her with surprise, but behind it was acknowledgment that indicated to her that he knew exactly what she was getting at. It bothered her that he didn't look in the least bit uncomfortable about it. He seemed at ease as he sat in front of her, the air of calmness around him thick like an invisible armor.

"Yes," he said.

She looked at him searchingly. She really didn't want to continue, but there was no going back now. She *had* to find out, once and for all.

She took a deep breath. "That time we talked, when you tested my power. You told me one truth, about your age. You also said one lie, about how many people you killed."

"Yes." He smiled.

"What about the third thing? The one about caring?"

His bold, direct look was unnerving. She quivered under it, feeling exposed as if he was able to see through her.

"Do you really want to know?" he asked.

She hesitated. She could turn and run away now. If she did, she'd never have to hear him say it. She'd never have to know that he didn't really care about her, that what he had said that time was a lie. But if she ran away now, she'd never learn the truth. She would never be a Keeper. Not that she ever wanted to be, but to think that she couldn't even face the truth about something so important to her…

"Yes," she said.

The smile faded on his lips. "It was the *real* test. It wasn't a lie. But it wasn't the truth either."

She stared. That wasn't what she expected him to say. In fact, she wasn't exactly sure what he was saying to her.

"What do you mean?"

He shifted in his seat. His calmness was unbearable. She wanted to see him unnerved, or at least a little bit bothered, but he was easy and relaxed, as if this conversation wasn't anything beyond the usual.

"I care," he said. "Just not the way you want me to."

She looked at him, the meaning of his words struggling to settle in her head and not quite succeeding.

"I don't understand," she whispered.

"You're a great person, Ellah," he said. "You are smart, and talented, and very brave. If I could have this kind of a bond, I would have liked to be your friend. But it could never be more."

She looked into his eyes searchingly. There was no laughter in their depth. He really meant it.

She felt dumbfounded. This simply *couldn't* be. She *loved* him, more than she could ever love anyone in the whole world. And he– he'd said that he *cared* for her. He said it wasn't a lie. It *had* to be the truth.

It was even worse because in the depth of her heart she knew he was going to say just that. Inside, she'd always known that Odara Sul and Mother Keeper were right. A man like him could never fall in love with a girl like her. Behind his dazzling looks, he was a ruthless killer, who put his deadly skill before everything else. He had been using her while it suited his purpose. And now, when it was over, he didn't want her anymore. He couldn't even allow her to be his friend.

She sat for a moment, looking at him, feeling all the bitterness inside her rise into her eyes with the itch of unshed tears. She wanted to hate him, but couldn't. The look of his blue-gray eyes as he held her gaze, made her feel so warm inside, even if its deep intensity and the special inner glow weren't really meant for her. Perhaps some day, when all of this was over, they could still become friends. Despite everything he said, perhaps he could even change his mind about becoming more.

She stopped herself. Thinking like that meant fooling herself, and she would never do that again. She had fooled herself enough chasing this fantasy, despite everything Mother Keeper had told her. If she ever wanted to pursue the dizzying knowledge she saw in the depths of Odara Sul's gaze, she had to learn to control herself and face the truth. She was going to do it, even if it shattered her heart.

"Tell me something," she said.

There was genuine surprise in Mai's face this time.

"Tell you what?"

She thought about it. "How old were you when you got your Diamond ranking?"

He held her gaze, recognition dawning on his face as he realized what she was doing.

"Nineteen."

She looked at him, her mind filling with a deep blue color.

"It's the truth," she said.

Then she got up and walked away.

52
SPIDER COUP

The nine seats around the council table were spaced so evenly that there seemed to be no possibility in accommodating an additional, tenth seat. Yet, it took Ayalla no more than a glance to send the servants scurrying, pushing the heavy ornate chairs out of the way to make room for a tangled chair-like contraption that seemed to be watching the activity in the room from the deep darkness of its woven branches. Evan suppressed a shiver as he saw it approach the table without any visible aid, positioning itself exactly opposite his chair, between the tall, lean seats of the two religious orders. A silent escort of Mirewalkers, led by Garnald and Alder, followed behind, planting themselves at the chair's back as Ayalla took her seat, her spider dress rustling about her.

Evan leaned back in his chair, watching the council members and their entourage take their places around the table. Some groups were so large that they barely fit behind the backs of the chairs they attended, including little Princess Aljbeda's seat, whose tall ornate back decorated with a red and gold lion of Shayil Yara harbored a full set of colorful Olivian ladies. Tanad Eli Faruh's place at her right elbow was prominently empty. Evan had used his authority to temporarily relieve the Olivian of his duty until his fate could be decided by Queen Rajmella herself. Instead, the place at the Princess's left side was now filled by a thin man with straight white hair and dark skin crumpled like a piece of old parchment – her teacher, Ravil El Hossan. His deep purple eyes held an alert and guarded expression, reminding Evan of the rumored wisdom and influence of this man, who had been single-handedly responsible for developing the Princess's incredible composure, knowledge, and the ability to hold herself far beyond her years.

A prominent gap in the royal gathering was obvious on Evan's left side, where the occupant of the green and gold chair carved with the Illitand's rivergull looked quite a bit smaller and more refined than Lord Daemur's imposing shape. Lady Celana graced her family seat with the quiet air of one well aware of her birthright, yet modest enough not to make it too obvious. Her smooth, porcelain face was calm, eyes surveying the gathering with an unreadable expression.

It had been a hard decision to exclude Daemur Illitand from this gathering. Evan was aware that sooner or later he would have no choice but to forgive the Duke, pretending that his entire adventure in the Illitand castle was no more than a ploy by a clever and evil enemy. Both he and the Duke knew how true this really was, but neither was willing to dwell on it for the sake of royal tradition in the kingdom and the future prospects of the two families.

Evan glanced at Kyth, seated in the Dorn family chair opposite Lady Celana. The Prince paid no notice to the royal lady's hopeful glances, his vision directed inward to the silent shape of Kara, who stood behind his chair next to Raishan. She wore no mask or armband, stripped of her Majat regalia, and that absence of distinction in itself made her slim black-clad shape ominous and menacing. For the moment, Evan could think of no better protection for his son. He hoped this status

ANNA KASHINA   465

quo could remain until they dealt with the enemy once and for all, and that no drastic measures from her Guild would leave his son vulnerable. If only Kyth didn't care for the girl more than a crown prince should care for his bodyguard. Evan looked away.

Mother Keeper's suite had a new addition. Ellah stood behind her chair next to Odara Sul, dressed in a white robe that resembled the Keepers'. Only the absence of the lock and key emblem on its left shoulder indicated her apprentice status. The thrown-back hood revealed the girl's pale, determined face, her hazel green eyes fixed firmly on the smooth table surface. She deliberately avoided looking at Mai, standing behind the King's chair next to Brother Bartholomeos.

Perhaps the most drastic change in the council's chamber was at the chair to Mother Keeper's left, an ancient seat marked by the chipped image of a black stallion galloping along the plain. The Cha'ori seat, the focus of their worries and hopes, now housed Dagmara, an impassive middle-aged woman with slanted, all-knowing eyes. A large group of the Cha'ori warriors crowded behind.

The High Council was in full assembly. Evan couldn't believe that they had actually pulled it off. Everything was ready for the Reverend Cyrros to make his appearance.

As the last council members settled into their seats, the doors to the Council Chamber rolled open, letting in a procession of robed men. Cyrros solemnly crossed the hall toward the table, throwing an uneasy glance at Ayalla, the crawling mass of spiders of her dress within easy reach of his narrow, armless chair.

"Welcome, Reverend," Evan said. "I am overjoyed to have you join this historic gathering, at which every council seat is occupied."

Cyrros pursed his lips, his eyes darting from Ayalla to Dagmara. "I am duly impressed by this show, Your Majesty.

However, I could not help noticing that some of these seats are taken by those who have no right to them." He paused his eyes on Kyth, then looked at Lady Celana.

"The Lady of Illitand is here in place of her father, who has been temporarily indisposed."

"Conveniently so," the Reverend murmured.

"Anyone else's seat you'd like to contest, Reverend?"

Cyrros raised his hands and pushed the hood off his face. Pulsing waves of power crept through the hall. They crept straight into the head, making it hard to concentrate.

"You think your pathetic assembly can contest the power of the Church?" he heard Cyrros say.

Struggling to remember what they were going to discuss, Evan looked around the table, meeting the same confusion in the others' eyes. His gaze was inadvertently drawn to Ayalla. He wasn't sure why she seemed so important to him. She was obviously powerless against whatever was going on because she made no move to resist, her gaze holding the quiet curiosity of a teacher, interested to see how a group of children was going to get out of a difficult situation they created.

In the stillness that ascended into the room, Kyth raised his head.

"You're using some strange power, Reverend Cyrros," he said. "It reminds me of another power I recently encountered. They call it 'power to control', don't they?"

Evan had no idea what he was talking about, but the pressure seemed to have eased a bit as the reverend's watery eyes rested on the Prince.

"I have no idea what you mean, Your Highness."

"I think you do, Reverend," Kyth said. "In addition to your title of Reverend Father, do you also, by any chance, have the title of a Kaddim?"

The reverend's eyes widened. The pulsing power subsided.

"What a preposterous thing to say, Prince Kythar," Cyrros said distinctly.

"Do you?"

The two men locked their gazes.

"The title you are referring to," Cyrros said, "is unfamiliar to me."

There was a stir in the back row and Ellah stepped forward, meeting Kyth's gaze.

"That was a lie," she said, her voice ringing clearly through the hall.

Cyrros jumped up from his chair and backed off. His men surrounded him in a protective ring. He drew himself up, spreading his palms parallel to the floor. There was a momentary stillness and the blast hit, so powerful that Evan shuddered under the blow.

Everyone in sight crouched, cowering under the pulsing force, but several figures remained still. Ayalla kept her back straight, surveying the scene with the calm detachment of an onlooker. Kyth half-closed his eyes, concentrating. But before he could do anything, there was a movement behind them.

Kara and Mai came into motion almost at once. They sprang forward like two black arrows, their slender, powerful shapes moving in unison. Steel rang as it left the sheaths. They spun around and stopped, coming from action to stillness on the same beat.

The flow of power from the reverend's shape subsided. He stood very still, blades crossed at his throat just short of piercing the skin.

"Won't you come back to the table, Reverend," Evan asked pleasantly. "Or, should I say, Kaddim Cyrros?"

The man glanced at the two Majat standing still at his sides, the angle of their blades suggesting that they could go in really deep in a really short time. He moved his gaze to Evan, but before he could say anything, Ayalla stood up.

"*Die*," she said.

Gray shadows darted away from her body, running across the floor toward Cyrros and the hooded men of his suite. Enough of the spiders disappeared to expose Ayalla's bare feet and the side of her long, slender leg, but no one paid any notice to this sudden display of flesh. The Forest Woman nodded and each spider struck, digging into their victim's skin.

Time stopped as the reverend and the men of his suite twisted and sank to the floor, rolling around in horrible agony. A shrill, inhuman wail rose to the ceiling and echoed in the giant stone vault. Ravil El Hossan, one of the few who kept his wits about him, stepped forward and threw his arms around the little princess, forcing her face into his shoulder to spare her the horrifying sight. The rest of them had no choice but to watch.

The men rolling on the floor disintegrated right in front of their eyes. It took minutes for them to stop moving, and what seemed like seconds afterwards before their flesh started peeling away from their bones, trickling onto the floor in a horrifying, reddish goo. More spiders streamed off Ayalla's body, their crawling mass covering the rest of the mess, hiding the dissolving human bodies from view. Fighting nausea, Evan forced his eyes to the Forest Woman, who stood absolutely naked, her eyes glowing with a deep, indigo fire. In a subtle way, the sight of her was no less horrifying than the sickening action going on at her feet.

Evan couldn't help looking onward to where Kara and Mai stood side by side in the very center of the turmoil, their faces so still that they looked like masks. Waves of spiders crawled around their feet, making it impossible for them to move. Evan wondered what kind of training it took to make them so controlled in the very midst of terrible chaos, when even the side observers around the council table were sobbing, retching, or nearly fainting.

When it was finally done, the spiders moved over, leaving nothing in place of where thirteen robed men had so recently stood, ready to attack their entire party. There was no trace of flesh, or even bones on the smooth marble floor. Heaped robes and metal orbens were the only evidence that none of it had been a dream.

53
THE NEW COUNCIL

The spiders returned to the council table and gathered at Ayalla's feet. They made no attempt to climb back up, surrounding the foundation of her chair with a dark velvety cloud. There was an awkward pause as she stood, peering down her own naked body, as if hesitating what to do. Then Garnald took off his patched forest cloak and stepped forward, wrapping it around her shoulders. She gave him a brief smile and closed it tighter, draping it around herself like an exquisite mantle.

Kara and Mai stirred and flicked their weapons back into the sheaths. They exchanged a brief glance and walked toward the table side by side. Evan could only imagine what it had been like for them, standing inches away from people being digested and eaten alive, but none of it showed in their neat, graceful postures as they took their places at the back of the appropriate chairs. The only indication of their possibly unsettled state was the fact that they had kept their weapons out so long after they had become unnecessary.

Around the table, people were slowly coming to their senses. Lady Celana, the first to regain her composure, sat very still, keeping her careful gaze on Ayalla. Kyth's face was paler than usual as he exchanged a long look with Alder standing at the back of Ayalla's chair. The Duke of Aeghor and Sir Orlon of Bengaw, the silent additions to today's council, didn't look well at all. Their greenish faces were shamed by the bright pink of Princess Aljbeda's cheeks as she disengaged from her teacher's embrace, looking at Ayalla with quiet curiosity.

The Forest Woman turned back to the table, as if nothing out of the ordinary had happened.

"We have very little time," she said. "The enemy is strong, and close. Much too close. Your Church is infested with them. A new Church leader must be appointed, to take care of things."

She looked across the table to Brother Bartholomeos.

"You," she said in the quiet commanding voice of someone who didn't consider disobedience to be an option. "Take the priest's seat."

Evan found it admirable that the old priest glanced at Evan and waited for a nod of acknowledgment before making his way around the table toward the empty chair. He took the seat with an uncertain look.

"To make this official, Your Majesty," Bartholomeos said, "I'll have to be elected by the Conclave, and this might prove to be a problem. Given my past history–"

"Your past history concerned your disagreement with Reverend Haghos," Evan said. "And he has recently been proven to be a renegade and a Kaddim Brother. You have the support of the crown, Father Bartholomeos. I'm certain the Conclave will see it this way. It has traditionally consisted of reasonable men."

Bartholomeos shook his head. "Your Majesty is talking of the men who elected two Kaddim Brothers in a row as Reverend Fathers."

Evan hesitated. He had no idea whether these choices were made willilngly or under the influence of Kaddim power, but Bartholomeos was right. They needed to find out how deep the problem went and how hard it would be to turn things around. If the Conclave, or some of its key members, were part of the Dark Order...

"We'll deal with them," he said. "But first, we have business to conclude at this council. We have a law to vote out."

"But first, there's another change due on this council," the Forest Woman said. She rose from her seat and ran a glance around the seated figures with a fond expression of a mother looking at her children seated at the dinner table.

"Since I cannot be here every time the council meets," she said, "it is my right to appoint an emissary, who can speak for the Forestlands in my stead."

She turned to Alder, standing on her left, and smiled. Then she stepped aside and pointed toward her empty seat.

"The seat's yours, fair one," she said.

"*Alder*?" Evan asked. "But he–"

The gaze of her deep indigo eyes stopped him.

"You have much to decide," she said. "And I can't possibly stay here with you all this time. My children need me. In my absence, you'll need a man to speak on behalf of the Forest."

"But *Alder*?" Mother Keeper joined in. "He– he hasn't even been properly trained!"

Ayalla held her gaze.

"If you mean training in what you call politics, Alder doesn't need any. You have too many trained people on this council. What you truly need is a man of the forest. A man with a pure heart."

She turned to Alder and nodded. Alder stepped forward with a stunned look and lowered himself into the seat.

"You are by far the oldest person in this room, Ayalla," Evan said, "and this seat is rightfully yours since the times before any of us can remember. We have no choice but follow your wish in this matter."

She met his gaze and smiled.

"You're right," she said. "You don't have a choice. And if I'm not mistaken, you still have business to conclude, don't you?"

Evan ran his eyes around the group.

"Indeed, lords and ladies," he said. "As your king, I move to abolish the Ghaz Shalan testing of infants at birth. Since, for the first time in centuries, this council is in full assembly, our vote today can decide the fate of this law. Does anyone wish to object?"

There was a silence.

"Then," Evan went on, "we hereby abolish the Ghaz Shalan testing. From now on, no gifted children in this kingdom will be put to death."

Nods came from various seats around the table and shocked glances from others, but nobody spoke. The only one whose face still held doubt was Bartholomeos.

"It would be a hard one to pass through the Church, Your Majesty," he said quietly. "Especially since my position here isn't exactly official."

Evan nodded. "It could indeed be hard if we encounter many of the Dark Order members in the disguise of priests. So, the *real* question is how far did our enemy penetrate our Church?"

"Aghat Raishan and I had recently paid them a visit," Egey Bashi said. "We didn't manage to catch Reverend Cyrros in the act, but things looked bad indeed. We barely escaped with our lives."

A movement around Ayalla drew Evan's eye. The spiders had started waking up from their stupor and climbing up her legs to regain their places on her body. They were scarce at first, but as more and more of them regained their strength after what must have been an extremely filling meal, they made their way higher, until she, once again, was clad head to foot in their exquisite intertwined velvet. She took off the cloak and handed it back to Garnald. There were a few spiders still clinging to it, but the Mirewalker took it without a flinch and put it back onto his shoulders.

"The enemy's strong," Ayalla said. "Things will get worse before they get better. But in the end, we all have a chance."

She ran her gaze over Kyth, and the Majat standing behind, then moved her eyes over the Keepers and finally rested them on Alder, giving him a fond glance. Then she turned back to Evan, her indigo eyes shining with deep intensity that made Evan shiver.

"Will you stand by our side in this battle, Ayalla?" he asked.

She slowly nodded her head.

"Then," Evan went on, "we do have a chance."

Kyth stood in his room staring out of the window at the distant activity in the castle courtyard. Prominent additions to the usual setting made the usually quiet grounds almost unrecognizable. Besides the Kingsguards and stable hands a large crowd of Cha'ori warriors milled around, attending to their horses, which they insisted on keeping outdoors, making the yard look like a rather disorderly extension of the stables. A group of snakewood trees took root by the castle wall, waiting for Ayalla to finish her business with the people, so that they could escort her back into the forest.

Kyth strained his eyes to see into the Majat grounds, but from this angle he couldn't make out much beyond the jagged line of the wall. He knew that Kara must be in there, polishing weapons with Raishan and Mai, or engaged in one of their strenuous training exercises, to which no outside observers were usually admitted. He longed to see her, to talk to her one on one, but he knew there was nothing he could do until she was ready to come to him herself.

He heard a click of the door opening behind him and turned to look. His breath caught in his throat as he saw the slim, graceful shape outlined against the doorway.

Kara.

She carefully closed the door behind her and approached, stopping by his side. He looked into her eyes, feeling warmth spread through his body at the mere sight of her.

"I came to say I'm sorry," she said, "for not being around all this time."

He paused. It was so good to be next to her once again that the past didn't matter anymore. All he wanted to do was stand and look at her. He slowly shook his head.

"You've been through a terrible ordeal," he said. "All because of me. I can't even imagine what it must have been like. I'm the one who should be sorry."

Her gaze wavered. "It wasn't because of you. The Kaddim Brothers – they *used* you to get to me. They wanted me out of the way. And, they almost succeeded."

There was a strain in her eyes that made her seem distant. Concern rose in his chest as he looked searchingly into her face.

"What will happen to you now?" he asked.

She hesitated.

"My future's uncertain," she said. "Such a thing has never happened before in the history of our Guild. There's no way to tell what they'll do if they find out I'm still alive. But for the moment," she went on, "I seem to be the only Diamond in the history of our Guild with freedom to do what I choose."

She reached over and touched his cheek. He shivered at the touch, a feeling so intense that he felt momentarily disoriented. He covered her hand with his, pressing it gently against his face.

"Is this what you choose to do?" he asked quietly.

She held his gaze. "No promises."

"No." He brought her hand to his lips and kissed the inside of her wrist. She shivered. Then she pulled her hand free and stepped into his arms.

Her closeness overwhelmed him. He held her, immersed in the feeling of her skin against his face, her sweet, maddeningly sensual scent that slowly reached into the deepest corners of his mind, filling him with the strength of a thousand men. It felt like coming home after being lost for a very long time. And more. It felt as if he was, once again, complete, as if, after being alone and lost, he had finally found his other half.

He didn't remember how, instead of standing upright they found themselves lying down on the bed, how the clothes separating their bodies was gone, so that nothing could possibly be in between them anymore. She shivered in his arms as he found his way to the ultimate closeness, so intense that he lost himself in it, letting his body take over from his weakening mind to yield to the overpowering passion that couldn't possibly be controlled.

It was late evening when they finally emerged from the world beyond worlds, filled with new strength and new weakness that left nothing else to wish for. He lay next to her, feeling her warmth against him with every bit of his skin, and hid his face in her soft golden hair.

Whatever the future held, when she was next to him like this, he wasn't afraid of anything anymore.

Around them, the sapphire shades of the evening deepened and the wind carried the distant boom of the bittern from the lake.

ACKNOWLEDGMENTS

This book would never have been possible without the support of numerous people over the years. First and foremost, I thank my friend, Olga Karengina, whose enthusiasm helped drive the first draft of this book, making the writing process even more fun than it would have been otherwise. I am grateful to the members of the Online Writers Workshop for Science Fiction, Fantasy, and Horror, especially Jennifer Dawson, Rhonda Garcia, Sandra Panicucci, Ariana Cordelle Sofer, Amy Raby, Siobhan Carroll, Abigail Carter, and Terry Jackman. While I received feedback on this novel from many others, these people gave me key advice (and key encouragement) where and when I needed them most.

I am very grateful to my husband, for his tolerance, encouragement, and support, as well as for his incessant ability to discuss the Majat weapons and fighting techniques at all the odd times of day and night.

I thank my editor, Lee Harris, and the Angry Robot team for helping me to realize my dream and bring the Majat warriors to life.

I dedicate the Majat Code series to Vladimir Keilis-Borok, my grandfather, best friend, and soul mate, who taught me everything I am.

An excerpt from

BOOK II OF THE MAJAT CODE
THE GUILD OF ASSASSINS

A VISITOR

Oden Lan, the Master of the Majat Guild, the Assassin of the Diamond Rank, forced his face into a calm mask as he stared at the object in his hand. A four-pointed throwing star, the large diamond set into its center glittering so brightly that it hurt his eyes. The intricate lines of the golden inlay at the base of the blades spelled a word in the ancient runic language, used in the Majat Fortress as a token of the Guild's unique ancestry.

Black.

In the Majat dialect the word was pronounced as "*Kar*" and sounded very close to the star bearer's name.

Kara.

Oden Lan's face twitched. It had been hundreds of years since the Majat Guildmaster had to arrange an assassination of one of his own, an elite warrior of the Diamond rank. The fact that he had to do it because Kara had betrayed her duty for the love of the sleek, blue-eyed Prince Kythar of the ruling House Dorn, made things worse. The Majat Warriors were not permitted to love. If they had been, Oden Lan himself would have never watched Kara grow up from a little girl into the most incredible nineteen year-old their Guild had ever seen without letting her know how he felt about her. And now, he would never have the chance. She was dead, killed at Oden Lan's orders by another one of the Guild's best.

A rustle of footsteps brought Oden Lan back to reality. He closed his fingers over the token in his hand, suddenly aware of the early morning chill creeping under his cloak, and the smother of the looming walls that made the courtyard adjoining the Guildmaster's tower seem dark and hollow, like a deep stone well.

"This had better be important," Oden Lan said into the gloom of the low archway.

A hooded figure separated itself from the shadows, its long, dark robe shuffling over the paving stones.

"Forgive the interruption, Aghat," the newcomer said in a deep, soft voice.

Oden Lan looked at him with curiosity. The way the stranger used the Guildmaster's rank as a form of address suggested familiarity with the Majat customs, yet Oden Lan was certain he had never seen this man before. Finding an outsider, unannounced, in the Guildmaster's inner sanctum, was so preposterous that Oden Lan couldn't even find it in his heart to feel angry. After all, no one in his right mind would come to the Majat Guildmaster, the man in command of the most impressive military force in the history of the known world, with bad intentions.

"Who the hell are you?" he said.

"A friend." The man stopped halfway across the courtyard

and pushed back the hood, allowing the Guildmaster a good look at his face.

He had heavy, gaunt features, his prominent eyebrows looming over deep eye sockets. His graceful posture spoke of warrior training, not sufficient, perhaps, to stand up to a Majat of a gem rank, but good enough to defend himself in a tight spot. His bulging robe suggested hidden weapons, perhaps a sword or a saber strapped across the back. But the most unusual thing about him were his eyes – so pale brown that they bordered on yellow. From the shadows of his eye sockets they stared at the Majat Guildmaster calmly, without fear or reverence that Oden Lan was used to seeing in the faces of his visitors.

"What do you want?" the Guildmaster demanded.

The man shifted from foot to foot, his calm look acquiring a touch of curiosity, as if he was studying a strange animal.

"I bring news of one of your Guild members," he said. "A Diamond, Kara."

Oden Lan's hand holding the throwing star clenched so tightly that the blades cut into his hand, piercing the skin. He kept his face steady, shoving the bleeding hand into his pocket before the strange yellow-eyed man could see it.

"I believe," he said steadily, "that I have all the news of Kara that I need. If you have nothing else to say–"

"She's alive."

In the silence that followed these words, the quiet rustle of the morning breeze seemed as loud as the howl of a hurricane.

"*What* did you say?"

"I'm afraid, the man you sent to do the job, Aghat Mai, failed to fulfill your orders."

Oden Lan kept the silence as the words settled into his head.

Alive.

Could it possibly be true?

It didn't seem likely. Mai, a Diamond whose incredible skill had made him a legend in the Guild despite his young age, couldn't possibly fail. Even less so would he disobey a direct order. The reports had been clear about this. Mai had used his famous blow – the "viper's sting" – on her. A blade between the collarbones. Instant death.

Unless…

Oden Lan turned to the man by his side, feeling the chill creep up his spine.

"Tell me more."

The man shrugged. "She and Aghat Mai are both at the King's court. I've seen them myself. Aghat Mai has resumed his duty as the head of the King's bodyguards – following your orders, I believe. As for Kara, she's spending her time getting familiar with the royal heir, if you know what I mean."

Oden Lan hesitated. Now he was beginning to think that the man was crazy. What he was saying was impossible. Mai was one of their Guild's best. If, for some unknown reason, he had failed to kill Kara the first time, he *couldn't* possibly just stay around her without trying again.

He should have this man executed for prying into the Guild's affairs. Yet, something kept him from calling the guards.

"Perhaps there's a mistake?" Oden Lan asked carefully.

"It was my impression that the Diamond Majat don't make such… mistakes."

"I was referring to you."

The man held his gaze with calm confidence.

"I wasn't there when they fought, and cannot be certain what happened, but I saw the two of them afterwards, fighting side by side. In fact, Aghat Mai took considerable risks to save Kara's life."

Oden Lan hesitated. This seemed crazy, and absolutely preposterous. Yet, it was clear that the stranger was certain of his words.

"You seem to be extremely well informed," he said.

The man bowed. "I pride on having good sources of information, Aghat. But I can see that you still don't believe me. Please, don't take my word for it. Ask the Jade who was on this assignment with Aghat Mai – Gahang Sharrim, if I am not mistaken."

Oden Lan stood back. For how unremarkable he was, the yellow-eyed man *did* seem to be well informed.

"Not that it is any business for an outsider," he said, "but since we are having this conversation, I don't mind telling you this. Gahang Sharrim brought back Kara's armband, and reported on a successfully completed assignment. In fact, he seemed to be quite proud of it."

"Question him again," the man insisted. "Ask him what kind of a blow Aghat Mai used to kill her."

"What does that have to do with anything?"

"I heard," the man said softly, "that Aghat Mai is rumored to have invented several special blows, which made him quite famous in your Guild. One of them is called 'viper's kiss'. Am I correct?"

Oden Lan froze. No outsider could possibly know this. This man was either a spy or –

He should call the guards. But the thought that, despite everything, Kara could still be alive, made Oden Lan's heart race. He *had* to know.

"How did you come upon this information?"

The man smiled, with the calm confidence of one who has the situation well in hand.

"This blow," he said, "looks exactly as deadly as the 'viper's sting', entering the body in exactly the same spot between the collarbones, but by a skillful tilt of the blade it merely sends a person into a deep coma, until the victim can be revived by a special pinch on the pressure points. The wound is still serious, of course, but with proper care it could be easily treated."

Oden Lan's skin prickled as he peered into the man's face. It would have taken a hell of a skill for Mai to use "viper's kiss" against an equal opponent. But if he did manage to pull it off on Kara, it was indeed indistinguishable from the "sting" on the outside. Even Sharrim, Mai's partner in the assignment and the best of the Guild's Jades, could have been easily fooled.

But why would Mai do such a thing, knowing that sooner or later the truth would come out? And how could this yellow-eyed stranger possibly know this?

"How the hell did—"

"Call in Gahang Sharrim," the man insisted. "Ask him."

"I fail to see how this would help," Oden Lan said slowly. "I heard Gahang Sharrim's report. You, on the other hand—"

The man waved his hand in dismissal.

"I am not your problem, Aghat," he said. "You have treason growing in your very midst. I came here with humble hope that bringing you this information could be considered a gesture of goodwill, and that in the future you would consider me a friend."

Oden Lan gave him a long look.

"What you are suggesting is ridiculous," he said. "But given the graveness of the accusation, I will question Gahang Sharrim again."

He signaled and a Majat guard appeared from the shadows at the edge of the courtyard.

"Take this man to the guest quarters," the Guildmaster ordered. "Keep him safe. Master...?"

He turned to the yellow-eyed man with question.

"Tolos," the man supplied.

Oden Lan nodded.

"Until we talk again," he said, "Master Tolos."

He turned and strode away.

The Jade, Sharrim, had curly red hair, freckled face, and a perpetual expression of childlike wonder that seemed odd in someone of his reputation as the best archer among the Jades. His superior, Gahang Khall, a pale man with straight black hair and piercing eyes, made a chilling contrast as the two of them stood in the Guildmaster's study with the solemn look of the men well aware of the due praise for a job well done. Looking at their silent forms, Oden Lan had trouble believing Master Tolos's accusations. Yet now, after summoning the Jades to his study, he had no choice but to proceed.

"Tell me how Kara died," he said, forcing his voice to stay level.

There was a puzzled silence.

"Is there a reason for–" Khall began.

Oden Lan looked up, nailing the man with a short glance.

"I choose not to take your words as doubt that I would ask you *anything* without reason, Gahang."

"But I already told–" Sharrim put in.

Oden Lan turned, his gaze forcing the younger man into silence.

"Tell me again."

Sharrim swallowed, his face losing several shades of confidence.

"After we received our orders, Aghat Mai and I caught up with Kara after ten days' chase. Aghat Mai engaged her, and when she was distracted, I shot her in the forearm. Then I stood back, like Aghat Mai instructed me."

"He instructed you to stand back?"

The Jade's face continued to show puzzlement. "He told me to stand down after the first hit. He said that one light wound would give him all the advantage he needed. And it did."

Oden Lan hesitated, searching Sharrim's eyes and finding nothing but honest pride at the successful assignment. He was beginning to feel like a fool. He swore to himself to have another conversation with Master Tolos after this was over.

"What happened afterwards?" he asked.

"After my arrow hit, it took mere minutes for Aghat Mai to get through. Kara lost a sword from her injured hand. Then, he struck her down. Death was instant, Guildmaster. Almost no blood."

Like the first time when he had heard this, Oden Lan felt his feet sway from underneath him. He summoned all his strength to appear calm.

Instant death.

When this was over, he was going to make an example of Master Tolos, to show everyone what it meant to pry into the Majat Guild's private affairs. How *dare* this yellow-eyed man come here to suggest such preposterous things and stir up the wound that didn't yet have time to heal?

"You told me before that Aghat Mai used 'viper's sting' on her, Gahang Sharrim."

"Yes, Guildmaster."

"How do you know?"

The Jade hesitated.

"We all learned what it's like, Guildmaster. It's Aghat Mai's signature blow. A deep stab between the collarbones, tilted left and in to go straight through the heart."

Yes, that was how "viper's sting" was supposed to go. Oden Lan had never tried it, but he heard enough talk in the Fortress five years ago, after Mai, a newly ranked Diamond at the time, had used it on his first kill. Mai had also used the other one, "viper's kiss", during the same assignment, to harmlessly get the victim's bodyguard out of the way. Mai's fame had spread like fire. Not many people in the history of the Guild had blows named after their token rune. *Viper*.

Oden Lan strained his memory to recall the details. There *was* a way to tell between the two blows, just not an easy one.

"You said there was no blood," he said slowly.

"Almost none, Guildmaster. A splash, no more."

A splash. Oden Lan's heart quivered, but he kept his face straight. "And what did Aghat Mai do right after the fight?"

"What do you mean?" Sharrim looked lost.

"Try to recall exactly, Gahang. *What happened right after the fight?*"

Sharrim licked his lips.

"I– I approached the body and checked that she was dead," he stammered, trying to speak faster under Oden Lan's urgent gaze. "There was no pulse. Then Aghat Mai sent me off to find her armband."

"He sent you off?"

"Yes."

"Why?"

Sharrim hesitated. "I was under his command. I didn't question his orders."

"Didn't you wonder why he stayed behind?"

"He– he said he'd take care of her weapons."

"And what did he do when you walked away?" Oden Lan prompted.

"He leaned over her, and…" Sharrim paused, his face going pale.

Oden Lan waited. After a moment, Sharrim spoke slowly, his narrowed eyes looking into the distance.

"He touched some points on the neck. Her body shook. I saw it as I left. And then, Aghat Mai said something to the boy, Prince Kythar Dorn. After Aghat Mai left, Prince Kythar wrapped Kara's body in a cloak and held it in his arms."

"He told the Prince to hold her, so that he could keep her warm," Oden Lan said. "Didn't he?"

Sharrim's blue eyes were suddenly dark like Khall's. His face lost its innocent expression and became cold and distant.

"I don't blame you, Gahang Sharrim," Oden Lan said. "You couldn't have known."

The two Jades went so still that they seemed inanimate.

"You may go," Oden Lan told them.

"What do you intent to do, Guildmaster?" Khall asked quietly.

Oden Lan turned to him, keeping his face so straight that it hurt.

"I'll do what I have to, Gahang Khall," he said. "Just like I've always done."

**The quest for the Arbor
has begun...**

HEARTWOOD

FREYA ROBERTSON

The quest for the Arbor has begun...

Miriam is on the road again, and this time she's expected...

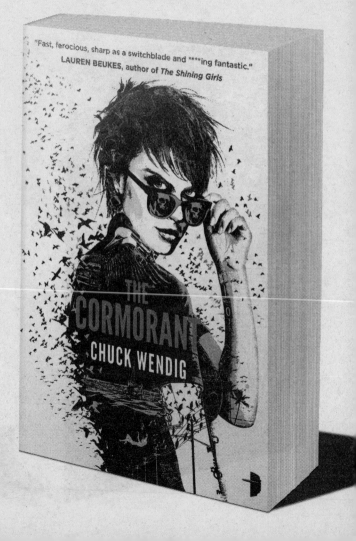

"Fast, ferocious, sharp as a switchblade and ****ing fantastic."
LAUREN BEUKES, author of *The Shining Girls*

THE
CORMORANT

CHUCK WENDIG

**Gods and monsters roam the streets
in this superior urban fantasy from
the author of *Empire State*.**

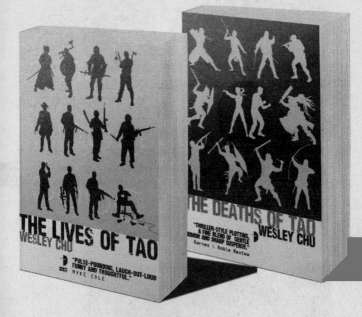

"Pulse-pounding, laugh-out-loud funny and thoughtful."
Myke Cole, author of Control Point

THE LIVES OF TAO
WESLEY CHU

"PULSE-POUNDING, LAUGH-OUT-LOUD FUNNY AND THOUGHTFUL."
MYKE COLE

THE DEATHS OF TAO
WESLEY CHU

"THRILLER-STYLE PLOTTING, A FINE BLEND OF GENTLE HUMOR AND SHARP SUSPENSE"
Barnes & Noble Review

"This is how historical fantasy gets dirty."
Douglas Hulick, author of
Among Thieves